Please, God, if you are there for such a wretched soul as me, Zeb prayed, *help me . . .*

He got his answer that night. It was not the answer he'd expected, or wanted.

Standing in the doorway that led into the tunnel connecting the cave to the castle above was a woman wearing a black tunic belted over tight black pants tucked into black boots.

Really tight black pants.

Numerous knives of various sizes were tucked into special sheaths in her belt, and she held one in each of her hands. A long black cloak, also fitted with weapons, was shoved back off her shoulders.

Her hair was red, and her skin smooth as cream. She looked just like . . .

"Oh hell!" he muttered. "It's Satan's sister."

"Think again, lackwit. I am Regina, the answer to your prayers."

By Sandra Hill

SANDRA HILL

A DEADLY ANGELS BOOK

GOOD VAMPIRES GO TO HEAVEN

AVONBOOKS

An Imprint of HarperCollinsPublishers

Excerpt from *The Cajun Doctor* copyright © 2017 by Sandra Hill.

GOOD VAMPIRES GO TO HEAVEN. Copyright © 2016 by Sandra Hill. All rights reserved. Printed in the United States of America. No part of this book may be used or reproduced in any manner whatsoever without written permission except in the case of brief quotations embodied in critical articles and reviews. For information, address HarperCollins Publishers, 195 Broadway, New York, NY 10007.

First Avon Books mass market printing: December 2016

ISBN 978-0-06235656-7

Avon Trademark Reg. U.S. Pat. Off. and in Other Countries, Marca Registrada, Hecho en U.S.A.
Avon, Avon Books, and the Avon logo are trademarks of HarperCollins Publishers.
HarperCollins® is a registered trademark of HarperCollins Publishers.

16 17 18 19 20   QGM 10 9 8 7 6 5 4 3 2 1

Prologue

What is your secret fear?

Satan came to visit me today.

Me! Zebulan, a mere Hebrew of no great fame, in the presence of the Boogie Man of Sin! And not a welcome mat in sight. Hah! If I had one, I'd try to hide under it. And I am not easily frightened.

You probably think that I mean Satan's visit as a metaphor for some bad deed I've committed. God knows . . . rather, Satan knows . . . I've committed plenty. No, I mean the real deal, scary-as-hell (pun intended . . . can you tell I'm losing it here?), evil personified, primo devil.

Really.

Can't you see him? He is standing right there before me.

In person.

Well, not "in person" precisely because, as everyone knows, the biggest, baddest of all demons isn't a person. Never was. Lucifer, as Satan was known in the beginning, existed as an archangel for eons, if not forever, before his fall from grace, never having started as a human, or so it is said.

People do not realize that angels were *created* by God, and that humans do not *become* angels after death, no matter how good they might have been. Blame the misconception on movies like *It's a Wonderful Life* with the line about angels getting wings every time a bell rings. Hah!

I am rambling, mentally, as you can tell. A defense mechanism, I suppose. It's either that, or scream with fright. You'd think there was nothing worse than the torture I have undergone this past year. I've grown at least two inches, thanks to the rack. (And I was already more than six feet tall.) Flaps of skin hang here and there from the floggings. (Needles and thread would come in handy, not to mention a nurse. I would do it myself if I could. But I am tied up at the moment. Ha, ha, ha!) No toenails or fingernails. (Ah, well. Saves money on manicures and pedicures, not that I've ever had either.) Barbed wire around my cock and round-the-clock porn shown on a ceiling screen. (Ouch! Gives new meaning to "Ring Around the Rosie.")

The only reason I still have eyes or a tongue is because Jasper, another fallen angel, wants me alive for centuries to prolong my agony. He thinks I betrayed him.

I did.

But back to Satan. Believe me, a visit from the Essence of Evil does not bode well for me, especially when he deigns to visit me in The Pit, this hidden cave deep in the bowels of Horror, Jasper's castle headquarters.

Jasper is king of all the Lucipires, or demon vampires (in case you didn't know), of which I have been one for the past two thousand or so years. Leastways, I had been until the Big Transgression. That's what Jasper calls my attempt to join the other team, as in vangels (Viking vampire angels). And, no, I am not a Viking. But I would try my damnedest to become one if it meant release from this demonic obligation. I'd even wear a ridiculous horned helmet, and learn to ride a longship, and eat that stinky gammelost, and . . .

"You find humor in my presence, Zebulan?" Satan's voice is so soft and beguiling one might be fooled into thinking his feelings are hurt. Does the Chief Devil even have feelings?

"No. I was grimacing, not smi . . ." My words trail off as I turn to look directly at Satan for the first time.

He is beautiful.

Holy hellfire! I'm not sure what I was expecting. Demonoid form, for sure. Scaly green skin and tail and drooling mung. Claws with razor-sharp nails. Blazing red eyes and fangs. A darting, snake-like tongue. Maybe even horns.

But, no, he is in humanoid form, and his appearance is so attractive it startles. Even Jasper, who stands in the background, still in demonoid persona, gazes at his master with awe.

Satan has long, silk-like red hair. Who would have ever guessed a demon redhead? But then, redheads do have a reputation for fiery personalities. His skin is the creamy color of aged ivory. A perfectly muscled, tall body is shown off in black leather tunic and tight pants tucked inside tooled ebony snakeskin boots. The chain belt around his waist is pure gold. About his neck is another gold chain from which hangs a crucifix, of all things, meant to be a sacrilege, I assume.

Satan carries not the caricature pitchfork portrayed in Christian images, but a long-handled whip with dozens of hair-thin, silver flails with weighted tails. The calm expression on his face is belied by the way he keeps tapping the whip against his knee, causing the metal to shimmer in the dim candlelight of the cave and make a metallic shushing sound.

Shush, shush, shush!

It is Satan's eyes that are the giveaway, though. Clear green orbs against a blood red background that almost seem to pulse with fury. They are mesmerizing in their attempt to draw a person into their cyclonic swirls of sin.

Shush, shush, shush.

The eyes and the repetitive rhythm of the whip hypnotize.

Shush, shush, shush.

I look away, afraid of what I might say or do if I fall under the devil's spell.

"Thou hast wasted enough time, Zebulan. 'Tis time to admit thy betrayal, beg for forgiveness, and promise to remain a Lucipire, never to stray again."

Shush, shush, shush.

Do a demon vampire's work for eternity? Continue to fight the vangels. Prey on human sinners. Kill, kill, kill. My body count is well over a thousand by now. The prospect of continuing that dark work is more horrific to me than anything Satan might do to my body. "No. Kill me and get it over with."

"You are already dead."

Shush, shush, shush.

"Just send me to Hell then. You can torture me there all you want." Brave words when I am shaking in my shackles!

Shush, shush, shush.

"Ah, that is the rub," Satan says.

Shush, shush, shush.

"Alas, I cannot take you home . . . yet."

Huh? I turn my head to look at Satan and, whoa! I understand immediately. This puts a whole new light on my situation. It almost makes the past year of torture worthwhile. Apparently, my eternal fate is in question. My good acts for the vangels must have gained me points up above. Oh, it wouldn't be enough to get me through the Pearly Gates, but maybe Purgatory's more tarnished portals. "My pal Michael must have put in a good word for me." I start to smile and stop when my dry lips crack and begin to seep blood again, my fangs cutting deeper. It's a wonder I have any blood left.

Satan hisses and lashes his whip across my chest. The metallic threads cause an excruciating pain, more like a searing burn. Thin welts immediately rise on my skin.

"You will not mention that name again!" Satan's red-rimmed, green eyes are now totally red. He is still beautiful, though, dammit.

Satan refers to Michael, of course, the archangel warrior responsible for kicking the fallen angels out of Heaven, including Lucifer, aka Satan.

"Michael, Michael, Michael," I taunt, foolishly, but with great delight.

The whip shoots out again, crisscrossing the chest welts. I probably look like a blank crossword puzzle. Give me a five-letter word for "person who taunts the devil." IDIOT. *My warped sense of humor is the only thing keeping me from crying out with pain.*

"Shall I send for Craven?" Jasper asks Satan. "My chief tortureologist has developed new methods of persuasion that are very effective."

Tortureologist? More like one sick bastard with more muscle than brain!

"Not so effective if this sinner can stubbornly refuse to surrender," Satan remarks.

Shush, shush, shush.

"Ah, but Hebrews ever were a stubborn race," Jasper points out.

Not a wise move! Even Zeb in his pain-riddled haze knows that one does not argue with Satan.

Satan scowls at Jasper. *Believe me, a Satan scowl is nothing to be encouraged. Better Jasper than me.*

"I mean, of course Craven has not been so effective in Zebulan's case, but . . ." Jasper attempts to backpedal.

"Watch and learn, Jasper," Satan snarls. "The best torture works on the victim's deepest despair. Their hidden fears. Their agonizing regrets. Their guilt. What might have beens. Their wish for do-overs."

Satan gives his full attention to me now, and I try to make my mind blank, to reveal nothing. At the same time, I brace myself, ignorant of exactly what he plans, but knowing I am in for something bad.

It proves to be worse than I can imagine.

"Do you remember Masada?" Satan asks me with well-honed cruelty.

How can I forget? That ancient rock fortress overlooking the Dead Sea, the scene of one of Israel's greatest massacres. It is the place where I lost my beloved wife, Sarah; and my twins, Mikah and Rachel.

"Would you like to see how your wife and children died?"

No! No, no, no, no, no, I cry silently. It is enough that I feel guilty over their deaths. That I mourned their loss every day of my human existence, which was not that long since I took my own life, but every day of my pitiful two-thousand-year-old Lucipire existence.

My eyes are forced shut and behind the lids I see Sarah, but she hardly resembles my wife with smooth, sun-kissed skin and dancing brown eyes. No longer is she the beautiful woman who strolled through the neat rows of our small Shomron vineyard, laughing up at me, teasing. No, this creature more resembles those pictures I have seen of Holocaust victims during World War II. Gaunt, skeletal, walking like an elderly crone, rather than her twenty-five years. I know then that I am seeing Sarah as she was during the year-long siege of Masada, before the final assault, before the fires set by Roman soldiers. Of which, for my sins, I had been one.

I arch my back on the rack, attempting escape. I scream, the first time in my captivity. A long wail of heartbreaking anguish.

"Or perhaps you would like to see how your children fared?"

When I do not respond, Satan says, "Everyone has a tipping point. Everyone."

What I see then pushes me closer and closer to the point of madness. And I know, deep down, that he will force me to view this scene over and over, flails to my very soul.

It is too much!

Chapter 1

The Norselands, AD 1250

There's a little bit of witch in every woman . . .

Regina Dorasdottir loved being a witch, but that had not always been the case.

Witchiness was in her blood, her mother and grandmother before her having practiced the black arts. For years, she'd fought her gifts, especially when she was teased and bullied by the village children and even the youthlings up at Winterstorm Castle, but then when she was fourteen, the ignorant village folks burned her mother, Dora Sigrunsdottir, while still alive and inside her forest hut, blaming her for a year-long famine. This, despite the fact that her sweet mother had been a good witch, providing healing potions to the sick, birthing babies, giving, giving, giving.

Regina could not claim the same goodness. After witnessing her mother's brutal death, a bitterness and rage grew in her like a festering boil.

She had to embrace her magical gifts, or explode. After a time, she rebuilt her mother's home in the forest . . . a hovel, actually, but she did not care. It was only temporary. Eventually, she came to excel at and enjoy all that she could do, uncaring if anyone got hurt, sometimes deliberately inflicting pain on those for whom she carried a grudge. And later, over the next eleven years, she did not even discriminate in that way. Yes, she helped a great many people with her healing potions, but that became incidental. If people paid, they got her services.

She loved the power. In a time when women were rarely given authority, she had a shadowy influence over many people.

She loved making money. Forget about being paid in chickens, or barley, or mead, as many healers and midwives were. She accepted only coins, thank you very much, preferably gold, but silver would do, and occasionally copper.

She loved pretending to be an aged, skinny crone with a huge wart on her hairy chin, skin splotches painted on her skin, similar to liver spots, which village cotters referred to as devil's spittle, and a not-so-lovely ashy gray hair. Best for a woman living alone in a remote area to appear as loathsome as possible. In fact, she had seen only twenty-five winters, her hair was an unfortunate flame red, also considered a sign of the devil. A raggedy gunna hid an embarrassingly voluptuous figure. Those folks who'd known her as a child were long gone, or unable to recognize this scary creature of the woods. They were suspicious, of course, but accepted her explanation that the original Regina was gone and she was a member of the coven (with the same name, would you believe it?) who'd come to take her place. The fools shivered at the word "coven" and asked no more questions.

She did not worry overmuch about suffering the same fate as her mother. She was hardier than her mother and more careful. Plus, she'd honed a talent with knife throwing over the years, and her knives were razor-sharp. She could pierce a running rabbit at twenty paces and gut a randy Viking bent on rape. Never openly. Best not to raise suspicions to another level.

Regina had no friends or family. She was alone, and that was how she liked it.

She enjoyed making jest of others, without their knowing. Especially fun were her threats of ridiculously impossible curses tossed at lackwit Vikings, like "Do as I command, or I'll make your cock the size of a thimble." Of late, she took great delight in being creative with her spells. "Have you ever seen a candle melt into a limp wick, Bjorn?" Or "Svein, Svein, Svein! May the winds blow so hard your braies fall off, and your cock gets twisted into a triple knot." Or "The gods are displeased at your misdeeds, Ivan, and they can turn your favorite body part black as night with running boils, stinksome as old lutefisk."

Men were so obsessed with their manparts, many of them coming to her with pleas for a magic potion to make theirs bigger, or thicker, or less ruddy. And they would try anything! Horse dung mixed with goat urine. Standing on their heads and chanting. Dipping their wicks in wax.

Never once did she have a man ask to make his smaller, not even Boris the Horse who was said to resemble his namesake.

Of course, women were just as bad. Always wanting love potions. Or ways to make their breasts bigger, or smaller, their buttocks less flabby, their hips wider. Half of them wanted concoctions to help them get pregnant, the other half wanted rid of the bairns already growing in their bellies.

None of that mattered in her longtime scheme of amassing enough wealth to buy an estate in the Saxon lands and become a grand lady. Well, mayhap not so grand, but at least respectable, in a class above the cotter class. She even had a particular property in mind, a small sheepstead with a barn and fields and a lovely stone manor house. But eleven long years of skimping and saving and still she didn't have enough. She needed a bigger influx of wealth to finally fulfill her dreams, and it would come soon with the arrival of the young Jarl Efram of nearby Winterstorm.

Ah, there he was now, just in time, leading his horse into the clearing.

"Come, come, my jarl," she said with an exaggerated cackle, motioning the fur-clad lording to follow her into her woodland hovel. Efram, new to the jarldom on the recent death of his father, was little more than a youthling at sixteen years. "You can tie your beast to yon tree, next to the boulder."

She could see that he was hesitant to go near the red-coated boulder, probably thinking the stains were blood. They were, but not human blood. She butchered her chickens and squirrels for the stew pot there. She cackled again, this time to show she noticed his squeamishness. Embarrassed, he looped the reins around the post, wiping his gloved hands on his braies.

With a sniff of distaste, Efram stooped to enter the low door of her home. He might be young, but he was tall. The ceiling, from which hung numerous bunches of herbs, almost touched Efram's blond hair, which he wore in a long, single braid. Her black cat, Thor, hissed and lunged for Efram's pant leg, and the boyling jumped, causing dried rosemary and lavender and dill to shower his head and shoulders with aromatic dried particles.

She chuckled, rather cackled, again when he shook himself of the chaff.

He was not amused and tried to kick at Thor who was already bored and scooting away to his woven pallet by the hearth, where he stretched out and proceeded to lick his private parts. Men, even feline ones, had no manners.

Inside the thatched-roof cottage was not much better than its wattle-and-daub exterior. The hard-packed dirt floor was uncovered by rushes, but she kept it swept clean and bug free. Not that the spoiled bratling, accustomed to finer fare, would notice such details.

"Where is it?" Efram demanded. "Did you make the potion?"

"I did," she said and sat down on the lone chair beside a small table that she used both for eating and preparing herbal remedies. That left only her bed if he chose to sit down, which he did not. Probably feared fleas or lice, little knowing he had more of such up at his keep than she did here. In fact, his servants were always coming to her for remedies to rid hair and beards and bedding of the varmints.

"Well, where is it? Give it to me! I came alone, as you insisted. I have to get back to the castle before my guests arrive," he said impatiently.

Guests, as in his uncle and entourage, who considered Efram too young and inexperienced for such a large holding. An uncle who would find out just how far his nephew would go to maintain an iron grip on his inheritance . . . if Regina helped him, that was.

"Where is my payment?" Regina asked with equal impatience. "Fifty mancuses of gold." Since one mancus was equal to a month's wages for a skilled worker, she figured this amount, on top of her savings equal to about two hundred mancuses, should carry her over until her sheepstead started producing income.

"You'll get your coin after I see if your potion works."

Hah! She'd known Efram would pull something like this. "You'll get no potion until I have my sack of gold. And don't be thinking of coming back and stealing back my treasure. I have friends in these woods with swords sharper than any blade of yours." Which was a lie, of course. She had no friends. "Besides, my cousin's cousin who works at Winterstorm has orders to poison your own drink if you even try to betray me."

"Why, you . . . you . . ." Efram sputtered, and his hairless cheeks blossomed with color. "How dare you insult me so?"

She shrugged. "'Tis just business, my jarl. Now, do you have the gold or not?"

Grudgingly, he parted his fur cloak and pulled out a leather sack tied to his belt. He tossed it on the table in front of her. "Do you want to count it?" he snarled.

"For a certainty," she replied with exaggerated sweetness. And she did in fact count out the fifty lovely coins.

While she was counting, his eyes darted about her small house, and his lips curled with distaste. "What is that horrible smell?" he asked, glancing toward the boiling cauldron over the fire.

It was cabbage soup, which was indeed smelly, but delicious. "Oh, just a porridge of rat tails, lizard hearts, pig snouts, sour milk, and oats," she told him. "Wouldst care for a taste?"

He gagged.

She'd counted the coins a second time and there were fifty. "Here is the potion then," she said, taking a stoppered pottery vial the size of a fist from a nearby shelf. "Be very careful. One drop would kill a war horse," let alone a full-grown man. 'Twas a mixture of deadly nightshade and water hemlock. "Because it is sweet, it will mix well, undetected, in any fermented beverage, like ale."

He nodded and reached for it, but she held it away from his grasp. "If you intend it for more than one person —" and she knew that he did. Not just his uncle, but everyone in his party. "—then you must be especially careful. This vial in a tun of ale could be accidentally tasted by innocent parties, even women and children filling the horns of ale.

Just one drop on the finger dipped on the tongue would be fatal."

Efram waved a hand airily and grabbed for the vial.

And Regina knew that he cared not who died in the process of his evil plot. She also knew that her own life was in danger once this was over because she was the only person who could disclose his plans. Ah well, she would be long gone by then.

Before nightfall, she had packed all her belongings, including her hoard of coins, onto the back of Edgar, her donkey. She'd bathed in a forest pool, tucked her bush of wild red hair into a thick braid, and donned one of the used lady's gowns she'd purchased in the market town of Kaupang. She would ride all night until she reached the harbor at Evenstead where she would sell Edgar. From there, she would take one of the merchant ships to the Saxon town of Jorvik.

She set her hovel afire before she left. Let the village folks think another witch had gone to her satanic grave. She'd tried to leave the cat behind because he would draw attention, but the lackwit creature refused. Instead of rubbing himself up against her and purring with entreaty, Thor had pissed on her new boots and spit up three hair clumps to emphasize his disdain for that idea. Cats were like that betimes.

She'd traveled half the night when her plans hit a snag. Thor, who had wrapped himself around her neck, his head and tail resting on her bosom, hissed an alert. Mayhap a cat companion was not such a bad idea after all.

Standing directly in her path, an apparition appeared, a full-body glow of light against the blackness of the dense forest. It looked like an angel Regina had seen one time painted on the walls of a Christian church in Northumbria.

"Have you no shame, witch?" the angel roared.

Double, double, toil, and lots of trouble . . .

Michael was sick to his archangel ears of Vikings.

He'd never been fond of the vain, arrogant, brutal Vikings. But then, five years ago, God assigned him to put together a band of Viking vampire angels (vangels) to fight Satan's evil Lucipires (demon vampires). His appreciation hadn't increased with close proximity to the bothersome creatures. Especially those seven Sigurdsson brothers who'd been guilty of the Seven Deadly Sins in a most heinous way. 'Twas like trying to herd cats.

And for his sins, Michael had to admit, he was not overfond of cats. His pal, St. Francis of Assisi, patron saint of animals, would be disappointed in him. But ever since that Noah and the Ark debacle, Michael just couldn't seem to abide felines. Truth to tell, two cats had entered the ark and seventy-five emerged when the floods receded. What did that say about cats?

And Vikings were no better.

Randy, crude beings, all of them!

Now, his boss (that would be God) expected him

to recruit a witch to the vangel ranks. A witch! A cauldron-boiling, potion-brewing, spell-tossing, broom-riding (well, maybe no brooms), cackling crone! Bad enough he had to deal with male Vikings, but now Norsewomen, as well, and a witch, on top of it all! It was enough to sour a saint's stomach.

Michael was in the dense forest of the frigid Norselands, freezing his holy skin under his white robes, more suited to a warm heavenly climate, when he saw his target approaching, astride a heavily laden donkey. Not a cauldron in sight, and she wasn't as cronely as he'd expected, but that was neither here nor there. On her shoulders was . . . (*What else! It was that kind of day!*) . . . a large, black, hissing cat.

Michael barely restrained himself from hissing back, but instead roared at the woman, "Have you no shame, witch? What wickedness thou dost brew!"

"Huh?" The cat bolted off for cover, the donkey balked, and the witch jerked on the reins and flew head over heels to land on the pine needle–laden ground.

"Regina Dorasdottir! Many men, women, and children died today at thy hands!"

"My hands are clean. I didn't poison anyone," she proclaimed, standing and dusting off her bottom. At least she wasn't denying that poison was involved. She knew exactly what he was talking about. The witch!

"Thou made the bane drink. Thou sold it for coin. It was used carelessly, not that careful murder is any less offensive. Many innocent people suffered painful deaths."

Immediately, he flashed a cloud picture in front of her so that she could see all the bodies in the rushes of the Winterstorm great hall, many of them lying in pools of vomit, others with blood emerging from their mouths and noses and even ears. Men, women, children, even the castle dogs. All of them dead.

Regina stepped back in fear, not at the sight of the dead bodies, apparently, but because she was seeing a picture in the air of an event that had already happened. "How did you do that? Are you a wizard performing some magic sorcery?"

"No sorcery. That is your business, witch, not mine. I am St. Michael the Archangel, and God is very angry with you."

"God? Which god would that be? Odin, Thor? Baldr?" She was taking careful steps backward as she spoke.

"There is only one God, lackwit!" He raised a hand, and a bolt of lightning shot from his fingers, hitting the woman in her heart. She clutched her chest and fell to her knees.

"Am I to be condemned for one . . . um, mistake?" She batted her long eyelashes at him in innocence. For a brief moment, he noticed that she was not unattractive, for a witch, that was. Her neatly braided red hair acted as a frame for a sharply sculpted Nordic face and green eyes, which would turn blue before this day was done, if he had his way.

But her appearance mattered not a whit, he reminded himself. Women were ever the devious ones, using their feminine wiles to persuade men to their designs. Hah! He was immune. "Mistake?

Mistake? Woman, thou hast committed many sins. Thy transgressions are so innumerable I can scarce list them. Dozens of babes killed in the womb, the addictive poppy used to make slobbering slaves of some men, and women, too, death potions for the elderly, murder . . . and, yea, killing men who came courting—"

"What? Those were potential rapists!"

"Not all of them," he contended. "Thou art also guilty of the sin of greed." He glanced pointedly at the leather sack attached to the donkey's saddle.

"Just compensation for services," she countered.

He arched his brows at that and showed her a cloud picture of her withholding a medicinal remedy for a starving family's baby with lung fever.

"Well, that is the exception," she lied.

"Then, too, there was fornication," Michael told her.

"One time. One stinking, unsatisfying time," she argued.

"Where in the Holy Book does it say that coupling has to be satisfying?" he asked.

"What about all the good I've done? There are many people I've helped with healing herbs."

"Not for a long time," he told her, then sighed. "On the celestial scales of good and evil, canst hear the thunk of weight on the one side?"

She ignored what he said and continued to argue, "And I never practiced any satanic rites, like some witches do."

"Satan comes in many forms. Some would say that practicing evil is the same as worshipping Satan."

"I still think—"

"Thou dost not think, that is thy trouble. Thou art a dreadful sinner, Regina Dorasdottir. Thou hast no morals. There is naught thou would reject doing if paid enough. If it were up to me, thou would burn in the fires of Hell."

She pulled a long-bladed knife from a belt sheath and glanced briefly at him, assessing the chances of escape. But then, her shoulders slumped as she took note of the full-body halo that enveloped him, and she dropped the weapon. "So, that's it then. I'm to die for my sins."

"Not quite."

Her head shot up at that.

"In his mercy, God is willing to give you a second chance for repentance."

She narrowed her green eyes at him. "What would I have to do?"

"Thou wouldst join the ranks of vangels, fighting in the Lord's army against evil forces."

"Me? An angel?" she scoffed.

"Not an angel. A vangel. A Viking vampire angel. Put on earth to destroy Lucifer's demon vampires, wicked creatures who prey on sinful humans, killing them before their fated time of death, giving them no chance to repent."

"Huh?"

"Explanations can come later. Dost thou choose Hell or vangeldom?"

"That's some choice! For how long?"

Michael was growing impatient. "As long as it takes. Centuries. Mayhap even until the Final Judgment Day."

"And I will live all that time, growing older and older, more feeble?"

"Dost deliberately misspeak, witch? Thou wouldst stay the same age."

"Oh. Really? Well, yes, then. Of course I agree." She paused. "But what exactly is a vam-pyre? Does it have anything to do with fire, or is—"

The time for questions had passed. She'd agreed. That was enough for Michael.

Raising both arms, he levitated her high in the air so that she twirled about, screaming as her upper jaw broke and restructured itself to accommodate newly formed fangs and her shoulder blades cracked open and grew bumps that might one day become wings. Her green eyes turned the clear blue of all vangels. *Now, do you understand what a vampire is?* At the same time, for his own pleasure, Michael sent the bristling, hissing familiar with her. *Take that, cat!*

"I changed my mind," Regina screeched.

Too late! The witch was flying through the air to parts unknown to take on her new role. And Michael was off to see what the Sigurdsson brothers were up to now. An archangel's work was never done!

Chapter 2

Transylvania, Pennsylvania, AD 2016

Beware of red-haired witches with fangs . . .

Aha! I've got him! He won't escape me now, the yellow-bellied son of a Norse boar!

Regina was in a rage.

And she'd finally trapped the one man who could help her. He wouldn't escape her this time.

"I've had enough of this glass ceiling!" she yelled up at Vikar Sigurdsson who was standing atop a twelve-foot ladder changing one of thirteen bulbs in the chandelier of the third parlor.

"Huh?" The Viking pivoted to look down at her, then had to use both hands to steady himself, which caused one of the bulbs to fall and shatter on the parquet floor.

He muttered something foul under his breath about fucked-up, bothersome witches. It was the kind of thing vangels were not supposed to say. At least he hadn't used the Lord's name as an expletive. That was a definite no-no. Still, he better hope Mike hadn't heard him. Mike was the rude nickname the vangels gave St. Michael. Not in his presence, of course. They weren't total fools. And anyway, why were male vangels always blaming the witch side of her nature for every little mishap; she was as much a vangel as they were, and that was the point.

Good thing she'd locked Thor in her bedchamber or the cat would also be blamed if Vikar came tumbling down on his fine Viking arse or his hard Viking head. Folks were always saying lackwitted things about witches, black cats, and stepladders!

"What glass ceiling?" Vikar sniped, now that he'd steadied himself. "I swear, we've replastered every ceiling in this damn castle, all hundred or so of them, and not one of them was glass." Restoration of the rundown castle was a sore point with Vikar, who had been attempting to make the crumbling ruin livable for the past five years. A never-ending battle, he was always bemoaning. Guilty of the sin of pride, Vikar still found it hard to reconcile that he was forced to live in a dump in Transylvania, of all places, and not Transylvania, Romania, either. This was the town of Transylvania, Pennsylvania, a corny, vampire tourist trap. If Regina didn't have other things on her mind, she would taunt him about his lowly assignment.

"You dope!" She probably shouldn't insult the head of their vangel clan, so to speak, but she was spitting mad. "Glass ceiling is a metaphor for the invisible barriers that keep women from rising to the top."

"Met-a-whore? What's that? No, don't tell me."

He rolled his eyes and muttered something about there being a reason why he avoided witches, and her in particular, all the time. He probably knew all along what a glass ceiling was, and a metaphor, too. "Holy clouds, woman! Can't this wait until I am off this death trap?"

"What difference does it make? You're dead anyway," she pointed out, arms folded over the chest of her tunic, tapping her foot impatiently.

Vikar noticed her foot tapping, and her attire, as well. The idiot preferred that the female vangels wear gowns in the ancient Norsewoman fashion, complete with ankle-length, open-sided apron, to distinguish them from the human females. Hah! She would wear an apron when Vikar started wearing ballet slippers, and she'd told him so, more than once. Regina much preferred leather braies and belted tunics. She looked good in such an outfit, too.

"What's your point, Regina? I let you put a Crock-Pot in your room."

"A Crock-Pot is not a cauldron," she asserted with affront. Vikar . . . in fact, all the Viking men . . . liked to mock her witchly activities. He probably thought she wanted to brew some bat wing and rat tail concoction, and not some healing remedy for bloody tongues. Vangels were always accidentally biting their tongues with their fangs. It was an occupational hazard, you might say.

"And even though I have rules against indoor pets, I have allowed your cat free rein of the castle."

Allowed? She'd like to give him "allowed" smack-dab in his hard arse which was pointed right at her as he climbed down the ladder. "Hah! Try and stop Thor from coming inside."

"I did, and it took two sennights for the scratch marks to heal. Anyhow, you are never happy, Regina. Didn't I give you that small room for drying your herbs and brewing your potions?"

"In the dungeon!"

"We do not call it a dungeon anymore. 'Tis the basement."

She counted to five in Old Norse to tamp down her temper. "You are not utilizing my talents, master." She'd added that master title to soften Vikar up, if that was possible. "For years I have been given the menial tasks. Guard the security gate. Act as backup for the front line team of vangels, which, incidentally, in case you haven't noticed, are all men."

"Have you suddenly become a feminist?" he tried to jest as he untied the tool belt around his waist.

Men and their tool belts. They could be fat as autumn hogs and smell like days-old gammelost, and still they thought the addition of a tool belt turned them into Svein the Sexy, with the usual, "Wouldst like to climb aboard and check out my longboat?"

Not in this century, or any other! "I have always been a feminist."

"Gloria Steinem of the Dark Ages, huh?" he quipped.

She would yank at her own hair in frustration if it hadn't taken her an hour to twist the red bush into a neat single braid down her back.

Vikar continued on his roll of humor. "Really?

I did not know they had bra burners back in the twelfth century. Or bras, for that matter. Mayhap they burned their chastity belts. Ha, ha, ha!"

"Very funny!" She was not amused. "I'm beginning to think you are a misogynist."

"A who? I do not do massages . . . well, unless they are for my wife in the midst of bedplay, and even then—"

"Aaarrgh! With all due respect, Vikar, betimes you are an asshole."

He grinned, probably thinking he'd successfully changed the subject and would be able to send her on her meek way.

"Even the American military, and those across the ocean, use women in combat today."

"We are not the Army, or Navy, or whatever. We fight for a higher power."

"I demand to be given a mission of worth," she said, jabbing a finger into his chest and backing him up until he hit the wall. It did not matter that he was six-foot-four and she a scarce five-foot-seven. A witch's finger could be a deadly weapon. In fact, just for a second, she pointed downward, and saw him shiver with dread. Viking men always feared her threats of a curse on their man-parts. Some were doubtful of her ability to actually put one in knots or curl it up into a little worm, but they took no chances.

Vikar put up both hands in surrender, laughing (but only halfway). "What exactly do you want, Regina?"

"I want an assignment that tests my talents. No more gentle, feminine jobs that keep me out of direct fighting. I have decided on just the mission."

"Oh?" he asked hesitantly.

"I am going to rescue Zebulan."

"No!" Vikar exploded and shoved away from her, stomping out into the hall and heading toward the kitchen. "No, no, no, a hundred times no!" he yelled back at her along the way.

She followed after him, doggedly, as they passed the office, the computer room, a small chapel, both a large and a small dining room. Everywhere vangels were at work, as they always were when not out on a mission, with brooms and mops, at computers, sanding mildewed wainscoting, sharpening swords, painting walls. In another parlor turned family room, Armod, the young Icelandic vangel who fashioned himself a Michael Jackson reincarnated, was teaching the young, human children how to moonwalk to the music of "Thriller."

When they got to the massive kitchen, she saw that Lizzie Borden, the cook, was chopping a deboned beef carcass into stew-size pieces with her culinary axe . . . uh, cleaver. (Yes, that Lizzie Borden. Enough said! If Regina had said it once, she'd said it a hundred times: Norsemen had a warped sense of humor, but then, mayhap angels did, too, since St. Michael picked those sinners to turn into vampire angels.)

At the other end of the fifty-foot center island, Lizzie's new assistant cook, Andrea . . . a pastry chef, actually . . . was baking something that smelled delicious. Cream-filled crepes, maybe. Or coconut and peppermint iced donuts. Andrea and her husband, Cnut Sigurdsson, were always salivating over those two flavors, for some reason.

Andrea had been an accomplished dessert maker before wedding Cnut, the last of the seven Sigurdsson brothers to bite the marriage bullet.

Andrea nodded Regina's way and then gave a surreptitious little fist pump at Regina. Andrea was aware of Regina's plan to "assault" Vikar today with her proposal.

Lizzie knew about Regina's plans, too, but Lizzie's suggestion had been that Regina shouldn't bother asking for permission, she should just put an axe to Vikar's neck and tell the Viking to give his approval, or else. Chop, chop.

Yeah, that would work. In a castle full of vangel soldiers! Regina would get about as far as the gazebo out back.

Vikar went directly to the commercial-size fridge and took out a carton of Fake-O, which he downed with a grimace in one long gulp. When vangels saved a sinner or killed a Lucipire, their skin turned a nice, healthy tan color. Otherwise, they had to feed on blood, or the fake synthetic blood invented by one of the brothers. Fake-O. That was another gripe she had for Vikar. With the lack of real fighting assignments, Regina was forced to drink more and more of the simulated crap, and it was repulsive to say the least.

"Back to Zebulan," she said to Vikar. "I have an idea that—"

Vikar put up a halting hand. "Zeb has been gone for more than a year. If it were possible to rescue the Lucie, I would have taken an army to do the job long ago." Lucie was the nickname that vangels gave to Lucipires, or demon vampires, of which Zeb was one. Well, leastways he had been until a few years ago when he'd turned double agent for Michael. He was still a demon, but a good one, if that were possible.

Cnut walked in then, coming up from the dungeon, rather the basement steps. He wore a T-shirt with the sleeves torn off and jeans, and athletic shoes. His head was half shaved on both sides and braided down the center in that ridiculous Ragnor Lothbrok style from the *Vikings* show on the History Channel. He was dripping sweat which meant he'd probably been teaching fighting skills to the newer vangels.

Wiping his forehead with a gym-style towel wrapped around his neck, he leaned over and kissed his wife, then said to Vikar, "Did I hear you mention Zeb? If anyone should go after him, it's me. After all, he traded himself for my sorry ass."

Vikar shook his head. "You know what Mike said. Zeb is dead to us. Gone to a place where he can no longer be helped. And he forbade us specifically from going after him."

Cnut nodded reluctantly.

But Regina had another idea. "Actually, what he said was, 'You men, all of you, are forbidden from rescuing Zebulan.' You know what that means, don't you?"

Andrea stopped piping whipped cream from a pastry bag into her delicacies. Lizzie stopped chopping the bloody meat. And Cnut turned inch by inch to gape at her.

It was Vikar who said, "What?"

"I am not a man."

Ding dong, the witch is here . . .

Regina had a plan for rescuing Zebulan the Hebrew.

Okay, it wasn't a plan exactly. More of a wish list for how things would work out. A wish list plan. *I know, I know. A witch wish list. Try saying that real fast. Don't laugh. At least I'm trying.*

And she was going to succeed, or die trying. Again. Since she was already dead, of course. *No, no negative thoughts. Focus. I am witch. I am vangel. I am woman. Hear me roar. Or cackle. Or something. Holy clouds, I'm so scared I could pee my skinny britches.*

Through a series of hits and misses, Regina had managed to make several wrong turns on the teletransport highway. *So sue me. I haven't had that much experience with molecular transfer, no thanks to the frickin' Viking powers-that-be, that chauvinist Vikar. And, you're right, I don't have a clue what "molecular transfer" means. Harek Sigurdsson, the smartest of all the vangels, taught me that phrase.*

In any case, she'd accidentally skidded through time and the world into some creepy castles where she encountered even creepier inhabitants. *Can anyone say Bran Castle, or Dracula? Now, that is one creepy dude! Or how about Moosham Castle in Austria, better known as Witches Castle, where several thousand young girls met their fate? Why does everyone pick on witches, by the by? And why fire? And then there was the Black Gate, which should have in no way been confused with a demon lair, but I somehow hydroplaned there. Yikes!*

But she had finally located Horror, Jasper's castle in the frozen tundra, far north of Norway. Check one off her list. *And remind myself to bring a fur cloak next time, instead of this silk-lined one, if there is a next time, please not, God! Brrr! And forget skinny jeans! Whoever invented them couldn't have been a woman. I'm cleaving my crotch here when I'm not freezing my buns off. If I bend over, I can't breathe, and any breath that comes out is frozen in the air.*

Get over yourself, Regina, she chastised herself. *You are where you wanted to be. On an important mission.*

Still, it would have been a lot easier if teletransport had GPS or if she had an iPhone with special apps. "Hey, Siri, where is Horror?" Or she could have googled Jasper's address, like that would be listed! "Jasper Lucipire, 101 Frosty Lane, North Pole." Or the Google search would have responded with an inquiry, "Did you mean Jasper Claus?" As if she was looking for Santa's evil brother! Not!

In the best of circumstances, Vikar or Mike could have drawn her a map, but they hadn't exactly given their blessings to undertake this road trip to Hell, so to speak. In her defense, she'd informed the vangel leader of her intentions regarding Zebulan, and to her mind that amounted to a permission of sorts, even though he'd said no. In fact, his last "No!" to her had been barely a shout. She figured she would have worn him down eventually, but she hadn't wanted to waste the time. Better to err and ask for forgiveness later than seek permission ahead of time. Or so she justified in her mind. *Some saint said that, didn't he? Maybe St. Augustine. No, he was the one who prayed,*

"*Dear God, let me be pure, but not yet.*" *Or some such thing. Whatever.*

As for Mike, he probably knew of her transgression by now since she'd been gone for two, almost three days. She declined to think what her punishment might end up being. *Surely, if I'm successful, there will be no punishment. Yeah, right. And I have a cloud to sell anyone who believes that!* She couldn't think about the future now.

Next, she'd had to case the perimeter of the vast building and grounds. More shivering! But check two on her list.

Infiltrating the castle had been easier than she'd expected. *I am vangel, watch me teletransport through two-foot, iron-studded doors!* Of course, vangels weren't supposed to use their teletransporting skills in such a light manner, when other means of entry might be available, and she was new at this advanced level, but she couldn't help but be delighted that she'd done it so well. *Yay, me!* Anyhow, check three for that one.

Now to find Zebulan's location, which she'd heard via the witch grapevine was inside a cave, presumably connected to or below the castle. Check four. And, yes, there were still witches around today, more than modern folks would believe. They blended in now, though. No more pointy hats or riding brooms, if there ever had been. And only an occasional cackle, which Regina thought was unfortunate. A good cackle could make the biggest man wet his braies with fright.

She'd been hiding in a broken, ancient elevator shaft all day, waiting for nighttime to come when the castle would presumably settle down, and she could explore. Actually, this far north and at this time of the year, mid-October, it was dark except for a few hours daily. Polar Night, it was called. So, it was more silence than light she was waiting for. Demons presumably slept sometime.

The walls of the wooden chute refracted sound, creating an echo of footsteps above and below, along with more than a few screams as new recruits were being tortured. Maybe one of them was Zebulan. No. Somehow, she didn't imagine him screaming, though everyone had a breaking point, as she well knew, having broken more than a few individuals herself in her time.

She'd never met the Hebrew in person, although she had seen him from a distance the few times he'd visited the castle in Transylvania. A handsome man when in human form. Tall. Lean, but well-muscled. Brown hair and eyes. Slightly aquiline nose. Like some ancient Hebrew warrior in a pair of blue jeans.

Silence finally overcame the castle. She waited several hours beyond that, past midnight, she guessed, and was about to emerge from her hiding place when a female voice whispered, "I smell witch."

Regina jumped back.

"*Mais, oui*, Patience, darlin'. Ah cain't help but notice the odor, too," a male voice drawled out in a strong Southern accent. There were several exaggerated sniffing sounds, whether from the male or female, Regina couldn't tell, but then the man resumed talking, "Smells lak the bayou. Ah declare, Patience, it reminds me of home. Toad and eye of newt, with a touch of banewort. Very swampy."

"You think everything smells like the bayou, Beauregard," the woman, Patience, said, drawing out the man's name so it sounded like Bow-rah-gahd. "Not all toads come from the swamp, you know. We had toads in Salem, too."

"Picky, picky! You said you smelled a witch, and you mentioned toads, and Holy Crawfish! Any Cajun with bayou mud in his veins would expect you meant swamp toads."

"Cajun, Cajun, Cajun! That's all you think about, Beau. I was about to mention that I also smell rosemary, thyme, and vervain," Patience sniped.

I smell like toad? Swampy? Are you kidding me? Regina unsheathed two of her favorite blades, and arranged her cloak off her shoulders to give her more arm room. She arched her back to get rid of the kinks from standing in one position for so long.

"Come out, come out, wherever you are, cackle, cackle," another female voice cajoled. Older sounding.

"'Tis not a game, Grimey," Beau chided the older woman. "We're not even certain of its witchliness."

"I'll give you Grimey, you worthless hordling. Scarce twenty years as a Lucipire and he thinks he can take liberties with his betters." There was a swatting sound, followed by a male "Ouch!"

So, this dude was a hordling. In other words, a young Lucie. In the social order of demons, there were high haakai, haakai, mungs, hordlings and imps, the foot soldiers of Hell, so to speak.

"Sorry Ah am, Grimelda," the man said, the twinkle in his voice belying any sense of apology.

Okay, this was getting ridiculous. Patience, Grimelda, and Beauregard? Maybe I'm not really in Horror Castle, but Bedlam, instead.

"Definitely a witch. Sniff, sniff, sniff," the younger female voice said. "But there's a different smell, too. Could it be . . . no, that's impossible. A witch vangel?"

"Ah've never heard of such before," Beau said skeptically.

"No worse'n demon Lucipires. Devil witches with fangs, angel witches with fangs. Could say we're kinfolk," the old lady laughed . . . uh, cackled.

Suddenly, three huge creatures literally fell into the shaft next to Regina, crowding her against the wall. They were demons, all right. Demon vampires with fangs and red eyes and scaly skin and claws and tails. But they also had the scent of witches about them. Such odors were only sensed by fellow witches. And, no, it wasn't the swampy, putrid odor of warty amphibians. More like a combination of wood ash and lavender.

She would have been frightened, except the three beasts were almost comical as they elbowed each other trying to fit into the tight space.

"Oh, spit," the younger female demon said . . . Patience, Regina assumed . . . as she morphed into human form. A twentysomething woman with jet black hair and eerie pale green eyes, wearing a modest muslin gown of seventeen hundreds vintage, with a wide, crisscrossed, white collar, and big-buckled black shoes. Very plain attire. Was she Amish? They had plenty of those living outside the home castle in Transylvania. No, not Amish. Puritan, Regina decided.

The other two followed suit, taking on human-oid personalities.

Beauregard turned out to be a lean, thirty-ish guy wearing a New Orleans Saints T-shirt hanging outside his faded jeans. On his feet were scruffy, flat-soled boots. His shoulder-length, dark hair was tied at his nape with a leather thong into a small ponytail. Dark mischievous eyes. Not bad looking.

Grimelda was eighty if she was a day, with straggly gray hair and rheumy, colorless eyes, wearing a black gunna with a long, open-sided apron in the old Viking style. They all exhibited fangs and reeked of a combination of dragon's blood, valerian, and sulfur, along with the usual ashy lavender witch scent.

"Who the hell are all of you?" Regina asked, encompassing all of them.

"Better question, chère, is who are you?" Beau countered.

Regina wasn't about to give up any information that could be used against her. "Just a visitor. Lost. On my way to . . . um, Skalgard."

"Hah!" Grimelda said. "More like yer on yer way ta trouble."

"We are a secret coven here at Horror," Patience revealed. "Have you come to rescue us?"

"Rescue? From what?"

"Lucipiredom," Patience said bleakly.

"You don't want to be demon vampires?" Regina inquired. Maybe Zebulan wasn't the only reluctant Lucipire.

"Does a skunk wanna stink? Does anyone wanna be a demon?" Beau scoffed, as if Regina might be dimwitted.

That fact was corroborated when Grimelda turned to her companions and remarked, "Must be she is daft? Mayhap she is not our savior, after all."

A savior? Me?

"Well, yes, many people do want to be Lucipires . . . in fact, most who come here . . . after many years of indoctrination," Patience pointed out.

"You sound like yer givin' a lecture," Beau observed.

"You sound like a dumb Cajun," Patience retorted.

"Some Lucipires really do like their, um, calling," Patience insisted. "Like Beltane, who's been a Lucipire for two hundred years."

"Beltane is Jasper's pampered assistant. Lak a lapdog, he is," Beau explained to Regina with disgust. "Ah've tried talkin' to the boy, as a fellow southerner, even brought him some sweet beignets from N'awleans. As my PawPaw always said, 'If it looks lak a possum, and smells lak a possum, doan be expectin' no gator.' The snot tattled ta Jasper that Ah was up ta something."

"Which you were," Patience pointed out.

"That's beside the point."

Figuring that introductions were in order, Regina told them, "My name is Regina."

And they introduced themselves as Beauregard Doucet, Patience Allister, and Grimelda the Witch.

"Actually, I *am* here on a rescue mission," Regina told them, "but only for one person, and he is not one of you. Sor-r-r-ry."

The three Lucies hissed with anger, but then

Grimelda cackled and told the others, "You know who she means, don't you? The Hebrew."

"Ah," Patience and Beau concurred.

"You'll never find him," Grimelda told her, wagging a bony finger in Regina's face. "Not without our help."

"And what would you want in return?" She eyed the three idiots through slitted eyes.

"Take us with you," Beau replied.

"I don't think so." *Not in a million years.* "Where would you go?"

"To your home," Beau said.

The castle in Pennsylvania? Oh, no, no, no!

"Back to wherever you vangels live," Patience elaborated, as if Regina hadn't understood what she meant.

Good Lord! I'll be in enough trouble as it is, assuming I'm able to get Zebulan out of here, let alone bring three lackwit demon witches with me. But Regina was no fool. She could use their help. "Sure," she lied.

"We'll take you ta him, but y'all kin only see him fer a moment. Can't risk gettin' caught until we have a plan fer a mass exodus," Beau said, rubbing his hands together gleefully.

Yeah, but Moses had God on his side when he led the Exodus. I don't even have St. Michael watching my back.

Soon, she was walking stealthily through a narrow corridor below the ground that led to a huge cavern. Stalactites and stalagmites abounded. The floors and walls reeked of ancient dirt. There was a wooden rack and torture implements sitting on battered cuttingboard-like tables. A massive Lucipire snored loudly in a reclining leather chair. And against one wall was chained a naked man, lying on a low pallet.

She gasped at his condition.

It was Zebulan, in humanoid form, but unlike the man she had seen in the past. His face was bruised black and blue and yellow with swollen lips and eyes. Patches of hair had been torn from his head. Flaps of skin hung here and there on his emaciated body. His fingertips and toes were bloody and without nails. There was a barbed wire wrapped around his penis.

Suddenly his eyes opened and connected with hers.

"Oh shit!" he muttered. "It's Satan's sister."

"Think again, lackwit. I am Regina, the answer to your prayers."

The Lucipire guard snuffled in his sleep. Regina couldn't risk waking him, or killing him, and thus alerting others who might come to relieve him, until she was sure of her exit route. She backed up and rushed away, but she would be back, as soon as possible.

As she sought her three witch cohorts, she mused on what she had seen. There was always much talk about man's inhumanity to man. It was nothing compared to the devil's inhumanity, she decided.

More than ever, Regina was committed to saving Zebulan.

Even if he did consider her Satan's sister.

Chapter 3

What's your worst nightmare?...

It was like an old-time movie reel playing over and over in his head, and on the walls of the cave, and on the ceiling. Even on the dirt floor. No escape. And it was driving Zeb crazy. No, not crazy. Madness might be a relief, actually. Anything but this continual amping up of his emotions to the point of either crushing shame or a raw yearning for what he would never have again, then slam-bang back to the reality of his cave prison. A brief respite. Then a repeat. Amp up, slam back, pause. Amp up, slam back, pause. Amp up, slam back, pause. Again. Again. And again.

Welcome to Hell on earth. Personalized torture. Only the most wicked mind could think of this type of torment.

Zeb had never considered himself invincible, but after a year of agonizing physical torture, he'd deluded himself into thinking he might just be able to withstand all that Jasper threw his way.

He was wrong.

Once Satan entered the picture, the game

changed. The essence of evil understood that, for some men, the worst torture involved the head, or the heart. Emotional zapping of the very soul, over and over and over. Pictures of the love he had had, and lost. Pictures of what he had done to gain riches, and how he had paid a price beyond measure.

If only he had been satisfied with his small vineyard in the Shomron valley which fulfilled the needs of his small family and half a dozen workers!

If only he had stayed at home and never bartered his fighting skills with the Roman Army in exchange for coin to purchase more land!

If only he had not returned to the wasting fortress city of Masada!

If only he had not killed, even indirectly, his sweet Sarah and precious twins Mikah and Rachel!

If only he hadn't taken his own life before he had a chance to repent, assuming he would have come to his senses, eventually!

Days ago, Zeb had been released from the rack. That should have been his first clue that the game had changed. He still had iron cuffs about his raw and bleeding wrists and ankles, but the chains linking him to the walls were long enough that he could lie on the filthy mattress.

He fought sleep, though, because every time he closed his eyes he saw a replay of his sorry human life. And not just the horrible end where he witnessed the dead bodies of his wife and children, and his role in their fate, but the early, happier days when they all lived together on the small plot of rich soil passed down through his family for generations of vintners, a property which had never been enough for his greedy ambitions. Of course, this agonizing replay of his human life was visible all around him, not just in sleep, like 360 degrees of HD television screens.

To make things more unbearable, Craven was always around as witness to Zeb's visual life. Like a peeping tom of the worst sort. Craven had once been a servant of the Marquis de Sade. Enough said!

Jasper joined Craven on occasion. Dumb and Dumber. Mean and Meaner. They would sit about in demonoid form in special recliners designed to accommodate their tails watching his life as if it were a fucking soap opera. They even ate popcorn and slurped on red slushies made with the blood of the latest human harvest.

Their running commentaries added fuel to Zeb's burning emotional torture. As intended, no doubt.

"Look at them titties," Craven said when Zeb was seen making love to his wife.

Slurp, slurp, crunch, crunch.

"I'd like a taste of that honey bush," Jasper added.

Slurp, slurp, crunch, crunch.

"Ah, look at the little kiddies, master." Craven was watching Zeb's children as they played tag among the grapevines. "Wish we had sweet morsels like that here at the castle. Wouldn't I love to prick some young skin!"

"Children are innocent. We want no innocents here, fool," Jasper replied.

Slurp, slurp, crunch, crunch.

Lucipires killed evil, irredeemable humans to increase their ranks, but they also preyed on those sinners who might have repented if given a chance to live to their natural deaths.

"I know that!" Craven said. "I'm just saying."

On the next screen was a view of Masada, and Jasper remarked, "I do like a hellish fire. Wish I had been there."

Craven nodded. "I do love the smell of burning bodies!"

After starving out the Jewish rebels at Masada, the Roman soldiers had set the bodies afire. That's when Zeb had arrived, just back from the Saxon lands where he'd been posted for the past two years, just in time to clean up "the mess."

Zeb screamed silently, and madness swirled and teased at his brain. Then abated. No such relief.

Please, God, if you are there for such a wretched soul as me, Zeb prayed, *help me.*

He got his answer that night when he was alone with only Craven, who slept in his recliner, snoring and snorting in his deep sleep, popping out noxious gases from his nether end. It was not the answer he'd expected, or wanted.

Standing in the doorway that led into the tunnel connecting the cave to the castle above was a woman wearing a black tunic belted over tight black pants tucked into black boots. Really tight black pants. Numerous knives of various sizes were tucked into special sheaths in her belt, and she held one in each of her hands. A long black cloak, also fitted with weapons, was shoved back off her shoulders. Her hair was red, and her skin smooth as cream. She looked just like . . .

"Oh shit!" he muttered. "It's Satan's sister."

"Think again, lackwit. I am Regina, the answer to your prayers."

Craven shifted in his recliner and appeared to be waking, but then he fell back asleep. When Zeb glanced back to the doorway, the woman was gone.

Had he imagined her?

The Lone Ranger and the Three Musketeers, all rolled into one . . .

"**A**h doan understand," Beau said after they left Horror's cave torture chamber, known as "The Pit," and were locked in a broom closet, all four of them! "How is watching movies torture? Ah love goin' ta the movies. Better yet, playin' videos on mah own TV. Ah have . . . *had* . . . a collection of DVDs that reached mah ceiling. After a day of trappin' down the bayou, ain't nothin' like a good ol' *Die Hard* flick while snackin' on some sweet tea and pork rinds."

He flashed a mischievous grin at them all, which made Regina wonder if Beau didn't put on an act as a dumb redneck. Even so, Regina had to remind herself that he was a young Lucie, only twenty demon years on top of his thirty human years. He would be familiar, somewhat, with modern technology, at least up to the age of DVDs.

"Fool!" Patience said. "That wasn't *movie* movies. Didn't you see that Zebulan was in those pictures?" Patience, on the other hand, had passed more than three hundred years, since the Salem witch trials, or so she'd told Regina this morning. Still, Patience had been a demon in modern times long enough to be aware of the changing world, somewhat, like Beau.

"Maybe they were home movies," Beau persisted.

Grimelda rolled her rheumy eyes. "Lackwits, all of ye! Didn't ye catch the scent of Satan down there? For a certainty, Satan don't do no entertaining of his victims."

They all nodded at that observation, including Regina.

It didn't take a rocket scientist, or even an above-average-in-intelligence vangel witch like Regina, after a few minutes in Horror's cave torture chamber, to figure out what all those flashing pictures meant. Satan had come up with a devious plan for driving Zeb crazy with tormenting pictures of his past life.

On that not so happy note, Regina agreed to stay in the broom closet during the day while the three demon witches went about their regular duties at the castle. They would meet together later that night to come up with a plan for Zeb's rescue. At the least, they would take Regina back to talk with him, if possible.

And so, twenty-two and a half hours later (*but who was counting?*), Regina found herself being driven crazy, just like Zeb, except her tormenters were three demon witches (*well, two witches and a warlock*) as she stayed hidden in the infernal broom closet (*ironical, huh? Brooms, witches, get it?*) waiting for the opportunity to approach Zeb again. The only sounds outside her locked door were intermittent screams coming from the distance.

Regina wondered if some of those screams came from Zeb. But, no, she was too far away, here in the castle itself, to hear him in the cave.

The space was actually rather large for a utility closet, about six by ten. Who knew that so many brooms would be needed for a castle or that there were so many types? Floor, fireplace, snow, whisk, push, angled, wet/dry, cobweb chaser. The only ones missing were racing brooms. Harry Potter cornered the market on those. *Ha, ha, ha.* It was a sign of her diminishing sanity that she could find humor in her situation. There were even demon-tail fluffer brooms. *Don't ask.*

Her three cohorts-in-madness never came to beleaguer her all together. One at a time was more than enough, believe you me. They were trying their best not to draw attention to her presence as they went about their daily routines.

Grimelda was working in the castle kitchens that day, and whew-boy did she stink of blood. Now, vangels were no different than demons in that they had built-in yearnings for blood, but the Lucipires overdid it, using blood in practically all their dishes. Not just the usual black pudding (sausage) or *blodplattar* (Nordic pancakes made with blood), substituting human fluids for animals. Everything had at least a dash of hemoglobin. Today, they were making meatballs and pasta with vodka sauce, heavy on the blood in the red gravy. Yuck, yuck, yuck!

"Try it. You'll like it," Grimelda said with a cackle, handing her a foil-wrapped meatball sandwich.

There was an overhead light in the closet which could be turned on or off with a long chain, thus allowing Regina to see the old witch clearly. She wore her usual scruffy black attire with the open-sided Viking apron, its white color splotched with red sauce (or blood). Her long gray hair was bunched up into a hair net (who knew demons were so fastidious?), and her fangs had a reddish hue today, presumably from tasting so much . . . well, you know what.

"Maybe later," Regina said, placing the sandwich on a shelf behind her.

"'Tis only half blood, half crushed tomatoes," Grimelda told her with a wicked gleam in her rheumy eyes.

Regina wasn't sure what that gleam implied. Probably that there were toad hairs or eye of newt in the sauce, too. Or that the crone had crushed the tomatoes herself . . . with her very own feet, or something equally distasteful.

She did take a drink of the bottled water Grimelda had brought with her, though, making sure to limit herself to a few sips. Otherwise, she would have to find a bathroom soon.

"Another hour and you should be able to visit the prisoner," Grimelda said abruptly as she examined a set of old-fashioned corn brooms. "I put a potion in Craven's beer. He should be out for at least three hours."

"What? Why didn't you tell me that to begin with?"

"I'm telling ye now."

"Why are you doling out potions without consulting me?"

Grimelda gave her a look that pretty much said "You're not the boss of me."

"Do Patience and Beau know about this?"

"They do now."

"Aaarrgh! I thought we were working together."

Grimelda had a long-handled broom in hand and was checking its heft, angling it this way and that, as if for flying. She just shrugged at Regina's consternation.

"I expect we will be out of Horror by tomorrow," Grimelda said. "Where do you plan on taking us?"

Regina had originally planned to take Zeb back to the castle in Transylvania, no matter what Mike or Vikar had said. She didn't think they would turn him away, not in his present condition. But Zeb *and* three demon witches? No way! First of all, she wasn't sure she could do a tandem teletransport with another person, assuming Zeb was able to handle his end of things, which was starting to seem highly unlikely. Somehow, she would figure a way to rescue him. But a five-person jump through space defied even the remotest possibility.

"Um . . . I was thinking that I would get Zeb out of here first, then come back for you three, one at a time," she said.

Grimelda just laughed, and it wasn't a nice laugh. More a cackle.

"Surely, you can see that all of us leaving at once would be impossible," Regina said.

"It's all or none, dearling. And lest ye be thinking I'm a frail old woman that ye could overcome, jist know there are potions and there are *potions*." She glanced pointedly at the water bottle that Regina still held in one hand.

"What? Did you put something in here?" She dropped the plastic bottle to the floor.

"'Course not," Grimelda said, examining her grimy fingernails. "But it would be a shame if ye were to have a bout of bloody bowel flux whilst in this closet, now wouldn't it?"

"You are a . . . witch!" Regina seethed, lunging for the old lady who managed to slip through the door, cackling. Outside, she could hear Grimelda talking to someone about the broom she must have carried out with her. Otherwise, Regina probably would have followed after her.

Minutes later, Patience showed up. Her mob cap was askew and her dress was rumpled. Regina didn't dare ask what her job had been for the day. "Do not be letting Grimey bother you," Patience advised when apprised of what she'd told Regina. "She means well."

"By threatening me with a laxative?"

"Well, not that, but by giving Craven a potion. I tried to seduce him away from the cave, but little good it did me," Patience said, waving a hand to indicate her manhandled apparel. "He was good for only five minutes. Not enough time for me to lure him away. The clod!"

Regina shouldn't have been appalled, but she was. Patience had engaged in sex with the beast, just to distract him long enough for Regina to talk to Zeb? It was more than she herself was willing to do. Probably.

"In any case, Beau will come within the hour to guide you back to the cave. You must determine whether the Hebrew is able to be moved. Not just physically moving him with all his injuries, but through space. Where will we be going, by the by? I mean, where exactly is the vangel headquarters?"

Regina wasn't about to give up that confidential information. "Oh, there are several headquarters. I'm not sure which one we'll go to. It's something I'll discuss with Zebulan."

Patience nodded. "I cannot wait to be out of here. Three hundred and twenty-seven years since I was burned at the stake, which was naught, compared to these three hundred and twenty-seven years of being a demon." There were tears in her eyes as she gazed at Regina.

Guilt overwhelmed Regina at the thought of leaving this woman behind, but what else could she do? Maybe she really could come back some-time later?

Yeah, and broomsticks can fly!

It was only minutes later, but seemed like hours, before Beau arrived. He had just showered and changed into the same attire as yesterday, though clean, explaining that he'd been in physical training to be a Lucipire all day long and had been stinky with sweat. "Ah smelled bad enough ta knock a dawg off a gut wagon," he said in his usual colorful way.

"As if that's important to me. You could smell like a toad for all I care," she snapped. "I need to get out of here."

"Keep in mind, *chère*. The best thing about us toads is we kin eat what bugs us." He waggled his dark eyebrows at her. "C'mon. Ah'll take you to the cave."

"Really? Just like that, I can leave now. Um, why don't you just point me the way, and I'll go myself." The sooner she was rid of these three yahoos the better.

But he wasn't buying that. "Darlin', you have as much chance of findin' that cave dungeon as a one-legged lady at an ass-kicking contest."

"Charming!" she murmured at his word choice.

Beau just grinned, took her by the hand and led her down the deserted corridor, looking right and left to make sure no one saw them. Once, he yanked her into a niche until two imps came tumbling by, talking enthusiastically about going to a game room. Regina didn't want to think about what games they might be playing.

Regina could probably handle two imps on her own. Imps were the weakest of all demons. If they had been mungs or haakai, that would be a different story. Even if these two imps were lower-level devils, it was best not to draw their attention. So, they waited, and Regina became aware of Beau's musky male scent, not unpleasant except for the sulfurous undertones.

After at least fifteen minutes of travel along the twists and turns, steps, and creaky iron doors, they came to the cave where Zeb was being held. Along the way, they'd seen other caves and other long-held victims whose conditions were beyond pitiful. It made Regina feel guilty that she just passed them by, but she couldn't help everyone, and, really, demons deserved what they got. Didn't they? Most of them anyway.

Craven was indeed fast asleep from Grimelda's potion, but Zeb's eyes were wide open.

"You again?" he said. "So I wasn't dreaming when I saw you last night?"

"No, you weren't dreaming, but you'll wish you were if you call me Satan's sister again."

Zeb grinned, or tried to with his raw, blood-seeping lips. "I know who you are now. A vangel. Regina the Witch. I saw you one time at . . ." He glanced behind Regina at Beau who was examining some of the torture implements. ". . . at the castle."

She nodded, understanding that he didn't want to give away any details about the vangel head-quarters, even to a Lucipire who appeared to be helping her.

"Why are you here?"

"To rescue you."

"Lord help me!"

"You better hope the Lord is on your side," she snapped.

"And the old witch who gave Craven the beer?"

"That was Grimelda. She's helping me, along with Patience Allister who's standing guard with her at the tunnel entrance. And Beauregard Doucet." She motioned toward Beau who was gawking at the walls where moving pictures were being shown of Zeb kissing a woman, with two laughing children tugging on their knees to be picked up, a loop of images being repeated over and over. She would have liked to look closer herself. Zeb appeared to be a really good kisser.

Beau shook his head as if to clear it (Regina did, too) and said to Zeb, "We've howdied but ain't shook hands yet."

There was the thing! In the short time Regina had come to know Beau, he had spouted enough Cajun colloquialisms to fill a book, one hokier than the other, even in the midst of dire danger. Did he deliberately try to appear dumb as a rock?

"The Cajun," Zeb said in recognition. Apparently, he'd been exposed to a few of Beau's sayings, as well. Then Zeb turned back to Regina. "Whose half-brained idea was it to engage three witch Lucipires to help you? They aren't called the Crazy Coven for nothing."

Well, that was rude. "Three witches do not a coven make," she remarked.

"We're recruiting," Beau said defensively, "but not everyone can be a witch, ya know."

"I know." *I really do.*

"Besides, we witches have a bad rep. All that toad's feet and eyes of newt crap."

Zeb interrupted. "Excuse me, but are you two here to rescue me or engage in witchy chitchat? I don't care if you join the Crazy Coven or the Book of the Month Club, just get me the hell out of here."

"If I were you, Zeb, I wouldn't be knocking Beau, and Patience, and Grimelda." *Or me.* "We need all the help we can get." She winked at Zeb, behind Beau's back, to indicate she had no intention of bringing those three with them. Zeb didn't seem to notice. He was too engrossed, painfully so, in his own motion pictures. Now, the children were gone, and he was doing more than kiss the woman. Aside from being a good kisser, Zeb was also clearly a good . . . well, never mind!

"Why didn't Vikar or one of the VIK come?" he asked. The seven Sigurdsson brothers comprised the VIK. "If they think I'm worth rescuing, why didn't they come themselves?"

"Uh, they were busy."

He narrowed his eyes . . . well, the one not swollen shut . . . at her. "They're not coming," he deduced with a sigh of disappointment.

"Not right away."

Beau snickered, but when she shot him a dirty look, she saw him still staring at the walls, like a pervert. And why not? He was a demon; perversion came naturally.

"It's been a year. Three hundred and seventy-five days, actually," Zeb pointed out. "Not that I ever expected Michael to relent, but, to my shame, I hoped."

"The Lord moves in mysterious ways," she replied evasively.

"And He sent you?" Definite hope in his voice.

"Um . . . you could say that."

"You mean, the VIK sent you at His direction?" Confusion mixed with hope now.

She hated deflating his balloon. "Not exactly."

"I'm afraid to ask what you mean by that," he remarked with a shard of misgiving sharp enough to pierce . . . a balloon.

"Then don't."

Pop, pop, pop!

"Are you sure Satan didn't send you, just to raise my hopes and dash them all in one demonic breath?"

"Don't start the Satan's sister nonsense again."

"Listen, you're wasting time."

"*I'm* wasting time? Well, you ungrateful—"

"Unlock my chains. The key is on the ring attached to Craven's belt. Then let's get the hell out of here."

"Can you even stand?"

"I don't know. They've been burning the skin off the bottoms of my feet. You might have to carry me."

Even with all the weight he'd lost, Regina doubted she could do that. "Maybe we can just teletransport from here."

"I seem to have lost my ability to teletransport. Don't you think I would have done that long ago if I were able?"

That made sense. "Does that mean you're not a demon anymore?"

"I don't know. Enough with all these questions! How long have you been inside Horror so far?"

She glanced at the watch on her wrist. "More than twenty-four hours."

"Oh shit! That long? You're going to get caught."

"No, she's not," Beau said. He had come to stand beside her, no longer entranced by the family videos. "We're guarding her . . . our new best friend." He attempted to put an arm on her shoulder, but she shrugged him off.

Instead of making a snide remark, Zeb asked, "Why? Why would a Lucipire offer a vangel protection?"

"Because she's taking us with her. With you and her." The steely look Beau gave Zeb was not at all hokey now. His expression dared Zeb to disagree.

Zeb let out a painful-sounding choke of laughter. "A five-person tandem teletransport? Or are we going to be like a kite with four tails?"

Regina didn't appreciate his mocking her.

"I don't know. I'm still working that out." She'd had enough trouble getting here herself, but she thought she might be able to manage one other person . . . Zeb . . . if he held on tight. On the other hand, Beau and Patience and Grimelda might have enough combined witch/Lucipire transport energy to carry them all, but then, that meant the three of them would be coming along for the ride. Oh, this was becoming way too complicated. "Some things will have to be decided on the spot. There's nothing wrong with winging it on occasion. Winging, vangels, angels, wings, get it? Ha, ha, ha." *I am losing it here.*

"Are you demented?"

More and more by the minute. "Are you rude? Really? I'm here to save your ass."

"Yeah, we're all gonna save your ass, big-time," Beau contended. "Ass savers, that's us."

Holy clouds! This was a goat fuck in the making. That was an expression Regina had heard another VIK, Trond Sigurdsson, and his Navy SEALs pals use on occasion. It meant one big mess.

"Sorry," Zeb said, not at all apologetic. "But where, pray tell, do you expect us all to land?"

"Well, I was thinking . . ." Regina started to say.

When she didn't go on, Zeb said, "Lord spare me from a thinking woman."

Definitely rude! She made a hissing sound of disgust.

"Sorry," he lied again. "Go on."

"I heard a rumor that you have a secret island in the Caribbean."

"Where did you hear that?"

"I overheard Trond Sigurdsson tell his brother

Vikar about it one day. Trond is a Navy SEAL vangel who—"

"I know who Trond is!" he shouted, then glanced at Craven to make sure his outburst hadn't awakened the sleeping giant. In a lower voice, he asked, "Did he say where it was?"

She shook her head. "No, but I figured you could maybe tell us how to get there. And once we arrive, I can maybe go back to the castle and maybe talk Vikar into convincing Mike to maybe come get you all."

"There's a whole lot of maybes in there."

"It is what it is."

"I hate that expression."

"I do, too. So, how does a Lucipire get to have an island?"

"It's my hidey-hole."

"Hidey-hole? What are you, like twelve years old?"

"It is what it is."

"Aaarrgh!"

"Holy Sac-au-lait!" Beau said then. He was staring down at Zeb's barbed wire–encased penis. "Ah bet that hurt worse'n a cat tail in a possum trap."

"Only if it enlarges."

"Man, ya'll better hope ya doan get a sudden hard-on. They come on me all the time, faster 'n a dog on a bone. A bone, boner, get it?"

Zeb groaned at Beau's lame attempt at humor. "I haven't seen anything worthy of an erection in ages."

"Is that meant as an insult to me?" Regina asked, giving him her best witchy stink eye. "Like I have any interest in your dangly parts!"

"So, Regina," Zeb said. "You, and me, and three other witches on an island?"

"Yes."

"Ménage à cinq?"

Zeb was either in shock, or he had a warped sense of humor, like Beau. But they were wasting precious time with this nonsense. "Sure," she said.

"Go for it," he said, dropping back onto the pallet and stretching out his manacled arms and legs. "What else have I got to lose?"

Chapter 4

The devil was in the details ...

Zeb had no interest in sex at the moment (hardly ever, for that matter), especially with a barbed wire cock. Not a one-on-one with the admittedly alluring vangel witch who resembled the red-haired, cream-skinned Satan, and certainly not a five-way that included the Crazy Coven, demon vampire witches who were clearly a dozen straws short of a full broom.

In fact, Zeb had every intention of ditching all four witches once he was out of Horror, assuming they got him that far. Alone, he might have a chance to regroup and escape to a safe place. With all that extra baggage, none of them would succeed.

His loner intentions weren't worth piss on a snowbank, he soon discovered, once they unlocked him and he tried to stand on his feet.

Apparently skin on the soles was essential for that mere task, as he'd suspected. The pain was so excruciating that Zeb's knees buckled and he almost passed out. Beau caught him just in time.

"I'll carry him," Beau said to Regina.

"What? No, no, no! My ribs are broken! No carrying!" Zeb tried to say. "A hospital gurney, that's what we need. Or a padded robe. Anything to protect my ribs."

No one paid him any attention.

"Y'all better secure Craven ta that La-Z-Boy, jist in case he wakes before we kin get outta Dodge," Beau advised Regina.

"Grimelda said the potion would last for three hours. That gives us another hour, at least."

"My PawPaw always said, 'Never trust a sleepin' gator.'"

"Oookay." Through the haze of his pain, with Beau holding him upright with both hands under his armpits, he saw Regina scurrying around looking for rope. The only thing she could find in short order was duct tape, which Jasper had used in the early days of Zeb's captivity to manscape his pubic hairs.

Ouch!

"That'll do. Duct tape is a guy's best friend. Ah even tied up a gator with duct tape one time," Beau said.

"Why?" Zeb asked, without thinking.

" 'Cause Ah could," Beau answered, as if that made perfect sense. "And mah cousin Rufus dared me to."

"I suspect more than a little home brew was involved," Regina said as she attempted to peel off a long strip of the duct tape and it kept getting attached to itself. After bunching up and tossing aside three tries, she finally got a first clear strip.

"Fer sure, darlin'."

So, Horror's tortureologist soon found himself duct-taped to the chair with about fifty yards of the gray stuff. Luckily, Craven stayed unconscious from Grimelda's potion during the whole clumsy process, including a wide swath across his snoring mouth. If anything would wake the mouth breather up, that would be it, but Zeb found himself unable to speak above a groan to point that out, especially when Beau hefted him not so gently up and over his shoulder in a fireman's carry. His cracked ribs cracked some more.

If he'd had anything in his stomach, he would have thrown it up. Instead, he just passed out. Which was a blessing, really.

Next time he awakened, the four crazies were standing at a crossroads of underground corridors arguing. Zeb could barely make out their faces in the dim motion sensor lights, especially from his upside-down position over Beau's shoulder, craning his head up and around. If he wasn't already bruised, battered and, well, dead, he would be soon from the pounding pain behind his eyeballs.

"Why aren't we going out the way we came in?" Regina wanted to know.

"There's been a change in plan," Grimelda said with a cackle of glee, presumably because she was the master of this change in plan. "We'll go down that corridor over there. It comes out about a mile or so outside of Horror."

What plan? They have a plan? I thought they were going to wing it.

"A mile!" Beau exclaimed, shifting Zeb on his shoulder.

Zeb saw stars at that move, and not the celestial kind.

"I'll carry him for a while," Regina offered.

That I'd like to see. Not!

"Not ta worry, darlin'. Ah kin handle it."

Darlin'? I'm in excruciating pain, and he has time for darlin's?

"Why don't we just teletransport from here?" Regina asked.

Yeah. Good idea! Let's do it. But wait. Teletransport where? Oh, damn, but my head hurts, and my ribs, and my cock in its barbed wire condom where it keeps bouncing against Beau's back. I want to kill somebody. I really do. Maybe myself.

"No, no, no! No teletransport inside the castle," Grimelda said. "I just found out, that new Lucipire . . . Gordon the Geek . . . set up a radar system for detecting every single teletransport into and out of Horror."

That's something new. Like a speed trap for escapees. Good, if you're a demon, to have such security, but not so good for those wanting to skip the joint. Like us. Uh-oh! We're going to get caught. Oh, hell! Oh, damn! Oh, shit! We're definitely going to . . .

They were on the move again. This time down another corridor. Bounce, bounce, bounce. Pain, pain, pain. Yak, yak, yak.

"Where's Patience, by the way?" Regina asked.

"Outside," Grimelda answered as she huffed along trying to keep up with Beau and Regina. "Blowin' up the balloon."

"Cool!" Beau said.

"What balloon?" Regina asked.

"Hot air balloon," Grimelda answered. "We got to get out of the radar, dearie."

"In a balloon?" Regina almost shrieked.

"What? You thinkin' we could all fly out on brooms?" Grimelda snarked. "We could have tried snowmobiles, but they make so much noise."

"Oh, Ah always want to go on a ski mobile," Beau said, clearly disappointed.

"Well, we ain't got no ski mobiles. We got a big balloon from the North Pole where Santa was savin' it for an emergency. Ha, ha, ha."

Regina rolled her eyes. "Are you people nuts?"

Zeb decided that he concurred with her sentiment and let his head drop to rest his cheek against Beau's shoulder.

"Wait! Don't fall asleep now. You need to direct us to your island," Regina shouted into his ear. Which gave him an earache, on top of his headache, on top of his rib ache, on top of heartache, on top of . . .

Zeb happily succumbed to delicious oblivion. Hopefully, when he awakened next time, this would all have been a dream.

Up, up, and away! . . .

Regina was high above the Norselands, drifting away from Horror Castle. Joy, joy! Yes, she was accompanied by three wacko witch demon vampires, and one high haakai demon (that would be Zeb), but at least they were beyond the range of the geek Lucipire's teletransport radar. Hopefully.

Of course, Jasper might very well launch a rocket or something at any moment, popping the balloon. But Regina chose to remain optimistic. No popping of her personal Pollyanna balloon.

The good thing in this latest step of what could only be called Regina's Great Adventure was that the hot air balloon had already been inflated. Apparently, a mission to capture some dire sinners in Denmark the day before had involved hot air balloon enthusiasts, and the Lucipire captors had yet to deflate the balloon.

The bad thing was that Regina and her gang didn't know diddly squat about steering an airborne wicker basket.

But wait. Regina was determined to remain positive.

Okay, another good thing was that Zeb remained unconscious.

On the other hand, that damned negative side of her brain disagreed, reminding her that they needed to wake him soon so he could direct them to his Caribbean island, via teletransport.

Assuming they *could* teletransport that distance. Five at a time!

After landing the balloon first so their launch was from firm ground.

Piece of cake!

Oh, boy!

Luckily, Zeb's body was covered with a warm white fur cloak. It was colder up here in the sky than . . . (no, she was not going to say "a witch's tit") . . . than a Viking whaler's butt in the North Sea. It was the Arctic, after all. In fact, Beau had had the foresight to toss in heavy outer apparel for all of them. Regina was wearing a red heavyweight wool cloak, making her look like a big red Popsicle. No matter! It covered her from neck to ankle, with an attached hood. Even so, it was still cold, but not as bad as it could be.

Unluckily, the cloak covering Zeb was precious white ermine, and one of Jasper's favorites. "How was Ah ta know that?" Beau had asked after being clouted with a broom by Grimelda.

(Yes, Grimelda had managed to snag a few brooms from the closet before leaving. Talk about priorities! No gun, but a floor broom, a hearth broom, and a whisk broom. Their enemies would face death by sweeping!)

Beau had continued talking while Regina's brain had been wandering with hysterical irrelevance, a sure sign of approaching insanity. Or terror. "Ah'm from the bayou. That fur could be skunk fer all Ah know."

Help me, Lord, Regina prayed at that point. *I had no idea it was so hard being an optimist.*

There was an ominous silence in her head. Not that God had ever talked to her personally. Or St. Michael, for that matter. But she could hope, couldn't she? Nope, Regina was on her own. Like always.

"While Zeb is unconscious, we should probably try to remove that barbed wire," Regina mused.

Zeb's one eye shot open at that. He tried to speak, but whatever he'd wanted to say came out as a squeak before he muttered a long string of words. It sounded like he was saying, "Lord spare me from Satan's Red Riding Hood!"

"Ah doubt anyone has wire cutters heah," Beau said.

"Good," Zeb commented.

"I have cuticle scissors in my purse," Patience offered.

Zeb made a choking sound again.

"You brought a purse?" Regina asked, as if that were important.

"Of course. A woman always carries her purse with her."

Regina glanced toward Grimelda who held up a tattered cloth bag to show she agreed with Patience.

Beau put up both hands. "Not me."

"Well, give me the scissors, and I'll give it a try," Regina told Patience.

"The worst thing that could happen is Zebulan becomes a eunuch," Beau offered with a chuckle.

Before Patience had a chance to move, Zeb managed to grasp Regina's wrist in a viselike grip. "Don't. You. Dare," he told Regina. "Later." On those difficult words, he dropped her hand and fell unconscious once again.

"Well, I guess we can wait," Regina said, rubbing her wrist.

For a few brief moments, she allowed herself to enjoy the peacefulness of floating with the mild wind currents as dawn began to rise on the horizon. At this time of the year, deep autumn, almost winter, there wouldn't be much sun. In fact, there would be a short window of opportunity before darkness fell again.

They were about a quarter-mile above the ground, but all they could see below, aside from the icy tundra, were the occasional wolves or caribou. Dark color against all that white. The magnificent polar bears blended in with the desert-like ice. In fact, after peering closely, Regina could see a huge, lumbering mama bear with three of her cubs gamboling toward a pool of water, a sight she would have appreciated if she weren't so distracted.

There was little or no turbulence, but the silence was deafening.

"I'm going to start to deflate," Patience said, then murmured under her breath, "if I can figure out how." She was the one steering the contraption. "You better wake Zebulan, for good this time," she advised Regina. "Oh, and be prepared. I think these things land on their sides. So, make sure Zebulan is on top, or the weight of our bodies will drive those barbed wires in like porcupine quills. We'll kill him for sure."

"He's already dead," Beau pointed out.

"So are you," Grimelda said with a cackle. "We all are."

"What's yer point?" Beau grumbled.

"Five dead people in a flyin' gondola tryin' not ta get killed . . . again. It's rather laughsome, methinks." Grimelda cackled some more. "We should take a picture ta have fer later. Does anyone have one of them eye phones?"

"Ya'll are weird, Grimey," Beau commented.

"No more'n you, boy," Grimelda countered.

"Anyways, porcupines doan have quills on their tooters, they have 'em on their tails," Beau added.

"How do you know?" Regina had to ask. "Did you ever check?"

"Ah ain't that dumb." Beau winked at her.

"Tooters?" Grimelda cackled. "That's a new one. I met a Viking once what called his Rooster. Just as bad, I suppose. His cock did do a lot of doodling. You know, cock-a-doodle." More cackling. "Do Cajun manparts make noise, like horns tooting?"

"Only when they're tooting their own horns," Beau joked.

Not for the first time, Regina questioned the combined IQ of her comrades in insanity.

"Would all of you be quiet so I can concentrate?" Patience said. "I wonder what this thing is down here." She pulled a lever and air began to whoosh quickly out of the balloon, causing the basket to lurch and sway from side to side.

"Holy Thor!" Grimelda exclaimed, clutching the side rail with boney, white-knuckled fists.

"I think mah tonsils jist shook hands with mah family jewels," Beau commented, also clutching the rail with tight fingers.

Regina was kneeling on the floor, trying to keep Zeb from rolling over.

Patience quickly pushed the lever back up. "Oops. Guess I know how to deflate now. Just a little more slowly."

"Zeb? Zeb, can you hear me? You've got to wake up. We're out of Horror and about to land soon. You need to guide us to your island."

He groaned and licked his dry, split lips. His one good eye blinked and then opened. He tried to sit up but only managed to raise his head. "What? Where am I? Am I in Hell?"

"We're in a hot air balloon. Floating away from Horror. Over northernmost Norway at the moment, I would guess."

"Yep, must be Hell." He closed his eye, about to fall back asleep.

Regina leaned forward and forced the eye to remain open.

"Ouch! Are you trying to pluck out my eyeball? Satan's latest torture technique? I was right the first time, wasn't I? You're Satan's sister, not a vangel. Red Riding Hell Hood."

"We're not in Hell, numbskull. Not yet. But we will be if you don't stay awake and help us." She grabbed his forearm and tried to pull him up.

He swatted her hand away and sat up himself, a testament to self-will or adrenaline energy or some such thing. It didn't matter why. The man was sitting up and gazing about him. At her kneeling at his side. At Grimelda holding one of her brooms like a baby and crooning some witchy chant. At Beau leering at Patience's backside as she manned the tiller, at the same time bending over to press the lever which was slowly deflating the balloon.

"Oh, fuck! We're screwed," Zeb said.

"We saved your ass, big boy," Regina commented. "A little gratitude would be appreciated."

"Thank you," he said, and appeared to be sincere. "Help me up, Doucet," he ordered Beau then. "Let's see what we can salvage from this SNAFU."

"What's a Sniff-You?" Grimelda wanted to know.

"Not Sniff-You. SNAFU, as in Situation Normal, All Fucked Up. It's a military term."

"Were you in the military?" Beau asked.

Zeb rolled his one eye, which was kind of comical, though it must be painful. "Not for a long, long time."

"Army? Navy? Mah cousin Leroy was in the Navy."

"Roman," Zeb said. "But I've been working with some Navy SEALs lately. It's a long story, and not important. Help me up."

Regina and Beau both helped him to stand with his back braced against one of the side rails and rope supports. The fur cloak fell off his body, puddling at his feet. "Please tell me that's not Jasper's hundred-thousand-dollar Hermès ermine cloak."

"I told you," Grimelda told Beau.

"Ermine, shermine! Enough with the fur crap, Grimey," Beau shot back.

"With everything else we've done . . . like escape from Horror with a prized prisoner . . . I doubt that Jasper is going to fixate on a mangy fur," Regina said with disgust, helping to cover his nude body once again. Otherwise, the jerk wouldn't have to be worrying about barbed wire. His you-know-what would freeze and drop off. Actually, that might not be a bad idea.

"Hah! You don't know Jasper." Zeb was still talking about the fur cloak.

The balloon was getting closer and closer to the ground, probably only a hundred feet up now, and decisions needed to be made. Zeb seemed to realize that, too. Shivering, he wrapped the cloak tight around himself, then surveyed the land they were crossing.

"Aim for that flattened area over there," he directed Patience.

"How do I aim?" Patience asked.

With a sound of disgust, Zeb took over and they made a relatively smooth landing where the basket did, in fact, tip over on its side, and he was, in fact, on top, facing upward so that his barbed parts

weren't pressed against anyone. When they all
alighted, they didn't think to grab onto the landing
ropes and the balloon began to rise out of reach.

Oh, well!

Zeb lowered his cloak so that he could stand
in his bare feet on the fur and not the icy ground.
The temperature was cold for all of them, who
shivered uncontrollably but more so for the nude
Zeb. In fact, he was turning a pretty shade of blue.

"Do you still think you're unable to teletransport?" Regina asked Zeb.

He seemed to be attempting a silent transport,
then shook his head. "No go!"

"Let's all gather around Zeb, team huddle style,
and try to teletransport out of here. Zeb, you concentrate on where you want us to go. No, don't
even think of sending us *there*. You'd be with us,
anyhow."

Thus it was that four witches joined arms, surrounding a high demon Lucipire and after what
seemed like an hour, but was only a minute,
began to swirl up into the sky. Already, the air felt
warmer in the currents of teletransporting. Then
the swirling reversed and they were spinning
downward.

Zeb gasped out, "The first thing I'm going to do
is find me a pair of wire cutters."

"At this point, I could do it with my teeth,"
Regina joked.

But Zeb turned inch by inch to look at her.
"Really?"

Honestly! Men and their manparts! Regina
made one last suggestion, "Maybe we should pray
first, for the success of our mission."

"We're demons," Beau pointed out. "We don't know how to pray."

Patience and Grimelda agreed with Beau. But, to Regina's surprise, Zeb arched his brows at her and said, "Good idea."

"But how?" Beau persisted.

"The words don't matter," Regina said. "Just the intent."

Thus it was, as the five of them swirled round and round toward the approaching ground, one communal prayer could be heard. "HELP!"

Chapter 5

She was red hot, all right ...

They landed face first on the shore of a small island whose narrow beach was more rock than sand. Bracing her arms, Regina raised her head and saw, to one side, beautiful turquoise blue waters, and in the other direction, up about a hundred feet, a cliffside, bamboo and banana-leaf-roofed dwelling, accessible only by a set of steep wooden stairs.

If it wasn't Zeb's "hidey-hole," it was a close second. Paradise!

Four of them got clumsily to their feet, spitting out sand and pebbles and feeling their faces and bodies for bruises. One of them did not stand. Zeb was still unconscious, and thank God for that, since his barbed wire penis was beneath him. Besides that, the rough landing had probably opened more of his wounds.

"We have to get Zeb inside and take care of his injuries as soon as possible," Regina said, taking command.

"Well, duh!" Beau was looking around, not

very impressed. He had probably been expecting a more luxurious island, maybe one with a boat he could confiscate and ride off into the sunset.

"Good luck with that," Patience said to Regina, staring pointedly at the high risers of the twenty-five or so steps. Patience ignored Beau altogether. She did that a lot, Regina noticed, when they weren't sniping at each other. Probably due to years and years of forced close association.

"We should have brought a gurney with us," Regina thought out loud. As if they could have fit one in the balloon basket!

"Too bad Zeb dropped that ermine cloak when we took off. We could have used that for a litter," Beau said, stretching his arms and arching his back to get out the kinks. Oddly, all of them had lost their outer garments in the transport. "Oh, what the hell! Ah'll carry him."

The rest of them looked at Beau with skepticism. The steps *were* steep.

"Ah'm stronger than Ah look." He flexed his muscles in a manner meant to be comical, but just looked silly.

"You look silly," Patience remarked.

"She likes me," Beau told Regina.

They were wasting time. "Beau, get serious! Can't you teletransport yourself and Zeb up the steps?" Regina asked. "It's not that great a distance."

"In case you haven't noticed, darlin', our landin' here on the island was less than smooth. Mah guess would be that the four of us couldn't move a sand flea now. Jasper must've discovered our escape."

"I still have fangs," Patience said, running her tongue along her upper teeth. "So, I must still be a demon vampire."

The other two did the same and concurred.

"Maybe Jasper is jist takin' some of our Lucipire powers away," Beau remarked. "Probably we're still Lucipires, right down to our sinful hearts."

"You're right. I don't feel suddenly pure," Patience agreed.

"Were you ever pure, darlin'?"

"Were you ever anything other than an asshole?" Patience countered.

"Enough!" Regina shouted.

No one paid any attention.

"I warrant we'll turn into those scaly beasts any minute," Grimelda said with a cackle, as if that would be funny. "How am I going to drag my fifty-pound tail up those steps?"

The image was enough to make even a hardened vangel shudder. Regina had no desire to be on a little island with three, maybe four, huge, slimy creatures. She would be Lucie soup by nightfall.

Zeb groaned and rolled to his side, which caused the three demons to go silent. Thankfully.

He was covered with sand and gravelly stones from forehead to bare, nail-less toes. He even had a piece of blue sea glass in the middle of his forehead, which matched his eyes. And wasn't that odd? Regina mused. She could have sworn Zeb had brown eyes. No, now that she looked closer, his eyes were still brown. It must have been a reflection of the brutal sun.

"Put . . . shield . . . up . . . NOW!" Zeb gritted out, then fell to his back with another groan.

"Shield? What shield?" Regina asked.

"He must mean that Jasper will locate us here if we don't put up some kind of shield. Oh, no! We can't have gotten this far only to be captured!" Patience was wringing her hands with dismay.

"Kinetic or magnetic?" Beau asked Zeb.

Huh? How would a Cajun moron know the difference? She certainly didn't. Not for the first time, Regina wondered if Beau was something other than he appeared to be.

"Both," Zeb answered Beau. "Hall closet. Red dial. Force field essential."

That effort knocked Zeb out again.

Well, holy moly! Zeb has some kind of kryptonite shields, or Star Trek-*type barriers, set up to avoid detection. He must be a regular Superman, or Captain Kirk.* She was impressed.

Nodding, Beau turned and sprinted up the steps, two at a time. Patience and Grimelda followed after him, more slowly.

That left her alone with Zeb. So much for Beau carrying Zeb up the stairs! Well, she wasn't a Lucipire; so, Jasper couldn't have cut off her powers, such as they were. The only one who could do that was God, or St. Michael, and presumably Mike was leaving her to her own devices. For now. More likely, he'd said something like, "To hell with her!"

With a deep sigh, Regina lay down on the sand next to Zeb. Even in his emaciated condition, he would be too heavy for her to lift. Instead, she wrapped her arms around him as best she could, and lifted one leg over his thighs. It was uncomfortable here on this rough beach but she managed to find a relatively smooth position. Tucking her face into his neck, she tried to concentrate on moving the two of them through space without actually standing.

Nothing happened.

Well, it might take time.

"You smell like cinnamon," Zeb said softly. "Those tiny red candies. Cinnamon hearts. Sweet, but then they zap you with a hot, spicy bite. Yes. Sweet zing."

She laughed. "Was that a compliment?"

"No."

"Well, you smell like rain. That probably sounds crazy. Especially after all your months of torture, without ever bathing. You should smell rank, like a rabid skunk. Instead, rain! You're probably thinking that rain doesn't actually have a smell."

Zeb moved his head in mild protest. "Yes, it does. Rain on a vineyard has a definite scent. Rain on a child's hair does, too. Raindrops in a woman's cupped hands. Rain after a long dry spell." He paused and smiled, despite his cracked lips. "Rain is a good thing."

Regina was surprised that he'd managed to string so many words together in his condition. Perhaps it was a good sign. "Cinnamon rain? Some combination," she remarked, trying to envelop him more closely without hurting him more.

And that seemed to be the trigger because with a rush of energy the two of them were levitating, twirling about above the bungalow like in the center of a typhoon, then suddenly they were inside, lying on a white-sheeted bed. Quickly, as soon as the dizziness left her, she extricated herself from Zeb's body (he'd landed with her one arm pinned under his shoulders) and adjusted his body better to the center of the mattress. Then she left the room and saw Beau standing before an open closet, studying a chart on the door and operating various switches. Patience and Grimelda were just coming in the front door, Patience sprightly, Grimelda huffing like a locomotive.

"Aren't you done yet?" Patience sniped at Beau. "You could have helped us up the steps. I had to half carry Grimelda most of the way."

"You did not," Grimelda said, leaning against a wall to get her breath.

"Bite me, Patience," Beau said.

"Sure. Just move your big fat head over here. One puncture and it will deflate. There's nothing but air in there anyway."

"Ha, ha, ha!" Beau said, then flicked a lever which caused a loud sound outside. He made a fist pump into the air before declaring, "Cajuns rule!"

Patience rolled her eyes.

"I need a basin of warm water," Regina interjected before they continued with their squabbling. "Wash cloths and towels. And some tools. Pliers and a wire cutter, if possible."

"Ah'll find the tools," Beau offered. "But first, Ah gotta turn on the generator so ya'll kin have electricity fer hot water and lights and such. A small solar generator kept the fridge workin', but the big, gas-powered one is turned off."

Regina wouldn't have even thought of such a thing. Nor known how to fix them. Showed how ill-prepared she was for this mission. She couldn't think about that now. "I'll check out the bathroom cabinets for any antiseptics and pain meds. I doubt if there will be any antibiotics, but you never know."

"I have herbs in my bag," Grimelda said. "I'll set them to brewing right away, soon as we get a fire going."

For just a moment, Regina was glad to have company. Others to help her. She glanced around for the first time at the large living room with glass doors leading out to a deck which overlooked the beautiful Caribbean waters. In the distance, she saw a couple of dolphins romping in the waves. Truly, a paradise.

The living room was sparsely furnished with a buttery yellow leather couch and two matching recliners. On the walls were fine paintings and a flat-screen television. Through a wide, curved archway she could see a kitchen with high-end appliances and red granite countertops. All very bright and cheerful.

Suddenly, she heard the sound of a motor turning over and then the hum of the overhead fan turning. The generator. Good!

She found antiseptic ointments in the bathroom, along with rolls of gauze, Band-Aids, and over-the-counter type pain pills. There was a wine cabinet off the living room, which was interesting but of no use to her at the moment. A bottle of whiskey above the fridge would come in handy, though.

She was about to return to the bedroom where Beau was exiting. He handed her a pair of needlenosed pliers and clippers more suited to pruning branches than delicate barbed wire penises. "He's becoming delirious, I think."

"Oh?" she said, walking into the room to see Zeb rolling from side to side, perspiration streaming down his face and beading his chest, despite the air conditioner that was starting to blow cool air and the ceiling fan. There was blood around the barbed wire.

"Red hot," Zeb pleaded. "Need red hot."

Jeesh! Even in a fever, he's smelling my cinnamon, or thinking he smells it.

"Is he talking about you? Does he call you Red Hot?" Beau asked.

"No! He's referring to those red hot candies. You know, cinnamon hearts? The kind that are sweet at first, but when you bite into them, they burn your tongue." She glanced over at Beau and bald-faced lied, with a straight face, even, "Some people in the midst of a fever crave cinnamon."

Beau looked dubious. "Ah never heard that before. And mah MawMaw was a *traiteur*. That's a folk healer."

"You learn something new every day," Regina said, laying out her tools and setting them beside the towels Patience had already brought in.

"Want red hot. Need red hot," Zeb continued to moan.

Tears welled in Regina's eyes for some reason. Maybe belated shock at everything that had happened today.

"Ah tol' ya he was delirious," Beau said behind her. "Goin' off the deep end."

Definitely off the deep end. And a weeping Regina, who could only smell the scent of cool, clean rain, appeared to be going with him.

*Whoever said "Pain makes you stronger"
never had a wired penis . . .*

Zeb alternated between agony and ecstasy.

First, soothing hands cleansed his body, all of it, head to toe, front and back, with warm water and pine-scented soap. It felt as if the washing went on for days. He wanted it to last forever.

Floating, floating. Warm water. Soft hands.

Like a *mikvah*, the ritual purification of his Hebrew religion, he mused. Not just a bodily cleansing, but a spiritual one, as well. Was there significance in that? A higher level of abrading away sin? A return to innocence?

Hah! Zeb had never been truly innocent. Not even when his father had taken him to the temple *mikvah* when he was a child and spoke softly to him of the laws set down for his people by Moses. As an eight-year-old, he'd been more concerned about a return to the running games with his cousins, or the honey oatcakes his mother had been baking that morning, or whether he should bash in the neighbor boy's head for teasing his sister Leah for bed-wetting.

"Zebulan, you must walk a straight path in your life dedicated to God."

No, no! Zig-zag is the best way, especially when being chased by Samuel. He runs like a gazelle.

"You must fast before the Shabbat, to show your discipline."

But Mother's oatcakes are so good!

"Love of Yahweh, that is the most important thing."

How about other kinds of love? He might be a mere eight years old, but he was a precocious boy, and he had heard things, and he knew about strange dreams that brought damp linens.

"Anger is never the answer. You must learn to turn the other cheek."

Hard to turn my cheek and throw a rock at the same time.

Would his life have turned out differently if his father had not died when he was ten? Perhaps a few more lessons in the *mikvah* would have molded him differently.

Water splashed on his chest, calling him back to the present, and he heard a female voice swear. This was no *mikvah*, he realized when he opened his eyes . . . both of them now since the crust had been softened on his one bruised eye . . . because women were not permitted in a male bath, and this was definitely a woman who was ministering to him. A red-haired woman. And a witch, besides!

"I am unclean," he said, not at all what he'd meant to say. The ritual cleansing should be male only, just as the female *mikvah* was for females only, menstruating ones. And he should not be touched by female hands in his sinful/dirty state. Plus, he was married. Well, not anymore, but still . . .

He could not say all that. Too many words! "I am unclean," would have to suffice.

But she seemed to understand and responded, "Aren't we all?"

"Not you. Vangels are the next thing to angels," he said.

"Hardly. And especially when it is discovered what I have done."

Uh-oh! "You will be in trouble for helping me?"

"Not so much what I did, helping you, but that I did it without precise permission."

In other words, you did what you knew would be forbidden. Just like a woman!

"I was once more guilty of pride, thinking I could do things on my own."

Just like a woman! Actually, I am guilty of the same sin. It's called conceit. "But you had help. Where is your help now, by the by? Gone back to Horror?" *I hope.*

"Don't you wish!" She continued washing and rinsing and drying off his legs as she talked. Very efficiently. Causing hardly any pain. You'd think she had been a nurse all her life, not a witch. "Beau is rechecking that shield thing you have around the island. Then he's planning to catch a 'bigass fish fer dinnah.' His words. Patience is making a bikini out of your kitchen curtains so she can go swimming. Being a Puritan, she never had an opportunity to wear such immodest garments, and even though she's been a Lucipire for a few hundred years now, she never had the occasion to need a bathing suit. You'd think this was Club Med or something. And Grimelda has a cauldron going on your patio barbecue, brewing up a potion that's going to cure all your injuries. I'm not sure what's in it, along with some herbs from that overgrown garden of yours, but I do know that she asked Beau not to throw away any fish guts." She gave the wash cloth a final wringing out and laid it on the side of the metal basin of water. "Which brings me to my biggest problem with Vikar and St. Michael. It's going to be that I brought not one, but four demons out of Horror."

"I'd like to be a fly on the wall when you explain that one to Michael."

"You'll probably be there with me. Be careful what you wish for."

He tried to smile, but then he noticed that she was examining his penis, trying to figure how to remove the wires which had become embedded with the jolts of their journey here. There was a time when a woman looking at his male part would have caused it to blow up like a . . . well, a balloon. Not now.

She pressed a glass tumbler against his lips and said, "Drink."

He sniffed. Tasted. Then exclaimed, "That's my fifty-year-old Genlivet. It cost me five hundred dollars at an online auction. You can't waste it on—"

She pinched his nose with the fingers of one hand and tipped the shot glass so he was forced to drink. "Don't argue. And drink it all. You're going to need it."

He was halfway drunk by the time he finished his second glass, so potent was the brew. But then his eyes went wide when she picked up several tools which she'd laid on the sheet beside him. A pair of long-bladed, pointy pliers, the kind used by electricians for fine wiring. *I always said I'm hot-wired different than other guys.* Cuticle scissors. *A manicure now? Or pedicure? Doesn't she realize that I don't have any finger or toenails left?* Tweezers. *My eyebrows do need a bit of shaping.* Some first-aid butterfly clips. *Uh-oh. I know what those are for.* A needle and thread. Alarm ripped through Zeb. *Seeing as I'm naked, there's nothing here to sew except . . . me.*

He tried to jackknife into a sitting position and barely managed to raise his shoulders. Beau stepped up to his one side, and Patience to the other, both pressing his shoulders to the bed. Wasn't Beau supposed to be off fishing and Patience off swimming?

"This is going to hurt," Regina said, taking the pliers in hand, like a sadistic dentist. At the first tug of the barbed wire, it felt as if his cock was being roasted over a red-hot flame, and someone was prodding it with a pointy poker. Here, there, everywhere, even his balls.

"No, no, no! Wait! Jesus, Mary, and Joseph!" he screamed and passed out again.

It was his wedding night, Zeb realized as he drifted in and out of a deep, torturous sleep. Well, not really his wedding night. He had been betrothed to Sarah for more than a year, which was as good as marriage (without the living together), and the consummation had taken place (embarrassingly short for him and painful for his bride), when they'd been wed seven days ago at the beginning of their marriage feast. But now, he led Sarah to the home he'd prepared for her over these many months. This humble house in the midst of a small vineyard would be a place of love and contentment for the two of them, and God willing, their many children to come over the years. But first, there was tonight. Just him and Sarah. And, oh, the plans he had!

Sweet dreams followed. Ones in which he and Sarah enjoyed the benefits of the marriage bed and their budding life together. Full of hope and goodness. Yes, there was goodness in those days. His love for Sarah grew and grew. Years flew by like butterflies. They had two children, twins, whom they adored. The small vineyard flourished, if not in the large quantities Zeb would have liked, but the wines were of such a quality as to be prized throughout Judea.

And then the drought came. Two years and no end in sight.

"I have to go. I have no choice," he told Sarah.

"You have a choice. Stay here with our people. Pray. Yahweh will bring us rain," Sarah argued with him.

"When?"

"When it suits His plan for us."

He threw his hands in the air with frustration. "It is a wife's duty to defer to her husband," he reminded her.

"Not when he is about to go off and fight *for* their enemy. How can you, Zebulan? How can you betray your own people?"

"That is your brother Benjamin speaking. He is a rebel whose head will soon end on the pike outside the Roman garrison." 'Twas true. Benjamin and his loud-mouthed comrades had staged one too many protests. At the bloodless expression on her face, he softened. "It is only for one year, Sarah, and I will not be fighting against any Hebrews. I have been promised."

"Roman promises!" She spat on the ground.

"I will be stationed in Briton where I am to build a fortress. Any fighting to be done will be against the Celts. I have General Julian's word on that."

"Words! All words!" She gazed at him sadly.

"This is not about the drought, but about greed. You want the gold coins to buy more hectares of land for your vineyard."

"Our vineyard, Sarah," he corrected her. "I do not deny my ambition, but my agreement to military service is about the drought, as well. The adjoining lands have a stream which has not gone dry, despite the drought. It is for my family, I do this. And that is the final word."

They made up, somewhat. Leastways, there were no more angry words, but there were tears. From his wife, as well as his two precious children. "Take care, my love. The workers will help you with the grapes." They had only two men, Caleb and John, but the vineyard was small. "Be safe, little ones. I will bring you presents. A surprise."

In the end, he was gone not one year, but two, and when he returned, it was to an abandoned vineyard and a burned-down house. What had happened? Where were Sarah and Rachel and Mikah?

He could not think of that now. It was too painful. Or was it the actual physical pain in his body. He was wracked with fiery torment in the region of his groin. No, his entire body was afire, like the time as a youth when he'd gotten a sunburn so bad his skin had broken out in blisters. Was it the drought with its merciless sun? Had the drought continued through those missing years? No, this was a different kind of heat. It came from within.

Confusion reigned.

And then there were the voices.

He tried to swim up from the hot fog that was

enveloping him, but he kept sinking back. He had a hazy recollection of being rescued by the vangel witch Regina, with the aid of the three witch Lucipires known at Horror as the Crazy Coven. Beau Doucet, Patience Allister, and Grimelda, whose surname he didn't know. He also recollected something involving a hot air balloon, then a wild five-way tandem teletransport to his island. That must be where he was now. He tried to open his eyes, but the lids were so heavy. Instead, he concentrated on the voices, trying to differentiate one from the other. Beau's was obvious, being the only male. Regina's was assertive and rather bossy, truth to tell. Patience seemed gentle and mostly quiet. Grimelda cackled so much that it was hard not to associate her with old age and witchliness.

His mental assessment of his present situation was interrupted.

"I can't get the fever down. We've got to do something. Now!" Regina said.

"I could brew another potion," Grimelda offered with a cackle.

"Please don't. The smell is enough ta make a possum puke," Beau said in a deep southern drawl. He was Cajun, from Louisiana, Zeb seemed to recollect.

"The only thing I can smell is summer rain. Sweet and pure and—"

"You're losin' it, Regina, bless yer heart. Patience, bring some more cool water fer Regina to bathe Zeb's body. Maybe that'll bring his temperature down. His skin is hotter 'n a Bourbon Street hooker on a Saturday night." Beau again. "He's already naked, and Ah doubt he's gonna rise ta the occasion if ya touch him intimate like. Not with them stitches. Ha, ha, ha."

"Why'd you use red thread?" Patience asked.

"It was all I could find," Regina replied.

"It looks cute," Patience said.

"Cute ain't what a man wants a woman to say when she looks at his favorite part," Beau pointed out.

"I once knew a man whose cock was red as a beet," Grimelda revealed.

"You people are nuts," Regina muttered.

Zeb agreed, but didn't have the energy to say so.

Much later, at least he thought it was much later, Zeb heard Regina say, "He needs blood."

"Grimey already put a bucket-load of fish blood in that brew of hers," Patience said.

"I did not," Grimelda protested with a cackle.

"Not fish blood, you fools," Regina snapped.

Zeb sniffed the air in her direction and realized that she smelled like cinnamon. Had he noticed that before? He couldn't remember.

"Ah could use a swig or ten of human blood," Beau remarked. "Ah swear, if a plane wrecked nearby and survivors came aseekin' some kinda Treasure Island, Ah'd have the whole lot of 'em drained before they could say, 'Where's Tom Hanks?'"

"You'd have ta beat me away first, with me own broom," Grimelda cackled again. "I have such a thirst, my fangs keep cutting my bottom lip. Good fer cutting off fish heads, though."

"Y'all think that's bad," Beau said. "Check these out." A hissing noise followed that Zeb recognized as the sound of fangs coming quickly out of gums. He'd done it a time or two (thousand) himself.

"You are always showing off, Beau," Patience observed, then added, "We must all still be Lucipires." There was disappointment in her voice.

"Of course, we're still Lucipires. Look at us," Beau said. "Great-lookin' scales, by the way. Specially the ones on yer boobs. I didn't know nipples came big as maraschino cherries."

"Moron! If your tail were any longer, you could screw yourself!" Patience sneered. Not so soft-voiced and gentle now.

"Ah already can," Beau boasted.

"I kin peel the skin off a toad with my claws," Grimelda bragged.

Zeb realized in that moment that the Crazy Coven must be in demonoid form. It must be crowded in here. His bedroom in the bungalow was not very big. More important, Regina better be careful. You never knew what a Lucipire might do. Even when they tried to be good, their inclinations were hard to control sometimes.

"I just thought that since we lost our teletransport powers, maybe we weren't demon vampires anymore." Patience sounded as if she were weeping.

"Dream on, baby!" Beau chided her. "Jasper would never let us go so easily."

"What if—"

"Aaarrgh!" Regina hollered so loud, Zeb's ears rang. "Will the lot of you get out of here? There's no space in the bedroom for me to work."

"What work? What're you gonna do?" Beau wanted to know.

"What I tried to say before you idiots interrupted me was, it's vangel blood that Zeb needs."

"Oh," several voices said as one.

"I've seen it happen before," Regina said. "Well, only among vangels. But when one of the vangels got badly hurt in a battle with the Lucipires, the only thing that cured him in the end was taking blood from another vangel."

There was silence for a moment. Followed by the sound of licking Lucipire lips. Beau said, "Lucky us, y'all! We just happen to have a vangel in this heah house."

"Out!" Regina shouted.

"Do you think you would have enough to spare for us to have a taste, too?" Patience asked.

"Out!"

"Bet it would make my maggot potion tasty," Grimelda cackled.

"Out!"

"Ah could make you," Beau said, and Zeb could tell by the steely tone of his voice that he meant it.

"You could try, but then you'd never have anyone to intercede with Michael on your behalf," Regina replied in an equally steely tone.

There was the sound of pushing and shoving and curses as several, presumably Lucipire bodies made their way through the door. Then, Zeb heard the door slam and the lock click.

He sensed Regina standing next to his bed (he could tell she was standing there by the strong cinnamon scent). She said, "Are you ready to party, big boy?"

You have no idea, he thought. The words wouldn't emerge from his battered body, but other things did. Like fangs slowly emerging in his mouth and although he didn't . . . couldn't in his present state . . . have an erection he did feel aroused down below. Sort of a hot throb. *Imagine that!* He wasn't surprised at the fangs, but he hadn't been aroused by a woman in ages, literally. Not that this was a sexual arousal. Just a reaction to the possibility of vangel blood, which had to be richer than a virgin human.

"I'm either going to kill you or cure you," Regina said, pressing her fingertips to his neck.

At the zing her mere touch caused, ricocheting with erotic, cinnamon ripples across his body, to all his extremities and the Happy Ground in between, he decided he couldn't care less. He was drowning in waves of pleasure so intense it hurt. The yearning for completion was sweet agony. Who knew a man could experience sexual bliss without a hard-on?

If Satan knew about this kind of pleasure pain, he would have surely employed it back in the Horror cave dungeon. And he would have wrapped it somehow in erotic memories of his wife and all he'd lost.

Maybe he was still in that torture chamber. Maybe this was all a dream.

Maybe Regina really was Lucifer's sister.

Chapter 6

Blood matters ...

"**I**'ve never done this before," Regina said to Zeb, though he was unconscious and probably couldn't hear her. "You could say I'm a virgin, ha, ha, ha."

She thought she heard a snicker, but when she looked closer, Zeb appeared dead to the world. Pun intended.

It's not that Regina hadn't taken blood before, or given it, during a human sinner saving. But that was different. When she came upon evil humans who wanted to repent, she needed to take a small amount of their tainted blood from their bodies, then inject a small amount of her more pure vangel blood into theirs. The blood ritual benefitted both the sinners and the vangels, sealing the sinners' redemption, saving them from becoming Lucies, but also making a vangel's skin stay a healthy tan color. Without it, vangel skin turned whiter and whiter, then almost translucent. Fighting and killing Lucipires had the same result. She remembered a time back in the early days of her vangeldom when she'd been living in a cave. One day, she'd noticed that she could see her veins and arteries through her transparent skin. Not a pretty sight! Talk about a jump start to getting her butt into vangel gear!

Of course, maintaining an attractive skin color was not the goal of the blood getting or letting. Saving sinners and killing Lucipires, that was the primary mission for a vangel.

Okay, now to the problem at hand. First, she better take out a little of his bad blood so that when she gave him some vangel blood, his bad blood would be diluted. Over and over the process would be repeated, every couple hours, until he lost the demon taint and his body's system would be better able to heal. Hopefully, this could all be accomplished within one day, or two at the most, and during this time period they would both have to eat or drink something with lots of iron in it to replenish their depleting blood supplies.

A vangel's fangs could work both ways, injecting and sucking. She lifted his arm and put his wrist to her mouth where her fangs were already elongated. The heat of his fever hit her skin like a hot bellows.

"Cheers!" she said.

It would be nice if she could say that the instant she tasted Zeb's blood, she swooned with delight, like a first sip of ice cold Pepsi on a hot afternoon. But that would be far from the truth. In fact, his blood tasted putrid, like the demon life source it was. How could a man who smelled like summer rain have a sewer running through his body?

She withdrew her fangs, spat in the wash basin, rinsed her mouth with whiskey, and spat again. After repeating the process six times, she figured that was enough. For now.

Then she prepared herself to give him blood. How to do that in his still unconscious state? She hated to bite herself and infuse him with some of her blood because it was such a slow process, a mere drip at a time into the mouth. It would be better if he took her blood himself, rather like a baby, being given eye droppers of milk or sucking on a nipple. "Blessed Lord, in this symbolic ritual, may my blood be as yours in the Holy Sacrament and give Zebulan healing sustenance. Amen," she prayed, then pressed her own wrist against Zeb's fangs, hoping he would instinctively bite her.

Nothing.

Not to be deterred, she fanged her own wrist and waited until droplets of blood rose above the surface. Then she held her hand, wrist downward, over his parted lips, letting one drop, then another, then another fall onto his tongue. (Can anyone say eye dropper?)

Nothing.

But wait. She thought she heard a moan.

With lightning swiftness, Zeb's arm snaked out, his fingers cupping her nape, and yanked her forward so that she fell across his chest. Before she realized his intent, his fangs sank deep into the curve of her neck, and she actually felt her blood rush to that spot, as if seeking nourishment, not giving it. Apparently he preferred neck veins over wrist veins.

After that, her world changed.

A blue mist seemed to swirl above, then settle around them like a cloudy cocoon. The rain aroma intensified, and for the first time she smelled her own cinnamon fragrance that Zeb had alluded to. Cinnamon rain, for sure. They ought to make a scented candle with that name.

Zeb's drinking from her was slow and rhythmic and only tiny sips at a time. But, oh, the bliss! It was both primal and sexual. No wonder vangels who mated sometimes fanged each other while making love. A fang fucking she'd once heard Trond describe it. His wife, Nicole, had smacked him for the crudeness, but she'd been smiling as she did it.

Regina arched her head back to give Zeb better access, an ageless gesture of female submission. How odd! That she would surrender anything to a man!

Only her breasts pressed against his battered body, the rest of her half on, half off the bed, her legs dangling over the side. Still, she adjusted herself so as not to hurt him, and in the process she twined the fingers of one of her hands with his, and she placed her other hand against his head, to hold him in place.

His hand still cupped her nape, but his other hand was making sweeping caresses over her back, from shoulder to rump and back again. Over and over. Even though she wore one of his old T-shirts and jogging shorts, she felt naked under his touch.

Regina was more aroused than she'd ever been in all her life. Not that she'd been inclined to lust very often. Once every century or so.

She wanted to climb atop his body and rub herself against him. Skin to skin. Breast to chest. Pubic bone to pubic bone. Thigh against thigh.

She couldn't. Even if she could, she wouldn't.

She wanted to kiss his lips and draw his tongue into her mouth. She would suck on him with child-like hunger. No, not childlike. Nothing childlike about the hunger she was feeling.

In any case, it was a moot point. It was hard to kiss a fanging man when only one set of fangs was involved. Two sets? Impossible! Wasn't it? They might even get locked together. Imagine Vikar's consternation if she arrived back at the castle fang-locked with a demon vampire, wanting him to unlock them. They would be the laughingstock of all vangeldom. Angeldom, too, she supposed.

She could imagine the jokes.

"How do two vampires kiss?"

"Carefully."

Better she concentrate on something else.

Forget his mouth and kisses. She wanted to examine his flat male nipples. To lick at them. Draw them into her mouth and suckle. Hard. And then she'd like him to do the same to her.

Whoa! Where did that thought come from?

As if he'd read her thoughts, Zeb's hand that had been cupping her nape moved down to hold one of her breasts from underneath and flick the nipple with his thumb. Repeatedly. Like a guitarist strumming an instrument.

Un-be-liev-able! Ripples of pleasure shot out throughout her body and lodged in her center where she exploded into a small orgasm. She gasped. That had never happened to her before.

She'd never climaxed so quickly and from only a touch. Good thing Zeb wasn't awake to witness her humiliation.

But that brought her back to reality, somewhat. She had to stop Zeb's drinking from her, for now, or she would be drained. Slowly, carefully, she pushed herself up and away, until his fangs withdrew from her with a small pop. He licked the skin, reflexively, to seal the wound.

"That's all for now," she said and rose off the bed. Her shaky knees almost gave out. How was she going to do this again and again until Zeb was healed? She would be a basket case. The most satisfied woman in the universe! Or the most stirred up and antsy for release! Yikes!

Zeb's eyes opened for a moment, and he said, "Thank you." Almost immediately, he fell back asleep, or unconscious. His body still threw off heat like an inferno; so the danger was not over. Still, she sensed that he was a little better.

She covered his body with a thin sheet, dabbed at the blood on his lips with a tissue (the fangs having retracted already), and finally replied to his comment, "No. Thank *you*!"

Who says there are no new ways to do it? . . .

Zeb hurt all over, but sometimes when the redhaired woman let him drink from her, he hurt so good. Regina, he reminded himself. The redhead was Regina the vangel witch who rescued him.

His poor, bruised cock failed to grow with the fangings, but it throbbed when she ministered to him. A pleasure-pain of throbbing, but no release.

Not that he was complaining! He'd probably burst his stitches with a hard-on. Yes, there were stitches in his most sensitive body part. Which of the four witches had done the stitching? He almost didn't want to know. Thank God he'd been unconscious when the sewing took place!

He was pretending to be asleep at the moment while Regina bustled around the room. If she suspected he was awake, she would force more of that awful, presumably iron-rich spinach and tomato juice slush down his throat to replenish lost blood. Meanwhile she munched away on iron-fortified oat cereal, sometimes plain, other times in a bowl with reconstituted dried milk. Crunch, crunch, crunch. Like fingernails on a chalkboard, she was, or fingernails on a wounded cock. He knew it was cereal she was eating because he heard her mention it to someone this morning, or was it yesterday. He'd lost track of time. Crunch, crunch, crunch. He felt like leaping from the bed and . . . and . . . he couldn't think what.

That was unkind. He should be thankful for her rescuing him. He *was* thankful, but that didn't mean she wasn't irritating.

"Zeb, you have to drink more spinach."

"Zeb, do you want to pee in a jar?"

"Zeb, I had to shave your head."

"Zeb, where's the toilet plunger?"

"Zeb, Grimelda caused a little fire on your patio with her cauldron."

"Zeb, Patience saw a shark today when she was

sunbathing in her bikini. The one made from one of your kitchen curtains."

"Zeb, Beau caught a seagull, and we're having it cooked Cajun style tonight. Is it true seagull tastes like chicken?"

"Zeb, Zeb, Zeb . . ." She was driving him crazy. And what was that about shaving his head? Surreptitiously, so she wouldn't notice he was awake, he put a hand to his head. Yep, bald. He couldn't really complain. Craven had done a job on him, pulling out clumps when frustrated with his torture. Zeb could only hope it would all grow out uniformly. But then, in the scheme of things, what did it matter how he looked?

"I know you're awake," she said.

Busted!

"How do you feel?"

He tried to sit up but sank back down. "Weak as cat piss."

She nodded. "The fever is gone, finally, but it's going to take a while for you to be back to normal."

"I think a few more fangings should do the trick," he said and took pleasure in the blush that swept over her face. He knew that the fangings aroused her sexually and that she even climaxed a time or twenty. At least someone was getting their rocks off.

"Do you really think that's necessary anymore?" she asked.

"Definitely."

She narrowed her eyes with suspicion. "Maybe more spinach slush would make you stronger."

He shuddered.

"Or if you're up to solid food, maybe some seagull livers."

He shuddered even more.

"Beau has developed a technique for catching the birds. He's planning to domesticate them, like chickens, and with proper feed, improve the taste of the meat."

It was his turn to narrow his eyes at her. "Just how long does he plan to be here?" But then, another thought occurred to him. "How long have we been here so far?"

"Four days!" He jackknifed up into a sitting position and about passed out from the pain. "What's happening in the world? Jasper must be raising havoc somewhere at our escape. And, bloody hell, what about Michael and your gang?"

"First of all, we can't get your TV to work, most of the time. The reception is horrible. If I see another *Die Hard* DVD, I'm going to puke. If that's not enough, Patience has played the *Mary Poppins* movie ten times so far. Really, Zeb? *Mary Poppins*?"

He ignored her jibe and said, "You need to jiggle the antenna on the roof."

"Beau has tried that. As for Michael and my gang, I don't know. For some reason, my telecommunication skills have died."

"Uh-oh! Not a good sign."

"Once you're better, I figure we should go to Transylvania and face the music, whatever it is."

"All of us?" He arched his brows at her.

"I was thinking we could leave them here until we can scope out the mood back home, assuming they would be willing to wait here."

"Dream on."

"What do you suggest?"

"For now, hop on up to the bed so I can fang you."

"I'm not sure I can do that in the daytime."

"Why?" He tilted his head in question, then guessed, "You've never had sex in the daytime?"

"Hah! I've hardly ever had sex, period, let alone in the daytime."

"Ah, then you have something new to look forward to."

"I liked you better when you were asleep."

"Yeah, but wait until I show you this new way of fanging. I put my mouth on your bare breast and pierce the edges of your areola with my fangs, at the same time laving and licking and sucking on your nipple. I've been told it's a great way to increase the blood flow." He batted his eyelashes at her. He had the longest eyelashes she'd ever seen on a man.

He could swear she just dampened her shorts, and maybe she'd even had a mini-orgasm, while she held onto the bedpost for support. But then, before she stomped off and slammed the bedroom door after her, she told him, "Why don't you go fang yourself?"

Or she might have used that other F word.

Zeb smiled. He felt better already.

Another war to end all wars! . . .

Jasper was in a livid, demonic uproar. He was about to declare war unlike anything humankind had ever witnessed before. People would think the Apocalypse was coming by the time he was done.

It all started when he'd sent Beltane to bring his ermine cloak after he'd gotten a sudden chill from drinking too many iced Bloody Marys (real Marys' blood, of course). And the cloak was nowhere to be found. The fact that the cloak was priceless was incidental to the fact that someone must have stolen it. It was not the kind of thing one misplaced.

But then, Jasper discovered other things that were missing. Like his prized prisoner and former friend, Zebulan the Hebrew, along with three witch Lucipires who'd helped some female vangel gain his prisoner's release. A vangel in his house and he hadn't even known it! He knew now what had happened because it was all caught on security cameras, much to his embarrassment.

The nerve! The audacity! The daring!

He seethed at the thought of the vangel witch who'd masterminded this plot. He had a special torture planned for her. She would wish she'd gone to Hell when she first died all those centuries ago. And she would turn into a Lucipire, that he guaranteed. Mayhap even his love slave. Hah! Hate slave would be more like it!

Then there was Zebulan. His former friend thought he'd been tortured before, but it was nothing compared to what was to come.

As for the three witch Lucipires . . . Beauregard, Patience, and Grimelda . . . who'd aided Zeb in his escape . . . there was no doubt Jasper would catch them. They were mere hordlings, no match for a high haakai like himself. They would regret ever leaving the comforts of Horror. Jasper planned to skin them alive and turn their flesh into purses.

He'd sell them on eBay for a fortune. The first ever demon bags. They'd be hotter than Coach or Michael Kors or vintage Chanel.

He'd already killed Craven for failing to secure the prisoner. His body had then been cut into bite-size pieces and fed to rabid wolves out on the tundra. He probably should have kept him alive for endless torture but he'd been in such a rage at the time, he had to vent his fury some way.

"Are the commanders ready?" he asked Beltane, his young assistant.

Beltane nodded and led the way to the conference room where Jasper's high council had been called to an emergency meeting. They passed through the Corridor of the Condemned, where normally Jasper would have paused to appreciate his special invention, life-size killing jars that lined either side. Based on the model of butterfly killing jars, these tall, glass cylinders held newly captured, naked sinners who would eventually turn into demon vampires. They were all alive, technically, with long pins through their hearts holding them in place, though only a few of them continued to scream and bang their bloody fists against their glass prisons. Others were already in a state of stasis. Usually, Jasper would have enjoyed watching his little pets being tortured into compliance, but not today. There was too much to do, and his mind was occupied elsewhere.

Beltane opened the double doors to the conference room.

The first person Jasper met was the Nazi, Heinrich Mann, whom he hated with a passion almost equal to what he now felt for Zebulan. Jasper put up a halting hand. "Do not speak, Heinrich. I am well aware of Satan's opinion on the matter at hand. I do not need your secondhand reports." Heinrich claimed to have a close relationship with the sin master, which he lorded over all of them. *No more!* Jasper vowed. He would stick a swastika up Heinrich's ass if he pulled any crap today.

Jasper glanced around the U-shaped conference table. Beltane stood on his right, between Jasper and Heinrich. Also standing (none would dare sit until Jasper gave the signal) were the high haakai Yakov the Russian Cossack; the pirate Red Tess; Ganbold the Mongol; and Hector, a former Roman general whose specialty had been feeding Christians to the lions. There were no other Lucipires in the room today. No veggie crudités or hors d'oeuvres, before or after the meeting. No live entertainment from pierced nubile Lucipire trainees. It would be strictly business.

Jasper called the meeting to order by letting out a mighty roar. They were all in demonoid form today, and they roared in reply. Then he sat down and the others followed suit in special chairs which accommodated their huge beast bodies and long tails.

"This atrocity that has befallen Horror . . . which is in effect an affront to all Lucipiredom . . . was caused by a vangel infiltrating our castle," Jasper announced right off.

A murmur of surprise and consternation passed through the room.

"What happened?" Hector wanted to know. "I thought extra guards had been set up to prevent any rescue attempts."

"Yes, we were on the alert these many months for the VIK to launch an all-out attempt to rescue Zebulan," Jasper said and couldn't even say the traitor's name with a tug of grief at his cold heart. Like a son Zebulan had been to Jasper, and then the betrayal. Ah, the pain! The pain! "What they sent instead was a female vangel who passed herself off as Satan's sister."

"Does Satan have a sister?" Tess asked.

"Of course not," Jasper answered. "This vangel will pay. Zebulan will pay. Every vangel in the world will pay," Jasper promised.

His words were met with cheers.

"This . . . is . . . war!" Jasper declared. "A war to end all vampire demon/angel wars! Our very own Armageddon!"

More cheers.

"This war will have three major goals: One, to recapture Zebulan, his vangel rescuer, and the three Lucipire witches who aided in the escape. Heinrich, you will lead that expedition. I know how efficient the Nazis were at finding the whereabouts of the Jews. This one Jew and his cohorts should be no problem."

Heinrich nodded his acceptance of the assignment, for once being deferential to Jasper. It probably wouldn't last any longer than he could get to a cell phone to call Lucifer and report all the doings here.

"Second," Jasper went on, "our mission will be to discover the hideouts of all the vangels in the world, including the VIK, and destroy those dwellings, whether they be cave or castle. Can you handle that, Hector?"

"Yes, master," Hector said. "I already have some ideas."

"Good, good. Now, last but not least, we are going to wage a grand war against all vangels. 'Tis past time we destroy these gnats in God's army. Every single one of them."

There were cheers and remarks of encouragement at those words:

"We have been too soft on them in the past."

"We are just as strong as they are, and we need not follow any moral compass."

"I need to sharpen my blade and season it with demon bane."

"Poisoned bullets in an AK-47 will work just as well."

"Wish I still had my ship. I'd have so many vangels walking the plank the seas would be littered with their corpses."

"Yes, but make sure you get them through the heart first. Don't let them make it to Purgatory."

"Is that a real place? I always thought it was a made-up place to appease the Christians."

"Of course it's real."

Jasper clapped his hands to get their attention. Not an easy task when a person had claws. Finally, he shouted, "Attention! There is more." He turned to his assistant who had a computer open before him. "Beltane, show us the map."

Immediately, with the click of a few keys (of a special computer keyboard designed to accommodate claws), Beltane was able to project an image on the opposite wall of a world map. It was divided into six different shaded areas. Jasper explained that each of them, himself included, Beltane excluded (not being a fighter of any skill), would be in charge of those regions. The territories were vast, of course, and he was quick to reassure them, "We have more than a thousand Lucipires on hand, fully trained, at the moment. Haakai, mungs, hordlings, and imps. But, in addition, Satan is sending us two thousand more demon warriors. Divided equally, that will put about five hundred Lucipires under each of us. Immediately, after we end this meeting, we must decide who will be the general, lieutenants, etc. among those ranks. I have a young Lucipire who is proficient with computers. Gordon will aid in the logistics of these plans. Do not hesitate to make use of his talents. Also, if we need more demons, Satan will send them to us."

"Should we increase the size of the command council?" Hector asked.

"Not at the present time. Sometimes less is better." Jasper had enough on his plate without screening candidates for the council.

"How long do we have?" the usually quiet Ganbold asked.

"One month." Jasper expected protests at that short period, but no one spoke up. They all realized the importance of acting swiftly. "One more thing. If possible, I want Zebulan and the seven VIK brothers delivered to me alive."

"As you wish, master," his commanders said then.

He stretched his arms out over them, prayerlike, and said, "May evil prevail!"

Chapter 7

It would be an unholy war ...

Vikar and his six brothers waited anxiously for the arrival of Michael. After the initial greetings and questions, they'd lapsed into silence. Probably praying. He knew he was.

The order to assemble had come at three a.m. with sharp words that awakened him from a restless sleep. There was no doubt in his mind that it had been Michael, and the archangel was angry.

It had been more than four days since Regina had disappeared, and, for his sins, Vikar had hoped to get her back on his own before anyone else needed to find out. His infernal pride!

He had to admit to not knowing where Regina was, precisely, or whether she'd managed to help Zeb or her pitiful self to escape, which was highly unlikely. Oh, Vikar had led a search party after her, as soon as he'd discovered her disappearance. He'd even gone so far as the frozen tundra where Jasper supposedly had a castle named Horror, one of many Lucipire headquarters with equally morbid names, such as Torment, Desolation, Anguish, Terror, and Gloom. He'd been unable to breach the shield that surrounded the Horror perimeter from miles around. He hadn't even been able to get a view of the castle.

Where was Regina? Had she somehow managed to get inside when no vangel ever had? Was she still inside? If so, in what capacity? Had she already been turned into a Lucipire? It would serve her right. No, it would not! No one deserved *that*.

Where was Zeb? Was he inside Horror? In what condition?

What should Vikar do? What *could* he do?

Acting as a double agent, Zeb had been their pipeline into Lucipire doings until his activities were discovered a year ago. There had been an unholy silence since then. Hard to imagine the torture Zeb was undergoing, or rather, he could imagine, and the possibilities were horrifying. Vikar himself had been captured by Jasper at one time, and he'd been held only a few days before his rescue. He would never forget the vile torture. Never!

If Regina and Zeb weren't concern enough, during the past twenty-four hours, there had been rumblings of murders and atrocities around the world, not all of them attributable to terrorism. A bomb had been dropped on St. Peter's Square in Rome, just missing the Pope who hadn't yet come outside for a morning blessing, but killing hundreds. Mass beheadings in Syria. A satanic cult in Colorado gaining publicity with its lurid, orgy-like activities that supposedly involved baby sacrifices. Cathedrals and synagogues being graffitied with what appeared to be blood. Rioting and looting in Chicago, Los Angeles, and Detroit.

The news media was going wild speculating on the cause of all these simultaneous activities. Of course, the press wanted to blame terrorists for everything. It was the easy answer.

But was there a connection? Who could be responsible?

Vikar had a suspicion. He knew terrorists, at least some of them, had another evil entity pulling their strings. It all came back to Satan.

Just then, there was a loud sound outside, like the flapping of wings. Lots of wings. Through the myriad leaded windows of the formal salon where Vikar and his brothers had assembled, Vikar could see a cloud of darkness pass overhead as the morning sun was shielded by all those feathery wingspans. Michael must have brought a legion of angels with him.

Their celestial mentor wasted no time as he entered through the wide, double front door, which had been left open, and turned into the large room. Only Vikar and his brothers were assembled. All the other vangels in residence and the humans attached to some of them stayed out of sight, but they would come forth if called.

Michael wore angelic garb today. A white, long-sleeved robe was adorned only with a twisted rope belt and a crucifix on a heavy gold chain. The massive wings were tucked in now at his back, but the glow of a subtle halo outlined his entire body.

Vikar and his brothers had been seated in a semicircle, but they all arose and bowed before Michael. He waved a hand for them to sit again. Vikar offered Michael a chair, one which he'd had specially built to accommodate angelic wings.

Michael chose to stand.

Not a good sign.

"What hast thou done?" he asked Vikar, without any preamble.

Me? What, exactly, is he referring to? Regina? Zeb? Or something else?

Not giving Vikar a chance to respond, he added, "Dost have any idea what thou hast unleashed, Viking?"

Uh, no.

"Did I not stand in this very room and order you vangels to stand back, not to attempt a rescue of Zebulan?"

"Yes, and I told Regina not to go, but she—"

"You knew about her plan? *You knew?* And you did not tell me?"

Vikar felt his face heat with color. "She came to me with some lackbrained idea for a woman, a female witch at that, having better luck gaining access to Jasper's hiding place. I told her that you had expressly ordered us not to intervene." Vikar still didn't understand why, but then it was not his place to question God, or His right-hand archangel.

"And?" Michael was pacing angrily while they talked, leaving a trail of flurrying feathers in his wake. "I named you leader of the vangels. Leaders exert authority. What authority did thou exert over your underling?"

"Regina pointed out that you said, 'You men, all of you, are forbidden from rescuing Zebulan.' She noted that you did not specifically forbid females." That sounded lame even to Vikar's ears, and he noted several of his brothers cringing at his ill-thought-out defense.

Michael stopped his pacing and glared at Vikar. "The nerve! The audacity! When will you Vikings learn about obedience? My words to you are law. And they are not to be picked apart for nuances. They are what they are!" He was shouting by now, and mostly at Vikar.

Hey, don't shoot the messenger, Vikar wanted to say, but didn't dare. "I never dreamt Regina would pull such a fool act."

"She is a Viking, isn't she?" Michael said, the implication being that anyone of Norse descent was a fool.

To his surprise, Cnut spoke on Vikar's behalf. "I should have gone to rescue Zeb. After all, the Lucie traded his life for mine. It galls to know that a female attempted what I did not."

"No," Trond said, "I should have gone. He was my friend."

"I'm smarter than all of you combined. I would have had a better chance of finessing an escape," Harek interjected. "I might have been able to break the code of the shielding at Horror, if that's where Regina went."

"What good is it being a berserker if I do not direct my anger toward a good cause? And what better cause than rescuing a would-be vangel?" Mordr bowed his head in shame.

"Well, if we're playing the blame game, I was the most logical choice for a rescuer, being a physician," Sigurd declared. "I could have ministered to Zeb's injuries, which would be massive, on the spot to aid in an escape. I can't imagine how a single female would have been able to carry Zeb's body out, assuming he is unable to walk with all the torture he would have sustained by now."

"Let's face it. There would have had to be an ingenious plan to get inside Horror Castle or wherever Zeb is . . . was . . . being held. Everyone knows that women cannot resist my charms. I guarantee a female Lucie would have opened the doors to me." Ivak, guilty of the sin of lust, who often self-proclaimed himself the best-looking of them all, probably believed his own propaganda. "I should have gone."

"Aaarrgh!" Michael tugged at his own long dark hair in frustration. "Would you listen to the lot of you? Idiots, all! If any of you had gone, it would have been in direct disobedience to my orders."

Silence followed.

Then Michael announced, "Regina managed to enter Horror, find the dungeon cave where Zebulan had been tortured these many months, and escape with him. The cave was in the bowels of the tundra there, undetectable . . . until now."

They all reacted at once.

"They escaped?"

"Wow!"

"That's wonderful!"

"I can't believe it."

"Where are they?"

"Are they okay?"

"This calls for a celebration."

"Regina deserves a promotion, Vikar."

"Or maybe not. Sorry, Michael."

"My wife is going to say, 'I told you so. Women rock!!'"

"Yeah, I'll never hear the end of it. Nicole is always saying the world would be better off if females ruled."

"Jasper must be having a bird. Beaten by a woman, and a lowly vangel at that."

"Don't forget she's a witch, too."

"Right."

"Wonder if she put a curse on Jasper's manpart while there? She was always threatening to tie mine in a knot."

"As if yours is long enough!"

"I'm plenty long enough."

"Somebody better go tell Lizzie to prepare a feast to welcome Regina home. Didn't she buy a big pig from that Amish farmer last week? Yeah, we could have roast boar to celebrate."

Michael shook his head at them. "There will be no celebration. I have no idea where they are. And if I did, there are a few words I have for the woman, and none of them would be 'Congratulations!'"

"I thought you knew everything," Trond blurted out.

"No, Trond, I do not know everything. Only the Good Lord knows everything, and He does not confide all in me."

Okaaay. At least Trond is the one blushing with embarrassment now, not me.

"I do not even know if they have survived. Last I heard they were in a hot-air balloon over the Norselands. And they were not alone."

This just got more and more bizarre.

Vikar and his brothers exchanged glances. "A hot-air balloon?" Harek mouthed, probably thinking that even he wouldn't have come up with that one. And what did Michael mean about them not being alone?

"Have you any idea what thou hast unleashed by not acting sooner?" Michael asked Vikar then.

Vikar wasn't about to argue about the unfairness of that statement, even though he considered it was unfair to blame him, totally.

"Jasper is in an evil rage. Satan's fury is even greater."

That is to be expected. And, frankly, yippee!

There were grins all around as the others silently shared his glee.

"They have launched an all-out war against all vangels, three thousand Lucipire strong and growing."

"Bring 'em on!" Trond, the bigmouth, said, even though they all thought the same thing. At first, anyhow.

But whoa! Last I heard from Zeb a year ago, there were a little over a thousand Lucipires. Now that number is tripled? Well, Jasper has a never-ending supply coming from Hell, I suppose. But they wouldn't be trained as Lucies, not so quickly, would they?

"Have you not seen the news? Wars, beheadings, bombs, every evil imaginable and some unimaginable to draw you vangels out into the open. Their goal is total obliteration of every single VIK and vangel and their human families."

Vikar and his brothers exchanged glances, not sure exactly what Michael meant.

"They are planning their very own Armageddon."

"Oh, Lord!" Vikar whispered.

Instead of being offended at Vikar's use of the expletive, Michael chose to view it as a prayer and said, "Exactly." Then he rubbed his hands together, as if getting down to business. "Vikar, I assume this castle is secure."

Vikar nodded.

"Make it more so. Double the shielding. Post more guards. Lock down and stay out of sight. Consider this a siege for those left behind when you all go out to battles, and, yea, there will be more than one battle at a time."

Vikar's mind was already working with plans for which vangel to assign to which task, and worry over his wife and the children.

"Ivak, how about your plantation? Do you have the shields up yet?"

"Not totally. It's a vast property," Ivak replied, beginning to get Michael's drift. "Gabrielle and Mikey aren't safe there, are they?"

Gabrielle was Ivak's wife, and Mikey was their son, who'd been named after the archangel.

"They are not," Michael said. "Get them out."

Ivak had already pulled out his cell phone and was presumably texting his wife.

"Sigurd? Your island hospital compound?" Michael asked.

"Good. Ivak, take your family and vangels there."

Sigurd ran a pediatric cancer hospital on an island in the Florida Keys, but it also served as a vangel headquarters. In an emergency, and this was definitely an emergency, the patients could be moved to a mainland facility, and the island would be turned into a fortress of sorts. He, too, was on his cell phone, texting his wife, who was there with his adopted daughter, Izzie.

Mordr was doing the same for his family in Las Vegas.

"First off, then," Michael said, "everyone must be gathered to this castle or the Florida Keys island. Everyone."

"But . . . but . . . there are a thousand of us, and more, including extended family," Vikar pointed out. "How will I fit five hundred of us here in the castle?"

Michael gave him a look that was almost a sneer. Very unsaintly. The expression pretty much said "Deal with it." Michael would probably be thinking that they had become soft, and that Vikar didn't recall the times they had no roof over their heads, let alone a huge castle.

Sigurd had probably wanted to ask the same question, but had held his tongue. Smart of him! Sigurd had a massive hotel on his island that he'd converted into a hospital and vangel headquarters.

"Since Satan obviously must be sending reinforcements to Jasper, will you be sending us backup fighters, as well?" This from Mordr.

Thank God, Mordr had asked that question, and not Vikar.

"No," Michael answered bluntly.

That was plain enough. Another unspoken "Deal with it!"

"I think I know where they are," Cnut said suddenly. "If they survived, that is. Regina and Zeb would probably go to his island hideaway. He took me there before going off to turn himself in to Jasper."

"I was there, too, at one time. Nicole and I both were," Trond said.

"Why didn't you say so before?" Vikar asked.

"Remember, Michael, you told us that Jasper had Zebulan," Cnut continued. "So, we had no reason to . . ." His words trailed off, realizing that placing blame on Michael might not be a good idea.

Michael rolled his eyes, as he often did when dealing with them. "Do you know how to get to Zeb's island?" he asked Cnut and Trond.

They both shook their heads.

"He was careful to make sure I didn't know the coordinates," Cnut told Michael.

"I might have been unconscious," Trond added.

Harek raised his hand. "For the sake of disclosure, I have to admit I knew Zeb had an island hideaway. It's what gave me the idea for my own island. I was never on Zeb's island, though."

Michael shook his head with disgust. "Can you figure out where it is located?" Harek was their computer genius. If anyone could figure out where it was, it would be him.

Harek bit his bottom lip, pondering. "Possibly. If Cnut and Trond give me any details they recall, I might be able to figure it out."

"Are you certain they aren't on *your* island?" Michael asked Harek.

Recently, they'd all learned that Harek had been harboring a secret island getaway, the one he'd just mentioned to Michael. Now, they began to realize that it was modeled after Zeb's own island hideaway, or the idea of it anyway. But Michael had found out about Harek's island, and it was now being trans-formed into a vangel electronics compound.

There were a whole lot of islands being dis-cussed today. Confusing!

"My island is safe, so far," Harek replied. "I came from there today, and no sign of Lucies. However, now that I think about it, I better pull in all my vangels from there, too. The island isn't secure enough yet if high-level haakai Lucies come poking around."

"Go with God," Michael said then. "Call for me if, and when, you have Regina and/or Zebulan back here."

On those words, he was gone, and all his angels with him. They would be sweeping up feathers outside for the next week. But that was of no im-portance. It was just like Michael to drop a bomb on them and then leave them to find a solution.

Like today. "Satan is waging a war against van-gels. Do something about it."

As if it would be easy, or even possible! But they had to try.

For a moment, Vikar was overwhelmed with all that he would have to do:

—Reinforce security at the Transylvania castle and
   make plans for housing and feeding all those additional bodies.

Alex could handle the logistics of accommo-dations with ease. She would probably draw up charts and everything. Right down to how many bars of soap and rolls of toilet paper per person.

And they would need to stockpile food for the duration. No ordering Domino's during the lockdown. Lizzie knew every farm and market within fifty miles. He was confident she could handle that task, though she would complain mightily. Cnut's wife, Andrea, was a chef; she could help Lizzie.

—Make sure the same was done for Grand Key Island.
—And secure Harek's island and Ivak's plantation, even though both places would be vacated.
—Rescue Regina and Zeb, if they were still "alive." Cnut and Trond could handle that. Or maybe Trond alone, thus releasing Cnut for other duties. No, they could both go, and hopefully accomplish the mission in short order and return for other orders.
—Develop battle plans against the Lucipires. Mordr could head that operation, being a seasoned fighting man. But he would need all the brothers, especially Harek, to develop specific missions for various parts of the world. Maybe Trond, with his connection to Navy SEALs, could engage the military's help in the terrorists' aspect of these battles.
—Training would commence immediately in the dungeon gyms and outdoor fields. They'd been lax of late. Vangels' earthly bodies must be continually tuned and fighting skills kept up to date. Like modern military special forces.
—Weaponry must be checked and new pieces seasoned with the symbolic blood of Christ. Swords, bullets, knives, throwing stars, whatever. The vangel Kurt Mortenssen would be good for that job.
—Order more Fake-O.
—Pray.

Vikar looked at his brothers who were on their cell phones, calling spouses and preparing to bring them all in, either here or to Grand Key Island. Then Cnut and Trond went into a huddle with Harek who already had his high-tech laptop out and was tapping away.

In that moment, Vikar realized that life as the seven brothers had known it was about to change, just as it had one thousand, one hundred and sixty-seven years ago when they'd first become vangels.

But where would that change put them next?

Chapter 8

And then they got company ...

Zeb was out on the deck, absorbing the sun's healing rays. He lay on a floral cushioned chaise lounge, made of natural cane by his own hands at one time, thank you very much, during an idle period twenty-five or so years ago when he'd fancied himself a woodworker. That was after his yoga period (meditation hadn't done crap for him, except make him more depressed), but before he'd turned to farming (being a grape grower was really just glorified farming), and thus the overgrown garden he had outside the cottage, up on the hill, being weeded at the moment by Grimelda, who might very well be planting pot for all he knew from the myriad seeds she carried in her bag. Or some kind of poison plants to put in the ever-boiling cauldron, aka his former canning kettle (*and, yes, I used to can vegetables and fruits from my garden, live with it!*) that she had placed on his patio barbecue.

Patience was probably in the rain forest shower in his bathroom, depleting their water supply, again. Good thing it rained a lot here to replenish the cistern tank. Zeb's hideaway might be a humble cottage, but he'd made sure it had all the modern amenities. Anyhow, as a Puritan, Patience had never experienced such luxuries before. And, as a lower-level Lucipire with no warrior skills, she'd never left Horror. A sheltered life, so to speak. But, no, he could hear her clanging pots and pans in the kitchen, preparing lunch, no doubt. She was probably wearing a bikini, also something new to her once modest lifestyle, and frankly Lucipires in the cold north didn't get much of a chance to sunbathe. Zeb would have no more curtains or tablecloths left if she kept sewing up more of the skimpy bathing outfits. She even made one out of the fabric of a broken red patio umbrella. Nicely water-repellent. Not that she'd gone swimming, at all, or even knew how to swim, for that matter.

As for Beau, Zeb could hear him, cursing and banging away, up on the roof where he was bound and determined to get some TV reception from the antenna. The boy yearned for a ball game, or even an old episode of *Swamp People*. Zeb referred to him as a boy, even though he wasn't that much older in human years, but he had him by centuries, even thousands of years, in Lucipire time.

In any case, Zeb had tried to tell Beau that it was a lost cause. Only occasionally was he able to get any reception, and even then it was intermittent and snowy. Same was true of cell phones. The Cloud didn't come here, apparently. The island's shielding probably didn't help, either.

Zeb stretched out his arms, or tried to. It was more than four days since the escape from Horror, and he was still so weak and wracked with pain that he couldn't walk or even sink into his whirlpool bathtub without help.

Demon vampires had no problems with sunlight, unlike angel vampires whose skin turned lighter and lighter, unless they got some blood from fighting Lucipires or saving sinners. Not an issue currently for Regina, whose skin had turned a creamy gold from the blood she'd been exchanging with him. And barely a freckle in sight. He knew. He'd checked. He could tell you precisely where all five of them were. Coppertone would love her for an ad campaign. "Who Says Redheads Can't Tan?"

Skin tone was the least of Zeb's concerns. He wore only loose boxer shorts to avoid chafing his still irritated penis. And forget about shoes on his raw feet, which were growing new skin, but not fast enough. He was still unused to his bald head which was smooth as a cue ball. In fact, he continued to be startled when he caught a glimpse of himself in the bathroom mirror, not recognizing the person who stared back at him. He didn't blame Regina for the shaving while he'd been unconscious. Craven had done a job on him, yanking out tufts of his long hair by the roots. This evened him out. A fresh start.

If only the rest of his life could have a fresh start.

He was not a demon anymore; he was convinced of that, which should give him hope. The proof, if he needed it, was that he was unable to teletransport or morph into demonoid form. The only thing about him that was the same was his fangs. Which should have been promising, a sign he was on his way to becoming a vangel, but, no, he didn't have angel bumps on his shoulder blades, the precursors to wings; so, he wasn't a vangel, either.

In truth, he didn't know what he was, and maybe he didn't want to know. It scared him to think that his lack of demon attributes might only be temporary, due to his injuries. He was certainly beginning to have unangelic feelings when he sucked Regina's sweetly erotic blood, despite his penis's inability to follow the lead. And thank the stars for that small blessing. If he got an erection, he'd probably pop a few stitches. Ouch!

While his body was far from healed, his mind was clear and he knew that time was their enemy. They had to get away from the island, to a safer place, hopefully in five different directions, or at least four, if he could convince his comrades-in-comedy to part ways with him and Regina, assuming she would take him with her to safety. That had been her original plan, after all. But no, the three demon witch vampires were hanging on to him and Regina like leeches. Which was unkind of him, considering their role in his escape. *See. I'm far from a vangel if I can be so mean-spirited. Right?* It was a sign of his unravelling brain that he carried on conversations like this with himself.

By now, more than four days in, Jasper would have all of Satan's powers at his disposal, and the shielding here would be frailer than tissue paper, no match for high-powered Lucipires. And he didn't need Regina to keep harping at him on the subject, either, as she surely would, he thought, as she came stomping out through the sliding glass doors.

"Well, have you thought of anything yet?"

"You mean, since you asked me fifteen minutes ago?"

"No need to be snide."

"Sorry." He had to keep reminding himself that he had much to thank her for.

They'd been sniping at each other ever since he'd been able to get up out of bed. From her side, he suspected it was because she resented getting turned on by their blood exchanges. From his side, he just wanted to be out of here, alone, without any help or any sidekicks. Besides, he was getting turned on, too. Except he didn't resent it. And he really couldn't do anything about it, without an erection; so, it didn't really count as a sexual transgression, in his clueless male rulebook.

"I'm not accustomed to making decisions for anyone other than myself," Zeb told her. "If we leave here, we've got to scatter, unless . . ." He gave her a questioning look.

"No way! I'm in enough trouble as it is, if I try to get you into the castle at Transylvania. You *and* three witch Lucipires would push Vikar over the edge."

"You're a witch, too," he reminded her.

"I know that." She glared at him. "What's your point?"

"No point." He shrugged. Then sniffed the air.

"Stop that damn sniffing."

"I can't help it. You smell so cinnamon sweet and spicy." *Makes me want to gobble her up. Or something. And, yes, I am wondering how a certain place on her body, her sweet spot, would taste. Would probably numb my tongue.* He didn't say that, though. He might be a dumb man and a dumber demon, but even he knew not to ask a witch if he could eat her. Not under the circumstances. Okay, not ever.

Instead, he turned the tables by blaming her and said, "Do you have to keep tempting me with sexy attire?" It had become a running joke between them . . . who was he kidding? . . . from his end only . . . that she was tempting him to sin with all her bloodletting. Little did she know, it was the truth. Blood fanging, cinnamon high, rescuer worship, red hair, sexual healing . . . he was on fire for her, and not in a fever sort of way. More like an I-want-you-so-much-my-broken-bones-ache-to-have-you kind of fever. But an I-can't-get-it-up way, too. *My poor penis must be so confused!*

Last night he'd told her, in a semi-serious tone of voice, as he prepared to fang her neck, "My train is definitely coming back to life. Good thing my engine is in sleep mode."

And she'd quick as spit replied, "I could always rewrap your engine in barbed wire."

No sense of humor.

Now, in response to his remark about her attire, she glanced down at his biking shorts that she wore (*yes, he'd tried biking once years ago, but he kept morphing into demonoid form and his tail got caught in the spokes*) covered by an oversized (*for her, not him*) Aerosmith T-shirt (*gotta love "Walk This Way!"*) that completely hid her generous curves (*but he had a good imagination*).

"Give me a break," she said and sat down on

the foot of a matching chaise lounge, facing him. Her red hair was pulled off her face and piled high on her head with a rubber band, thus leaving her neck exposed, where he could see the faint scars of his last fanging.

He felt an ominous lurch down below. Holy shit! That's all he would need. To get his mojo back in the midst of all his other troubles. Well, not really mojo, that would imply sexual appeal. More like sexual hunger.

I am in such trouble, he thought.

And he could swear he heard a voice in his head say, *You have no idea.*

"What did you say?" he asked her.

"Nothing."

"There is one thing that might work," he told her. "If Beau were to open the shield for a moment, long enough for you and me to slip through, and then close it right away, we could teletransport to the vangel headquarters, assuming you still have the ability to teletransport. I don't." *Or I would have been out of here by now.* "Once we figure out the lay of the land, so to speak . . . how Vikar and Michael are going to react to me, rather us, assuming we will be forgiven . . . we could come back for Beau, Patience, and Grimelda, assuming Michael would permit that."

"You have a whole lot of assumptions in there, buddy. Yes, I believe Beau has the skill to open and close the shield. He's lots smarter than he pretends to be," she said.

"He was a petroleum scientist," Zeb informed her.

"Really? I was thinking redneck alligator wrestler, or something equally low class. Does that make me a bigot?"

"Against alligator wrestlers, rednecks, or just good old southern boys?" he asked.

She made a face at his teasing. "What happened to him?"

"He got involved with some voodoo priestess, Lilith, and she turned him into a witch, or warlock, or whatever you call male witches."

"I should have known. The way he figured out your diagrams for the shielding right off!"

"Oh, don't go getting mushy over Beau," Zeb advised her. "He and his voodoo babe had a running business in dead bodies down on the bayou there for a while, murder for witchly hire. But then Jasper got a whiff of his evil scent and that was the end of that. Of course, Lilith managed to escape detection. The same old story, really, women causing men's evil. Goes right back to Adam and Eve. If it weren't for Eve, Adam would still be lazing about the Garden of Eden."

"You're delusional," she concluded.

"Probably," he agreed . . . amiably, in his opinion.

Which didn't warrant at all her snide remark, "Dumber than dirt." She quickly added, "Forget that idea, though. Beau and the others are never going to let us go off without them."

"Not even if the alternative is Jasper breaking the shield?"

"I don't think so. They'll say all or nothing. Five of us, or none of us, can leave."

Zeb rolled his eyes.

"As for five of us going through the shield, and then going off in all different directions . . . forget that, too. I already discussed it with the coven. Grimelda threatened to put a curse on us that would turn our brains to oatmeal. Patience said she could put something in our food that would keep us on the potty for a week. Beau's working on some kind of rope device that would bind us all together like beads on a rosary."

"We could take them by surprise, open the shield and take off, leaving it open behind us," Zeb pointed out.

"I'm not sure I could pull off a tandem tele-transport with you so quickly," Regina said.

"And that would be uncaring of what happened to those left behind," Zeb remarked. "Not very vangelic of you?"

"Weren't you thinking the same thing?"

"Well, yeah, but I'm not a vangel."

"What *are* you?"

"No clue," he said. Then, "So, nix that idea?"

She nodded. "Here's something else to worry about. Our three friends are showing more and more demonic attributes. They've even burst into demonoid form a few times before mentally changing themselves back."

"And that is a worry . . . because?"

"Because, aside from the chaos it's causing, they might just kill us, accidentally."

"What chaos?"

"You don't want to know."

"Yes, unfortunately, I do."

"For one thing, Beau is in full lust mode," she explained. "He's hit on everyone, except Grimelda so far. I mean, big-time. He doesn't even try to hide the fact that he's horny as hell."

"All guys are like that, sometimes." *Or all the time.*

She shook her head. "All guys are not demons, who take what they want when they want, even if that means rape. And, hey, don't think you're excluded from his radar. When you're in one of your unconscious states, he could take you on."

Zeb was appalled, but she was right. Demons . . . including demon vampires . . . had no morals. And they could be bisexual. Any sexual, really. The more perverted the better. "What else is contributing to the chaos?"

"Patience isn't making things any better by walking around in those skimpy bikinis," Regina went on. "She thinks when she gets out of here that she might try her hand at becoming a Victoria's Secret model. She says it's all those years as a Puritan, then being stuck in Jasper's various households without spreading her wings, so to speak."

She was right. Chaos. "And Grimelda?"

"The scary thing is, I don't know. She keeps to herself, in that garden of yours. She's up to something, I suspect. Bottom line is, the blood urge is still in them. Yours is satisfied by my letting you take little sips of mine. And mine is satisfied because I am presumably saving you. I'm afraid the three of them are going to gang bang fang me sometime when I least expect it. And drain me in the process. Then where would we be?"

"In other words, we need to decide something fast. Even if it's the wrong decision."

She nodded.

But then, the decision was taken from their hands.

Beau, clearly distraught, came scrambling down off the roof. Luckily, he was in humanoid form, wearing a pair of Zeb's jeans, and nothing more. If he'd been in demonoid form, he would have probably fallen through the roof.

"Someone, or something, is trying to break the shield," he said hurriedly. "Offshore. Then from above." He sucked in a breath. "Doesn't seem to be a horde. Only one or two." He bent over at the waist, hands on thighs, and inhaled deeply to calm down.

Zeb grabbed a bamboo fishing pole he'd cut in half to use as a cane, levering himself into a sitting position, then standing. "Get weapons, Beau; they're under the floorboard in my bedroom closet. And, Regina, call Grimelda inside. Tell Patience to close and lock all the windows and doors."

They rushed inside. Well, Beau and Regina rushed. He hobbled. And was about to close the sliding doors after him.

"Wait!" Regina said. She went back outside and was standing at the rail, sniffing the air.

"Are you trying to smell my rain again? Bad timing, sweetheart!" he called out to her.

"Don't be an idiot. It's vangels."

"What?"

"It's vangels trying to enter."

"Are you sure?"

"As rain. Or dumb men."

Zeb turned to Beau. "Open the ocean side

shield, the number six lever, but only until they enter. Then close it immediately." He would have gone himself, but Beau could move quicker. "And, Regina, gather the weapons. Just in case."

Thus it was that, a short time later, Trond and Cnut Sigurdsson came rushing into the bungalow in full VIK mode. Long black cloaks over tight black T-shirts and black jeans and black athletic shoes, carrying swords in one hand and pistols in the other. Trond had his usual military haircut. Cnut still sported the Ragnor Lothbrok look with the sides of his head shaved, and an intricate dark blond braid running from his forehead, across his crown and down to his nape where the tail was caught in a leather thong. Rambo and Thor. Vangel warriors.

Zeb could only imagine how they must appear to Cnut and Trond. Him standing, well, leaning on his broadsword as a cane, having dropped his bamboo cane coming inside. And next to Zeb, a red-haired vangel witch, spread-legged in a military defense mode, knees slightly bent, holding forth a rifle. Beau had an AK-47 at the ready. Patience, in her red-and-white-checked bikini, had a long-handled ladle, the one she'd been using to make fish chowder for lunch. And Grimelda, the aged, cackling crone, carried a garden rake and muttered something that sounded like "Bring it on!"

"Well, well, well," Trond said with a grin. "What have we here?"

Cnut answered for them, "I smell witch. Must be Zeb and his very own coven."

"We're called the Crazy Coven back at Horror," Beau informed him with a grin.

"That'll do," Cnut said.

"By the by, Zeb," Trond added. "You look like shit. What bulldozer ran you over?"

"Jasper."

"Ah," Trond and Cnut said as one.

"Did you know you're bald now? Was it lice?" Cnut asked. "Not a bad look."

"You would think that with your hoity-toity Viking hairstyle," Trond remarked.

"Hoity-toity my ass!" Cnut responded, giving his brother the bird, openly.

"It's probably a sexual thing." Trond waggled his eyebrows at Zeb. "You know what they say about bald men and how they can please women in certain sexual positions?"

"Do tell, brother," Cnut said.

"NO!" Regina interjected. "Don't tell."

Zeb tried for his own levity. "Don't the Navy SEALs have a saying when they rescue someone, Trond? 'We are the Navy SEALs. Uncle Sam has sent us to bring you home.'"

"The only problem with that, my friend," Trond said, "is that we, at the moment, are vangels, not Navy SEALs, and Uncle Sam is Michael the Archangel, and home, meaning the castle in Transylvania, is currently in lockdown."

Uh-oh! Lockdown. What does that mean?

"Regina, have you any idea what you have unleashed?" Cnut asked then.

She shook her head slowly from side to side. "We've been cut off from the rest of the world here, no cable or Internet or cell phone reception."

"In a nutshell, Jasper has declared a war against all vangels, and he has three thousand Lucies and demons at his disposal."

Zeb could have predicted that; so, he wasn't shocked. Regina and the others were, though.

"Plus, he wants you and Zeb, alive," Cnut said.

She shivered but raised her chin. Defiant witch!

"How 'bout us?" Beau asked.

"Dead or alive. Either way, you'd end up in his hands." Cnut didn't look at all concerned. Why would he? Zeb asked himself. They were demons, after all, and Cnut didn't owe them anything, like Zeb did.

"Then you have to rescue all of us," Beau said, raising his weapon, as if that would do any good.

"Is that a fact?" Trond fingered his own weapon.

"Lower the piece, Doucet," Zeb ordered in a soft voice that brooked no argument. "Everybody, settle down. Let's sit down and talk this over. Surely, there's a solution."

"Do you have any beer?" Trond asked.

"No. Beau drank the last of it," Zeb replied.

"There were only six bottles," Beau said defensively.

"I have plenty of wine, though," Zeb said.

"That'll do," Trond said. Just then, he seemed to notice that Patience's bikini matched the curtain on the second set of windows in the kitchen. He looked at her, the curtain, then Zeb. And grinned.

Zeb just shrugged.

Grimelda left the room, trailing her rake after her. She said she had a boiling cauldron that needed tending on the patio.

"What is that smell?" Cnut said then, sniffing the air.

"Grimelda?" Regina asked. The old lady *was* a bit ripe.

Cnut shook his head and continued to sniff.

"Patience was making chowder," Regina offered.

Cnut shook his head some more and continued to sniff. "No. It smells like rain. Do you think a storm's coming?"

"It's me," Zeb admitted, feeling his face heat. "I supposedly stink like a friggin' rain forest."

"No, not rain," Trond said to Cnut, ignoring Zeb's comment. "I smell cinnamon. Like those buns the Amish sell down at the market." Trond tilted his head in question toward Regina.

"Rain and cinnamon? You guys are imagining things." This from Beau, who was helping Zeb into one of the recliners.

Suddenly, Trond and Cnut made the connection. As one, their gazes fixed on Zeb, then Regina. They let out hoots of laughter.

"Lifemates! Can you believe it?" Trond said.

"The witch and the demon! What a combination!" Cnut remarked.

Regina understood before Zeb did. "Oh, no! Absolutely not! I don't even like him."

"You do so," Zeb said, before thinking. "You said last night that my bald head is hot."

"I did not!"

"Well, you implied it. Besides, why did you rescue me if you don't like me?"

"I did it for me, not you, idiot!" She glared at Zeb. "Why are you arguing? Do you want a lifemate?"

"Hell, no! I mean, absolutely not!"

"Cinnamon rain . . . has a nice ring to it, doesn't it?" Trond said to Cnut, clearly to annoy Zeb and Regina.

Regina stomped off.

And Zeb asked the two Sigurdssons, "Is there any way to undo a lifemate connection?"

"If I were you, I would be more worried about how we are going to get all of you out of here," Trond said.

"Right," Zeb agreed. "Escape first, broken heart later."

Trond was surprised at his answer. "Will you have a broken heart?"

"I always have a broken heart."

Chapter 9

Preparing for a road trip ...

Ⅽnut and Trond spent the next few hours giving Zeb some of their blood to speed his recovery. Vangel blood was like a triple dose of antibiotics and a miracle drug combined. There had been cases of vangels near death who'd come back to life after such ministrations, and quickly, too. Plus, the two VIK members were older and stronger vangels than Regina, and their blood presumably more potent.

Oddly, Regina missed the blood-giving task.

And, no, it wasn't the lifemate nonsense. There was just something that spoke to a woman's maternal side when nurturing a sick man. Didn't matter if it was the flu or a terminal disease laying a man low. Not that Regina felt anything close to maternal about Zeb. Far from it! But she'd gotten him this far, and she felt a responsibility for carrying through her mission. Who was she kidding? She wanted to be the one to take him back to the castle. Package delivered. Pride of accomplishment. I-told-you-I-could-do-it! End of case. Instead, Trond and Cnut . . . *men* . . . would probably brag that they had to rescue her . . . a poor weak woman . . . and pick up the pieces. Not that she needed rescuing, much. She was handling things just fine. Mostly.

At least, that's what she tried to tell herself.

Meanwhile, she and the others were preparing to close up the bungalow. Which was probably a futile effort. If Jasper discovered the hideaway, he would no doubt raze it to the ground in frustration.

Regina had ordered Grimelda to take a shower or Regina wouldn't take her with them. While the old crone was in the bathroom, tossing curses right and left, Regina put Grimelda's dirty garments into the washing machine. They would probably disintegrate from age and filth. She could match Grimelda curse for curse anyhow, and Regina had told her so.

And Regina had ordered Patience to ditch the bikinis, for now, at least. She doubted Michael would look too kindly on the demon witches, to begin with, but a half-naked one would surely push all his archangel buttons. Patience was also doing a lot of grumbling about Regina and her bossy ways.

Beau needed no ordering. He was smart enough to know his future was on the line, and he was behaving as well as a demon could. In fact, he was being downright ingratiating toward Cnut and Trond, who were taking advantage of him by having him fetch and carry for them. Beau's model behavior was only temporary, of course. Regina suspected Beau was planning a trip "down the bayou" as soon as he could manage to slip away from the castle. A little redneck retribution was in line for the voodoo priestess Lilith, assuming she was still there.

"How is he?" Regina asked when Cnut and Trond came out of Zeb's bedroom.

"Asleep," Trond said, "but better."

"We'll give him an hour or so, another shot at fanging, then we hit the road. Time to blow this Coke stand," Cnut said. "Is everyone ready?"

"As ready as we'll ever be."

"I still can't believe he had barbed wire around his cock . . . I mean, penis," Trond said for about the hundredth time. "Wish I coulda seen that."

"Me, too." Cnut put a hand reflexively over his groin.

"It was awesome," Beau contributed. "Ah knew a guy one time who pierced his cock with an industrial bolt, said it enhanced his lady's pleasure. Gave new meanin' ta screwing, that's fer sure."

Trond and Cnut bent over laughing.

"I don't imagine Zeb's wiring would have pleased a woman, though," Trond speculated, once he wiped the tears of mirth from his eyes. "Too sharp."

"Ouch!" Cnut concurred.

Really, that's all the men wanted to talk about regarding Zeb. Forget about all his other tortures, they were fixated over wires poking manparts. How it felt. Was it unbearable? Did he see stars? Was there blood? How many stitches did he have? Who sewed up his penile wounds? Did he think it would impair his sex life in the future? How about erections? Could they watch when the stitches came out?

Men!

Regina had something more important on her mind, like herself, but she didn't dare ask what her fate would be when they returned home. So, instead, she homed in on other subjects. "The castle will be crowded, I assume, with all the vangels being called in."

"Yep. Almost five hundred, but I expect we'll be going out on missions almost immediately. In and out. Probably no more than a hundred in residence at one time. I should be there now, helping to plan." Cnut was known as a great battle strategist. She could see why he would resent time wasted here, not to mention the fact that she was responsible for this whole debacle to begin with, by initiating an unauthorized rescue of Zeb.

Regina couldn't feel guilty about that, though. She just couldn't.

"And I need to get back to Coronado," Trond interjected, coming from the kitchen where he'd nabbed a carrot which he was chomping on. "Gotta come up with a way to involve the SEALs without telling them exactly what's going on. A bit of force multiplication on the home front."

Chomp, chomp, chomp.

Trond could be so annoying sometimes, and Regina's nerves were already on edge.

"Do you think Vikar will send me out to fight on one of these missions?" Regina asked.

Cnut and Trond looked dubious.

"It's the brig for you, babe," Trond said. Chomp, chomp, chomp. "That would be my guess."

He was probably joking.

Chomp, chomp, chomp.

If she had some barbed wire handy, she would wrap it around something, probably Trond's tongue.

"How about me?" They all turned to see Zeb standing in the hallway. It was the first time he'd gotten up on his own, and he was looking better than he had hours ago. Not back to normal by any means, but surprisingly better. In fact, he'd even put on a sweatshirt and jeans and had flip-flops on his sore feet.

Without thinking, she glanced toward his crotch. The denim material might irritate the stitches.

Catching her glance, Zeb grinned and said, "I put a sock on it."

He was probably teasing. Still, she hated the heat that filled her cheeks, probably his intent. After all the intimate parts of his body she'd come to know, it was a miracle that she could still blush.

Apparently, she was the only one who'd heard Zeb's remark, and he had already turned his attention back to Cnut and Trond, repeating, "What about me?"

"What do you mean?" Cnut asked.

"Will Vikar use me? Surely, my insider information could help."

"We'll soon find out," Cnut said.

And they did.

Less than an hour later, they were down on the beach, where three vangels and a coven linked arms around a hard-to-categorize former demon and tried to focus on moving their bodies through the air.

"Praise the Lord!" Regina prompted.

And they were up, up, and away.

No matter the danger, no matter the
circumstance, it still comes down
to a man and his penis . . .

It was barely past dawn, but Vikar was up and about, in the castle kitchen, having a carton of Fake-O, enjoying the quiet before the daily madness began. Alex was still sleeping when he'd left their bed. Likewise, their children, Gunnar and Gunnora, in their adjacent nursery.

He was staring idly out at the back courtyard, still not fully awake. Throughout the quiet castle, especially down below in the former dungeons, where most of the vangels were accommodated, he heard the rustling sounds of awakening . . . soft footsteps, toilets flushing, loud yawns, farts, water running. He had really good hearing.

Soon, he would get down to final plans for the war to end all wars with the Lucipires, which would be launched two days from now. One of the dining rooms had been turned into a war room, with maps laid out on the long table, several computers and printers, and wall charts showing a division of not only the various planned campaigns by geography but by those who would command and serve in those divisions. Vikar and his brothers had been working on the plans nonstop the past few days, as well as battening down the security here at the castle and on Grand Key Island.

Michael, who was a warrior himself, or had been, could have been of so much help, but, as usual, he had stepped back to let them blunder on their own. "Be strong and be of good courage, that is what God said to Joshua before going into battle," Michael had reminded him.

As if Vikar were in Joshua's league! When he'd repeated Michael's words to Mordr, a skilled fighting man, he'd likened Joshua to the NFL and they were mere Pee Wee players. Vikar wouldn't have gone that far, but still . . .

There was so much to do, and so few vangels for such a monumental job. Yes, a thousand Viking warriors sounded like a lot, but he could use ten times as many, and still not feel confident of the odds. Five hundred of the vangels were currently crammed in every corner of this castle and its grounds. Four hundred and fifty of the five hundred being temporarily housed on Grand Key Island would be returning here day after tomorrow when the vangels' aggressive missions against the Lucipires would commence.

Trust in God, he kept hearing in his head. And that's what he would do. Except he was reminded often by Trond of that old military saying, "Trust in God, but pass the ammunition."

Lizzie came in, yawning, and nodded at him. Within minutes, she had the commercial-size, automatic coffeemaker brewing, and Vikar prepared to take the first mug. Coffee was a brew unknown to Vikings of old, but he'd come to rely on its morning kick start. Mayhap he was just getting old. Ha, ha, ha.

Suddenly, he was jarred to alertness, and not by caffeine.

There was a loud noise outside.

Cnut and Trond must have returned. Praise God! Now they could complete their war plans.

But then, Vikar's jaw dropped with astonishment at the scene unfolding before him.

They'd left an open "fold" in the shielding around the castle in anticipation of his brothers' return. Only they knew how to access that opening, and it would be sealed after them. However, this was not a soft landing he was viewing out in the back courtyard. In fact, Trond ended up in the pool, Cnut on the gazebo roof, and Zeb lay on his back in the grass with his knees drawn up to his chest, moaning in pain.

But it was the other three, no, four characters that drew his incredulity. There was Regina, and she was certainly more voluptuous than he'd ever realized as she raised her butt to get up off the ground and arched her back to ease some bruising from the fall. It was probably her attire, which was unusual for her, a pair of skin-hugging, knee-length shorts and a T-shirt that proclaimed "I Love Devil Dogs." Her red hair, which she usually had pulled off her face in a ponytail or braid, stood out like a flaming bush.

Turning, she helped an old lady to stand. The gray-haired witch—and that's exactly what the old hag looked like in a long black gown with a long, black, open-sided apron in the Viking style—held a broom in one hand and a burlap bag in the other.

Then there was a pretty, black-haired wench in a Puritan costume. Leastways, that's what it looked like to him. But what did he know about female clothing. Maybe it was Quaker. Or even some new Amish group. She was adjusting her apron and dusting off her backside, having landed in the children's large sandbox.

And, finally, a dark-haired, dark-eyed guy, wearing jeans, a denim shirt, and Zeb's Blue Devils baseball cap, strolled confidently toward the others who gathered at the far end of the patio, talking among themselves.

Vikar opened the French doors and got a good whiff of . . . sulfur! "Holy shit! They're Lucipires!"

"No, they aren't," Lizzie Borden said, coming up to his side. "They're witches, and they better not be coming into my kitchen."

"Huh? What?" Vikar looked again. "Witches? Like Regina?"

"Not exactly. They're demon witches."

Michael is going to have a bird!

As Regina came forward, Vikar said, "What have you done?" And he didn't just mean going off to rescue Zeb and setting off a war.

Regina bowed her head and said, "Master Vikar, I beg leave to enter the castle."

"Bullshit!" Regina didn't consider him her master any more than did her cat, Thor, which must have escaped from the pantry where it had been locked because it now hurled itself, not at Regina, but at the old crone who dropped her broom and bag to open her scrawny arms wide. "There's a pretty. Come to Mother." She smiled . . . and Vikar doubted she had more than two teeth, and both of them fangs . . . and petted the cat which was already draped around her shoulders.

Regina didn't look at all put out at the disloyalty of her cat. In fact, she muttered, "You're welcome to him."

"Is baby hungry? Does he want a little mouse to eat?" The old crone glanced toward the kitchen.

"His name is Thor," Regina told her, as if that mattered. "And this is Vikar." She nodded toward him, then told him, "This is Grimelda."

"How do you do?" he said as politely as he could muster. Then in a misguided attempt at humor, he asked, "Do people call you Grimey for short?"

"Only if they value black tongues and bleeding hemorrhoids." She waggled the fingertips of one hand at him as if wielding a curse. And she cackled, of course.

Lizzie straightened with indignation, or as much as she could with her short frame, and not about Regina's failing to introduce her. "There are no mice in my kitchen. I keep a clean kitchen, that I do."

Not to worry. Grimelda, or Grimey . . . *what a name for a witch*, he thought . . . reached down into her burlap sack and pulled out a dead rodent (long dead by the dryness of the thing) and gave it to the cat. It probably came from Horror and was a demon mouse. Thor, pleased at his prize, took it in his pointy teeth and jumped off her shoulders to go off and devour the treat.

Vikar had always been told that cats only eat live prey. Perhaps witch cats were different. Yuck!

Grimelda was off, as well, brushing past Lizzie into the kitchen. "I need a cauldron. Where do you keep the cauldrons?"

"No, no cauldrons!" Lizzie screeched, rushing after the witch. "Don't touch anything. And leave that filthy broom outside."

Andrea, Cnut's wife and a pastry chef, who helped Lizzie in the kitchen, walked in then and stared after the old woman who was surprisingly quick on her feet and cackling up a storm as Lizzie chased her around the long kitchen island. Andrea wore a white chef's coat over black jeans. Must be she was preparing to bake for the masses today. His stomach rumbled at the prospect of her warm bread spread with butter and peach jam from the Amish market.

Vikar would notify Michael of Regina and Zeb's arrival, and the archangel might very well be here to confront the two of them by this afternoon, or maybe tomorrow. He would have to tell Andrea to bake some of those chocolate-filled croissants that the archangel favored. Yes, even heavenly beings had sweet tooths.

A huffing Lizzie gave up on her chase and came over to them. "She's a witch," Lizzie whispered to Andrea.

Andrea arched her eyes in surprise, but not too much surprise. She was a human, not a vangel, and, during the year or less she'd been here, there had been lots more, bigger surprises than a mere witch.

Grimelda, who was standing a short distance away, must have heard the remark, though, because she eyed Andrea's attire which would seem odd to her, and instead of remarking on her white coat, she asked, "Ya got any eye of newt around here?"

She was probably kidding.

Wasn't she?

Quick to react, Andrea replied, "Just the eye of my husband Cnut," and waved to the vangel who had jumped off the gazebo and was grinning as he walked toward her. By the gleam of lust in Cnut's blue eyes, you'd think he had been gone a year and not just a day.

"Well, one new witch down, two more to go," Vikar said to Regina. "What were you thinking? Bringing witches here. Demon witches."

She shrugged. "I had no choice. They helped me rescue Zeb."

"You had a choice, all right, girl. Starting with your decision to leave this castle without permission."

"I am sorry."

"You are not!"

"Well, I'm sorry that I had to defy your orders . . . implied orders, I might add. You never actually said that—"

"Do not play word games with me," he practically shouted. "There have been vangel transgressions over the years, but none so serious as yours. And none with such monumental consequences that affect us all. God only knows what your punishment will be. If it were up to me, it would be banishment."

"No!" she cried. "Let me explain—"

The young male witch interrupted them now, stretching out a hand to Vikar. "Y'all mus' be Vikar Sigurdsson. It's a privilege ta meet you. Mah name is Beauregard Doucet from La-fay-ette, Loo-zee-anna. At yer service. Call me Beau."

Vikar shook his hand, before withdrawing it quickly with distaste. Vangels did not willingly touch demons, and there was no doubt this man was still a Lucipire. He reeked of it.

"And this heah is mah friend, Patience Allister."

The plain-dressed lady with the white apron (a regular apron, not the Norse kind) stepped forward and bowed her head at him. "Greetings, sir," she said.

"Patience usta be a Puritan, but now she jist wants ta become a Victoria's Secret model," Beau told him with a wink.

Patience elbowed Beau. "Fool!"

"We three are known back at Horror as the Crazy Coven," Beau continued. "We doan mind if y'all call us that, too, jist so you let us stay."

That is just great. I can see it now. "Michael, I'd like to introduce you to the Crazy Coven." At a loss for words, he just nodded at the man, but then he told Regina, "Take these new friends of yours to my office and make sure they stay there until I have a chance to make a decision." Implied in his words was the directive that the door be locked and that she keep them from leaving, or moving about the castle. "And make sure you grab that old crone, too, before Lizzie wields her hatchet at her." Before she left to do his bidding, he added for Regina's ears only, "Only you would dare to bring a coven of witches into a vangel lair!"

"Maybe misery loves company," she sniped at him. "Maybe I'm tired of all the witch jokes around here." On those words, she stomped off.

"Maybe we're tired of all the witch curses on our manparts," he called after her.

He could swear she gave him the finger over her shoulder. But he was probably mistaken. He turned back to the patio.

A dripping wet Trond was helping Zeb walk toward Vikar. Cnut left Andrea's side and went over to help. Zeb was in bad shape. Battered would be the best description and that didn't even take into account his gaunt, half-starved body and shaved, bald head. Vikar could only imagine how bad he must have been when Regina had first found him. But the teletransport must have drained Zeb's energy even more.

The interesting thing was that the three witches Regina had brought here carried the demon scent, heavily. No question they were still Satan's disciples of one sort or another. If they'd wanted to escape Horror, it wasn't out of a burgeoning distaste for the Lucipire life.

Unlike Zeb, who carried no scent at all. Not sulfur. Not lemon, which was the odor of dire human sinners. Nothing, except maybe a fresh scent of something like rain. Where that weird thought came from, Vikar had no idea.

Zeb, whose arms were now wrapped around Trond's and Cnut's shoulders, holding him up, raised his heavy lids to Vikar. "Lord Vikar, I would beg leave to enter your domain."

Vikar didn't know if by "domain" Vikar meant his castle or vangeldom, in general. Either way, it didn't matter. He was here. For now.

"You may enter," Vikar said. "Looks as if Jasper has used you for a whipping post."

"If you only knew!" Trond interjected, and blurted out, "Zeb had barbed wire wrapped around his cock for the past year. And the TV tuned to nonstop movies, probably porn. Leastways, that's what Regina said, not about the porn but the movies. Like a barbed wire condom, I'm guessing."

Vikar's eyes went wide.

"Regina took the barbed wire out and had to give him some stitches," Cnut added.

Vikar's eyes went even wider.

They all looked down at Zeb's groin area.

"Wish I could have seen that," Vikar said.

Within the hour, while Zeb lay passed out in one of the third-floor bedchambers, word of his barbed wire penis passed among all the vangels. Some even had the nerve to ask Regina if she could draw a picture of how it had looked, but they'd only asked once before having one of her famous curses laid on them. Even so, jokes on the subject abounded.

"What looks like a metal condom and hurts like a metal condom? Must be Zeb's phallic sculpture."

"Gives new meaning to the word Tickler."

"How many cuts can a barbed wire make in one penis? Depends on the size of the penis. Size matters, dontcha know?"

"There are times when a needle dick comes in handy."

"You could say it was a male chastity device."

"Mayhap it was a lightning rod for demons flying during a storm."

When Vikar's wife, Alex; and Trond's wife, Nicole; and Mordr's wife, Miranda; and Harek's wife, Camille; and Karl's wife, Faith; all in residence at the castle for the duration, heard the jokes, they said as one, "Men!"

Chapter 10

*The best laid plans of mice and men,
rather demons and angels ...*

Zeb couldn't stop smiling.

He was by no means safe. From the Lucipires, the vangels, or his own weak body. But he had escaped from Horror, and there was hope. Hope was everything.

Vikar, Harek, and Mordr had given him blood "transfusions" all day yesterday and through the night to supplement what he'd already received from Cnut, Trond, and, of course, Regina. This morning, he was a new man. And he was hungry as a bear, lured by the scent of frying bacon and coffee coming from down below.

After showering and shaving (his face, not his head), he donned some clothing left in his small bedchamber and made his way down the back stairway to the kitchen, the one originally intended for servants. The fact that Vikar hadn't locked him in didn't surprise Zeb. They knew good and well that he had nowhere else to go, and besides, Zeb had made it known for years that he yearned to become a vangel.

Slowly, and carefully, he moved, holding onto the rail. They were steep steps, and his legs were still weak and his soles not completely healed.

There were several people standing about, or sitting on stools at the long island. He had eyes only for the one whose cinnamon scent swirled about and hit him like a cloud of welcome. She wore a long dark blue gown, plain, with no adornment, belted at the waist, but loose, and her red hair hung down her back in a thick braid.

"Why are you dressed like a nun?" he said, coming up behind her.

She turned quickly and almost spilled the glass of juice she held in one hand. "You're awake, finally," she said, ignoring his remark about her attire. "Everyone's been waiting for you. Michael will be here soon."

Ah, so that was the reason for the modest attire. Trying to impress the big guy. Little did she know, but her restrained appearance could not compensate for her recent actions in rescuing him. She might as well be wearing Wonder Woman tights with a winged *W* on her impressive bosom. "I Am Woman, Hear Me Roar." Or something like that.

"Stop looking at me there," she sniped.

"Okay," he said and continued looking.

"How are you feeling?" she asked.

"Almost human," he replied, and they both laughed at the irony of his remark. He would never be human again, and he wasn't sure he would want to be.

She glanced at his groin area. "Are you ready for me to remove the stitches?"

He grimaced at the prospect. "Doctor Sig came

in last night. He already did it. With a topical anesthetic." Sigurd Sigurdsson was an accomplished physician who maintained a vangel headquarters on a Grand Key island, which also housed a pediatric hospital.

"Great!" Regina said, but appeared disgruntled. Had she wanted to take on the task herself? Probably. Not because she wanted to handle his goods, but she was a woman who wanted to be in control of everything. Fat chance in a castle full of men! Including a physician.

"By the by, did you have to use red thread?"

He could tell that his question caught her off guard. She even blushed. "It was all I could find."

"Before Sig removed the stitches, every vangel in the house insisted on viewing the spectacle so they could mock me. Some said I looked like a candy cane."

"I didn't think about how your precious part would look. I was more concerned about saving your fool life." She raised her chin defiantly.

He should have stopped provoking her, but he was on a roll. "With your cinnamon breath and cinnamon body odor, I have to wonder if you were putting your mark on me."

"What? Don't be ridiculous," she said and gave him a shove, which caused him to grab for a nearby stool and sit down. She sat down next to him.

He wasn't sure why he enjoyed prodding Regina so. He just did.

A serving girl vangel came over and placed a mug of coffee and plate of bacon, eggs, and toast in front of him. She gave Regina a cup of coffee, as well, and took away her half-empty juice glass.

Regina motioned toward a sugar bowl and creamer with a raised eyebrow, but he shook his head. He liked his coffee black. She did, too.

"Where is everyone?" he asked. Those in the kitchen were mostly lower-level vangels. None of the VIK or warrior vangels he'd come to know in the past. Nor their families.

"Everyone has eaten already, in shifts. There are so many here. The children and their mothers are in the family room watching cartoons or playing video games or reading with ear plugs in. Mostly the vangels are either in the weight rooms in the basement or outside in the fields practicing their fighting skills. Still others are dipping weapons in the symbolic blood of Christ. In truth, everyone here is doing some kind of work to help in this war effort."

Except her, apparently. "Dare I ask about the Crazy Coven?"

"Locked in one of the dungeon cells. Thor is with them."

"Who's Thor?"

"My traitorous cat. He's developed a love connection with Grimelda."

"Oh boy!" he said. Then, "They have dungeons here?"

"Onetime dungeons. Never used for that purpose, I'm sure. But now they've been renovated into dorms and training rooms."

"They must be climbing the walls, or planning some mischief."

"The 'cell' they're in has padded walls for Close Quarters Training."

"Good. Just in case they revert to demonoid

form and try to fight each other," he guessed. It was a real possibility.

"My thoughts, exactly."

"Are you sure they won't teletransport out of here? They helped you bring me here. So, they haven't lost that ability, like I have."

She shook her head. "They'd never be able to break through the shielding around this place. The only reason we got in was Vikar ordered an opening so that Cnut and Trond could return."

"You should still keep an eye on them," Zeb advised. "They can create trouble inside the perimeter, too."

"We will. Well, not me precisely. I'm on a kind of in-house parole until Michael makes a decision about my fate."

Ah, so that's the reason for her idleness.

"You, too, I suppose. On parole, I mean."

At least!

"But anyhow, if they were let loose, I suspect Beau would shoot off to Cajun land the minute he got an opening, to enact some Cajun vengeance on that woman he blames for his becoming a Lucipire. And Grimelda is dying . . . ha, ha, ha . . . to test out one of Lizzie's cauldrons, and as for Patience, she will be . . ."

"Off to model swimsuits," Zeb finished for her, "or plant herself in the Playboy Mansion, but, no, that doesn't exist anymore, does it?"

They smiled companionably, knowing they were responsible for the oddball witches. In a way. Until the Lucipires' future was decided, too.

As Regina talked and sipped at her coffee, he began to realize that she was a very attractive woman, when she wasn't being sarcastic or downright mean. Odd that he'd never noticed her on his earlier visits to the castle. Did she deliberately try to make herself invisible? Yes, he was sure that was her ploy. Except that her true nature came out in her witchy outbursts of biting observations and constant threats of curses on male parts. Trond had told him one time that Regina had at least fifty different, inventive curses for the male vangels who taunted her, including knotting one man's penis into a pretzel and not the salty kind.

In any case, her skin had that creamy glow some redheads had, and as he'd observed before, only a few freckles, one of them on her right earlobe, which fascinated him. Another to the left of her mouth. Her fangs were hardly noticeable, except when she smiled, which was rare, and even then, they did not detract from her beauty. He especially liked her lips, which were full and bruised looking.

Enough! No more on Regina's appearance! He was ravenous and soon consumed every bite on his plate, and was sipping at a second cup of coffee. Cnut's wife, Andrea, came over and placed a warm, iced cinnamon bun in front of him. Maybe that's what he'd smelled when he entered the kitchen, and not Regina's spicy scent. "For good luck," Andrea said. "We're all rooting for you."

They were?

Who did she mean by "all"?

It didn't matter. He would find out soon enough. Besides, he reminded himself, he had hope.

And then he took his first bite of the sweet bun

and almost swooned with pleasure. "Now, this is heaven."

Regina laughed. "Close to."

When he'd scarfed down the whole thing and was licking frosting off his fingers . . . to Regina's fascination, he noted . . . he asked her, "And the brothers . . . the VIK . . . where are they?"

"In the war room . . . the dining room, actually."

"Why aren't you there . . . or somewhere working? Oh, I remember. You mentioned parole." Something occurred to him then. "You're being punished for your efforts to save me," he concluded.

She shook her head. "No doubt there will be punishment, but not yet. Not until Michael arrives. In the meantime, I've been waiting for you. They'll send word when I'm to bring you to the meeting."

He listened to what she said, and what she didn't say. "They're still suspicious of me, aren't they? That's why they're meeting now . . . to decide if they can trust me?"

"Something like that."

He drank his coffee slowly, savoring the strong brew. Time enough for the serious business at hand. He could help in the upcoming fight with all his inside information, if they'd let him, but first he wanted to address an issue important to him.

"Thank you," he said simply.

She didn't ask for what. She knew. "You're welcome, but, as you know, I did it for myself more than you."

"Doesn't matter to me. You got me out." That must rankle some of the male vangels who hadn't, or couldn't, do what a mere female vangel had accomplished. Even if it had been against protocol, aka Michael's wishes. "Kudos, babe."

"Thanks, *babe*," she said and shared a smile with him. She had a very nice smile when it wasn't coated with biting cynicism. "You smell good," she added.

"The rain crap again?"

"Oh, yeah! Summer rain on a fresh mowed lawn. Autumn rain on leaves. Slashing rain. Gentle rain. Fresh. Clean."

"That's me. Mr. Clean. I thought I smelled your cinnamon spiciness again, but then I realized it must be those sweet rolls Andrea baked. No lifemate nonsense from my end."

"You don't have to look so happy about it."

"Regina, I have enough troubles as it is without a woman. And you don't even like me."

"I don't dislike you as much as I did before, but, God forbid, I have no use for a man. It would cramp my witchy style."

Zeb laughed. "Anyhow, I'm thinking about becoming a priest."

She was the one to laugh now. "Get serious."

"I am serious. Here's my thinking. Michael is already on the fence about me becoming a vangel. Not just because I was a demon, but I'm not a Viking and so far, all the vangels have been of Norse descent. I've been practicing Viking, though. Truly, it would be points in my favor if I could show him that not only have I been a double agent for him, and not only did I give myself up for Cnut, and not only can I be devout and celibate, and—"

She put up a halting hand. "You're overthinking this. Besides, Michael has probably already made up his mind."

"Oh," he said, his shoulders slumping.

"Besides, do Jews become priests? Shouldn't it be a rabbi, or something?"

"I didn't think of that. Are Vikings ever rabbis? Probably not."

"I hesitate to ask, but how do you practice Viking?"

He straightened and grinned at her. "Well, before my recent incarceration, I tried braiding my hair and walking with my shoulders thrown back, like I owned the world."

"That's a start."

"Arrogance comes easy, but I'm not too hot for boats. I get seasick."

She shrugged. "Modern Norsemen rarely go a-Viking these days. No need to ever step foot on a longboat. Besides, plundering is against the law."

"I developed a taste for wild boar, even though we Jews are supposed to avoid pork."

"Too gamey, if you ask me."

"I like mead, but it's a bit sweet for my taste buds. There's nothing like good old Bud Light."

"I prefer Diet Pepsi myself."

"I would even wear a horned helmet if that would convince Michael."

"Vikings never wore horned helmets. They would have given their enemies a handhold during battle. No, that's a myth that started with Wagner's opera about Beowulf."

"Thank God! A helmet would probably chafe my bald head. Oh, and I've been practicing dance steps to the Michael song."

Regina smiled at that.

The vangels had a fondness for the movie *Michael* in which John Travolta played a rather unflattering, cigarette-smoking Michael the Archangel. In particular, they'd learned the dance Travolta did in that movie to the song with the lyrics "chains, chains, chains." It was a sight to see when the seven brothers did their unchoreographed version.

"I'd like to see that."

"I'm not ready for prime time," he said. "Anyhow, that's about it for practicing Viking, or vangel. I'm open to other suggestions."

She rolled her eyes. "You got the 'dumb as a Norseman' down pat."

"See." He winked at her.

"Don't do that."

"What?"

"Wink."

"Why?"

"You have such long eyelashes."

"And . . . ?"

"Your wink gives me flutters."

Zeb had no time to ponder that amazing revelation because the young vangel Armod came moonwalking into the kitchen, wearing a red jacket and short black pants that exposed his white socks. Zeb knew from previous visits that the boy fashioned himself Michael Jackson reincarnated. He must have healed from the Lucipire bite he'd gotten last year on a Montana ranch where ISIS terrorists and Lucipires were engaged in some devilment. The poison of a Lucipire bite was normally fatal, even for a vangel. "The boss wants you," Armod said.

By "boss," he assumed that Armod meant Vikar, and not the musician, which wouldn't have been a stretch with the young music addict.

When Zeb entered the dining room, he saw that all of the brothers were there, even though Sigurd and Ivak and their families and vangels were staying on Grand Key Island. They must have left them behind to come here. In addition, there was Karl Mortenssen, two other higher level vangels, Svein and Jogeir, as well as Trond's wife, Nicole; and Harek's wife, Camille; who were female SEALs. The five or so others he did not know.

"Michael will be here this afternoon," Vikar said.

And Zeb's heart dropped. That would be a life-changing moment for him.

"But in the meantime," Vikar continued, staring directly at Zeb, "we would like your input on some of our plans." Vikar motioned Zeb to enter the room where maps and charts covered every surface of the long table and all the walls. Harek sat before a high-tech computer that looked as if it could do everything except fly a jet, or maybe even that.

"So, you have decided to trust me," Zeb stated. It was not a question.

"Somewhat. We took a vote," Vikar responded. In fact, a few of the vangels stared at Zeb with outright hostility, and he could guess how those vangels had voted. Clearly, it had not been a unanimous decision. Somehow aware of Zeb's conclusion, Vikar added, "You had advocates speaking on your behalf."

"I did?"

Vikar nodded. "Trond and Cnut. And Regina, earlier today."

Zeb glanced to his side where Regina stood, apparently staying for the meeting. She ignored his gaze and stared straight ahead. *So, I have one more thing to thank her for.* Zeb did not like being beholden to a woman, to anyone, really. And he did not like the bond that seemed to be growing between them. Happily-ever-afters had died for him with his wife's passing. And he hadn't totally put aside the priest idea.

"Let's start here," Cnut said, motioning for Zeb to come to the middle of the table. "How does this look? It's a map showing the various command centers for the Lucipires and their haakai leaders."

Zeb took one look and shook his head. "Out of date." He picked up a marker and showed them the changes. "Heinrich is in Siberia at Desolation, which had been Yakov's headquarters. Hector is still in Rome under the Vatican at Terror. Yakov took over my old territory in the Greek volcanic caves called Gloom. Ganbold the Mongol took over Haroun's old stomping grounds in the Arab lands. Red Tess the Pirate, a new addition, handles the northern United States, from Maine to Washington State, up to and including Canada. I have no idea if Jasper replaced me in the southern United States yet. I was assigned last year to a territory running from Virginia to California and Nevada. I can't imagine that he hasn't. Or even added more commanders with all the extra demons you say have come in. Oh, I can't forget. Jasper still maintains Horror, his castle in the north."

Everyone in the room gathered around to view the changes. While they did, Zeb gave them background information on each of the Lucipire commanders, past and present.

"Was once a Silk Road merchant active in the slave trade . . ."

"She loved snakes, so much that . . ."

"A Russian cossack who still has a taste for horse blood . . ."

"Serving under Genghis Khan, he was partly responsible for a million deaths . . ."

"Liked to feed Christians to the lions . . ."

"Looks like an angel but made 300 or more victims walk the plank . . ."

"A Nazi general who has a close bond with Satan . . ."

"Jasper has to suspect that you're with us and sharing information," Sven said. "Wouldn't he have changed all those dynamics by now? I mean, those headquarters may be empty and relocated."

"Eventually, he would have, but not yet. You have to understand the order of Lucipires. Haakai, mungs, hordlings, and imps. The majority of Jasper's forces are in those lower orders, the foot soldiers of Satan, and they love unruliness and disorder. They thrive in it. Nothing happens quickly with imps, and hordlings aren't much better."

"And you were a haakai?" Vikar asked.

Zeb liked that Vikar had used the verb "were." He answered truthfully. "For my sins, I was. For almost two thousand years. Almost as long as Jasper himself."

The fact that he was older in demon/vangel

years than any of them did not go unnoticed. Regina was practically gaping at him. Hadn't she known that about him? Obviously, not.

"Well, let us hope your experience can help us," Trond said. He was the brother who'd had the most association with Zeb. Almost a friend, you might say.

Zeb nodded his thanks at Trond.

Then, while everyone sat down in chairs on both sides of the huge table, Harek stood and updated them on all the happenings around the world the past few days that were believed related to the Lucipires.

"Islamic extremism abounds in the world, without any Lucipire influence, as you all know. Unfortunately, terrorism is Jasper's fastest and most efficient conduit for evil deeds. He has already infiltrated more than 500 of his Lucipires into dozens, maybe fifty, ISIS cells. They're in Boko Haram, too. And al-Qaeda. The result is even more murders and atrocities. Not to mention the bomb dropped on St. Peter's Square in Rome several days ago, or the continued widespread beheadings in Syria, or rioting in major cities, or the satanic cult in Colorado that got so much publicity because of its orgies and human sacrifices."

Everyone was grim-faced at Harek's report.

"Yesterday alone, fifty more girls were kidnapped in Nigeria, gang raped, and left for dead," Harek continued. "Lions were let loose in French, Spanish, and London zoos, devouring some children and maiming numerous adults. A town occupied by special forces in Afghanistan was bombed. An American airplane headed for

Israel was hijacked and its whereabouts is still unknown. At least a thousand females in cities across America, Europe, and South America were seized overnight and believed sold into the white slave trade. Some whackjob guy, who claims to be the Antichrist, is on the Internet calling for Satan worship in order to gain world peace. He already has a million followers. And that's only the beginning," Harek concluded. "I guarantee it's going to escalate even more."

This was bad, very bad. Worse than Zeb had expected.

"And this is all my fault. I unleashed this," Regina said with dismay.

"You may have been the trigger, Regina, but this was going to happen sometime," Cnut told her. "It's like nibbling away at ducks. Eventually the ducks rise up and either fly away or attack the hunters. That's what we vangels have been . . . the hunters. And we're seeing now what havoc the ducks have created."

"Cnut is an expert on ducks," Trond teased his brother.

"Quack, quack," Ivak said, also teasing Cnut.

"Bite me," Cnut replied.

"Back to my report," Harek said. "That was the outside news. Now for what's happening with regard to us vangels. Regina and Zeb, you have to know that Jasper is searching for you everywhere."

They nodded.

"The Crazy Coven, they don't care so much about, although if they catch them, there will be witch stew, for sure."

"At the moment, they are in demonoid form and clawing each other. The Close Quarters room reeks of demon mung," Svein reported.

"That's Michael's problem," Vikar said, then immediately added, "I mean, we should do nothing more until Michael decides their fate."

"Once again, back to my report," Harek said. "Zeb, I am sorry to say that your island hideaway is no more. As of last night, it was razed to the ground."

Zeb was sorry about that, but he didn't figure he'd have much opportunity to go there again anyway, no matter what Michael did with him.

"Ivak, your plantation is no more, either. It is as if a tornado swept the grounds. All your renovation work for naught."

"Oh, shit! Wonder if I'll have to rebuild after this is over?"

No one answered his question because, frankly, they weren't sure they would be the victor in this battle of good against evil.

"They haven't discovered Harek's or Sigurd's islands yet, the shielding there being triple reinforced."

"So what do we do about all this?" Nicole asked. She was wearing a Navy WEALS T-shirt over camouflage pants and sand-colored boots. WEALS was the name of the female SEALs unit, Women on Earth, Air, Land, and Sea. She must have come directly from Coronado.

"Mordr and Cnut can speak better on campaign strategy," Harek said and sat down, while Mordr and Cnut stood.

Mordr, who had once been a berserker, spoke

first. "Nicole, you and Trond and Camille will return to the SEAL compound and update them on certain aspects of the terrorism plots, not mentioning Lucipires, of course. You can say you have intelligence from Cnut's Wings International Security firm. Bottom line, we need their help to handle the normal terrorist activities, as compared to the Lucipire-influenced frenzy."

She nodded.

"Keep in mind, their goal is to destroy terrorists. Ours is to save evil humans, even terrorists, if they repent. But mainly our target is the Lucipires. So, our interests converge and diverge."

Nicole nodded again, as did Trond and Camille, also in military attire.

Cnut spoke then, asking Harek to project something onto the one wall which was clear of maps. What came up was a different kind of map of the world. "Consider Jasper's operation like the spokes of a wheel," he said, "with Horror as its hub. Out from the spokes you will see the various satellite headquarters, those we know about. In the United States, Greece, Italy, Siberia, and the Arab lands. We are going to work from the wheels inward. Five commanders . . . myself, Vikar, Ivak, Mordr, and Harek . . . will command troops of one hundred vangels each to hit each of those targets. Destroy the nest and the rats have no place to scurry home."

"What about me?" Sigurd asked.

"And me?" Trond added.

Jogeir, Svein, Regina and others asked about their roles, too.

"Sigurd, you must stay on Grand Key Island

and hold the fort there. I guarantee Jasper will discover your whereabouts," Cnut said.

Sigurd agreed, reluctantly.

"And Trond, you, of course, will be the liaison with the SEALs, as I already said," Cnut explained. "If you find your presence unnecessary at some point, you will join one of the other operations."

Trond nodded, too.

"Karl, you will stay here at the castle and take steps to reinforce all security," Mordr said. "Do not under any circumstances let a single Lucie enter the perimeter." Mordr was of course concerned about his wife and five adopted children who had moved in here for the duration.

The other vangels who had family here were equally concerned, as were Sigurd and Ivak with their brood out on that island.

"This will not be a defensive campaign," Mordr told them. "Our end game will be the destruction of Lucipiredom. Jasper and all his demon vampires must be obliterated."

Zeb wondered idly what would happen if they were successful. If there were no more Lucipires, would there be a need for vangels? Well, that was a question for later.

For the next hour, there was much discussion about additional missions to subvert Jasper's plans, headed by other vangels.

"And, remember, everything is fluid, subject to change, as we gain more intel," Harek emphasized.

Zeb couldn't help but note that he and Regina were not included in any of the announcements. Which was a moot point, really, because just then

Armod stuck his head in the door and announced, "Michael is here."

Even more ominous, he added, "He wants to see only Vikar, Zeb, and Regina in the first parlor."

Regina looked at Zeb and said, "This is it."

Zeb nodded, but the question remained. What was "it"?

Chapter 11

Judgment Day wasn't what they expected . . .

Regina was surprised to see Michael already in the parlor, sitting in one of the wingback chairs. The archangel was in human appearance today with his hair clubbed at his nape in a low ponytail. He wore a blue oxford collar shirt tucked into Levi button fly jeans, legs crossed at the ankles, and on his feet were a pair of high-end Nikes. It was a well-known fact that Michael had a weakness for modern athletic shoes. He probably had a collection of footwear up above that rivaled that of Imelda Marcos.

None of that mattered. What did matter was the expression of barely suppressed fury on his handsome face. In fact, the glow . . . rather full-body halo . . . seemed to shimmer. His posture said relaxed, his demeanor said, "The you-know-what is going to fly."

Zeb appeared to be stunned. In awe. As he should be. Regina wasn't sure, but this might be the first time he'd ever met Michael, in person. No, he had to have met him a few years back when

Michael offered Zeb a deal he couldn't refuse: act as a double agent for fifty years and then maybe he'd let him become a vangel. Even if Zeb had met Michael before, being in the presence of an archangel was always . . . well, awesome.

He did not invite them to sit. Not a good sign, not that they'd been expecting happy greetings. Thus, the three of them just stood, edgy and nervous, the way Michael wanted them.

"You first, Vikar. A captain is responsible for a sinking ship."

Does he consider this a sinking ship? Another bad sign.

"I blame you for this debacle, Vikar. For this sin, I give you a thousand more years as a vangel."

Vikar's eyes went wide, but he bowed his head and said, "As you say. And I apologize for not being a better leader."

"As to that, I considered demoting you and raising another of the VIK to rule the vangels. But there is no time for that with all the evil that Jasper is stirring in the world. So, thou wilt remain as leader, but consider thyself on probation."

"As you wish," Vikar said, his face flushed with high emotion. Vikar was a prideful man, and Michael's opinion of him had to cut deeply.

"Or I could send you back to the Norselands as a human to continue thy life as a ninth-century Viking and see if thou hast learned anything from all your vangel years. A second chance to correct your mistakes, in person. Like Cnut was given." Last year, Cnut somehow traveled back in time to his old estate in the midst of a famine, and he was able to correct some of his earlier human sins. Not many people were given a chance for do-overs like that. In fact, none that she knew of, other than Cnut.

"But . . . but what about Alex and the children?" Vikar asked.

"They would stay here to live out their natural lives."

Without hesitation, Vikar said, "I choose probation as leader of the VIK, provided I have the choice."

Michael nodded.

But whoa, whoa, whoa, Regina thought. Vangel punishments usually ranged in the hundreds, never a thousand years. And that business about sending Vikar back in time, separating him from his family, that was harsh.

Regina and Zeb exchanged a quick look. This was not at all what they'd expected. Vikar taking the brunt of the blame? It didn't seem fair, but as Michael always said, "Who says life must be fair."

The "penance" levied against Vikar raised a whole lot of other questions, other than the injustice of him paying for her crime. Like:

- —If Vikar got a thousand years, would she get two thousand? Or more? What if she got banished? Where did banished vangels go anyhow? It had never happened before.
- —Would there still be vangels in a thousand, or two thousand years?
- —If Michael dealt so harshly with Vikar, one of the good guys, how would he treat Zeb, a demon, whom she'd forced on him with her unauthorized rescue? And, holy clouds! Who knew he'd been a demon for so long?

—Should she step up and express her regret for her actions, sort of a preemptive defensive move? The only thing was, she wasn't sorry, not for the end result.

"Regina Dorasdottir," Michael called out then.

She jumped. He hadn't shouted, but to her ears it sounded like he'd used a bullhorn.

"Your servant," she said, bowing her head in deference.

She thought Michael made a scoffing sound. But then, he demanded, "What dost thou have to say for thyself, witch?"

Okay, addressing me as "witch" and not my name is another bad sign. "I saw a need, and felt that I could do the job." That sounded arrogant even to her own ears.

"Didst think thou could do the job better than anyone else? Better than Vikar, for example?"

Vikar's head shot up at that, and he glared at her.

"Not necessarily better. But no one else was stepping up."

Vikar glared some more.

"Admit thy sin, woman! Thou initiated this action for thy own ends. 'Twas pride and ambition that drove you. You wanted the praise of your fellow vangels. You were raising a flag for womanhood and female superiority."

All of that was true, and, in fact, many vangels had come up to her in private and given their congratulations.

"It started that way," she admitted. "But once I'd entered Horror and saw Zeb . . ." She shrugged. There was no way to explain how her motives had changed on seeing his pitiful condition, and being inside a castle that reeked of evil. At some point, her motives had changed to a need to rescue the man, for his own sake, not her own pride.

Michael nodded. "Witnessing evil has that effect betimes." He was silent for a moment, and seemed to be recalling in his mind some horrendous memory. But then, he shook his head and asked, "And what of the three demon witches you brought here? Just because I allowed one witch to become a vangel," *meaning me*, "does not mean I have a fondness for the creatures." *Well, that's not nice, calling us creatures. And his attitude regarding women stinks, too. Best I not tell him that now, though.*

"Do you like witches?" Michael asked Vikar.

Great! Now he was being sarcastic.

"Not a bit," Vikar replied.

The traitor. Just when she'd been planning to take the blame off him and onto her own shoulders.

"I had no choice but to bring them here," she said.

"Thou had a choice!" Michael boomed. "There is always a choice."

"Well, the three Lucipire witches . . . the Crazy Coven . . . helped me rescue Zeb, and it seemed the better of the alternatives. Besides, there are good witches."

"Tsk, tsk, tsk! When will thou learn? Those three down below are demons. Like you, they helped Zebulan escape for their own reasons. And while I might be able to forgive your transgression, being a vangel, what should I do about three demons in the midst of five hundred vangels? Once a demon, always a demon."

Regina had no answer for Michael, and the most alarming thing in his statement was that demons could not change. What did that portend for Zeb? As Zeb stiffened at her side, she could tell that he had the same thought. And why did Zeb suddenly smell like rain in a tropical forest? Talk about bad timing! She glanced at the others, but no one else seemed to notice.

"We will come back to your fate and that of the three witches later," Michael said to her. Then he turned to Zeb and said, "Shalom, Zebulan ben Judah."

Interesting that Michael knew Zeb's full Hebrew name, when none of the vangels had ever heard it. Well, of course, Michael would know. He was God's right-hand man.

"Shalom!" Zeb said back at the archangel, who had his future in his celestial hands.

"Thou hast suffered much," Michael observed.

"I have," Zeb choked out.

"Why?"

The question surprised Zeb and for a moment he did not answer. Then he realized, as she and Vikar did, that Michael was asking why Zeb hadn't just surrendered to his tormentors, to end the agony.

"I just could not bear to be a demon anymore. It was too much," Zeb replied.

"Too much what?"

"Evil. Cruelty. Filth. That's why I resisted the torture for so long."

"Vanity, thy name is man. Did our Lord have naught to do with your withstanding so much torture?"

"I'm not sure. I sensed . . . perhaps I imagined . . . that He was there with me at times."

"He was," Michael confirmed.

For the first time, Regina began to feel hopeful.

Zeb blinked those incredibly long lashes of his to hide the tears that welled in his eyes.

"Vangels have always been Vikings. Thou art not a Viking," Michael pointed out to Zeb.

Regina willed him not to mention all that practicing to be a Viking crap.

Luckily, it seemed as if he heard her, and all he said was, "I know."

"And you are not a Christian. You are a Jew."

"Jesus was a Jew."

It was Michael now who said, "I know." He tapped his fingertips on the arm of the chair, thinking. "You are no longer a Lucipire, or even a demon, you know?"

Hallelujah! A good sign. Finally.

"I suspected," Zeb said and his lips twitched with a smile, which he suppressed. He wasn't out of the woods yet. "What am I, exactly?"

"That remains to be seen," Michael said. "Do you still wish to become a vangel?"

"Oh, yes, please."

Surely, it couldn't be as easy as this, Regina thought. There had to be a catch. There always was with Michael. She'd like to warn Zeb about an upcoming trap, but got no chance with Michael watching.

More tapping of Michael's fingertips on the chair as he studied Zeb. "Vangels have always been Vikings. Thou art not a Viking," Michael pointed out, just as she and Zeb had discussed earlier. "But mayhap there is a loophole in the regulations." Odd that Michael could use such archaic words as *thou* and *dost* and then pop out a modern one, like loophole.

"A loophole?" all of them said.

"Perhaps you could marry into the family, so to speak. Yes, that might work. In the old days, back in Judea, arranged marriages were often the norm. Marrying *into* a family was often considered an asset."

At first, they were confused.

"Zebulan could marry his rescuer, Regina, and thus become a vangel by marriage."

What? Michael had always opposed vangel marriages, not facilitated them. In fact, he'd forbidden them in the beginning before vangels discovered lifemates.

The archangel seemed pleased with himself. He'd probably had this idea up his saintly sleeve the whole time.

But she couldn't allow him to get away with this preposterous idea. "No!" Regina cried out.

"No way!" Zeb cried out.

"Hmmm," Vikar said with a decided grin on his face.

"I have no particular liking for men," Regina tried to explain.

"Oh?" Michael arched his brows. She could practically see his brain spinning, wondering if he was going to have to deal with a gay vangel on top of everything else.

"Not like that! I've just had some bad experiences with men in that way." That sounded lame; so, she tried again. "Overall, they are more trouble than they are worth."

"Zeb is trouble, and yet you went to such lengths to rescue him? Hmmm." Michael was being difficult. Surprise, surprise!

"Zeb is not so bad, but sharing a bed with him, yuck!" That slipped out before she had a chance to bite her tongue.

Zeb and Vikar both turned to stare at her.

She refused to acknowledge their stares, and besides, at the same time she'd made that unflattering statement, she recalled her carnal response when giving Zeb blood. No yuck there!

No matter!

"Surely there have been men who treated you well, Regina. Thou art an attractive woman, for a human," Michael said. "Isn't she, Vikar?"

That question startled Vikar. After a brief hesitation, he answered, "She is not bad when she is not being snarky."

"Mayhap thou could tone down thy snarkiness," Michael advised Regina.

Aaarrgh! This is not going well. If it were anyone but Michael saying that, she would show him just how snarky she could be.

"I rather like her snarkiness," Zeb inserted.

Huh? She gave the dumb man a disbelieving look.

"See?" Michael tossed his hands in the air in a voilà manner.

Regina really, really, really wanted to tell three people what they could do with themselves and their opinions. Well, not people precisely. A lackwit ex-demon vampire, a lackwit vampire angel, and a lackwit archangel.

Realizing his mistake, Zeb tried another tactic. "It is a moot point, anyhow. I'm already married."

"Not anymore," Michael snapped. Realizing the callousness of his response, he added, more softly, "Thy wife and children are in a good place, Zebulan. Even if I allowed you to die right now, thou would not be joining them. Thou would be sent to another place."

"Hell?" Zeb asked, suddenly ashen-faced.

"No, not Hell. Purgatory. Or perhaps Tranquility." Michael didn't explain, and Regina wasn't sure if Zeb knew that Tranquility was the place dead vangels went, when they passed before their sentence was completed.

Was that another good sign? That Michael might place Zeb in a vangel place? Maybe.

Zeb was still not convinced. "Besides, I was planning to become a priest if I were made a vangel."

Vikar glanced sideways at Zeb with an incredulous expression.

Regina groaned. She'd told Zeb not to try that ploy with Michael.

In fact, Michael laughed. "So, thou were planning a celibate life?"

"Yes!" Zeb said quickly, thinking he'd won this battle.

Hah! He didn't know Michael.

"Are you sure thou art not a Viking?" Michael asked in that disdainful tone he usually reserved for Vikings. Then he turned to her. "And thou sayest that relations with a man . . . with Zebulan . . . would be repugnant to you?"

Well, not repugnant with Zeb, exactly. Just not welcome. Still, she gave a blanket "Yes."

"See?" Michael said, as if everything was going

according to plan. "A perfect solution. A celibate marriage. The best kind. Holy matrimony."

Whaaat?

"Oh, please, can't you reconsider? This is not a good idea," Regina pleaded.

"C'mon, are you serious?" Zeb scoffed.

Maybe Zeb was right about Michael not being serious. Maybe this was an archangel joke. A celestial *Candid Camera* moment.

No such luck. Michael didn't crack a smile.

Meanwhile, Vikar was bent over laughing. "Perfect, Michael, perfect! A demon-vangel union. I can't wait to tell my brothers."

"So, it is decided," Michael said with satisfaction, glancing first at Zeb and then her. "Consider thyselves betrothed."

Regina and Zeb were stunned into silence.

Vikar was still chuckling.

"We will have the wedding after this war against Jasper and the Lucipires is settled."

"Does that mean we will be successful?" Vikar asked hopefully.

"That is not for me to say," Michael said in his usual enigmatic way. "Show me your battle plans before I go, Vikar. I brought Joshua with me as an advisor. And I have some warrior skills myself that might be helpful."

Joshua? The Biblical warrior of Jericho fame? And St. Michael, patron saint of all fighting men, as an advisor? Holy clouds! Maybe it wouldn't be a losing battle of good fighting evil, after all.

"Before that, though, take me to those witch demons thou brought out of Horror," Michael ordered Regina. "I would settle their fates afore they revert to their demonic selves and wreak havoc.

"I still must decide on your punishments, as well." Michael looked at both her and Zeb.

What? Marriage isn't enough of a punishment? she thought, not daring to say the words aloud.

"Some appropriate punishment," Michael continued. "Hmmm. I will have to think on that."

They were back to bad signs.

Michael looked at Zeb then and said, "Mazel tov!"

Was he joking? Wishing Zeb "Good luck!" and in Yiddish, yet, seemed rather odd. But then, this whole situation was odd.

As Vikar led the way, Zeb hung back and whispered to Regina, "You planned this, didn't you? I was to be your prize all along."

"Get over yourself," she snapped. "You are no great prize."

"What a mess! And I don't even know if I'm a vangel yet." He turned sideways and said, "Check my back and see if I have shoulder bumps."

"I am not touching you!"

"Two days ago you had my cock in your hands."

"Crude moron!"

Suddenly, they were awash in the scent of cinnamon rain, and they heard Michael say ahead of them, without looking back, "I feel a storm coming on."

And Zeb who probably hadn't said anything very Yiddish in hundreds of years, muttered, "Oy vey!"

Chapter 12

Devil-may-care, they were not . . .

Zeb thought he'd been prepared for what they'd find in the Close Quarters Combat room in the basement, but he was shocked. As were Michael and Regina and Vikar.

When the door opened, the three Lucipires glanced over, claws raised, ready to fight them, as well as each other. The three Lucipires, in full demonoid form, along with a crazed cat, fur standing on end, had shredded the mattresses which lined the wall, floor, and ceiling of the room where vangels presumably honed their fighting skills. It had been modeled on a Navy SEALs program, CQC, which taught hand-to-hand combat techniques. These three beasts must have been in combat, all right. With each other.

Leave a demon alone for an hour, and this is what happened. If they didn't have humans or vangels to fight, they fought each other.

The fools were covered with seeping wounds and bruises which would show up better when they transformed into humanoid form. There was mattress batting everywhere. In the air, caught in the scales of their demon skin, piled on the floor, in Thor's tail. The room reeked of sulfur and cat piss.

"Son of a star!" Vikar exclaimed.

"Can't you three behave, even when your lives are on the line?" Regina chastised them.

"I'm not surprised," Zeb said.

Michael pointed two arms at them and yelled, "Satan, begone!"

Immediately, the three demons reverted to humanoid form, looking dazed and then shame-faced at the archangel who held their destinies in his hands, which were no longer pointing at them.

Michael shook his head from side to side and made a tsk-ing sound of disapproval.

Meanwhile, the cat . . . Thor, he believed it was called . . . had its back arched and appeared ready to launch itself at them all.

Michael gritted out, "Do. Not. Dare!"

The cat hissed at him. Then had the nerve to walk over, cough up a lint ball on one of Michael's athletic shoes, then dart out the open door, off to hide, no doubt, or lick his balls.

It was amazing that Thor, who'd been with Regina for hundreds of years, didn't give her even a passing glance. That was cats for you! Loyal as their options. Like men, some women claimed.

Michael gazed at his shoe with disgust, then turned that disgust on the three Lucipires who were picking clumps of lint off their clothing and out of their hair.

"Come with me," Michael ordered, and led them to a small anteroom where there were a table and chairs, a coffeemaker in the corner, and a glass-fronted fridge full of Fake-O against the wall.

Zeb had tasted the vangel beverage one time, and it was putrid. He supposed he'd have to develop a taste for it if he ever became a vangel. Small price to pay, of course.

The few vangels who were taking a break there hurried out, without being directed to do so, sensing danger. Who wouldn't, seeing Michael's stormy expression.

Michael sat down wearily, still shaking his head from side to side at the three Lucipires who sat down across the table from him, even though Michael hadn't invited them to do so. Dumb as . . . well, demons. Since their sitting didn't seem to bother Michael, Zeb and Regina sat down on one side of Michael, Vikar on the other.

Beau and Patience fidgeted in their chairs, nervous, or maybe they were just anxious to be off somewhere. Grimelda couldn't have cared less, still picking mattress batting off her black gown.

"The three of you still carry the demon taint," Michael told them. "Even if I had considered making you vangels," he pretended to shiver at the prospect, "that would preclude thy joining those holy ranks."

Whoa! That raised two big questions in Zeb's mind. First, did that mean Zeb no longer carried the taint, since Michael had only said that those three carried the taint? A quick glance told him that Regina and Vikar had the same question.

Second, vangels were "holy"? *Who knew! Holy Vikings? Does that mean, if I become a vangel, I will be a holy Hebrew? Ha, ha, ha! I'm not sure I can live up to being holy. Even if I become a celibate, I don't think I can be perfectly pure. But then, the seven Sig brothers are far from perfect, or even remotely close to pure.*

"Ah reckoned our helping Zebulan escape would count fer somethin'," Beau said to Michael, clearly surprised and disappointed.

"It did, but not enough to remove the taint completely," Michael told him.

"Does that mean we have to go back to being Lucipires?" Patience cringed.

"I ain't sucking blood anymore, I don't care what you say," proclaimed Grimelda with a chuckle. The old crone was probably a little bit looney, or suffering from dementia, to argue with an archangel.

"Tell me, why did you want to leave Horror?" Michael asked the three of them.

The question seemed to surprise them.

Finally, Grimelda said, "I'm too old to be dragging a tail around. And they won't let me make my potions, just the same old demon recipes. And everything has blood, blood, blood in it. I get heartburn every time I do a fanging these days."

Zeb had never heard the old lady string so many words together before. Not that he'd had much contact with her over the years. Usually she was assigned to the kitchens which were in a part of Horror he rarely visited.

"I'm tired of being forced to spread my legs for every visiting haakai demon," Patience said. "I want to be able to pick my own lovers . . . like I did when I was human . . ." She seemed to realize how inappropriate her statements were for an angel, or a Puritan, and her words trailed off.

"And killed them off afterward," Zeb finished for her.

"I don't mind the taste of blood, though," Patience continued, licking her lips for emphasis. "And fanging is fun."

"Maybe you would just be happier if you'd been given a promotion," Michael offered. "From hordling to mung, maybe. In time, even a haakai."

The stupid woman nodded vigorously, not realizing the trap she'd set for herself.

"And you, Beauregard?"

"Initially, Ah wanted ta escape so that Ah could go back and wring the neck of that voodoo priestess, Lilith. She deserved to be a Lucipire more than Ah did, or so Ah've always thought. Ah'm still tempted, but lately Ah keep thinking about the way mah life was, pre-Lilith, pre-witchcraft. That's what Ah want. Doan get me wrong. Ah was no saint, but Ah wasn't evil."

Beau exchanged a glance with Zeb, wondering if he'd said the wrong thing. Hard to say. At least Beau was being honest.

"This is what I have decided regarding you three," Michael said. "For thy efforts in helping Regina to rescue Zebulan, I will offer you Lucipires one option, and one option only. Go back to thy old lives as humans, not as Lucipires. A second chance to live a good life and make up for thy evil. Chances are you would make the same mistakes. But who knows? Thou may surprise me."

Why wasn't I offered that choice? Zeb wondered. *Oh, to be able to go back to Sarah and my children, to stay in the vineyard and never join the Roman Army. A do-over. I probably would have died at Masada, like the others, but at least I would have been with my family at the end.*

Alas, he had not been offered that choice and probably never would be. He did not even want to think about the option that had been offered to him, remarriage . . . and to a witch, no less. All right, a vangel witch, he conceded. But still . . .

"Back to the old Norselands?" Grimelda scoffed. "It's hard living there. Cold. Snaring food. Making potions. Did you ever try to gather snails' tails in the middle of winter? And possum cooked over an open fire tastes worse than blood."

Michael shrugged, not caring about the old crone's discomforts.

"And I would go back to Salem where every other woman is accused of witchcraft?" Patience appeared horrified. "I don't think I could bear being burned at the stake again. I had to screw every man in town then, too, just to have food to eat. They deserved to die. All twelve of them! The bastards!"

There went any hope of Patience being a swim-suit model.

Zeb had figured that Patience had not been a model Puritan, but he hadn't known the details. Now, he did.

"What if we don't accept this offer?" Beau asked.

"You would be cast out into the world, visible to any Lucipire with a nose for thy demon lure. You would probably be back in Horror within a day. Mayhap Jasper would give the lot of you a second chance, after unbearable torture. I doubt it."

"Talk about an offer you can't refuse!" Beau commented.

"But Salem in the seventeen hundreds? Pfff! I refuse to go back there," Patience said. "How about modern-day Massachusetts?"

"I'd rather be a Lucipire than live in that hut again," Grimelda said.

It became obvious that these two had not learned a lesson in Horror. They would complain and resist living their old lives over until they ultimately committed grave sins again. Even Zeb could see that. Michael undoubtedly saw much more.

In a blink of an eye, Patience and Grimelda were gone. Poof! No smoke. No abracadabra. Just gone.

"I hope she took Thor with her," Regina murmured.

"I doubt it," Zeb murmured back. "You're stuck."

"We're both stuck, if we get married. Ha, ha, ha!"

"Wouldst thou care to share the joke?" Michael inquired.

Zeb and Regina went mute.

"Whoa!" Beau said, putting his hands up in surrender. He was still reacting to the abrupt disappearance of his comrades in sin. "Ah accept, Ah accept. Ah know which side mah biscuit is buttered on."

"As you say," Michael pronounced. "Resume thy old life then, Beauregard Doucet, back in Louisiana. Make sure to remember where thou hast been these past twenty years. As a young Lucipire, mayhap the evil has been too far embedded in you."

"Ah intend ta try harder," Beau said. "Ah think Ah'll move ta Alabama, put myself far away from Lilith so Ah'm not tempted ta wring her evil neck."

"Good idea," Michael agreed. "One other thing, if you do decide to stay in the bayou, go visit a woman named Louise Rivard, best known as Tante Lulu. She is a good friend of St. Jude, the patron saint of hopeless causes. She might be able to help you."

"Ah know her!" Beau said. "Everyone up and down Bayou Black, in fact, throughout Loo-zee-anna, knows Tante Lulu. And Ah certainly qualify as hopeless, guar-an-teed."

"Go with God, then."

And Beau was gone, too, leaving just the four of them in the room. Zeb, Regina, Vikar, and Michael.

What now?

They all stood, three of them rather stunned at how quickly Michael had acted. And how dramatic . . . no, miraculous . . . his actions had been.

"Vikar, we will go upstairs now where you can show me the battle plans. I heard there were more bombings in Lebanon this morning and a sulfurous smelling fire burning down an entire block in Las Vegas." Michael turned to Regina and Zeb then. "I'm sure you two have much to discuss about thy future plans."

What? No! No plans! "Don't you want my input?" Zeb asked.

"Later," Michael said.

"How about me? Haven't I proven that I have some skills?"

Michael arched his brows.

"We need each vangel brain and body we can get," Vikar surprised them by saying.

Does that mean Vikar considers me a vangel now? Zeb wondered.

Michael conceded, "Zebulan, you do have information that could aid in the campaigns. And, Regina, disregarding thy sins of stubbornness and lack of obedience, you did get inside Horror when others could not."

Stiffening with affront, Vikar was about to protest, to repeat that he'd only been following Michael's orders not to rescue Zeb, but he stopped himself, just in time. Zeb would have to learn such restraint.

Michael studied Regina and Zeb, pondering. "Yes, you two may join in the planning, but later. Whether you join in the fighting will be up to Vikar, your leader."

Vikar bowed his head in acknowledgement of Michael deferring to him on this point.

"For now, as a newly betrothed couple," Michael continued, "I am sure you two have much to discuss between thyselves, personal plans."

"But—" Zeb started to say.

She jabbed him with an elbow.

Thus, he was left alone with his . . . dare he say, fiancée.

"I still don't see why Michael is insisting on marriage," Zeb complained.

"Because you're not a Viking, and vangels have always been Vikings, and marriage to a vangel would make you a Viking-by-marriage."

"That's stupid."

"Would you care to tell that to Michael?"

No, he wouldn't. "What are we going to do?" he asked her.

She didn't need to ask what he meant. She knew! "I don't know what we *can* do. We have to find a way of turning lemons into lemonade, I suppose. Forgive the lemon association. Finding some good in a bad situation."

"So, if we're married, what are the benefits . . . the lemonade, so to speak?" Aside from the obvious, and he wasn't even going there.

Several vangels looked in the room and were about to enter, then turned away when they noticed the room was occupied.

"C'mon. Let's go outside. There's a back exit through the parking garage," she said and led him through several rooms and doorways, passing vangels at work. Mostly physical training or checking out weapons. Breaking down guns, oiling them, and putting them back together. Sharpening swords and knives. Taking out extra ammunition for weapons. Then making sure they had all been dipped in the symbolic blood of Christ.

Zeb didn't recognize most of them, but Regina nodded here and there, or spoke briefly about Michael and the activity upstairs.

There were also strange men in their midst, giving quiet instructions or demonstrations. Most of them wore ancient attire, similar to what he'd worn as a Roman soldier. Thigh-length leather tunics with thick belts and cross-gartered sandals. They carried heavy swords or lances. An aura surrounded them, not unlike the full-body halo of Michael's, but much fainter and more subtle. They also had a hint of wing bumps under their clothing.

"Archangel warriors," Regina whispered to him.

"Of course," he whispered back with a note of sarcasm. Why wouldn't there be a legion of angels hanging out in the basement of a vangel castle?

She darted a reproving glance his way.

Just then, Regina's cat shot out of a doorway, paused in front of them, hissed at Zeb, got in a position as if it was going to pee on his shoe, but ran away when Zeb said, "Don't you dare!"

"Damn! Thor is still here," Regina said.

"Your cat doesn't like me," Zeb told her.

"Thor doesn't like me, either." She shrugged, not at all offended.

He wasn't either.

Finally, they got to the underground garage, obviously a new addition to the castle, and it was massive. He could only imagine Vikar supervising the work on this project, cursing and complaining the whole time at yet another of the seemingly endless improvements or restorations needed for the castle.

At least six dozen vehicles were parked there, lots of SUVs and pickup trucks, and a few luxury sedans, like a BMW and a Lexus. Even some motorcycles.

"All of them are black or dark-colored, I notice. Designed not to attract attention?" he asked.

"Right. Although, being located in a town known for flaunting its vampire character, being invisible almost makes us more visible."

There was an odd logic in her illogic.

"Why would vangels need motor vehicles, if they can teletransport?"

"Vangels only teletransport in emergencies. We're encouraged to use modern methods, wherever possible. Cars, trucks, trains, planes. And not just to appear normal to humans, but because teletransporting drains a vangel of energy."

He'd known that, actually. He was just making conversation. Moving on to another subject, he remarked, "Seriously, Regina, why didn't someone mention to me that you vangels would have archangels covering your backs in the fight against Jasper and his hordes? That puts a whole new perspective on the chances for success."

She shook her head. "They're only here as advisors. Once Michael leaves, they will, too."

"So, no hometown advantage? A heavenly second team waiting in the background?"

"None," she answered.

They emerged through a series of tunnel-like corridors, reinforced with steel (more kudos to Vikar and his renovating efforts), up some concrete steps, and out onto the back lawn, beyond the swimming pool. Normally, on a warm day like today . . . mid-September, but balmy weather . . . there probably would have been children and some adults in the still-open pool and surrounding patio, taking advantage of the last days of what was known as "Indian Summer." But, in deference to the pandemonium out in the world and Michael's visit here, almost everyone seemed to be staying inside. Except for some vangel gardeners working on landscaping. Zeb could hear a lawn mower in the distance. Still others were using nets to clean the pool and hose down the patio. And wait . . . in the distance, a field held dozens of vangels, who wore leather armor, practicing swordplay. They would all transform into fighting men and women, when called to battle, even the gardeners and pool boys.

When they got to the gazebo, Regina sat down on a cushioned wicker chair and motioned for him to do the same in an opposing one. He was, frankly, glad to get off his feet. All the vangel blood he'd been given had improved his health immensely, but he was still not back to normal, and he felt it in his weary, battered bones. His ribs, especially, were aching and his feet hurt from all the walking he'd been doing in the castle since he awakened this morning. He would need several more vangel "transfusions" today, and tomorrow, too.

Maybe Regina would . . .

No, he couldn't go there, not with the new betrothal business.

For a moment, he closed his eyes and just relished the peacefulness of the setting. He hadn't felt so calm and hopeful . . . and clean, truth to tell, inside and out . . . since the days when he'd owned his own small vineyard and had been satisfied with just a modest harvest and enough wine to sell to take care of his family. But this was not Israel. And the scent was not of grapes, but late-blooming roses filling the air, except for the occasional wafts of cinnamon.

"Are you smelling rain?" he asked suddenly.

"Oh, yeah."

He'd been expecting her answer, but still it bothered him. He wasn't sure why. It was amazing to him that he could be so opposed to a union with this woman . . . any woman, really . . . but so attracted to her scent. "So, what's this lemonade idea of yours?"

"We could be partners. Vangel partners. Combine our talents. Brainstorm ideas. Fight side by side. I could see that working." There was excitement in her voice.

Ambitious wench! "Batman and Robin? Mulder and Scully? Holmes and Watson?"

She smiled. "Whatever floats your boat."

"You think I'm a vangel, then?"

"What else?"

"I still don't have shoulder bumps. I checked when I showered this morning."

"Stop fixating on wings. None of us have wings so far, except maybe Vikar who flew one time when Michael helped him escape from Jasper."

"I'm looking for proof, that's all. Shouldn't I feel different if I'm a vangel?"

"Different how?"

"Gooder."

"What?" She laughed. "That's not a word."

"More good. Purer. Angelic."

"Vangels aren't angels, Zeb. Never will be."

"I thought—"

"Nope."

"So you think we should try working together as vangels? A team?" Zeb commented. "No offense, but it seems to me that benefits you more than me."

"How so?"

"Being a woman, you're more likely to get plum

assignments if you're joined at the hip with a male, especially one of my superior fighting skills." He waggled his eyebrows at her.

He was teasing, but he could tell she didn't appreciate the sexist nature of his remark. Even if it was true. Point of fact, there were no high-level female vangels. It was probably because the seven VIK members were Vikings, and Vikings were known to be rather chauvinistic. Leastways, they had been in the old days.

About to backtrack, and explain his poorly chosen words, he saw that it was too late.

She bristled and made a hissing sound through her clenched teeth.

He couldn't help observing, "You look just like your cat when you do that."

"Best you be careful then, that I don't spit a hairball on you."

And he knew just where it would land. She was staring right at his crotch. Trond had told him in the past how Regina was known for throwing her witchly curses on men's male parts when they offended her in any way.

"Don't even try it, Regina. I'm immune to your curses."

"I wouldn't count on it."

"Listen, sweet witch," he said, having no clue why he referred to her with that half-assed endearment, "my cock was already in sleep mode for a long time before Jasper got hold of it. There isn't much more you could do to it."

"Hmpfh!" she said. Then, "As for one-sided marriage benefits, here's one for you. If you're married, women might stop hitting on you."

"What makes you think women hit on me?"

"Are you kidding? You're gorgeous, even with a bald head, which is starting to grow out, by the way. You already have a little fuzz. Besides, your eyelashes alone are enough to make a saint swoon."

He grinned. This was fun. "You think I'm gorgeous?"

"Don't let it go to your head. There are lots of good-looking vangel men. They're Vikings, after all. That doesn't mean they get to spread the love."

"Spread the love," he choked out. "Not even to their wives, if they're married?"

She narrowed her eyes at him. "What's your point?"

"I've been thinking. If I'm going to have to be married, if Michael won't let me be a priest, I am damn sure not giving up celibacy." He had no idea where that thought came from. He certainly didn't mean it.

"But you said . . ."

"I've reconsidered." *No, I haven't. I'm just kidding. Honest. Why won't my tongue correct itself?*

At first, she looked alarmed, but then she said, "Don't you think that's a two-way decision? And I can tell you right now, I'm not interested."

"I could convince you." *Damn, my tongue has a mind of its own.*

"Hah! You could try."

"Okay." *Who's driving this runaway train of a tongue of mine? Not me!*

"What?"

"You invited me to seduce you. So that's what I'll do." *Why don't I just lie down and surrender . . . to whatever or whoever is pulling my puppet strings?*

"You never mentioned seduction."

"Convince, seduce, same thing."

"Are you freakin' kidding me?"

"Yes," he said, finally gaining control of his unruly tongue.

"Idiot!" she said. "Here's my idea if you'll let me finish a sentence. Michael said we would marry *after* the mission is over. All we have to do is pretend to be compliant, and then we can do lots of good things to change his mind. Time is our friend."

"It might work," he said. "First of all, the mission might not succeed. We might all be destroyed. Then, our marriage would be a moot point. Second, it would give us time to come up with worthy arguments against our wedding."

"Exactly."

"The only thing is," he hesitated, "in the Jewish religion, as it was when I was human, a betrothal was as legal as an actual marriage. Oh, not consummation or love play of any kind, but for the year or so between engagement and wedding, the man and woman were considered man and wife."

She pondered his words, then concluded, "You're not in Kansas anymore, Toto."

"What in bloody hell does that mean?"

"Times have changed," she explained, standing. Apparently, their meeting was over. In her mind, anyway.

He stood, too, and said, dubiously, "If you say so."

"It's a deal then," she said, extending a hand for him to shake.

Which was a big mistake.

The second his flesh touched hers, palm to palm, a blue mist of cinnamon rain emanated from their clasp and swirled about, enveloping them in an erotically charged cocoon. Really. It did. Like magic, or something weird.

Every hair on his body stood on end, even the fine bristles on his head. Carnal caresses seemed to sweep over his body, in slow motion, like feathers.

She moaned.

He groaned.

And then he succumbed to the need that overwhelmed him, tugging her closer. He even felt a jolt down below.

She succumbed as well, stepping into his embrace.

The kiss that followed defied description. Lips met lips, then shifted reflexively to get the best angle of fit. Turns out fangs against fangs was no problem, after all.

Zeb didn't touch her, except for his fingertips on her upper arms. Her hands were pressed, lightly, against his chest.

But you would have thought they were joined in the most intimate way. His brain seemed to melt, and all logical thought was gone. He was just one big mass of throbbing need. For what, he wasn't sure.

He moved his mouth against hers, then tasted her with his tongue. Sweet. And spicy. Cinnamon with a bite. And the perfect match to his raging hunger.

She sighed and kissed him back, licking at his lips and fangs, then inserting her tongue into the hot sheath of his mouth.

He breathed into her mouth.

She breathed into his mouth.

He felt tears well in his closed eyes at the utter pleasure/torment of their kiss. It was wonderful. It was terrible.

Then, the unthinkable happened. Reflexively, he turned her head and sank his fangs into her neck.

And she let him.

He drank deeply. Only for a second. But it was enough to feel as one with this woman. He could swear they melded together. This fanging was more intimate than an actual mating.

Was she truly his lifemate?

Did he have no say in the matter?

Was she Eve to his Adam, tempting him?

Or was he tempting her?

What did it all mean?

Surely, pleasure this intense is of another dimension, he thought, and had no idea where that word *dimension* had come from.

With an inner strength that he didn't know he had, Zeb drew away from her.

She stared up at him, dazed.

And he responded, finally and belatedly, to her question, the one posed when she'd first extended her hand for a shake. "It's a deal," he said. "God help me, it's a deal."

Chapter 13

They were a sight to behold ...

Regina waited with Zeb on the lawns in front of the castle where nine hundred or so vangel warriors had gathered. Mostly male, but there were some female vangel soldiers, as well, Regina included. A hundred vangels remained on Grand Key Island where they provided defensive security for Sigurd's and Ivak's families. Both men were here now, but Sigurd would return to the island shortly.

Yes, nine hundred was a large number of bodies, but the fields surrounding the Transylvania castle covered several acres, and some of the vangels had arrived only this morning. Despite the appearance of disarray, or one huge crowd, there were prearranged military groupings, based on a vangel interpretation of army rankings. Today, Vikar, Ivak, Trond, Mordr, Harek, Cnut, Jogeir, Sigurd, and Karl would act as generals. Under them would be captains, and lieutenants/soldiers. Regina and Zeb would be captains serving under Jogeir.

It was a huge clearing, mostly grass, on the flat top of the mountain, not unlike the motte and bailey castles of old. The man who'd built this castle, an eccentric lumber baron, must have spent a mint just leveling this area.

The vangels, regardless of rank, wore long black cloaks over their apparel, whether it be denims or tight braies. Easier to hide weapons that way. And they were all heavily armed. And all of them had elongated fangs, a reflex preparatory to battle. Some of them had braided their hair, or beards, in the old Viking style. Some had even put temporary tattoos on their faces and arms. At least, she thought they were temporary. Mike would have a fit over body embellishments like that, considering it another sign of Viking vanity.

She could only imagine what they must look like from above. A huge flock of ravens, about to take wing. Although there was not a wing in sight.

And Regina fit in perfectly. She had chucked her demure gown, after Zeb's teasing, and wore a black turtleneck shirt tucked into black jeans which were tucked into black ankle boots. Her wild red hair, the bane of her appearance, in her opinion, was twisted into a tight braid and wrapped around her head in a coronet. Being adept with knives, she had an assortment sheathed in specially sewn inner pockets, along with her compact M11 Sig Sauer, and a few throwing stars. She'd never been very good with swords.

Zeb, of course, had no hair to braid, and he was concerned about reflections on his bald pate. So he camouflaged it with dirt and fireplace soot. He, too, wore the long vangel cloak over black attire, in his case black T-shirt, black jeans, and black athletic shoes. He carried a sword as well as a foldable AK-47. Extra mags holding up to thirty bullets each were stored in specially designed pouches of the chest rig he wore. In other words, he looked hot, as in sexy as hell. Like a bald Magic Mike would look in vangel attire.

Even though they didn't touch, she was very aware of his proximity. Ever since the kiss, she'd avoided getting too close to the rogue. Zeb had told her that they were already married in his old religion. *My husband,* she thought, testing the words on her brain. They weren't as repulsive as she would have expected.

But she couldn't think about any of that now.

Vikar, clipboard in hand, stood on the wide front steps of the castle with his brothers. As he called out the various mission assignments, groups of vangels along with one of the brothers or other high-level vangel commanders were expected to either disappear into the air via teletransport, or go off to the long driveway or the parking garage to get their vehicles.

There was no joking around or hum of conversation, as there normally was before an operation. This was stone-cold grave business, literally.

"Karl, as mentioned before, will stay at the castle. He will keep a hundred vangels with him here. It's not the building so much that needs protection, but the precious occupants." He referred to his family, as well as Karl's, Cnut's, and Mordr's.

"Got it," Karl agreed and led his contingent in

a file around Vikar, up the steps, and through the open double doors into the castle.

"The rest of you, leave as your assignments are announced. You already have instructions. If you complete your mission, contact me on your secure phones, and I'll direct you to where your help is most needed.

"Our first stage is intended to destroy all of Jasper's strongholds and the Lucipire council commanders who hold them, Horror Castle being the last and final battle of phase one. This will not happen in one day. In fact, it may take as much as a week. Take as long as necessary."

All this, Vikar had explained in group meetings the last two days. But it bore repeating.

"We will all gather at Horror after completing our initial assignments. After Horror is destroyed and all its occupants, we will gather back here to develop a new plan for phase two. Hitting those countries not yet covered by the first phase where Lucipires may still be hiding. Spain. Nigeria. Iceland. Wherever. Presumably, by then, all the leaders will be gone, but there will be strays. And like roaches, leave one and they will multiply again.

"Phase three will involve another sweep of every country in the world for every single demon vampire.

"This is war! Our ultimate goal is: 'NO MORE LUCIPIRES!'"

They all cheered and raised their fists or swords in the air, shouting, "NO MORE LUCIPIRES!"

Vikar bowed his head then, and eight hundred vangels followed suit as Vikar prayed, "Dear

Lord, be with us today and always as we fight in Your army to destroy evil. Amen!"

The crowd repeated, "Amen!"

Vikar cleared his throat and announced, "Trond, Nicole, and Camille, you will go with the SEALs to Nigeria or whatever terrorist hot spot they are hitting this week. Take a hundred vangels with you, but keep them hidden. Remember, while the SEALs engage the terrorists, you are after Lucipires. This is not a mission for saving sinners."

Camille gave her husband, Harek, a quick kiss, and the three headed for the first vehicle in the driveway. Since Camille and Nicole were not vangels, it had been decided that they would all fly back to California, rather than piggyback on Trond's teletransporting. They would catch a plane out of Philadelphia International Airport. The hundred vangels working with them disappeared and were presumably back in Coronado already, scattered in various hiding places until called to action.

"Sigurd, go to your island, and be safe. Call for us if you need help. Remember, a good defense is as good as an offense." Sigurd had been chagrined not to be involved in any of the assault campaigns. "Any vangels who get injured will be sent to your hospital for care."

Sigurd nodded, and he was gone, too.

"Mordr, find Tess, the pirate recently added to Jasper's council. She may have established headquarters in your part of the country." Mordr had a home in Las Vegas where his wife was a psychologist. "Wipe out the entire nest. Your family will stay here at the castle.

"And Svein, you and your hundred vangels will begin a sweep upward from the southern United States, Florida, Louisiana, and so on until you meet up with Mordr. Then the two of you and your vangels will head to Horror for the final battle."

Mordr and Svein nodded, and disappeared along with their vangels. Mordr had already said his good-byes to his wife and children while inside the castle.

Likewise, Ivak, who was being sent to Syria, a hotbed of ISIS terrorism, and therefore a haven for Lucipires, as well.

"Harek, you are familiar with Siberia. Go to Desolation and wipe out Heinrich, that Nazi piece of shit, and his contingent. Take Armod with you. He can moonwalk on the tundra."

Everyone laughed, including Armod.

Harek nodded at his assignment, although it was well known the time he'd spent in that frigid part of the world had been a punishment, not to his liking at all. He would complete his task quickly and get out of there as soon as possible. He also took a hundred vangels with him, including Armod.

By now the lawns were half depleted of vangels.

"Cnut, take a hundred vangels with you to Italy. Rout Hector from the catacombs under the Vatican, then sweep out to other parts of Europe, except for Greece. France, in particular, reeks of Lucipires lately. And Germany, too. We will leave South America and Australia for another time, as well as more thorough screenings of Asia, Africa, and Antarctica. I wouldn't be surprised if the stray Lucies flee to South America or Australia."

Cnut kissed his wife and was gone, along with another hundred vangels. Which left only three hundred or so vangels, along with Vikar, Jogeir, Zeb, and Regina.

"I will take a hundred vangels with me to the Arab lands, which seem to have the most concentration of terrorists these days. I may meet up with Trond and the SEALs there, or any others of you who find yourselves with operations completed. Hopefully, I will get a chance to fight Ganbold the Mongol there in his own territory.

"But first, Jogeir, I would have you take Zeb and Regina with you to Greece, where Yakov has taken over Zeb's old headquarters in the volcanic ruins."

Regina had already been aware of which assignment she would get, and that Zeb would serve at her side, also that Jogeir would be keeping an eye on them both. It did not matter. Much. At least, she was being permitted to fight, not restricted to the castle.

"A hundred vangels should suffice for your task, Jogeir. You can then either join me in Afghanistan, or go on to the Norselands, and Horror. We can decide that as we go."

Jogeir just nodded, solemnly, as did Regina and Zeb. She knew that Zeb was just as glad to be given a job in this war as she was.

Vikar walked up the castle steps then and embraced his wife, Alex, who was standing in the doorway.

And then he, too, was gone, along with a hundred more vangels.

"Are you ready?" Jogeir asked Regina and Zeb. "We are."

Zeb took her hand, and Jogeir took Zeb's other hand, just in case he wasn't strong enough yet to teletransport. Turned out he was.

In the midst of whirling fogs and fast-moving clouds, and the feeling of g-force currents hitting the abdomen, they arrived in a remote area of Greece. At least she thought it was Greece, except that the region looked like a dystopian landscape after an atomic bomb.

It was the volcanic ruins where Zeb had until recently—for a period of many, many years, centuries, even—maintained a headquarters. Its name was Gloom. And what an appropriate name that was! Everywhere she looked there were black, porous rocks and pumice stones. Only a few bushes grew on the slopes of the funnel-shaped hill. It had been three centuries since the volcano had erupted but there was a dusting of ash on the ground and every surface. They would come away from this battle covered in the stuff.

Thus far, there was no sign of human or un-human habitation. According to Zeb, the nearest village was ten miles away. No one wanted to rebuild on this site for fear of another eruption, and superstitions said it was haunted. By demons, of all things. There had to be an irony in Jasper wanting a stronghold of demon vampires in a spot already known for demons.

She glanced over at Zeb and saw him staring sadly at his surroundings. Regina's heart tugged with sympathy. What a lonely, depressing life he must have led when residing here!

As if he'd read her thoughts, Zeb stepped up next to Regina and said, "Honey, we're home."

"Very funny!" she replied.

Jogeir raised a hand to silently signal that the vangel troops should scatter out like a net before closing in on the various openings that Zeb had outlined for them. They'd already studied maps of the site and had tactics planned out.

That's when the long-dormant volcano began to erupt, spewing out, not lava, but Lucipires, like ants from an ant hill. Really big ants! And leading them was the powerful haakai, Yakov. Zeb had given a detailed description of how the Lucipire would look in both demonoid and humanoid forms. If he had been in humanoid form, which he was not, he would have worn a long tunic-style coat and beaver hat, or else shaved head with small pigtail in back. Prominent high Slavic cheekbones. Most of all, and visible in both forms, like now, was the traditional Cossack weapon, a curved, long-bladed sabre, known as a shashka.

"Go with God!" Jogeir hollered. Then, raising his broadsword high, he added, "To war!"

War stinks . . .

Zeb stabbed his sword repeatedly into one Lucipire after another, making sure to get them through the heart with the specially treated blade. That would ensure they could not return as demon vampires, but were sentenced instead to eternity in Hell.

When a Lucipire was destroyed, it melted away into a puddle of slime. When a vangel, or human, was killed by a Lucipire, its body dissolved on the spot with no slime and was immediately transported to Horror, or the nearest Lucipire stronghold. Already the ground near him was covered in slime, which would mix with the ash to form a godawful mess. There was no help for that.

The fangs were of no use today. Normally, a vangel would give a sinner that had been fanged by a Lucipire a chance to repent, and if they agreed, the vangel would fang the sinner, offering another chance to live a good life. Surprisingly, most of them refused. But there was no time to make those offers today. Besides, a fang redemption probably wouldn't work on a Lucipire.

Zeb wondered idly if he had the vangel power to redeem a sinner. He would have to try, when he got a chance.

Sadly, scanning the battlefield, Zeb saw several vangels go down, then disappear, leaving their clothing and weapons behind. Hopefully, when the vangels led by Vikar got to Horror, they would be able to release the injured vangels who'd been taken captive. Also hopefully, the Lucipires would be too engaged in battles to have time for torture in an attempt to turn them into Lucipires.

The injured vangels would be taken to Grand Key Island for hospital care. If they'd died while still vangels, they would already be in Tranquility until the Final Judgment Day.

Maybe Zeb should try to get injured. Tranquility didn't sound too bad. No, that wouldn't work. Michael would never allow it.

One advantage the vangels had in this current battle was that the Lucipires were so huge they made big targets. At the same time, their size was a disadvantage for the vangels because the Lucipire beasts were extra strong and did not tire easily.

Zeb, like many of the vangels, had dropped his cloak, for ease of movement. They would gather them all later.

Already having downed a dozen Lucipires with his sword, Zeb decided it was time to get out the big guns. Unfolding the AK-47 strapped to his body, he prepared to mow down a new batch of the creatures storming toward him. They'd been coming in waves with a short respite in between. At least a hundred of them so far.

He couldn't lose focus, but still he glanced quickly toward Regina who was lobbing a vast assortment of knives to pierce the Lucipires' hearts. She was an excellent marksman with the blades. If she ran out of knives, many of which hung in loops sewn onto her black denims, she had the powerful M11 handgun in a shoulder holster. She looked like some kind of Norse goddess as she stood her ground.

He felt an odd pride in her appearance and abilities.

He spotted Jogeir moving toward Yakov who stood alone on a small rise of rocks. Jogeir and Yakov were soon engaged in a fierce swordfight, Jogeir with an ancient broadsword, and Yakov with an equally ancient sabre. Jogeir was an accomplished warrior, but still Zeb made his way toward him, to offer his help. Yakov's power couldn't be underestimated. Besides that, the stone-covered ground could cause even the most nimble man to falter, giving the advantage to his opponent.

A brief glance from Jogeir was the only acknowledgement that he knew Zeb was at his back. Because the broadsword was so heavy, it couldn't be used in a thrust and parry mode, like a long sword. Rather a wide arc. Which made the combat rather cumbersome. No wonder Vikings had such powerful shoulder and upper arm muscles. The sabre, too, was designed for cutting blows, not thrusting.

Just then, Yakov noticed Zeb and roared, "Ah, the traitor arrives." With a huge clawed paw, Yakov knocked Jogeir to the side and Jogeir dropped down on one knee.

Even so, Jogeir was able to swing his broadsword upward, two-handed, across Yakov's beastly chest. Yakov glanced down at himself with surprise at the blood already seeping through his scaly skin. He wasn't done for yet and could still do some damage if left to die slowly. Plus, his heart probably hadn't been pierced.

Zeb was no fool, and all was fair in love and war, as they said, so he felt no need to use blade against blade. Instead, he raised his AK-47 and rat-a-tat-tat, Yakov was shot through the heart. At the same time, one of Regina's knives flew through the air, over his shoulder, hitting Yakov in the same spot. Yakov clutched his chest and fell backward to the ground with a crash, crushing some of the coarse pumice rocks with his weight.

At first, the beast just lay on its back, looking up at Zeb with hatred in his red eyes. Then he snarled, "I will meet you in Hell, Hebrew."

"I sincerely hope not," Zeb said.

"And you, bitch," Yakov choked out, looking at Regina, "Jasper has a special torture planned just for you."

Over my double-dead body, Zeb thought.

Yakov was soon gone, his gnarly body melting like butter on a hot stove. Yakov's slime made a particularly putrid stink.

"That's a real coup, Jogeir. Congratulations," Zeb said.

"You and Regina helped, too," Jogeir replied. "We all did."

"You're the leader of this fight," Zeb pointed out. "Killing Yakov is huge, Jogeir, and a good number of his minions, as well. Mission accomplished."

"Not totally. We're to wipe out every single Lucipire," Jogeir reminded them. "I don't think we've got them all yet . . ."

Zeb leaned over and gave Regina a quick fly-by kiss on the cheek before she could swat him away. "Congrats, wifey."

"Are you going to kiss Jogeir, too?" she sniped.

"Only if he grows a pair of breasts and smells like cinnamon."

They did a three-way high five then, before turning to engage in the tail end of fighting. There weren't many of the enemy left. Having lost their leader, many of the Lucipires were scattering, running off to the hills, or teletransporting to another of Jasper's outposts. Where they would, unknowingly, be met by another vangel team.

An hour later, Zeb and Regina were inside the Gloom cave, which had been renovated and enlarged by Zeb over the years. Yakov hadn't made any changes during his short time here. Jogeir was outside assessing damages, and making a tally of Lucipires killed by counting the number of slime puddles. A crude method of accounting, but the alternative was having each of the vangel survivors tell how many individual demon vampires they had got through the heart. Jogeir had directed them to make sure the cave was a good enough stronghold for the vangels until they decided what to do next. Zeb had assured Jogeir that it was secure, but they were double checking.

"Wow," Regina said when she first entered the cave. The wide, medieval-looking door was hidden from view to outsiders by a wide overhang of porous rock requiring a visitor to stoop before even seeing the entry.

He led her down a long corridor which was stark and dreary even with overhead lighting and sconces along the walls. He'd chiseled much of this by hand himself. But then they came to the large living room, which was warm and inviting, if he did say so himself, with cushiony, low couches, recliners, coffee tables, and end tables with lamps giving a subdued, soft lighting. Persian rugs in jewel tones covered the bare stone floor. Paintings and framed prints adorned the stone walls. There was a sixty-inch flat-screen TV, and a gas fireplace.

"Wow!" Regina said again. "How did you do all this, especially without garnering any attention?"

"Worked mostly at night. And, hey, I had a lot of years to complete the project. At first, it was only a cave-like opening. That was back in the 1860s, same time as the American Civil War was going on. Jasper had a heyday with some of the corrupt officers, not to mention vicious slave owners. Anyhow, I had no backhoes or drills or other modern equipment. Just sweat and blood. Later, I made sure the Lucipires on my team had some particular skill . . . electrical, plumbing, engineering."

She looked at him as if impressed.

And he had to admit to being pleased with her appreciation of his efforts. He showed her the modern kitchen then, the two spacious bedrooms, and a bathroom that rivaled many spas. There was also a pantry that had a ton of nonperishable food, like the most sophisticated bunker. "The kitchen alone took me a century to complete, especially since the appliances date themselves almost as soon as they're put in. Can anyone say microwave, or K-Cup coffeemaker or ice maker?" He smiled at her.

And she smiled back. "I wouldn't have the patience. Obviously. As indicated by my recent actions, which some . . . namely Vikar and Michael . . . would call impulsive. Jumping in to rescue you because I couldn't bear to wait for others, more qualified, to get off their butts and act . . . yeah, I rubbed some noses the wrong way for my recklessness."

"And thank God for that!"

There was also a huge cave-like section, which he showed her, containing dorm-like bedrooms, lounges, a kitchen, and three communal bathrooms to handle up to twenty-five Lucipires . . . and now vangels. The digs back here were modest, but comfortable. Besides that, a room in the far back held a massive generator for electricity because a drain on municipal lines would be noticed. In addition, there was a cover and a complicated mechanism leading to a well for water. "It took me ten years to find a natural underground spring and run water lines. Try doing that at night so no one will notice."

"I still can't believe you did all this, on top of your island hideaway," Regina said.

"Like I said, I've been around a very long time . . . almost two thousand years. Lots of time between missions. And occasionally, like I said, when I had enough space carved out, I had Lucipires to help me."

Jogeir came in then with several vangels who needed to take a shower to remove some Lucipire mung. Jogeir was given the tour, too, and was equally impressed.

For some reason, Zeb didn't bask as much in Jogeir's compliments as he had with Regina's. "Love the TV. Bet a Phillies game on that screen would be awesome."

Regina muttered something like, "Men!"

"What did you say?" Jogeir asked.

"I said, 'Men!' They see a marvel of architectural ingenuity, carving a home out of rock, and all they can comment on is the TV."

Zeb grinned at her assessment. *Me? An architectural genius? I'm going to remind her of that the next time she snarks at me.*

"Well, it is big," Jogeir said defensively. Then, "I wonder if Mike will allow you to keep this cave. Possibly as another vangel outpost."

"I didn't think of that," Zeb said.

The question in all their minds, though, was: Would there continue to be vangels when this war was over?

Then Jogeir gave them a post-op report. "Thirty Lucies destroyed and off to Hell, ten Lucies killed but no heart piercing; so, they're back at Horror by now and will come back as Lucies once again. We lost five vangels. I pray to God we will be able to rescue them when we hit the target there. Hopefully, the Lucies will be too busy out on field missions to torture them right away."

Regina cringed at the prospect, having witnessed firsthand Jasper's torture room. "Speaking of which, will we go to Afghanistan or directly to Horror?"

"Um, that's the thing," Jogeir stammered. "You two and fifty vangels are going to stay here."

"What?" Zeb and Regina said at the same time.

"The possibility was discussed back at the castle, but a definite decision was handed down when I relayed to Vikar your remark, Zeb. You know what you told me, about how the Lucies would return here after an initial retreat?" The vangel leaders were able to communicate with each other via specially designed wireless devices, similar to cell phones but much more secure and with wider ranges. "We have to get every single one of them. I'm sending my half of the vangels on to Fallujah right away, but I'll stay until tonight, just to make sure everything is secure."

In fact, when Zeb scanned the area, he realized that half the vangels were already gone. They must have already teletransported out. Quick work, that. But then, these were important, and dangerous, times for vangels. Timing and manpower were everything.

Jogeir gave Zeb and Regina pointed looks. "Like I said, you two will remain, equally in charge."

"Pfff! Cleanup work! You're doing this because I'm a woman," Regina snarled. She made as if to attack Jogeir, but Zeb held her back by tugging on her braid which had come loose during the fighting. She didn't struggle against his restraint, so he assumed she'd meant no harm, just an aggressive motion to show she was as much top dog as any man.

"Not at all." Jogeir put up both hands in surrender. Then he crisscrossed his hands over his groin to ward off one of Regina's famous cock curses. He was probably teasing. No one really believed that nonsense. Did they?

"It's important work, Regina, for a man, as well as a woman," Jogeir continued. "And I made the final call, if you want to blame someone." Zeb noticed that Jogeir still had one hand casually over the crotch of his pants.

Zeb was just glad to be given any job at all as a vangel. Or almost-vangel. Or whatever he was.

"Keep in mind, we could just destroy this cave headquarters, thus taking away a Lucie nest, but, as we discussed earlier, this could be a valuable vangel outpost. Plus, we don't want to alert all of Greece that we're here with an explosion, even one that implodes. Even if they think this old volcano is erupting, it would be attention we don't want."

"Got it," Regina said.

Zeb nodded his agreement.

"One more thing," Jogeir said, hesitating.

Uh-oh!

"I'm going to take a few vangels to recon for a few miles' radius and make sure the villagers in that town about ten miles from here aren't alerted to our presence. You two are going to have to clean up that mess of slime and abandoned clothing and weapons out there. Sorry to leave you with such a dirty job, but we can't risk some humans seeing it. Even a plane passing over might notice the scene and alert authorities."

"See!" Regina snapped. "Women's work. You give the cleaning job to a woman."

"Shut up, Regina," Zeb said.

That got her attention, and that of Jogeir, who grinned.

"It's not just a woman he assigned this task. It's me and fifty vangels out there, as well." Zeb patted her shoulder to show he understood her chagrin. "Besides, there are two other female vangels in this contingent."

She shrugged his hand away. "Still . . ."

The witch just couldn't let go. Persistent, she was, and stubborn.

Then she told Jogeir, "Sorry if I overreacted." But to Zeb, she said, "Jerk!"

Zeb grinned now, too.

"How long do we stay here?" Regina asked Jogeir in a calmer voice.

"I would think two days, three max, would be more than enough," Jogeir answered. Then he turned to Zeb. "What do you think?"

"Sounds about right. They'll be back, for certain. It's the pattern most Lucipires follow in battle. Retreat and Return."

"Like the Navy SEALs expressions 'Spray and Pray,' or 'Escape and Evade,' or that well-known 'Shock and Awe.'"

"Exactly," Zeb concurred, adding, "In addition to wanting to continue the battle, they won't abandon a long-held nest, and this is a valuable location to them. It probably won't be until tomorrow, though. They'll need time to regroup and add other Lucies to their troop. Without a leader, there will be initial chaos."

Jogeir nodded his understanding, and Regina, now that she was over her initial pique, inserted, "We'll be on the alert today, however, just in case." Clearly, Regina was asserting her authority.

That was all right with Zeb.

Jogeir gathered his team, and they were soon gone on the scouting mission.

"Okay, Regina, we have some decisions to make. Cook or clean?"

"What?"

"Are you going to make some kind of meal for all of us, or are you going to lead the project to clean up the slop outside?"

She frowned at him. "I pick slop."

Chapter 14

Home, Sweet, Home . . .

Slime, slime, slime.

Phew, phew, phew!

She had only herself to blame. She knew that, but still she persisted in muttering rude insults regarding Zeb, and zapping curses on various parts of his anatomy.

Not that he could hear her or that her curses worked. She was in the shower with its rain forest showerhead, washing away foul-smelling slime and Lucie cooties, with tepid water since a large number of vangels, those most covered with the goop, had already depleted the hot water. In the end, they'd given up on digging holes and shoveling the slime in. Instead, they shoveled ashes, which were in plentiful supply thanks to the volcano, over the slime. It would have to do.

Regina expected to come away smelling fresh as . . . well, rain, after her shower, half hoping that soap would be the answer to Zeb's compelling scent. But, no, there was just Irish Spring body wash. If it was in all the bathrooms, the whole company would be smelling like a pine forest, she thought, smiling to herself. Regardless, it was good to be clean.

The washing machine was also running non-stop for the worst of the vangels' apparel. Zeb had given them all clothing from his own supply to use in the meantime. After her shower, she donned sweatpants, a sweatshirt, and her combat boots. It wouldn't do to walk barefoot on these stone floors.

Despite their seemingly relaxed attitudes, all the vangels kept their weapons ready at all times. Regina's cloak with all the knives she'd retrieved from the battlefield lay across a hamper. Later, she would clean and sharpen all her blades.

The delicious smell of tomato sauce, which Zeb was making in a huge pot, wafted through all the nooks and crannies of the "cave," heavy on the garlic and basil.

"I thought vampires were supposed to be repelled by garlic," she had commented when she'd seen him chopping numerous garlic cloves.

"I'm not that kind of vampire," he had replied, waggling his eyebrows at her. Which caused her to notice, for about the hundredth time, his incredibly long eyelashes.

It was odd to be doing these mundane tasks in the midst of a war, but Regina and Zeb had set up a schedule whereby twenty-five vangels would be on guard duty, outside, all around the volcano setting, while the other twenty-five inside, rested. There would be a rotation every four hours to make sure the vangels were alert. Jogeir was out there now, having not yet left for Afghanistan.

Zeb intended to take the ten-to-two shift; she would be two-to-six a.m. By six, they were all to be on alert for returning vangels.

It was only five p.m. now, and Regina heard her stomach rumble with hunger. She made her way to the kitchen where Zeb, with a chef's apron over his jeans and T-shirt, was ladling out sauce from a big pot onto heavy paper plates of fettucine. A long tray of warm garlic bread sat on the counter.

There were about fifteen vangels sitting around the living room, eating, or reclining on couches, or even the floor. The rest of the twenty-five were back in the other lounge or taking a quick nap. Trond had told her one time that SEALs had a knack for sleeping whenever they could grab a few minutes while on a live op, even standing up. She felt like she could do that herself.

Unable to stifle a wide yawn, she sat down on a stool by the island to watch Zeb work. He turned to look at her, having doled out what seemed to be the last plate to be filled, for now. "Hungry?" he asked.

"Famished," she said, and watched as he plated pasta and sauce and topped it with a slice of bread. He also gave her a small bottled water, which was marvelously cool. "Umm, this is really good," she said taking the first bite. "What is it?"

"Pasta Puttanesca, which means 'in the style of a prostitute.' It was a dish that was quick and easy for the ladies of the night to make between clients." Zeb sat down beside her on another stool and took a swig of his own bottled water. He had taken a shower as well, and smelled not of Irish Spring, but of fresh rain.

"You're making that up."

"No, it's the truth," he said. "There's no meat in it. So, it wouldn't spoil while . . . you know?" More eyebrow waggling.

She continued to eat. Maybe it was just that she was so hungry, but the mixture of tomatoes, garlic, basil, black olives, capers, cheese, and, yes, anchovies, which she usually hated, was salty and spicy and better than anything she'd ever eaten. She moaned with appreciation at every bite.

"Please don't do that," he urged.

"What?"

"Moan."

"Why?"

"Because it's causing me problems."

"Like what?" He wasn't making sense.

He hesitated, and she could swear he blushed. "It appears as if I'm getting my mojo back."

It took her a second to realize what he meant. Then she blushed, too. "It's probably just adrenaline rush from the battle. I've heard lots of men claim the need for sex after fighting."

"Uh-huh," he said, clearly not buying it.

"Really, it's a normal reaction. I don't take it personally. Probably any woman would garner the same reaction."

"I didn't feel the same way when Inga and Dagmar were here a little while ago." Those were the other female vangels on this mission. They were Norse sisters who'd joined the vangels about a hundred years ago.

"Maybe because they're a mite older than you," she said, trying to be kind when what she thought was, *and homelier than bulldogs.*

Zeb leaned closer to her and dabbed at the side of her mouth with a paper napkin. Then he didn't draw away, but leaned even closer so that she felt his breath when he murmured, "Do you have an answer for everything?"

At the moment, she couldn't think of a thing to say, so wrapped was she in the aura that seemed to surround them. As for him getting his mojo back, she was feeling a tug in that region, as well. Her lady parts were coming to attention in a way they hadn't for centuries, if ever. Whoo-boy!

A change of subject was needed, Regina decided. "Tell me about your life, what you did before . . ."

She could tell that he knew what she meant without her finishing the sentence. She half expected him to evade the question or tell her it was none of her business. Instead, he was forthcoming.

"I died in the year AD 76. A suicide. Unfortunately, a Lucipire was nearby . . . in fact, a young Jasper, it was . . . young in demon vampire years, I mean. I probably would have gone to Hell anyway, but he harvested me for his own group."

"I had no idea. No wonder Jasper is so outraged by your rejection."

Zeb nodded. "He often said I was like a son to him. Creepy, huh?"

"Did you ever feel any affection for him? Or any bond?"

"Never. In the beginning, I was too stunned by everything that had happened to my family, and my role in it, to care where I was. And, believe me, it was primitive living in the early days. No castles or luxury accommodations. We came to favor caverns around the world. They were roomy and hidden. Most humans feared entering them. But the bats! I shudder even today when I see one of the flying creatures."

She had to smile at that. "A demon afraid of a little harmless bat?"

"We all have our phobias." He shrugged. "What's yours?"

"Snakes. I hate snakes." She shivered with distaste.

He smiled then. "I rather like them. They eat bugs in my garden."

She wasn't to be diverted. "Tell me more. Why did you commit suicide, if you don't mind my asking?"

He got up to help two newly showered vangels to food and bottled waters. They spoke briefly about the mission and the game on TV. After they went over to the living room to sit down with their food, he poured two cups of coffee, bringing them back to the island. He'd remembered that she took hers black.

"I had a good life, a wonderful life, but I couldn't see that for the greed that blinded me. I adored my wife, Sarah, and two children, twins, Rachel and Mikah. I had a small vineyard passed down in my family and a modest house. We were not wealthy by any means. In fact that was the crux of the problem. I should have been happy with what I had, but I coveted my neighbor's land with its water access which would have made such a good addition to mine."

"The grass is always greener," she injected.

He nodded. "I wanted that land with a passion that should have been spent on my wife and children. I took every job I could find, but it was never enough. And I had little time for my family. Obsessed, I was."

"It's not uncommon," she told him. "The downfall of many men."

"Yeah, well, I didn't see that at the time. I got the idea to join the Roman Army, which was offering a great number of coins to those who could serve in higher-ranking positions. I had some experience with Hebrew fighting in the region."

"Really? I thought the Romans were the enemies of the Jews then."

"They were. But I did not intend to join the Roman armies fighting Hebrews or Christians. There were other Roman soldiers building a wall in the Celtic land across the waters. Which is Britain today."

"I've seen remnants of that wall," she was excited to tell him. "Just think, you helped build that. Amazing!"

He shrugged, as if it was no big deal. "My family tried to dissuade me from what they termed my 'madness.' Especially my brother-in-law Benjamin, who tried to tell me of the atrocities being committed by the Romans, not nearby but in distant cities and villages. I discounted Benjamin's ravings because he was known to be a hothead rebel, always in trouble."

"And so you went." It was not a question.

"I did. For two years. And I returned to my little vineyard, my pocket full of bloody lucre, full of pride in myself. Now I could buy the additional land. Now I could devote more time to my family. Everyone would be so happy." His voice choked on those last words, and he bowed his head.

She put a hand on his arm. "You don't have to go on."

He raised his head and his grief was hard to look at. Soul deep. In his sad eyes and in the slight furrows between his brows and beside his mouth. He cleared his throat and went on. "My vineyard and home were burned to the ground, as were all the neighboring properties. There was no one around. I went mad for a while, tearing at my hair . . ." He put a hand to his bristly head for emphasis. "Pounding the earth . . ." He pounded the island's granite top with a fist and caused a roomful of vangels to look his way, then return to watching the ball game. "Screaming to the heavens."

He paused, then continued, "Finally, an elderly man came out of hiding and told me what had happened. Benjamin and his band of rebels had been harassing the soldiers in the distant city. Incensed, the soldiers came into that region, which had seemed safe for so many years, searching for the rebels. They found them, and took out their anger on everyone else for miles around."

"They were all killed? Your family?"

He shook his head. "That would have been kinder, but, no, they escaped to Masada where they eventually died of starvation, then were set afire. The Romans besieged them in that setting, you see."

"I remember hearing something about Masada one time. I think there was a movie."

"Yes, but none of the books portrayed the real happening. I got there a little too late. The fire was still burning, and I actually saw the bodies of my wife and children. They were so thin, like Holocaust victims."

Tears rolled down his face, which he swiped away with the back of his hand. "I went on a rampage then, killing every Roman I could find, even their women and children. And then I killed myself."

She was holding both of his hands in hers. "It wasn't your fault."

"Yes, it was. I as good as set the fires myself. By taking a place in the Roman Army in Britain, I relieved other soldiers to war against my people in Judea."

A moment of poignant silence ensued. Regina wasn't sure what to say.

"So, that is my story," he said.

"Do you know, your eyes are blue now?" she remarked.

"Really? Like all the vangels?"

She nodded.

"Little by little, I am becoming one of you, I think. But did my eye color just change now?"

"I think so. When I sat down, I was admiring your eyelashes again—"

"These fool eyelashes!" he said with a grin.

"—and I know your eyes were brown then."

"Hmmm." He probably thought she was trying to make him feel better.

"Maybe it's a sign that you're forgiven," she proffered.

"I'll never be forgiven," he declared. "Never! I'll never forgive myself."

"That's not for you to say."

"Quite the religious zealot, are you?" He chucked her under the chin playfully, an attempt to veer away from his painful revelations, she was sure.

He got up to help some vangels refill the coffeemaker and then went off somewhere, probably the bathroom to check his eyes in the mirror. Regina didn't have the energy to get up herself. She yawned and thought about going into one of the bedrooms to lie down for a while, but it was only six p.m., and she doubted she'd be able to sleep.

Many of the vangels were not having that problem. Some had already gone to their beds, while others slept on couches or the floor as the TV hummed on. They were wise to rest when they could. Fighting took a lot out of a man, or woman, physically *and* emotionally.

Zeb came back and poured himself another cup of coffee. She put a hand over her cup to indicate she wanted no more. He sat down again and said, "Yep. They're blue." He seemed pleased at that. "And I think my hair is coming in blond."

"No, it's not." His hair was brown, normally. "And you don't have to be blond to be a vangel, anyhow. There are brown-haired and black-haired Vikings and redheads, too, for that matter." She put a hand to her own mop which was still damp from her shower, but was probably frizzing up already. She would braid it when she got a chance.

"Your turn now, Regina."

"For what?"

"Tell me your story."

She waved a hand airily. "My life was not nearly as interesting."

"Hah! Interesting is not how I would describe mine." He jabbed her shoulder with a forefinger and prodded, "C'mon. Spill. How does one get to be a witch?"

"You don't *get* to be a witch, you're born that way. Usually. You either have the gift, or don't."

She could see his skepticism at the word "gift." She couldn't take offense. Most people felt that way.

"My mother was a witch, and my grandmother before her. But, despite our serving the people, we lived apart from them. In a hut somewhere in the woods. Also, despite the villagers and even upper classes coming to us for help, medicinal or otherwise, they feared us. They burned my mother's hut down, with her in it, for some infraction, real or otherwise, doesn't matter. I just managed to get away."

"Oh, Regina."

"Don't pity me," she said, pride rearing its head. She hated people pitying her. "I built up my own business, and I managed to defend myself better than my mother had."

"What business?"

"There are good witches as well as bad, you know?"

"Were you a good witch?"

She shrugged. "In the beginning, I was. I dealt in healing herbs, spells to help people overcome some problem, even acting as midwife on occasion. But there was no money in that, I realized over time. And as I grew up and realized how the people used me, I also saw how separate I was from them. I wouldn't have admitted it at the time, but I was desperately lonely. So, I set a goal for myself. I would amass a vast amount of coins, enough to buy a home for myself in the Saxon lands, where I was not known. Nothing fancy. A farmstead where I could raise some sheep. But to accumulate that kind of wealth, I needed to expand my business. That's when I became a black witch, dealing in potions that killed, curses that caused harm, draughts to abort babies, that kind of stuff. My last black act involved giving a young jarl a potion to kill his conniving relatives, but instead he killed the whole party, women and children included."

"And that's when Michael rescued you?"

"Well, rescue isn't quite how I'd describe it. But, yes, he gave me a second chance."

"You're an attractive woman, Regina. Wasn't it dangerous living out in the woods, alone? Didn't men bother you?"

"They did, in the beginning. The first time I was raped, I couldn't fight back. I had no skills or weapons. I hadn't perfected my talents yet. The second time I was raped, I killed the bastard. After that, I became proficient with knives, and no one bothered me. In that way."

"Ah, Regina! How old were you?"

"The first time? Fourteen. And don't you dare spout some pity pap at me. It happened. I'm over it."

He smiled, and she realized she was being overly vehement.

"And you're still fighting against the restrictions of your life. Then, it was the restrictions placed on a witch. Today, the restrictions on a female vangel."

She was going to argue, but he was right. "I think I'll go get my clothes out of the dryer and lie down for a while. Things seem to be quiet outside. Will you call me if . . . when . . . the Lucies return?"

"I will," he said, then added, "It was good talking to you, Regina."

She agreed and as she walked away, she mused to herself, *Maybe it isn't so bad being married.*

A voice in her head said, *See! I told you so!*

Chapter 15

Cuddling is just another form of foreplay ...

All was quiet as Zeb worked with a couple of vangels to clean up the kitchen and living area. He had no idea what would happen to this space after tomorrow, or whenever they departed. If it would be used by the demon vampires or the vangels, or not at all. Just in case the vangels decided to keep it, he didn't want to leave it a dump.

He supposed he'd become a neat freak. Like a soldier who still kept his room excessively ship-shape, who folded his socks and hung his shirts a certain way years after leaving the service. In his case, it came from living alone for so long, often in tight spaces. By necessity, he told himself. If he'd become, or was about to become, a vangel, would he be able to abide living with others who might not be so fastidious?

Silly, it was, to dwell on such a minor point.

Jogeir came in, having just returned from his scouting foray, and drank a cup of coffee, standing. This was Jogeir's first time heading a large mission, and he took it seriously. As he should.

"I sent patrols out five miles in six different directions and nothing, so far," Jogeir reported. "No alert in that village, either."

"I scouted myself, too, after you left, and nothing," Zeb told him. "But that doesn't mean they won't be back. I've talked with Vikar, and there are Lucipires in large numbers causing trouble all over the world, at the same time. Jasper has to be tearing his hair out, trying to set priorities."

"And where would this place . . . um, Gloom . . . be in terms of priorities?" Jogeir had trouble referring to this cave-like home, no matter how comfortable, by the distasteful name of Gloom.

"High. It's a strategic location for them. They might not be here tomorrow morning, or even the next day, but they'll be back." Zeb had told Jogeir all this before, of course. It needed repeating.

"Hmmm."

"On the odd chance they don't show up, how long do you think we should stay?" Zeb asked.

"Depends on how much Vikar needs us on other operations. Certainly, he'll want every vangel with him when he hits Horror."

Zeb wanted desperately to be there when that mecca of evil was taken down. Please, God, that would be done! Even now, Zeb was anxious to get moving. He knew it was important to safeguard Gloom, but he would still like to be somewhere in the midst of the action, more action than they'd seen here. Perhaps it was vain of him, but he felt he had much to offer the vangels, and he was being underutilized. Ah, well, it was not his decision to make.

And by the by, they would have to change its

name of Gloom if the vangels took it over. Maybe Glory.

"You find humor in this?" Jogeir asked.

Zeb must have been smiling at the idea of giving this cave a pretty name. "Hey, we get our yucks wherever we can."

"Well, I'm off then," Jogeir said. "I just talked to Vikar, too, by the way, and things are wild in the Arab lands. The news media is going crazy, not sure what's going on. They blame it all on terrorists, of course. Only we know how much Lucies are involved, too."

Zeb nodded. "Be safe," he told Jogeir.

"And you, as well." And just like that, Jogeir was gone.

Zeb yawned. He hadn't realized how much of a toll the day had taken on him. Health-wise, he felt almost back to normal, and, like the vangels, his skin had turned a healthy tan after killing Lucipires. Another clue that he might not be one of them anymore.

He went down the hall to the "dorm" area where two dozen vangels were sleeping or resting with books or television or music headphones. All was well. After that, he checked the second bedroom where the two female vangels, Inga and Dagmar, were soundly asleep. Inga opened her eyes and raised herself up on an elbow, whispering, "Is anything amiss?"

"No," he whispered back, putting a fingertip to his mouth so they wouldn't awaken Dagmar.

Next, he checked his own bedroom where Regina slept, although she had sworn she would be unable to do so. Through the dim light of a low-watt lamp, he saw that she'd put her hair in a ponytail, and it hung in a swath over one shoulder. Probably she'd been too tired to braid it.

It was a big bed, and Zeb didn't hesitate. He removed his boots and slid under the sheets, fully dressed. Regina was dressed, as well. He would just close his eyes for a second, he promised himself.

But her cinnamon scent enveloped him, even from across the space that separated them. He inhaled deeply, and felt so sleepy. It was as if a weight had been lifted off his soul by revealing his history to Regina. His sleep promised to be deep and peaceful, which would be rare for him. In fact, he rarely slept more than a few hours each day. Maybe Regina really did have witchy powers and had put a spell on him.

Usually he awakened at the slightest sound, but it was Regina who shook him now.

He jackknifed to a sitting position. "What? Did something go wrong? Is it time for my shift?"

"Neither of those," she said. "It's only eight o'clock."

"I have two more hours then." He plopped back down, wanting to burrow back into that soft, peaceful sleep.

But she leaned over him. "You smell so good," she said in a low, husky voice that every male recognized. Female arousal!

That thought caused an instantaneous reaction down below, and there was nothing halfway about it this time. He was wide awake now and tried to calm himself down as she continued to lean over him, enveloping him in her own spicy scent.

"Some men would take offense at being told they smell," he told her. And couldn't help himself from reaching up and stroking several loose strands of her hair behind her ear.

She arched her neck, like a cat being petted. In fact, she made a low, purr-like sound.

"What are you doing, Regina?" he asked.

"I don't know," she said, nuzzling against him, her face now resting on his chest, and one knee raised over his thigh. "Something woke me up and told me to touch you."

"The devil made you do it?" he teased.

"No, I think it was someone else."

"What? God . . . or Michael . . . told you to put the moves on me?"

"I'm not putting the moves on you," she said, even as she tucked a hand under his T-shirt and ran a fingertip over one of his many scars, this one running from his rib cage to his navel. "I'm just cuddling."

To keep himself from rolling her over and taking her like a randy war horse, he made a silent count to ten in Old Hebrew, then Latin, then two different versions of Arabic. When he could finally speak above a squeak, and had pulled her hand out from under his shirt, he said, "Hah! Cuddling is just another word for foreplay."

She was running a forefinger over his bare forearm now. Up, down, up, down. Then she asked with a coyness he didn't know she had in her, "Does that mean you object?" And she made a quick pass over the bulge in his jeans. It might have been an accident. It probably wasn't.

"Bloody hell, no!" He tugged her over so that

she lay fully atop him, his hands resting on her butt. "Am I going to lose my chance to become a vangel if I do *this*?"

"We don't have to do *that*. Besides, we have our clothes on."

"Surely you're not so naïve as to think sex can't happen with clothes on." *Can anyone say "dry humping"?* He decided not to share that crude expression with her.

"Well, clothes *are* a deterrent." She sniffed at his neck.

Not much of one, at the moment. Damn, damn, damn! Her scent is killing me!

Her fangs were elongated, he noticed.

So were his.

He groaned, trying his best to resist her temptation. Forget counting to ten in various languages. He thought about Lucipire slime, Jasper's fury, oatmeal, which he abhorred, rap music, prunes, bad wine, soap operas. Nothing worked.

"I have an idea," Regina said then as she very slowly moved her hips from side to side over his crotch . . . his very happy crotch.

Beware of women with ideas! Or was that, welcome women with ideas! He never could get that straight.

"Trond always claimed to have invented something called 'near sex' that was allowed for vangels, or leastways not forbidden. Did he ever explain it to you?"

Did he ever! "He might have," Zeb admitted.

"Show me," she demanded.

Zeb was no fool.

*Amazing what two people could
do with their clothes on! . . .*

Regina might be a witch, but it was Zeb who
was casting a spell on her. It was either that, or she
was losing her mind.

What possessed her to awaken from a sound
sleep with an urge to have sex? *And I don't even
like sex.*

What possessed her to be the aggressor, the one
to suggest sex play? *I wouldn't know sex play if it hit
me in my lady parts and played the tuba.*

What possessed her to suck in fresh, rainy air
like it was life-giving oxygen? *Oxygen is overrated,
in my opinion.*

What possessed her fangs to elongate and
throb? Well, not really throb. More like, become
overly sensitive. *Semantics!*

Regina was lying atop Zeb (*how did that happen?*),
and his talented hands were alternately caressing
her back under her T-shirt, where he magically
undid the clasp of her bra, and then they crept
inside her sweatpants and panties, both at once,
and were cupping her bare behind, urging her
to move against him in ways she couldn't have
imagined. *Who knew? Who knew?*

"So soft, so soft," he murmured against her
neck. "I forgot how soft a woman's skin is."

Is he thinking about Sarah?
Do I mind?
Only a little.

His palms ran from her shoulders to her thighs,

and back up again, under her clothing. "How sweet it tastes!" He licked her neck.

I think my bones are melting.

She wanted to stroke the scars that she knew crisscrossed his back, but he was pressed to the mattress. So she examined with her fingertips the soft bristles of new hair on his bald head. "There's something sexy about a bald man," she whispered against his ear.

She could hear the laughter in his voice as he replied, "Then I'll have to continue shaving it."

"I also like long hair. You looked good in long hair when I saw you last year."

"Well, then, I'll have to alternate. Anything to please my lady." He nipped at her ear as he spoke, then laved it with his tongue.

Yikes! His breath in her ear was as erotic as the most intimate act. And she thrilled at his calling her his lady, even as she realized how pathetic and needy that must make her. She did not care. These feelings . . . these wonderful, torturous, too-good-to-be-true erotic sensations . . . were too hard to resist.

Totally new to her.

And totally unexpected.

Who knew there was such a sensual side of her just waiting to be unleashed? She knew exactly what it was. She'd been asleep her whole misbegotten life, and now she was awakening into her newborn self. Not unlike her cat Thor after a long nap. Stretching out, arching, unfurling. Layer upon layer of new senses.

Zeb cupped her nape then and drew her mouth to his. At first he adjusted them from side to side so they fit just right. *(Those damn fangs!)* But then he forced her mouth open and plunged his tongue inside. Before she had a chance to protest that she did not like tongue kissing, he withdrew. Then in again, and this time, it wasn't so bad. By the third time, she was welcoming him. Hot, wet, hungry kisses ensued. She gave as much as she got.

When she moaned her pleasure and rubbed her breasts against his chest, reflexively, he groaned his pleasure back at her, and slid both hands under her shirt, brushing her loose bra aside. Then he lifted both breasts from underneath and used his thumbs to strum the nipples to life. As if anticipating her response, he held her head in place with one hand so he could kiss her, hard, and she cried out into his mouth her sheer bliss. He would not stop. He continued to play with her breasts with one hand as she was forced to endure his deep kisses by his hand gripping the back of her head.

She stiffened her legs and tried to forestall the climax that was fast approaching. How embarrassing! To come from mere kissing or touching!

"No, no. Don't fight it. Let yourself go. Let me see you melt." He put his mouth to one of her breasts, right over the T-shirt fabric and sucked. Rhythmically.

Oh! Oh! Oh! She did, in fact, melt into unbearably tantalizing spasms that emanated from between her legs—which had somehow become even wider spread with Zeb's erection pressing against her—and rippled outward throughout her body in waves.

She gasped for breath and said, finally, after

calming her racing heart, "What about you?" It was obvious that he hadn't come to orgasm himself, as evidenced by the continuing erection that still nudged her center and the slight panting that emanated from his parted lips.

"I'm okay," he said, raising his head upward a little to kiss her softly.

He was not okay, she could tell. He was frustrated, sexually, and trying not to show it. "Oh, no, you don't. I'm not going to make a fool of myself with a one-sided sex show, and you just lie there like a loaf of bread."

"Are you kidding? It wasn't one-sided at all. I got as much pleasure as you did. Well, almost. And I participated, too. In fact . . . oh, Lord . . . what are you doing?"

She'd slid down so she was sitting on his thighs and was in the process of unzipping his jeans. Parting the pants, she could see a sizeable erection through the thin cotton of his briefs.

"Someone's happy to see me," she said and ran her fingers from his balls to the tip of his penis.

He said a foul word as he arched up and moaned.

"Did that hurt?"

"Hurts so good," he gasped out. "Do it again."

She stroked him then, varying her hold on him and the pace of her movements. She didn't know about him, but this wasn't enough. They didn't dare remove their clothing, though, for fear they would be called to action quickly.

Finally, he put a hand over hers and said, "Stop. I can't ejaculate."

She sat back on her knees and asked, "Why?"

He shrugged. "I don't know. Maybe it's the long years of celibacy, and my cock doesn't know how anymore."

"Bull!" she said, and quoted him that old saying about never forgetting how to ride a bicycle.

"I think this is a little bit different," he said, but he was smiling.

"Are you sure you didn't take Viagra? Don't they warn about four-hour erections or something?"

"No, Regina, I haven't been popping any little blue pills. And I won't be having a four-hour erection, either. I'll go take a cold shower in a few minutes. There's probably only cold water left anyhow."

"Maybe the injuries from the barbed wire have made you permanently . . . um, impaired."

"Maybe," he said doubtfully. "If we were in a different place and had more privacy, I'd damn sure keep on trying but . . ." He shrugged again. "Don't worry about it."

Regina glanced at the watch on her wrist and pressed the button to light the dial. Nine o'clock. They'd been fooling around for an hour. "It's another hour until your outside shift," she told him.

"I don't think I could fall asleep again. In truth, I don't need—"

She interrupted him. "You know, Zeb, I can go from naked to fully dressed and armed in a minute. How about you?"

"Forty-five seconds." He smiled when he realized her meaning.

She smiled back at him.

They were both bare-assed (*and I mean that literally*) naked within thirty seconds.

As time goes by . . .

𝕿his was not a good idea.

In the twenty-seven and a half seconds it took him to remove all his clothing, Zeb thought:

I could be jeopardizing my future as a vangel.

But she's my wife . . . or as good as.

I didn't think so before.

If I do this, will it be the same as giving my consent to a lifemate marriage?

Haven't I already done that?

Yes, but reluctantly.

Am I suddenly not reluctant?

Definitely, when it comes to sex. Not so much when it comes to marriage.

Is there still a chance Michael could be convinced to ditch the marriage idea once this is over?

Maybe.

Even if we have sex?

Make up your mind, man.

His mind was made up for him when he glanced over at Regina who stood, naked as a jaybird (*whatever the hell that was*), proud as a Norse goddess with her red hair loose from its ponytail and forming a nimbus of red flames about her head. Or was she Xena Warrior Woman? Or that Celtic Queen Boudicca, who was rumored to have knee-length auburn hair and led an army against the Romans? No matter!

Regina was more voluptuous than he'd expected, covered as she usually was with loose clothing. Breasts which were ample but high and firm. Nipples a rosy hue, matching her kiss-bruised lips. And, yes, her hair was red down below, too. A trim waist. Wider hips. Long, muscle-toned legs. And, oh! Lookee, lookee! Sweet curved buttocks that begged to be cupped in male hands, his, in particular.

The die was cast.

He was a goner.

If he was stuck with this woman forever, so be it, and God bless.

"Are you done ogling me?" she sniped.

He smiled. Even when aroused, she maintained her snarkiness.

"Not nearly enough. Turn around."

"No way! You're wasting time, Zeb. Five minutes have gone by already. Your clock is ticking."

"More than my clock is ticking," he said and palmed himself.

"Crude lackwit!"

"And yet you want me," he teased. Then, before she could snark some insult back at him, he closed the few feet between them, picked her up by the waist and tossed her onto the bed. Then he crawled up and over her, making sure he spread her legs in the process, and he pressed her arms over her head by lacing their fingers.

"I've got you now," he said, raising his upper body so he could look down at her.

"The question is: What are you going to do with me?"

"Everything," he promised.

And he did.

That same fog of cinnamon rain seemed to swirl around them, and he could swear that hazy blue wings sprang up from Regina's shoulders. He wondered if the same were coming from his shoulders. "Do I have hazy blue wings?" he asked her.

She nodded, still stunned by his tossing her onto the bed. Or maybe it was his erection which stunned her, as it continued to grow between her legs, as if it had a life of its own.

Forget his penis. For now. There were increasing signs that he was becoming a vangel, or already was. The haze of wings being the latest. A sudden thought came to him. "What color are my eyes?" He widened them so she could see better.

"Blue, I think."

There was light in the room, but it was dim. Maybe she was mistaken.

"Are you sure?"

She peered closer. "Yes. Sort of blue. Blueish gray, I think."

Hallelujah! His eyes had been fluctuating between brown and blue, but now mostly blue. He would have done a high five if his hands hadn't been otherwise occupied.

He relaxed with relief, or as much as he could relax being nude with a lady who was also nude, and his cock resting in her happy place.

But then, he noticed something else. All his senses were heightened to a remarkable extent, he realized. Like smell. And it wasn't just the aroma of coffee which still brewed in the far-off kitchen, or the spicy cinnamon scent of his bed companion, but also the shampoo Regina must

have used on her hair, plus the natural scent of
her skin heightened by his Irish Spring soap, and
her woman musk. He could even discern his own
fresh rain body odor. "I love the way you smell,"
he said, nuzzling her neck. He would sniff her
down below, too, but he was pretty sure she would
smack him. This early in the game, anyhow.

"Likewise," she said. "I'll never see rain again
without thinking of you."

He was studying . . . okay, playing . . . with her
breasts with his one free hand (the other arm now
being braced by the elbow beside her head), but was
able to talk at the same time, multi-tasker that he
was. "That would be interesting . . . if rain is now
a sexual trigger for you. Really, Regina, think about
the possibilities. You wouldn't be able to help yourself from seeking me out every time a storm comes."

She smacked him playfully on the shoulder.
"That's not what I meant."

When he pressed his lips to hers, he murmured,
"You taste like hunger."

"Does hunger have a taste?" she asked, licking
one of his fangs.

He saw stars, figuratively speaking. Fangs had
to be the most erotic of the erogenous zones on a
vangel body. "Yours does," he squeaked out.

His sense of hearing was also especially tuned
now. In fact, he could hear distant conversations,
even through the half dozen walls separating
them. And the burbling of the coffeemaker in the
kitchen. The rustle of the sheets. And Regina's
softest sigh.

"Are you ready?" he asked then.

"I was ready ten minutes ago."

Snark, snark, snark. He swore to himself then that he was going to love the snark out of her. Not love-love, he was quick to amend. Making love-love, as in screwing. Whew! That was a close call. He might have said that aloud.

He proceeded to examine and worship her body, every inch of it, from her forehead to her pretty, long toes, and all the interesting places in between. The curve of her neck. The muscles in her upper arms. Her breasts which were gorgeous, simply gorgeous. The sweetest navel he'd ever seen, tiny and inverted. Her pubic curls that were soft as a baby duck's down. The delineation of muscle and sinew in her thighs and calves.

Then he rolled her over and did the same to her back, from nape to heels and all the interesting places in between. Her shoulders, which did indeed have swirls of a blue haze rising from the bumps. The small of her back. The swell of her buttocks. The dimple at the top of the crack. The crease behind her knees.

When he put her on her back again, he thought she would berate him for wasting time, but instead, she said, "Have you put a spell on me?"

"You're the witch, Regina. You're the master of spells and curses. I'm equally ensorcelled, you know."

"Really?"

He nodded. "In fact, remember what you said before about bicycles?"

"Yes," she said hesitantly, confused by his question.

"It's true." He rubbed his erection along her thankfully slick channel. "A guy never forgets how."

"To ride a bike?"

"No." And he used a graphic word to explain what he meant.

"Then why are we talking?"

"Sweet snark," he growled, then lifted her hips and entered her with one long thrust. All the way to heaven, or so it seemed.

She welcomed him with rhythmic grasps, all along his length. Inside her tight sheath lined with warm honey, her inner muscles shifted and moved to accommodate his size.

It had been a long, long time since Zeb had been inside a woman, but it had never been like this. And it wasn't just years and years of celibacy that made him think so. He wasn't sure what it was, exactly, but he recognized that this wasn't just sex.

He got down to the serious business of love play then. With both elbows now braced on either side of her head, he was able to kiss her at the same time that he began his long strokes. In, deep, deep, deep, slow, slow, slow, then out almost completely. In again, a little faster, but still slow and deep, but not so deep. Over and over, he completed his strokes until he was pummeling her with short, hard thrusts.

He tried to mimic the sex act with his tongue, but lost his rhythm when she began to suck on him. He gazed down at her, and was further stimulated when he saw the fierce arousal on her face. *I did that,* he thought with inordinate pleasure. *She is excited by me.*

He wasn't sure if he would be able to come to orgasm this time. He felt like it, but he couldn't be sure. He would be embarrassed if he had any sense left at all, which he didn't. Two weeks ago, if someone had predicted he would be having hot sex with a vangel witch, he would have said they were crazy.

Regina grabbed his head. He thought she wanted to play with his bald head. It seemed to fascinate her. And, frankly, he was discovering that the stupid hairless pate had some of its own erogenous zones.

But, no. Sly wench . . . uh, witch . . . uh, woman . . . that she was, Regina not only had his head in her hands, but was tilting it to the side. Then she did what vangels did instinctively. She fanged him, and sucked softly on his neck.

Every one of the heightened senses in his body exploded. He might have hollered. Leastways, he knew for sure he groaned, real loud. It was the most intimate thing any woman had ever done to him. It was especially stimulating because he was buried in her to the hilt. And then . . . miracle of miracles . . . he was ejaculating like he hadn't in at least three hundred years.

Regina withdrew her fangs and arched her hips up as she surrendered to her own powerful climax. When she was done, she just stared up at him. For once, no snarky remark at the ready. She appeared both stunned and a little frightened at the same time.

He felt the same way.

He wanted to ask her what all that fanging combined with spectacular sex was about. Did it happen every time a vangel had sex? If so, wow! That had to be the best kept secret. Instead of questioning her on the subject, though, all he could come out with was, "Thank you."

"My pleasure," she said, running her hands over the numerous welts across his back.

As he dressed then for his shift, he realized that only forty-two minutes had gone by since they'd started this madness. With three minutes to spare.

So much had happened.

It was not nearly enough.

For his sins, he couldn't wait until the next time.

Did he have regrets?

Not a single one.

Yet.

Chapter 16

*In the midst of battle, a man's
mind turns to ... sex? ...*

The next day, the Lucies returned. A whole horde of them in demonoid form. Thirty at least. She didn't know if that qualified as a horde or not. Scary beasts, to be sure. But Zeb, Regina, and their forty-some vangels were ready for them.

Zeb assured them that these weren't high-level Lucipires, ones who would have had many, many centuries of experience and therefore unimaginable strength. These were only hordlings and imps, with a few huge mungs thrown in. That didn't mean they weren't frightening in appearance and dangerous. Still, things could have been worse. Jasper, and his commanders, probably hadn't expected any vangels to have remained at Gloom.

The whole battle took only a half hour before the Lucies began to retreat again, but the vangels couldn't allow that. Not again. Zeb led a contingent to follow those escapees, while Regina and the remaining vangels took care of the few demon vampires left. Slime city!

Zeb was almost fanatical in his fighting, swinging his sword right and left, never pausing before he moved forward. Regina guessed that he was trying to chalk up points in favor of his becoming a vangel, or staying a vangel after their indiscretion. Or maybe she was underestimating him. Maybe he was just that powerful of a warrior. After all, he'd been doing it for almost two thousand years.

That number boggled Regina's mind. Hard to imagine what it would be like to be a vangel for that long. Even harder to imagine the horror of being a demon vampire for so long. She couldn't help but admire Zeb for rising out of that mire of evil and filth, wanting to be a better person. Or leastways a vangel. He must have felt like he was sinking in quicksand for centuries, unable to move anywhere but down. Michael had thrown him a rope.

Zeb wasn't the only one who'd been yearning for change. In truth, if Regina had ever wished to be part of the vangel fighting forces, her wish had more than come true. She'd tossed more knives and shot more bullets and destroyed more Lucies in the past twenty-four hours than she had her entire vangel life. The stink of Lucipire was firmly lodged in her nostrils, the sight of red eyes, super big fangs, scaly skin, claws, and tails was imprinted on her brain.

They'd tidied up the scene at Gloom, now renamed Glory, the volcanic cave in Greece, after wiping out the thirty Lucies who'd returned to the scene. A few more vangels had been injured and one was lost to Horror in the process. The sooner all the vangels got to that arctic castle the better, not just to destroy Jasper once and for all, but to save the vangels who'd been taken in not just the Gloom/Glory endeavor, but the other missions as well. Regina figured it must be close to fifty by now.

By noon, they were preparing to shut the cave down. Regina had no idea if any vangels would ever return here. When they turned the lights out, going out the door, the lights might not ever be turned on again.

Zeb told her that he didn't care one way or the other, which was amazing, considering how much work he'd put into it. "This place holds too many bad memories for me."

Regina had to wonder if he included their lovemaking in the bad memories category. She had to be realistic. He must have regrets about what they'd done. After all, he had the most to lose.

And, yet, she'd noticed him watching her at various times during the day, even during brief breaks in the fighting. And there didn't seem to be regret in those stares, more like confusion, trying to figure her out. He was remembering.

Just like she was. What had come over her? What was continuing to plague her about the man? She caught herself checking him out, too. But she knew exactly what intrigued her. The man had hidden talents! And she might have initiated the action last night, but he'd enjoyed himself, too. She was sure of it! Men couldn't fake *that*.

While they waited for Vikar to call and tell them where to go next, they were watching CNN, along with a dozen vangels, including Inga and

Dagmar, who kept giggling every time Zeb looked their way. Smitten, they were, Dagmar confided to Regina. An old-fashioned word, to be sure.

Regina understood. She was a little smitten herself. Ha, ha, ha! Who was she kidding? She was neck-deep in lust overload.

But she digressed.

The news on the TV was dire for the entire world. Religious leaders were claiming the End of Times was coming, and she could see why they might think that. While half the world was rushing to churches and synagogues and mosques, the other half was reveling in the depravity. Evil and pandemonium reigned. And government leaders and police officials were running around like chickens with their heads cut off. "The sky is falling, the sky is falling," was practically their refrain. And yet no one had any answers, except for piecemeal putting out of fires, figuratively speaking. In other words, defensive actions.

What they saw on the TV screen *was* horrifying. Bombings. Sanctioned rape by terrorist groups, including all the nuns in a French convent, even the elderly ones. Multiple fires in the vicinity of the Twin Towers. Beheadings in the Middle East with production line precision. Cannibalism forced on political prisoners. Acid thrown on innocent people in a mall. Crucifixions. Tongues sliced in half, eyeballs plucked out. The atrocities went on and on.

And then there was Satan worship on a grand scale. What had probably started out as a lark for young people had turned into the real thing, all of it multiplied a thousandfold by Internet social media, which called it a religion no different than Christianity.

"What do those idiot followers think is being sacrificed on those satanic altars?"

"Doll babies?" she guessed.

The anchors, clearly agitated, interviewed every official and so-called expert they could get in front of a microphone, but even the specialists had no clear answer to what was happening, except to blame it on "terrorists." The Republicans blamed the Democrats, and the Democrats blamed the Republicans. The blacks blamed the whites, the whites blamed the blacks. The Muslims blamed the Christians, and vice versa. Politicians said it was all the fault of immigrants, or oil prices dropping, or the economy, or lagging defense spending, or climate warming. Whatever. In other words, no one knew.

There were also strange cases of puddles of slime showing up in the areas of these criminal activities. The FDA and CDC were investigating.

"Good luck with that!" Zeb laughed. It wasn't the first time that the public had discovered a pile of Lucie slime and took it to authorities for analysis. Nothing showed up.

"And I know from experience how hard it is to shovel that crap up," Regina added.

Zeb shook his head in disgust and got up to check his cell phone again. It sat on the kitchen counter, ominously silent. Her phone hadn't rung yet, either, although she and Zeb had given Jogeir, and in turn Vikar, a report two hours ago on the outcome here at the volcano. Jogeir had told them to sit tight until they got new orders.

Regina was tired of sitting tight. Fighting must be in her blood . . . pun intended . . . because, despite the rigors of their earlier "battle," she was anxious to get into the fray again. At least that was the explanation she'd come up with for the antsy feeling that was making her squirm in her seat.

Zeb went into the pantry off the kitchen, probably to check once again that no perishable foods would be left behind. He called out to her then, "Regina, could you come here a minute?"

She put her cell phone into the back pocket of her jeans and went over to the pantry. Zeb was standing before a mountain of paper towels. He glanced her way and said, "Shut the door."

Huh? He must have gotten some message and didn't want the others to overhear. She closed the door, which caused the interior light to go out.

But Zeb reached up and pulled a cord to turn the light on manually. He walked over to her then, and reached around to lock the door.

Definitely something secret and confidential. "What have you heard?" she asked anxiously.

"Not a thing."

Huh?

He was standing close to her, really close.

She could probably count the number of incredibly long lashes on his lids which were at half mast, as if, as if . . . "Son of a cloud, Zeb, do you have to crowd me like this? Your fresh rain scent is like an aphrodisiac to me," she blurted out.

What was wrong with her, that she could divulge something like that? The same something that had caused her to practically assault the man last night. That made her lick her suddenly dry lips now, then inhale deeply.

He smiled.

"Forget I said that," she hastened to add.

"Not a chance!" He chucked her under the chin. "I've been on a cinnamon high nonstop all day. What do you suppose I should do about it?" He trailed a fingertip along her jawline, from her ear to the center of her chin. Then, he inserted the same fingertip into her mouth, took it out, and tasted it himself.

Holy frickin' hormones! "Uh, I thought you were having regrets."

While she'd been distracted by words and his wicked fingertip, he'd been more into action. Other action. She was backed up against the door, and her jeans were unzipped before he lifted her and wrapped her legs around his hips.

He pressed himself against her core. "Does that feel like regret?"

For a guy who'd recently suffered major damage to his package, he sure was coming back with a vengeance.

A wash of hot lust swept over her, and she put her arms around his shoulders. Still, she had to ask, "Do you really think this is a good idea?"

"No." He was licking her neck.

"Then why?" She arched her neck to give him easier access.

"Regina, Regina! Has no one ever told you that if you feed the tiger, it will come back for second helpings? And third? And fourth?"

She was no longer listening to him as she felt him shove her panties to the side, undo the buttons on his own jeans and shrug them down just enough so that he could enter her. She made a keening sound of pure pleasure, especially when he pressed a thumb down to the place where they were joined, causing a hair-trigger orgasm to explode from that special spot, shooting out like sparks to her whole body. At the same time, her inner muscles clutched Zeb's already thrusting erection.

"So good, so good, so good . . ." he kept moaning against her ear.

Good didn't begin to describe the sensations that were flowing over her body in waves. If he hadn't been holding her up with his hands under her butt and if her shoulders weren't pressed against the door, her knees would have surely given way.

When he had himself embedded inside her to the hilt, and came to completion, ejaculating into her body, he rubbed his pubic bone against hers, and she climaxed again, even more explosively.

Did I mention he is a talented fellow?

"Was that as good for you as it was for me?" Zeb teased.

"Do you have to ask?'

"Back to being snarky, are you?" He nipped at her neck, and she felt a thrill . . . even after all the thrills she'd already experienced . . . as his fangs pressed but didn't quite pierce her skin.

He lowered her to the floor then, and her knees did, in fact, buckle. He caught her just in time.

They were both adjusting their clothing when they heard a buzzing noise. Looking around, they were unable to locate the source of the noise until Regina felt a vibration against her butt.

She glanced up at Zeb with dismay as she pulled the cell phone out, and realized that the device was on. Putting it on speaker phone, she heard laughter.

She must have butt dialed someone while being thrust against the door.

Then Jogeir said, "A rain aphrodisiac, Regina? Ha, ha, ha."

And Vikar joined in with, "Eye of the tiger, Zeb? Or was that cock of the tiger? Ha, ha, ha."

They would be the laughingstock of all the vangels.

*They worked well together, and
did other things well, too . . .*

Zeb felt as if he was twiddling his thumbs in Nigeria while he would rather be going after the big guns in Lucipiredom . . . those remaining anyhow. Yes, he had been instrumental in killing Yakov in Greece, and apparently Mordr and Svein had taken care of Red Tess in the United States. Two down! There were still Ganbold in the Middle East, Harek in Siberia, Hector in Rome, and of course, Jasper, back at Horror.

It's not that he didn't understand the importance of the Nigerian mission for the SEALs. But, having been forced to participate in unimaginable evils over the centuries, he had a personal dog in the fight to bring the leaders down. And that dog was in the far north, about thirty-five hundred miles from here, as the bird (or the angel) flies.

Ah, well, the sooner they completed the job here, the sooner they could move on. After settling things in Greece, Zeb and Regina, with their remaining vangels, had teletransported to the Sambosa Forest in Nigeria. They'd joined up with Trond, Nicole, and Camille, who were with the Navy SEALs fighting Boko Haram, who had once again kidnapped a contingent of young girls. Unlike the past where the terrorists kept or sold the girls as sex slaves, this time they were executing them one by one for no reason other than to set an example. In other words, depravity.

It wasn't the first time Trond and the SEALs had come to this region to target these particular terrorists, but this execution crap was a new twist on wickedness, and the Lucipires clearly had a hand in manipulating the bad guys into being even badder. The SEALs were determined to wipe them out this time, which was probably an unreachable goal, at least in the short term.

While the SEALs dealt with the terrorists, or tangos as the special forces referred to bad guys, Zeb and Regina had led their troop of forty or so vangels to join with Trond's vangels, to clean out the Lucipires. Simple as that, especially since there was no major haakai leader in command here at the moment. Unlike other missions, the vangels were not to try saving those sinners who might have a last ditch wish to repent.

Twenty more Lucipires were now residing in Hell, in addition to the sixty already decimated by Trond. Small numbers when compared to the frightening four thousand demons Michael had mentioned to them.

Sometime during this particular mission, Zeb had come to a realization, which was both alarming and gratifying at the same time. He and Regina made good fighting partners. He, who had always worked best alone, watched her back, and, amazingly, she watched his back, as well, and did a damned good job of it.

Once, he'd been engaged with a huge mung Lucipire, sword to sword, when he slipped in some slime, and ended up in a bear hug . . . rather demon hug. Ugh! Regina had aimed one of her longer knives at the beast's back, and the blade went straight through to its heart. Zeb had landed on top of the creature as it already began to dissolve. Laughing, he'd saluted Regina, and the witch had saluted him back.

Another time, Regina had been backed up against a tree, the semiautomatic revolver at her feet, the clip apparently depleted of bullets. She'd had only one knife in her hand. The question had been, which of the three Lucipires in humanoid form surrounding her, would she target.

One of them, he'd recognized. Claude Bouclet, a French nobleman who had been a pal of the Marquis de Sade. He'd been taunting her with what he would do to her back at Horror, while his buddies enjoyed the show.

And Regina, bless her witchy soul, had been trying to ignore his taunts by waggling the fingers of her free hand at them all and tossing out curses at their manparts.

"I will keep you chained in my dungeon for years. Naked, of course," Claude had said. "You will serve me and any man or beast I bring to you."

"Abracadabra, mud of a bog. Screw you, demon, turn into a frog."

The three Lucipires had laughed. It had been a rather pitiful curse.

"Every opening in your body will be filled by my cock and the assortment of dildos I keep for that very purpose," Claude had continued. "I especially like the expanding ones."

"Effa, sola, inda, sarce! Demon dick like a dart!"

Claude had glanced downward.

At that brief lack of focus, Zeb, who'd been behind the Lucipires, had swung his broadsword in a wide arc, decapitating Claude. At the same time, Regina had thrown her knife at one of the other Lucipires. And Zeb had taken the third one down. He and Regina had both ensured that the blades had gone through the demon hearts so they couldn't return as Lucipires.

Afterward, as they'd cleaned their blades on a patch of moss, Zeb had looked at her and smiled. "Dick like a dart?"

She'd shrugged and smiled back at him. "I'm a bit rusty on curses. Haven't had occasion to use them lately."

Without thinking, he'd hugged her to his side and they'd walked off to find Trond and the two family WEALs. They met up with Trond, Nicole, and Camille, who were taking a brief rest in a forest clearing. All their vangels were there as well, but hidden in the thick foliage or up in trees.

They updated each other on the campaigns to date.

"Good work in Greece," Trond said to both Zeb and Regina. "I understand you cleaned that site totally, and most important, sent Yakov to Hell."

"It wasn't just us. Jogeir led that mission," Zeb was quick to correct.

"But Zeb took care of a huge number of Lucies on his own," Regina added.

Zeb glanced at her, with surprise. It was not like the snarky Regina to compliment a man, at her own expense.

"I'm just saying," Regina added, blushing.

That was also surprising. Regina, blushing?

"I just got news from Vikar," Trond went on. "Mordr and Svein and their crew arrived in Afghanistan last night, after having wiped out Red Tess in the United States, as you already know. Ganbold the Mongol is a formidable opponent, and thus far Vikar hasn't been able to pin him down. Ganbold has even been seen in Syria, where Ivak is in charge. So they have roughly three hundred vangels there. They need more. Turns out Harek took care of Heinrich in Siberia and will be bringing his vangel troops there, as well."

"Damn! I wanted to be the one to confront Heinrich," Zeb said. "I'd been hoping to be sent there next."

He could see that was a surprise to Regina.

"I'm a Jew, he is . . . was . . . a Nazi. The Holocaust." Zeb shrugged. Enough said!

"Nicole and I will be going back to the SEALs and WEALs to complete our assignments here," Camille informed them. "We'll need to make an excuse for Trond not returning with us. He'll of course be going to Afghanistan. Maybe we'll say that Trond captured a small contingent of terrorists he wants to bring in."

"Or we could say he was injured and is off being treated by medics. In the confusion, no one will notice right away." Nicole added, "It worked once before." She looked at her husband. "Remember, babe?"

"You got it, babe." Trond leaned over and kissed his wife.

Zeb kind of envied the easy affection this married couple showed each other, even in public. Not that he was envying marriage. It was just nice that some married men and women acted that way. In fact, he had a sudden memory of his mother and father standing out in the vineyard. He was only about five years old at the time. But he clearly recalled his father kissing his mother on the forehead *and* placing a hand on her behind.

He also remembered holding Sarah's hand as they walked to synagogue on Shabbat. Just holding hands, but so intimate.

Odd the thoughts that came to a man at the most inopportune times. And talking about . . . thinking about . . . inappropriate. He had a sudden inclination to kiss Regina's red braid and palm her ample bum.

"Where will we be going now?" Regina wanted to know, calling him back to the matter at hand. "Afghanistan?" she asked hopefully.

Trond shook his head. "Cnut is having trouble cornering Hector in Rome. Part of the problem is those never-ending catacombs under the Vatican, but also the large numbers of humans congregating there. He doesn't want to call attention to the Lucies or the vangels, and he doesn't want innocent people to be caught in the fray."

"So you want us to go to Rome?" Zeb asked. "Both of us?"

Trond tilted his head to the side. "Yes. Unless you have a problem working together."

"No," Regina said hesitantly. Zeb knew that it wasn't himself she was hesitant about, but a yearning to be part of the bigger action.

"No," Zeb said, not so hesitantly. He wouldn't mind being part of the action to destroy Hector . . . a former Roman Centurion who fed Jews, Christians, and anyone they didn't like to the lions.

Besides, for his sins, Zeb was wondering when the next opportunity would pop up where he could engage in sex again. With Regina. He had lots of ideas and centuries to make up for.

Chapter 17

The dead visiting the dead? ...

And so, Regina found herself in Rome. Under Rome, actually. Okay, under Rome's outskirts.

Here she was, plodding along the hundreds of miles of catacombs, which were underground burial crypts. In this case, for an unbelievable six-plus-million dead people, including a few martyrs.

Regina shivered and moved up closer to Zeb, who was leading the way through the narrow, underground tunnels, followed by their vangels, who were muttering about the disturbing atmosphere of their surroundings. They all carried flashlights or wore headlamps.

"Is it strange for a vangel to be creeped out by dead people?" she asked Zeb.

"Yep, especially since vangels are also dead people."

"But we're different kinds of dead people, right?"

"I don't know. I would think that, from the perspective of those Up Above, we're all the same."

"Eew!" someone said behind her.

They'd just passed a monk—roughly five hundred years old, give or take—standing upright in an alcove, fully clothed with a monk's cowled robe over his skeleton. The empty eye sockets seemed to be glaring at them for disturbing the deadly quiet.

"And so we find the origin of the hoodie," Zeb joked.

Regina heard Inga and Dagmar giggle behind them a ways. Zeb's voice did carry. They better be careful or they would wake the dead, or some hidden Lucies.

And then Inga said, "Wouldn't it be funny if there were demon vampires hiding in some of these crypts?"

And Dagmar countered, "Not!"

They both giggled some more.

Hard to believe that these two dingbats had once been prostitutes.

Changing the subject a bit, Regina said, "I'm becoming quite the world traveler, though basement of a Roman crypt is a new one for me."

"I, on the other hand, have seen my share of graveyards, mausoleums, or even the pyramids," Zeb remarked.

"Actually, until a few years ago, vangels traveled back and forth in time and all over the world," she told Zeb. "Then Michael assigned us to set up permanent headquarters in modern times, and we could move forward in time only as humans do. He said there was enough corruption in the contemporary world to keep us more than busy." She was babbling nervously.

Zeb said, "I can't argue with that. I contributed to a lot of that sin."

"That was before you changed teams. You have a clean slate now." Clean except for their not one, but two, recent indiscretions, which she wasn't about to bring up.

"Hopefully." Zeb gazed at the frescoed walls and decorative stone tombs they were passing, ones yet to be discovered, the so-called "lost tombs," those six and more stories beneath the surface of the earth. "This really *is* amazing. To think, someone . . . probably a slave, or lots of slaves . . . carved this all out ages ago, long before power tools. I feel a little like Indiana Jones, coming down here."

Actually, Zeb looked better than Harrison Ford ever did, even with a bald head. "Yeah, but Harrison Ford was in catacombs under Venice, which were nothing as grand as the real deal here. And he was looking for the Holy Grail. We're just looking for demon vampires," Regina pointed out.

"You're probably right. The Vatican is very strict about opening these tombs to the public. Of the fifty or so known catacombs, they allow tourists in only a few, even though there are even actual churches belowground in some cases. And all those known catacombs are on higher levels than where we are now. Talk about digging all the way to Hell!"

"You sound like a travel brochure."

"Maybe I'm as nervous as you are."

"No one is as nervous as I am."

A half dozen voices behind her chimed in, "I am!"

That made her feel a little better.

"Anyhow, I doubt the Papacy, even a hip, modern Pope like Francis, would ever permit a film company to tramp around down here, Indiana Jones or not. And definitely not a troop of angel vampires," Zeb remarked.

"Not to mention presumably pagan Vikings, except for you."

"I thought I was going to become a Viking-by-marriage?"

"No, that was a vangel-by-marriage." Had she just indirectly agreed to this crazy wedding idea? She felt her face color.

He turned and winked at her to show that he understood her obvious dismay and that he'd been just teasing. Which caused her to blush even more. Those blasted long eyelashes of his!

Zeb took her hand as they entered one slightly wider channel. It wasn't meant to be an intimate action, but it felt that way to Regina. And, yes, she smelled fresh rain, not the dust and cold stone of the ages.

After they'd left Nigeria and before they'd teletransported to Rome, Regina had used Nicole's laptop to do a bit of quick research. She'd discovered that the catacombs had been carved by slaves beginning almost two thousand years ago out of tufo, a soft volcanic rock which hardened on exposure to air. Mostly, there were wall graves, arranged vertically, one on top of the other, like stone drawers, each holding one or several bodies. But there were also burial rooms for families that allowed for meals to be eaten belowground with the dead. *Seriously!* And chapels. All with beautifully decorated frescoes and sculptures.

The immensity of this was exemplified by the Catacomb of St. Domitilla, which, alone, was spread over nine miles and contained four million skeletons and an amazing fresco of *The Last Supper*. Not to mention its own basilica.

Then there was the Bone Chapel, or Capuchin Crypt, whose chapel was lined with the bones of 4,000 monks, including several still in priestly, hooded garb, arranged upright in alcoves, staring down at any visitors who stepped into the chamber. Eerie!

If that wasn't enough, this arrangement of crypts and chapels was repeated on at least four different known layers or stories, connected by narrow steps. Truly, the catacombs earned their title of City of the Dead.

Regina and Zeb and their vangels were, of course, nowhere near the public areas. In fact, they were so far down, there were several stories of tombs between them and those already discovered.

Finally, they emerged into a large clearing, which was actually an underground church or chapel. "This is it," Zeb said, looking at a map in his hand which he'd drawn up after talking with Cnut earlier today.

They all walked hesitantly into the immense circular space, and were stunned at what they saw.

On second glance, Regina noted that the room was not really circular, but twelve-sided, with a diameter of roughly a hundred feet. Above was a vaulted ceiling that rose into a high dome. On the center hub was painted the Resurrection, or Christ rising to Heaven, surrounded by angels.

"Holy shit!" Zeb muttered, and pointed to one particular section of the fresco. "Is that who I think it is?"

Yep. Good ol' Michael was peering down at them from behind a cloud. The artist must have had a personal acquaintance with some of the heavenly hosts. Heck, maybe the artist had been an angel.

The magnificently detailed frescoes on the spokes depicted the twelve disciples. There was no natural light here, of course, but the beams of their flashlights and headlamps reflecting off the colored stones that lined the panels appeared like stained glass windows, just as they would have by candlelight when this artistic masterpiece had been created.

"Oh, Zeb!" was all she could say.

"Don't touch anything," Zeb said when one of the vangels was about to pick up a gold chalice. His voice echoed around the room, the acoustics designed to enhance the chants of the clergy who once worshipped here. "The oils in the skin would cause these objects to degenerate or lose their historical integrity. Just our being here would horrify archaeologists."

Regina gave him a glance of surprise. Of all things for him to be worried about!

"I'm just sayin'," he replied with a blush coloring his cheeks, evident even in the dimness of their artificial lights. She loved when she could make him blush, which wasn't often.

Some of the vangels had already dropped to their knees and were praying. The room had that effect on them all.

Beneath the twelve spokes were niches carved into the wall. Small wooden chests sat in each of the openings, the kind that might very well hold the bones of the saints, or some religious article that belonged to them. Certainly the apostles themselves weren't buried here; Regina didn't think so anyway.

"I bet there are relics of the apostles here," Dagmar whispered, to no one in particular, but her voice carried.

Regina recalled that some of these old domed churches had "whispering galleries," certain spots in the space where sound was deliberately echoed.

"You may be right," Zeb agreed. "The Christians were big on having churches built on even one tiny bit of bone. Some of them were ridiculous, like a toe of the baby Jesus."

Zeb's jest seemed almost sacrilegious in this "holy" place.

"Well, some of them were real, too," Dagmar countered.

"I can still smell the incense they used here," Inga said. She sniffed the dry air. "Like cloves, it is. No. Cinnamon."

Zeb looked at Regina and grinned.

"If it starts to rain, we're in trouble," she said to Zeb.

"You're right. I don't think having sex in the middle of a church with the angels and Jesus and twelve disciples looking down on us would be a good idea."

"What? Who said anything about sex?"

"Yeah. Who said anything about sex?" Cnut asked, coming into the chapel space, from a doorway on the opposite side.

Regina was pleased to see that Zeb was still blushing, as much as she probably was.

Cnut was in full vangel warrior garb, like all of them, but he stood out because of that Ragnor Lothbrok hairstyle he'd adopted lately, shaved on the sides with a dark blond braid running from his forehead to his nape, then tied off with a leather thong. Rather nice, actually, and a wonderful contrast to Zeb's almost bald head, which was, truth to tell, equally attractive. Actually, more so.

"Follow me into the sacristy. I need to discuss a change in plans." Cnut motioned with a forefinger for Regina and Zeb to follow him.

Before they left, Zeb repeated his warning to those left behind. "Don't touch anything. When this level of catacombs is discovered sometime in the future, if it is, we don't want to have left evidence that we were here."

"That includes the candles," Regina said to Inga who was about to pocket one of the votive candles sitting in a rack of several dozen. At one time, every Catholic church had these candles that parishioners could buy and light with a small donation to get special favors.

"Where are your vangels?" Zeb asked Cnut.

"Back in a large, half-cleared space about a quarter mile from here. It was probably going to be another worship area eventually," Cnut answered.

They stepped into the small sacristy, a room

used to store church vestments and sacred objects and, of course, candles. Lots of candles. Even after all these years, the room smelled of beeswax.

"Don't touch anything," Zeb repeated, for their benefit now, too. "Sorry," he added when she and Cnut looked askance at him, as if they needed that kind of reminder.

"It's just that vestments like that laid out over there have remained relatively intact, but will probably degrade just from our breathing in here, let alone touching," Zeb said defensively.

Regina wasn't knowledgeable about the combination of moisture, temperature, and whatnot that affected historic fabrics, but Zeb was probably right. "I hope we're not going to be fighting the Lucies here, on this level," she told Cnut. "It would be a shame to destroy that beautiful chapel." She waved a hand to indicate the space they'd just left.

"No. That's what I wanted to discuss." Cnut pulled out two rolled-up pieces of stiff paper and spread them over a table in the center of the sacristy that was probably intended for folding vestments or filling holy oil cruets. He also turned on a high-intensity, battery-operated lamp that he must have carried with him so they could see better. Regina recognized the two maps, which Zeb had been responsible for drawing up while they were still back at the castle. Not that Zeb had ever been here before, not for centuries, anyhow, but he'd seen many diagrams, he'd told the VIK. And he had a good memory! Add to that the fact that when he'd gone rogue demon, he'd secreted many documents out of Horror and copied them for his own insurance.

The parchments showed in detail the labyrinth of catacombs, not just the ones known to the public or the Vatican, but the "lost ones," as well. "There isn't any way that we can fight the Lucies down here. First of all, they know these passages better than we do."

"You got that right. Hector has maintained a headquarters here for about four hundred years," Zeb said. "Calls it Terror."

"What an odd place for a demon headquarters, though. Below the Vatican. Hardly an unholy place," Regina observed.

"Are you kidding? All those sinners coming to Rome for forgiveness . . . a gold mine for Lucipire harvesting," Zeb told her.

"That's sick."

"That's life."

"If you two lovebirds are done squabbling," Cnut interjected.

"Huh?" she and Zeb said at the same time. And both blushed.

"There are no secrets in vangeldom, my children," Cnut said and winked. "As I was saying, we can't fight the Lucies in these catacombs because they know the passages better than we do, even with maps, which are only as good as Zeb's memory. But also, if they're in demonoid form, the spaces are too tight for fighting. Don't get me wrong. We've taken down a ton of the beasts, but it's been one at a time. Slowly. And no sight of Hector. We have to lure them aboveground."

"How many Lucies does he have with him?" Regina asked.

"I can answer that," Zeb said. "Unless things

have changed dramatically the past six months, he doesn't have any more than a hundred Lucies, and only a few of those are haakai. For obvious reasons. The logistics of these catacombs don't require large numbers."

The first map showed a cross-section of the catacombs, down ten levels. The other map showed diagrams of the tunnels on each of the levels. "This is where I think Hector has his headquarters." Zeb pointed to a large clearing in the center of a series of corridors on the eighth level. That was two levels above them. Regina and the vangels were on the tenth "story" down.

"I have close to seventy-five vangels stationed outside the perimeter of Rome along the Apian Way. Let's use the twenty-five I have inside and your forty or so to push the Lucies out. See all these X marks. Those are exits, twenty-seven in all. That's where we'll have two vangels posted at each one. There are no other means of escape."

"And what's your plan for forcing them toward the exits, instead of taking a stand inside," Zeb wanted to know.

"I thought you'd never ask," Cnut said with a decided twinkle in his blue eyes. He went over to a pile of canvas bags stacked in a corner. Out of one of them he took what looked like a plastic pistol along with some tubing and a heavy plastic bladder."

"A water pistol?" Regina asked with disbelief.

"I know what this is," Zeb said, picking up the bladder, which must be filled with some liquid because it made a sloshing sound. "A CamelBak. Navy SEALs carry this on their back, with the tubing over the shoulder so that all they have to do is turn their heads to take a drink."

Cnut was grinning like the cat who swallowed the canary and a few mice as well. "You know how Lucies hate holy water. Sprinkle a little on them and their skin starts to sizzle. Sprinkle a lot and their skin can actually catch on fire. What if we arm all the vangels inside with these water pistols and a gallon of holy water in reserve? The Lucies would run, not stand and fight. At least, that's what I'm thinking."

Zeb was examining one of the units, which he'd put together, and then grinned as he squirted it at Regina.

Regina swiped her face with a sleeve and said, "Grow up, cowboy."

"I think this just might work," Zeb said with a smile. "Not for any length of time, of course. The water would run out. But just to get the Lucies running toward the exits? I love it!"

Zeb and Cnut gave each other high fives.

"Where are you going to get all these gallons of holy water?" Regina asked. Someone had to be practical here.

"There's a natural spring behind the chapel altar, and one of my vangels is a former priest. He's blessing water as we speak." Cnut was obviously pleased with himself.

"And what's that big X that's circled on the map?" Zeb asked.

"That's my mark, and that's the exit I think Hector will emerge from. It's the widest, allowing for him to bring a troop of Lucies with him," Cnut explained.

"So, you're the one who gets to confront Hector?" Clearly, Zeb was not pleased. He hadn't been given first shot at Yakov and now Hector was taken out of his crosshairs, too.

Hey, Regina wasn't too happy, either.

"Damn right I am," Cnut answered Zeb. "After being staked out here for two days, I get first dibs on Hector."

Neither Regina nor Zeb disagreed with him, not out loud, anyhow.

Regina frowned as she studied the maps, though. "What's to stop the Lucies, including Hector, from just teletransporting out of here once they recognize the threat?"

"Ah, I know the answer to that," Zeb said, exchanging a glance with Cnut. Both men looked at the pistol. "Holy water, even a sprinkle on a Lucie's skin, prevents the ability to teletransport, as well as burning them."

She nodded. "One more thing. Sorry to be the doubting Thomas here, Cnut, but even if we vangels have been quiet as mice, both inside these catacombs, and on the outside, wouldn't Hector have been long aware of our presence by now? Especially with you being here for two days already."

"Probably, but not as quickly as you might think," Cnut answered. "We have two levels of unexcavated catacombs separating us that act as a sound buffer. As for the outside, believe me, my vangels are well disguised as tourists and Catholics making a religious pilgrimage. You should see Armod. He's leading a troop of Michael Jackson impersonators. Believe me, they've been thrilling the crowds with their antics."

"I thought vangels were supposed to lay low and not attract attention," Zeb said.

"In most cases, that rule holds true, but if you'd ever seen Armod moonwalk, you'd never in a million years suspect he was a vampire. Or an angel," Cnut replied with a laugh.

"Or a Viking, for that matter," Regina added, also with a laugh. "Remember last Halloween when he had all the children . . . Gunnar, Gunnora, Izzy, Mikey, and Mordr's five kids . . . made up as zombies, and they entertained the whole castle with their rendition of 'Thriller'?"

"How could I ever forget? Gunnar had guts dripping from his mouth." Cnut pretended to shiver with distaste. "It was actually spaghetti and red sauce," he explained to Zeb.

"You vangels are a little weird," Zeb remarked. "Is that it, then? Can we get this show on the road?"

"ASAP." Cnut pointed to the large canvas bags on the floor. "The holy water pistols and water bladders are in there, for you two and your vangels. Let's synchronize our watches. Two hours from now, you should all be in place. Let's say thirteen hundred hours?"

Cnut rolled up one of the maps and tucked it under his cloak. Regina took the other one; she would need it to explain positions to the other vangels.

"Go with God, then," Cnut said.

All three of them bowed their heads for a moment.

And then Cnut was gone, teletransported to the outside.

Zeb looked at Regina and then at the bare table, then back to her. "I was thinking . . ."

"Are you crazy? In a religious place?"

"You're the one who started me on this track. You're the one spreading your cinnamon lure like a pheromone perfume. You're the one who looks like Wonder Woman in those black jeans and turtleneck."

She just gaped at him.

"Besides, this isn't a religious place, like the chapel out there," he said defensively.

A fog of fresh rain scent swept through the room, and Regina almost swooned with sudden yearning. "Maybe later," she conceded.

The holy water idea worked remarkably well. Regina worked with Dagmar, and the two of them managed to herd at least a dozen Lucipires through their assigned corridor out toward the exit. It was not to say they didn't engage in any fighting. Especially in the beginning when the Lucies were in demonoid form, making them clumsy and big targets. Soon they were transforming themselves into humans with deadly swords and firearms.

One particularly stubborn Lucie looked Mexican and spoke with a Spanish accent. Regina didn't speak Spanish, but Dagmar apparently did, and she loosely translated his words for Regina. "He's saying: 'Whores! I will see you in Hell.'"

"Not today, Jose," Regina said to the dark-skinned man who had one ridiculous gold front tooth. She wielded one of her knives in a direct hit to the tooth, causing it to pop back into his open mouth. Her next blade went into his chest, which was already burning from the squirts of holy water from Dagmar's gun. He began to dissolve into slime almost immediately.

Stepping over him, she and Dagmar smiled at each other.

Most of the Lucies ran away on seeing them coming, especially when they got sprayed by the long-range water pistols. Or maybe they ran on the sight of these two strange women who were whooping and dancing down the halls like this was a game. It was. A war game.

Once they exited onto a wide lawn, it was a totally different game, though. A to-the-death battle between the vangels and Lucies who were engaged in one-on-one combat as far as Regina could see, to her left, and to her right, even across the highway. Any tourists or passersby still on the scene were scattering like frightened cats. Pretty soon the police or news media would arrive. They would have to end this battle quickly or there would be a whole lot of explaining to do.

Regina noticed that all the vangels, herself included, had blue, misty wings at their backs. Fangs were elongated on the vangels, as well as the Lucies. Vangels had no reason or inclination to fang a Lucie. That was intended for human sinners wanting to repent, not an option for these deadened souls. But if one of the demon vampires bit a vangel, the poison would travel quickly through the body, putting it in stasis. That was the time when a vangel was taken back to Horror for the torture transformation to Lucipiredom. Not happening today, she hoped. These "dead" but not bitten vangels would be healed if treated soon enough, or they would go off to that holding place for vangels . . . Tranquility.

Dagmar rushed to help her sister, and Regina made her way, popping off Lucies with her revolver which had a silencer on it, toward where she saw Zeb and Cnut trying to get closer to Hector. The former Centurion was in full battle gear from the Roman era. A white, knee-length tunic was covered with leather armor, front and back, tied on the sides, with cap sleeves, a bronze chest plate, shin and wrist guards, sandals, and a red-plumed helmet. In one hand, he carried a long sword, already dripping with vangel blood, and in the other, a large metal shield with some family crest on it.

He looked frighteningly strong and cruel, which he was, of course, having been a Lucie all these centuries, and a high-level haakai at that. A number of dead or mortally wounded vangels lay scattered around him, a testament to Hector's military might. Hopefully, the vangels would be the winners today, and they could take these wounded back to Dr. Sig's island hospital for medical aid or send them on to Tranquility. The alternative . . . a trip to Horror . . . would be, well, horrifying.

Cnut was equally strong, having been a vangel since AD 850. Yeah, Hector had a good eight hundred years on him, but Cnut had higher powers on his side. Hopefully.

Regina worked her way toward Zeb, fighting Lucies right and left. She'd packed dozens of her knives before coming to Rome, and she had almost a full round in her firearm, which she'd checked before exiting the catacombs. Afterward the vangels would do a cleanup of all these loose weapons and shells. Assuming they were "alive" to do so.

There was no time for thinking then as the sounds of battle took over. Grunts, occasional screams, war cries, expletives, the clash of metal against metal, the pop of weapons with silencers (because of the public setting, all the vangel fire-arms had noise suppressors on them today), and the occasional Viking shout of "To the death!" or the military "Hoo-yah!"

Soon they'd cleared the way for Cnut and Hector to engage each other with swords. It was a lost battle for Hector by now, with few or no Lucipires left to back him up. Even if the Roman managed to over-power Cnut, there were enough vangels regrouping and surrounding them that he had to know the end was near. And teletransport back to Horror to re-group wasn't a choice for Hector, either, as evidenced by the holy water burn marks on the exposed skin of his thighs, calves, elbows, and forearms.

He wouldn't go down easily, though.

"So, Cnut, dost think you can better me just be-cause you have a Pretty Boy Viking hairstyle?" Hector raised his shield to deflect the thrust of Cnut's long sword.

"Nay, Roman, I will better you with my su-perior skill." Cnut made a deft twist of his wrist while lunging which caused the tip of his blade to slice the shoulder strap on Hector's breast plate. The chest covering was now hanging lopsided.

"Ah!" Zeb said at her side. "I see his strategy now."

Regina did, too. Just killing a demon was not enough. In order to destroy Hector, totally, so he could never return as a Lucipire, there would have to be a direct piercing of his heart by a blade or bullet that had been treated in the symbolic blood of Christ. The breast plate prevented that from happening.

Hector parried Cnut's next strike and countered with a strike of his own. He missed but the flat side of his blade whammed Cnut's thigh, bringing Cnut down on one knee.

Ouch! That was going to leave a bruise. Good thing the blow didn't pierce the skin. Lucie blades were also specially coated . . . theirs with a deadly mung.

The crowd of vangels gasped with surprise, but Cnut was almost immediately back on his feet, and now he was angry . . . angrier than he had been before. He fought fiercely, at one point managing to flick the breastplate aside and off Hector's body, totally.

It was thrust, slash, clash, retreat, metal against metal, over and over until Cnut finally grunted out to his vangels, "Clear . . . the . . . area. Wasting . . . time!" In other words, stop gawking at him and clean up all the vangel weapons and, yes, bodies, before the authorities arrived. Sirens could already be heard in the distance.

"You're wasting time, for a certainty, Dead One," Hector snarled, misinterpreting Cnut's words.

Regina was about to leave and secure the catacomb entrances when Cnut deliberately feinted with his sword, pretending to aim right, but actually going left.

Hector deflected the sword with his shield, spun on his heels in a skillful move, and made a sweeping arc with his own sword, which sliced across Cnut's chest. To her surprise, and delight, Cnut was wearing body armor underneath . . . thick padding which prevented what would have been a heart-stopping blow.

Surprised, Hector was caught off guard when Cnut immediately countered with a head butt that knocked the Roman back, sending him to the ground. His shield slipped from his fingers, and he struggled to adjust the sword in his other hand. Too late! Cnut knocked the high haakai's weapon aside with his foot.

But instead of ending Hector's demon vampire life in one pierce of the sword tip through his evil heart, Cnut slashed off one of the Centurion's arms.

Hector screamed.

"That is for all the Christians you sent to the lions."

Then Cnut cut off the other arm.

Hector screamed again.

"And that is for all the innocent Hebrews you slew in your marches through Judea."

Holding his sword by the hilt with both hands, Cnut slammed it down on Hector's genitals.

Hector only groaned now.

"And that is for all the women you raped and tortured. Men, too, you evil sod!"

Hector opened his reddened eyes and spat at Cnut. "I will fuck you in Hell, too, one day, Viking. That I promise."

"I. Don't. Think. So!" Cnut said, pulling his bloody sword out of Hector's body, then thrusting it through his heart, pinning him to the ground.

Closing his eyes, Cnut seemed to be saying a prayer. Then said aloud, glancing around the battleground, "It is done!"

Within ten minutes, just as the police and news media were screeching onto the scene, Cnut and the vangels gathered together. They'd cleaned up the perimeter as much as they could. The only things remaining were piles of slime. Lots of piles. Which should have the authorities puzzled for a long time to come. Not to mention an occasional water pistol. How would they explain those?

The injured vangels had already been picked up and taken via teletransport to the Grand Key Island hospital. The dead ones rested in Tranquility by now, bless their souls.

"Let us thank the Lord for our victory today," Cnut told them all. Then he shouted, "To Horror!"

The vangels immediately began to disappear as they teletransported to the last and undoubtedly biggest mission of their vampire angel lives. It wouldn't be the final battle of good against evil in this world. There was still Armageddon to come someday. But it would be the biggest to date.

Zeb came up and took Regina's hand.

"Are you ready?"

He was panting for breath.

She was, too, and not totally from the exertions of war.

"You have no idea," she said.

Just before Cnut melded into the stratosphere,

he passed Regina and Zeb and remarked, "Holy clouds! I miss my wife. I can almost smell Andrea's cinnamon buns."

Zeb chuckled. "I'm thinking about buns, too."

Not to be outdone, Regina said, "Me, I'm in the mood for rain."

It was a good day.

So far.

Chapter 18

It was like D-Day for vangels . . .

At last, at last! Zeb felt as if he'd been waiting for this day for centuries, perhaps since the day Jasper first made him a Lucipire almost two thousand years ago.

He'd been biding his time these past few days. At the castle in Transylvania, Pennsylvania, in Greece, in Nigeria, in Rome, and now here in the far northern Norselands, he'd done the work he'd been assigned and done it well, if he did say so himself. Now, he was about to reap his reward, and he didn't mean becoming a vangel. Finally, he was to confront Jasper and put an end to the demon, who had started Zeb on his wicked path and kept his claws deep in Zeb's soul all these years.

Vikar was the general in this assault on Horror Castle. He and about a dozen of his lieutenants were huddled in a crude hunting lodge going over last-minute plans. Zeb would join them in a moment; he was playing an important role in this final lap of the Lucipire/Vangel race, having more knowledge of the castle layout and who might be found where. But he'd gone over these details numerous times before, both back at the Transylvania castle days ago, and here this morning in the far north of the Norselands.

For now, Zeb stood with Regina, both of them viewing the battalions of vangels as they set up their posts outside of Horror. Because of the cold temperature, the vangels had changed to fur-lined hats and gloves and cloaks, which were outfitted for weapons and ammunition, like their regular capes were. Fire pits had been set up at different places for them to warm themselves when the cold got too much for them as they awaited the beginning of the battle.

But that wasn't what had Zeb and Regina transfixed. And, frankly, amused. The engine of an aircraft could be heard as it droned overhead in a wide circle around the circumference of the Horror Castle grounds, about one hundred yards from any of the buildings. The fixed wing aircraft was actually an air tanker, piloted by one of their very own vangels, and it was water bombing the grounds with . . . what else? Holy water! It would ensure that the Lucipires inside the periphery would not be able to teletransport out.

The former Russian military plane had already made a previous trip the short distance back to Svalbard, an archipelago near the North Pole, actually the northernmost settlement in the entire world, where it refilled its retrofitted tanks by skimming the Arctic Ocean. At that point, the water was blessed by the same vangel priest who'd handled the water pistols back in Rome.

The tanks only held several thousand gallons of liquid.

"From hot air balloons to water bombing," Regina mused, recalling the last time she'd been here at Horror. It seemed like ages ago. Zeb had to wonder if Patience and Grimelda were inside, and whether he or Regina would be the ones to kill them. Not a job either of them would relish, but they would do it if it meant an end to Lucipiredom.

"I wonder whose idea this was?" Regina mused.

"Probably Cnut's. A play on his holy water pistols," Zeb answered.

"You've gotta give the vangels credit for having imagination," Regina commented.

"And a sense of humor," he added.

"There's nothing funny about this, though, is there?" she said.

"War is never funny, and this is war."

She looked at him for a long moment, then said, "Everything will be different after this, won't it?"

He nodded. No matter the outcome today, vangels would face an uncertain future. No matter the outcome today, he and Regina would face an uncertain future. He knew she wanted assurances from him, but he couldn't make any. Not yet. Maybe never. Squeezing her hand, he said, "We better head back into the meeting. We'll talk later."

When they entered the primitive hunting lodge where reindeer heads and polar bear skins adorned the log walls, he heard Vikar giving the group of leaders some final words. "We have an army of nine hundred vangels here today, counting the hundred more brought in from the two safe headquarters."

"I'm still afraid that won't be enough," Svein said.

"It will have to be, but I think it'll suffice." Vikar glanced over to Cnut, their battle strategist, for confirmation.

"There could very well be more than three thousand Lucipires inside," Cnut pointed out.

"They got to be packed arse to elbows, even in a castle this big," Vikar added.

Cnut nodded and continued, "So, be prepared to be outnumbered. But remember, it's not the numbers that matter here. A herd of sheep is no match for a sharp-toothed wolf. David beat Goliath, after all."

"I'm fresh out of slingshots," Jogeir called out.

Much nervous laughter followed.

"The numbers might be daunting, but keep in mind that many of them are imps and hordlings, who are practically useless without leaders," Zeb inserted. "And—"

"And most of the leaders are gone," Cnut finished for him.

"Right," Zeb agreed. "All the members of the high council are gone, except for Jasper. And Beltane, who is no warrior. Residing in Hell at the moment are Yakov, Red Tess, Heinrich, Hector, and Ganbold."

"And may they never rest," Vikar said.

"Amen," the others concurred.

"Also, many of those inside right now are demons sent by Satan, but not demon vampires," Zeb told them.

"There has to be mayhem inside, then," Harek concluded, "which is to our advantage."

"The majority of the fighting will take place outside, hopefully. But many of us will have to go inside as well. And the hardest part will be our entries. Once inside, we should be evenly matched. Quality versus quantity. Tanks versus BB guns. Horses versus puppies. Sheep versus wolves." Cnut should stop while he was ahead, with all these foolish metaphors.

"I wish we could just detonate the whole she-bang." Trond had become quite the explosives expert since he became a Navy SEAL, but despite his enthusiasm for big noises, even he knew that would not work in this case. "Yes, yes, I know, we have to protect those vangel captives inside." Fifty-two of them had been taken in the past few days, and everyone was concerned about their condition.

"Afterward, assuming we are successful in this venture, you can blow the castle to dust, Trond," Vikar said. "Remember, you can't rely on tele-transport to save your asses today. Teletransport has been cut off in the immediate vicinity, for us and for the Lucies. In that respect, at least, there's an even playing field."

"Warriors do not play, they fight," Mordr corrected.

"Whatever!" Vikar replied to his usually dour brother.

"Another reason why we can't bomb the hell out of Horror . . . actually, two reasons," Vikar told them. "One, we don't want to draw attention to our presence here, especially before we get the job done. And, second, we need to pierce each of these Lucies through their slimy hearts. Bombs don't necessarily do that. Without those chest blows, they'll just come back again as Lucies in a day or so."

"That's not true of the regular demons that Satan sent here, by the way," Zeb was quick to add. "Kill them any way you want, and they'll be off to their fiery lairs."

"How will we know the difference between the Lucies and regular demons?" someone in the back asked.

"Believe me, you'll know," Zeb said. "Think red skin, red eyes, forked tongues à la Gene Simmons, razor-sharp claws, long, pointed tails. Some, not all, have hooves and horns."

"How attractive!" Regina commented.

Zeb shrugged. "In humanoid form, they can be very attractive, even beautiful. In fact, last time I saw Lucifer, he looked a lot like you, sweetheart."

Zeb couldn't believe that he'd used that endearment for her, especially in a room full of Vikings. He could tell that she couldn't believe it either. He was in for it!

"Holy shit!" someone muttered.

"I'd like to see that," someone else muttered.

"I always thought she had a bit of the devil in her," still another vangel muttered.

"That's neither here nor there," Vikar said, clearly fighting a grin.

Regina elbowed Zeb. "Fool!" she muttered.

Zeb couldn't help but grin, too. "Sor-ry!" He winked at her, to make up for his slip.

Not even close, her scowl told him.

Vikar turned his attention to Harek then. "That geek Lucie still has a force field around the castle that prevents teletransport in or out of the castle proper. You're a geek, Harek. Can't you remove it?"

"I'm not that kind of geek," Harek said, indignant that Vikar would think he could do such a thing, from this distance. Vikar was pushy that way.

Vikar shrugged.

But then Harek conceded, "Once I'm inside the castle, I'll find the electronics guru from Hell, or his equipment, and disengage the barrier. That, I guarantee."

"Good," Vikar said.

"Just give me time," Harek griped.

"Time is our enemy," Vikar quipped.

Harek, and several others, rolled their eyes. Zeb hadn't been a vangel for long, but even he recognized that when Vikar started with the proverbs, it was never just one.

"Enter, engage, and run the hell home."

More eye rolling.

"God might give us guns, but we have to supply the ammunition."

"Puh-leeze," Regina begged.

"You might want to toss out a few of your witchy curses while you're at it, Regina," Vikar added with a grin.

Regina needed to learn that it was a mistake to call attention to herself. It was a lesson he'd learned early on in Lucipire 101. Invisibility wherever possible.

"I'd especially like to see a few Lucies go back to Hell with their cocks tied in a knot and their tails up their arses," Vikar said, thus proving Zeb's invisibility theory.

"This is what you've done to me," she hissed at Zeb. "No one takes my curses seriously anymore."

Oh, that was unfair!

Regina murmured something under her breath about what Vikar could do with his own appendage.

Vikar just grinned and continued, "In any case, we'll storm the castle at twelve hundred hours on the dot. Once we've breached the entries, expect a mad rush of Lucies to come out all at once. Most of the fight will take place outside. I expect a field of slime by this evening. By the way, Zeb, do dead demons leave slime in their wake, too?"

"Nope. Just a lot of stink."

They all checked their watches. It was already ten hundred hours and they had to get to their assigned assault and defensive positions. "Aside from destroying every single Lucipire we encounter, we've got to be on the lookout for the captive vangels who were taken the last few days. Their safety and return to Transylvania or the hospital on Grand Key Island, if they're injured, is paramount. They'll have to be led, or litter lifted, or carried over our shoulders till we're outside the castle perimeter for teletransport."

Everyone nodded grimly. Many of these were close friends, who were being held as prisoners. And God only knew their condition if Jasper and his minions had begun torture.

"Let us pray," Vikar said then.

All heads bowed, and they took each other's hands, raising them.

"May the Lord be at our backs, and may St. Michael guide our sword arms, as we begin this battle of good against evil. Death to all Lucipires!"

"Amen!" everyone replied. "Death to all Lucipires!"

Svein dropped Zeb's left hand. Zeb squeezed Regina's right hand before releasing it.

"Remember, Jasper is mine," Vikar said for about the dozenth time since they'd arrived, and he ended the meeting.

Zeb didn't argue but he had every intention of being the one to end Jasper's days as a demon vampire. He had an ace in the hole that would ensure he gained that access. It wasn't just the satisfaction of being the victor that Zeb craved, but there were a few things he had to say to the king of the Lucipires before he met his final reward. Questions that needed answering.

Just then, he noticed Regina staring at him oddly, especially at his clenched fists. The woman saw too much. He unclenched his fists and smiled at her.

She didn't smile back. "What are you up to?"

"Nothing," he lied. "We better go find Jogeir." He and Regina had been assigned to Jogeir's team once again. Their assignment was to enter the castle through the dungeon corridors, the way Regina and the witches had rescued him not so long ago. Well, Jogeir and Regina didn't know it yet, but he wouldn't be with them. Not the whole time, anyway.

He put an arm around her shoulders as they followed the others out of the building and on to their various assigned posts. Everywhere he looked he saw vangels swinging their fur-lined capes back over their shoulders, exposing swords or guns or lances, even twin-bladed battle-axes. And in Regina's case, knives.

And, oddly, or perhaps thankfully, many of them appeared to have hazy blue fog at their backs. Would this be the day that some vangels earned their wings? Would he still be a vangel at the end of this day?

"Just in case things don't go well today—" Regina started to say.

He put his fingertips to her lips. "Stop."

She kissed his fingertips and shoved them aside. "I have to say this. Just in case things don't go well today, I want you to know that I have . . . that I have . . . come to love you and I probably wouldn't mind if we *are* lifemates."

"Regina, not now."

He could tell she was disappointed that he didn't reciprocate her declaration. In truth, he wasn't sure how he felt. Oh, there was a bond between them. Lust, for sure. And something else. Whatever it was, would it still be there when the fever of war receded?

Suddenly a group of vangels marching off to their respective assault positions separated them, and Zeb knew he had to take this opportunity to launch his own secret plans. "Later," he yelled to her, but she probably didn't hear him.

He hoped there would be a later for him . . . for them both.

Sweeping up devils was dirty work ...

Regina was with Jogeir and fifty vangels at the entrance to the castle dungeons. The same place she'd stood not so long ago when three witches had helped her bring Zeb out of Horror.

Déjà vu?

Yes.

Except there was no hot air balloon.

Except that Zeb wasn't here.

And she wasn't surprised. For some reason, she had been suspicious of him all morning. He hadn't been acting quite right. She realized that he'd never intended to join them in this last foray through the dungeon corridors.

Where was he?

She found it impossible to believe that he'd been deceiving them all along, that he'd been deceiving her personally, that he was still a Lucipire. But what, then?

All questions had to be postponed as they saw their first batch of Lucipires approaching from the dungeon chambers. What followed was a frenzy of fighting. One beast after another, and some of those beasts in humanoid form. Still others . . . the regular demons, if a demon could be called regular . . . were almost scarier. Yes, they had the red skin and sunken red eyes and flicking reptile tongues and long tails and sharp claws which Zeb had described, and the overpowering sulfur scent of rotten eggs, but many had emaciated, bent bodies and sharp, jagged teeth, not unlike that character Gollum in *Lord of the Rings*. In fact, they made a scrabbling sound as they rushed over the stone floors, like a herd of rats. Still others were huge with hooves and horns, obviously the more powerful of these evil beasts.

One of the demons had guts hanging from its mouth, like the zombies on *The Walking Dead*. And it looked like it had deposited a pile of shit, right there in the dank corridor.

If she had the time, she would bend over and vomit, but Regina barely had time to remove her knives before another Lucie or demon was in front of her. Soon she switched to her revolver, especially handy since any mortal wound would do on the non-Lucie demons. She could see all her teammates, Jogeir leading them, facing the same seemingly unending deluge of demons, but popping them off. Bang, bang, bang!

Regina had never seen so many elongated fangs, from both Lucies and vangels. Nor had she seen so much slime and gore. She knew how a berserker felt now. Death, death, death was the only focus her brain could handle. Onward, onward, onward. Keep on fighting. Don't think. Just kill.

She couldn't even stop for those vangels who fell along the way, either killed or injured. Those killed would go on to Tranquility, no danger of being tortured by Lucipires into becoming one of them if the victors. The injured would be taken to Grand Key Island after the battle was over. Again, assuming the vangels won, however. If not, all bets were off.

They got as far as the dungeon where Zeb had been tortured for all those months. It smelled of evil . . . that rotten egg, sulfur odor associated with demons and hellfire and all things wicked. The dungeon was empty, which gave the vangels a chance to take a breath and regroup. Regina went back and picked a dozen of her knives out of the slime and brought them back to the gathering of vangels where she began to wipe them off with an old rag. Both the demons and Lucies were already evaporated.

"Where's Zeb?" Jogeir asked right off. This must be the first time Jogeir had noticed Zeb's absence, or the first chance he'd had to ask.

For her sins, Regina lied and said, "He's back a ways, taking care of a few stray Lucies in the side corridors."

Jogeir nodded, but she could tell he wasn't convinced. "How many of ours lost?"

"Three dead and three injured," Regina answered.

"Bring the injured in here and make them comfortable," Jogeir told one of the male vangels. "We'll take care of them later. No time now. We need to have the teletransport barrier removed first. Plus, we've got to move up to the main floors of this friggin' castle."

And then they were off and up the stairs into the next level of the castle. Through a window, she could see a major battle taking place outside. Hundreds and hundreds of the evil enemy spilling out of the castle onto the already slimy lawns where they were met by vangel swords, and axes, and firepower. Even from here she could hear the sounds of battle. Metal clashing. Guns firing. War cries. Screams and grunts.

On the main floor of the castle, Regina and her

group joined up with Vikar, who was driving Lucies from the other end of the long, extra wide gallery-style corridors that held those disgusting "killing jars" of Jasper's, the ones that still held not-yet-turned sinning humans who were killed before their time. As far as Regina could tell in passing, none of them were vangels. In addition, the vangels were fighting Lucies and demons who came out of the various rooms along the way . . . offices, lounges, conference rooms, whatever.

Cnut and Mordr and their teams were handling the Lucies on the second and third floors where the demon vampires slept in specially designed beds to accommodate their tails. The lower-level Lucies had their own TV and game rooms . . . games, as in torturing newly turned humans or activities attuned to the dark side of demons. Such as live dartboards, eyeball pool, thrustmaster exercise machines with female and male orifices in strategic locations, televisions showing nonstop sadomasochistic porno movies, a water dispenser that shot out not H_2O but blood, real blood, a vibrating recliner that was not used for relaxation but something else, a fireplace where it wasn't marshmallows roasting on long sticks but toes and fingers. The depravity went on and on.

It was more than an hour before they got these floors cleared, and Vikar had already ordered some vangels to make up litters and take the injured vangels outside beyond the no-teletransport zone. Harek hadn't yet broken the force field code. In the meantime, Svein and Trond were scouring any hidden spaces inside where Lucipires might be hiding.

But still, there was no sign of Jasper. There had been powerful haakai and muscle-heavy mungs, and plenty of imps and hordlings. But the big guy was missing.

"Where is he?" a furious Vikar demanded, coming up to Regina.

"What? Who?"

"Zeb, that's who."

"Um . . . I don't know. Isn't he around?"

"She told me he was in one of the side corridors in the lower level handling some Lucies," Jogeir said.

Regina blushed. She thought about lying, but knew she was caught. "I haven't seen him since we left the lodge meeting this morning."

Vikar wagged a forefinger at Regina in an "I'll handle you later" manner and turned to his brothers.

"Zeb has Jasper," Harek concluded.

"What? I didn't think of that. So, Zeb isn't a traitor, after all. Whew!" Regina said.

"What? Are you crazy? Do you have reason to think he's a traitor?" Vikar demanded of her.

"Uh, no," she conceded, feeling foolish, and guilty, for having doubted Zeb's integrity.

"He is in such trouble," Vikar said, angry that Zeb had taken away his prize. "No sooner made a vangel than he transgresses."

"Yes, but not the wrong kind of trouble," Regina argued. "And not the worst kind of transgression, surely."

"You are in trouble, too," Vikar warned. "Watch yourself, witch, I can throw a few curses, too."

She smiled, she couldn't help herself. Zeb wasn't a traitor.

Oh, the choices we make! ...

Zeb found his ace-in-the-hole cowering under a table in the third-floor grooming salon, the place where Lucipires went to have their claws clipped, their scales thinned, and overall toiletry services. Including having their tails cleaned. It was amazing what a dragging tail could pick up, and they were too long for the creatures to reach back and clean themselves.

Beltane had been Zeb's informant for years now. Sort of a double agent to a double agent. Jasper hadn't a clue. To all outward appearances, the Creole hordling was a devoted servant and the newest member of the High Council, in a rather secretarial role, never having been trained in fighting skills. As evidenced by his hiding under a table during the Battle of the Ages.

"Where is he?" Zeb asked right off.

The boy, in the humanoid form of his nineteen-year-old self when taken from the 1700s Vieux Carré, New Orleans's French Quarter, crawled out from under the grooming table and pointed upward. "He's been outside all this time. Fighting like a madman. I saw him lop off two vangel heads. There's no escaping him when he's in this berserk mode. Best you go hide, Zeb. He has evil plans for you. I'm afraid what he'll do to me."

"Stop the babbling, Beltane. Jasper isn't going to hurt you anymore." At least, Zeb hoped he wasn't. "Now, where is Jasper, exactly?"

Beltane shook his head. "On the roof. Assessing the casualties. Making plans. He sent me to find

Gordon, that geek who set up the teletransport shields. I saw the IT guy trapped in the computer room with Harek Sigurdsson, who was carrying a big sword. Pfff. Gordo has fewer fighting skills than I do."

Zeb shook Beltane to stop his rambling account. "Jasper," he said once again.

Beltane nodded. "Up on the roof, like I said. He has two haakai with him, a mung, and a few imps."

Zeb was about to go back out into the hallway, then up the stairway to the roof when Beltane asked, "How soon can I leave?"

Glancing back, Zeb saw that the boy had packed a suitcase and it sat tucked under the table. He couldn't imagine what a Lucipire would want to take with him.

Before he could answer, Beltane added, "Will I become a vangel, like you?"

"What makes you think I'm a vangel?"

"Those blue wingy things on your shoulders."

Wingy? Zeb tried to look over his own shoulders, and there was in fact a blue mist there. Which made him feel guilty. Here he was, being given the second chance he'd yearned for all these years, and he jeopardized it all with his need to confront Jasper on his own. He also jeopardized something else. Regina. But he couldn't think about that now. He needed to focus.

"Beltane, I never promised you that you would become a vangel. Nor did I guarantee your safety once you were outside this castle."

"I know, I know," Beltane was quick to backtrack. "But you did promise to speak on my behalf to . . . to . . ." He glanced upward.

Did the fool think Zeb had an inside connection with God, or St. Michael? But something else occurred to him then. If Zeb was in fact a vangel now, maybe he could try saving Beltane, although he wasn't sure a vangel could do a fang-saving of a redeemed demon. Usually it was evil humans on the brink of death-by-Lucipire. If it were that easy, surely Trond or one of the other vangels . . . Regina, his supposed lifemate, for example . . . would have completed the process on him long ago.

It was worth a shot, though.

"Beltane, are you sorry for your sins?"

"I am, I am."

"Do you promise to go henceforth and sin no more?"

Beltane's eyes went wide at that. Zeb could tell he wanted to ask him to define sin. But, instead, he wisely answered, "I do."

"Come then," Zeb motioned, and before Beltane knew what he was about, Zeb sank his fangs in the boy's neck. He sucked out some of the vile blood, spit it on the floor, then fanged him again, this time infusing him with some of his own purer blood.

After the fanging was over, Beltane just gaped at him. "Is that all?"

Zeb nodded. He had no idea if his actions would help Beltane. "Go with a pure heart," he said, which seemed like a good thing to say. "Now hide again until this is over."

He left and made his way toward the roof. On the way, he removed his AK-47 from the inside of his cloak, unfolded it and rechecked the magazine. Half full. Good enough! He had extra clips stored in his chest rig. In addition, he carried an old short sword he'd picked up on his way here; that had been his weapon of choice back when he'd served in the Roman Army. Having made those last-minute checks, he tossed his cloak aside, for ease of movement. And opened the door slowly onto the roof.

At first, Jasper and the others didn't see him. In humanoid form, in full military gear, they were all leaning over the gaps in the stone crenellations of the roof. From this viewpoint they could see for many miles around. The snowy tundra was dotted with the dark shapes of the cloaked vangels engaged in swordplay with escaping demons and Lucipires. Blood and wet patches that must be slime splotched the white ground.

Without giving any warning, Zeb propped his sword against the wall and raised his right arm, bracing his assault weapon on his shoulder. The deep, popping sound of the AK-47 echoed as all the Lucipires except Jasper fell to the ground. Rat-a-tat, rat-a-tat, rat-a-tat! Over and over, Zeb shot until he was sure he'd gotten them all, not just deadly wounds, but through the hearts with the specially treated bullets. Occasionally, with an efficiency usually reserved for the military, he had to pop out a used mag and insert a new one with up to thirty bullets.

Jasper, who wore what must be an Army general's camo uniform, just stared at him, his fangs elongated, the only sign of his vampirism. Same as the vangels. Well, except for all the wispy almost-wings he was seeing today. Jasper, too, carried an assault rifle and a sword. He had to know that this would be a one-on-one fight, but that Zeb had something to say first. He also must be sensing that he had lost this final fight and that he would soon be facing his maker . . . Satan.

In fact, Jasper was probably up here awaiting the opening of the teletransport shield so that he could leave voluntarily. Zeb couldn't allow that because, sure as sin, Jasper would be back on earth sometime in the near future putting together another army of Lucipires.

But first, he had other issues to settle.

"Spit it out, traitor. What have you to say, Zebulan?"

"Back then, before I ever joined the Roman Army, did you have me in your crosshairs, even then?"

"Of course."

"And you primed me on a path of evil so you could eventually pick me off?"

Jasper shrugged. "You know the routine of a Lucipire. Get the scent of a sinner, or someone contemplating some great sin, and prod them on. Offer temptations. Encourage evil deeds. You, with your greed, were already prime pickings."

In other words, the devil was on his doorstep even before he went outside. So to speak. Oh, Zeb knew his great sin had been his own fault, but he'd just wondered if there had been some kind of push.

"And my wife and children?" he choked out.

Jasper smiled. "The side benefits of being a demon. Being able to view the destruction humans can do to themselves. Your downfall would not have been half so satisfying if I hadn't been able to steer your loved ones toward a pitiful death. Your little Rachel was especially sweet as she took her last breaths. And

your wife, did you know she cursed you in the end
for having abandoned them to such a fate?"

Zeb felt wet tears on his face. The agony of his
guilt was almost more than he could bear.

"I came to love you, Zebulan. Like a son."

"Pfff! What father forces his son to do the things
you've had me do over the centuries?"

Jasper shrugged. "It is what demons do."

"Do you never regret what you gave up? Being
one of God's favored angels?"

"Only every second of every minute of every
hour of every day of every year of every century,"
Jasper admitted. "But I love sin more, and that is a
fact. You cannot really kill me, you know. Yes, you
can destroy my Lucipire self, but I will still be one
of Satan's disciples."

"I know," Zeb said and realized that Beltane
had come up and stood beside him.

Jasper's eyes went wide. *"Et tu, Brute?"*

Beltane had both hands on a pistol which he
had aimed at Jasper.

Zeb hadn't even known the boy could handle
a weapon.

With a shot to Jasper's leg, Beltane said, "For
the first time you sodomized me."

The second shot went to Jasper's right arm
which caused his sword to drop to the stone roof.
"For the times you forced me to sodomize others."

He shot off one ear and snarled, "For making
me drink blood, and liking it."

Jasper wasn't even fighting Beltane's attacks. At
this point, he probably welcomed death.

"For giving me Marie as a partner fifty years
ago, then sending her off to Hell for refusing to

service a troop of visiting haakai whilst I was
gone." This shot went directly to Jasper's groin.

Zeb gave Beltane a sharp look, and realized
that the young Lucipire looked half-crazed. His
eyes were blazing, spit drooled from his mouth.
Had Zeb's fanging pushed him over the edge, or
was it just too many years under Jasper's thumb?

In any case, none of Beltane's bullets had been
specially treated, and Zeb feared the master Lucipire would die, and come back again as a demon
vampire. Raising his short sword now, Zeb used
both hands to thrust the heavy weapon directly
through Jasper's heart.

The demon just smiled as he began to fade into
a puddle of slime. "I will see you again," he promised. And laughed.

Just then, a group of vangels blasted out of the
door. In addition, some others, including Vikar,
flew up and over the top of the battlements. How
did they do that? Oh. Zeb noticed that they had
white wings. How cool!

"What in bloody hell is going on here?" Vikar
demanded to know. He took one glance at the
beasts whose features were fading, but were still
discernible. In particular, Jasper's grinning face.
"You dared? You bloody hell dared to disobey my
orders?" Vikar was livid.

"And who the hell are you?" Vikar had turned
on Beltane and sniffed the air, confused.

Beltane smelled of Lucipire, but not. He smelled
faintly of something else, too. Not vangel. Not
human. A mixture of good and evil all in one,
human and inhuman, Zeb decided.

Looking from Zeb to Beltane to Zeb again, Vikar

asked Zeb in a steely voice, "What did you do?"

Beltane, meanwhile, was staring at the dissolving mass that had been Jasper with tears welling in his eyes. To Vikar, Beltane must have appeared in grief over losing his master.

"I did what I had to do," Zeb said.

"Aaarrgh! Take him into custody and lock him up back at Transylvania until I . . . rather, Michael . . . can decide what to do with the rogue."

"Which one?" Mordr asked. "Zeb or the idiot?"

Beltane did, actually, look like a half-brained idiot, stunned, no doubt, by what he'd actually garnered the nerve to do. His shoulders were slumped and his arms dangled at his sides, the gun having fallen to the floor.

"Both," Vikar snarled.

"Did you know you have actual wings now, Vikar?" Zeb couldn't help but remark. "Really nice, white ones."

"Bite me!" Vikar said, not at all appeased by Zeb's compliment. But Zeb noticed him glancing back over his shoulder to check for himself.

Just then, Regina came through the door. With a quick scan of the area, she took in what had happened. Then she tilted her head in question at Zeb.

Zeb didn't need to be a rocket scientist, or even a body language specialist, to recognize the expression on her face. Profound hurt.

She must consider his actions a betrayal, a rejection of the love she'd professed for him a short time ago. Because, even if they were lifemates, and that was yet to be decided, his failure to follow orders meant he did not care what happened to himself. Or to her.

Chapter 19

Strange doings, down on the bayou . . .

For two weeks, Regina traveled about the world with one team or another to rid the world of any remaining Lucipires. She could have returned to the castle occasionally for some of the celebrations, but she couldn't bear to see Zeb. His betrayal had cut too deep. She might not ever recover.

He must have been using her during their short time together. How he must have laughed when she'd told him she loved him! What a fool she'd been, to think a man like him would care for a woman like her. A witch!

She should have put a curse on him right from the start. She'd become soft. No more!

Vikar remarked whenever he saw her now, "Regina's got her snark back." And he wasn't the only one who teased her on the subject of her scowling countenance.

"I never lost it," she shot back every time, and usually accompanied her retorts with a waggle of her fingers toward their male parts.

Unfortunately, no one took her curses seriously

anymore. They just laughed. She blamed Zeb for that, too. He'd made her a laughingstock.

She never asked anyone about Zeb, but she overheard others talking about him. Apparently, he was confined to a tower room on the fourth floor of the castle, shunned.

Good. Better yet, he should be boiled in oil, or exiled to the remains of Horror Castle, or . . . or . . . something.

Zeb's fate, like all the others of the vangels, awaited Michael's final decision, which would be announced at the Final Reckoning to be held in two days.

And wasn't that an ominous-sounding title for their meeting with Michael?

For that encounter, she would have to return to the Transylvania castle. Not everyone would, though. Not right away. They were being asked to come in shifts of fifty each. In the meantime, some were on Grand Key Island, or Harek's small telecommunications island, or the ravaged plantation in Louisiana where Ivak had erected a sort of tent city, until the property's ultimate fate could be determined.

She decided to go to Louisiana in the interim. Maybe she could charm a few snakes there, as a side offering of her witch business, or she could bring a few back to Transylvania to slip into Zeb's room.

That was mean of her. She hated this slide down to the dark side of her personality. She wanted to be happy and content, like other people. She wanted to rejoice in the demise of the Lucipires. She wanted love, dammit! She wanted to be left alone. She wanted to be part of a family. She wanted, she wanted, she wanted! And wasn't that what had gotten her into trouble in the first place?

"It's that bad, huh?" Ivak's wife, Gabrielle, asked, as she came up to the porch of one of the restored slave cabins where Regina was staying. Although Jasper's minions had destroyed all of Ivak's work in restoring the plantation mansion, appropriately named Heaven's End, he'd left the slave cabins alone . . . all twenty of them. They were really quite charming little log cottages, if you managed to forget their original purpose.

Regina motioned for Gabrielle to sit on the other porch chair and offered her a glass of iced tea from the pitcher that sat on a small table between them.

"I don't know what you mean," Regina lied.

"Honey, you look like someone shot your dog, and your cat, and your parrot, all in one day. And, by the way, did you know your cat Thor has taken a shine to Zeb, and he keeps him company in his tower room all the time?"

No, Regina hadn't known that. But it figured that even her cat would betray her. Regina hated that she was still wallowing in pity, and that it apparently showed.

"Don't worry, though. Things will work out. They always do."

Gabrielle was a lawyer who handled pretty much the most hopeless cases in the legal system, and she was married to the world's most womanizing vangel, before they were married, of course. Now, he just had an eye for every female who passed by, or rather they had an eye for him, the handsome devil . . . uh, angel . . . uh, whatever.

How Gabrielle managed to remain such an optimist was beyond Regina.

"Where's your little one today?" Regina asked,
instead.

"He's with his daddy over at the prison."

Regina arched her brows at that. Ivak was
a chaplain at Angola Prison, of all things (for a
Viking guilty of the sin of lust . . . enough said!),
when he wasn't off doing vangel stuff.

Gabrielle laughed at Regina's astonishment.
"There's a concert there today, and Ivak figured
Mikey might be an inspiration to some of the
more redeemable inmates."

"If you say so," Regina said dubiously. Everyone
knew that Angola contained some of the worst of
the worst criminals, but then the vangels knew
better than most that second chances do work.

"Zeb asks everyone about you," Gabrielle said.
"He must care. And he keeps sending you letters—"

"—that I return unopened." There was nothing
that Zeb could say now that would erase what he
had done. When Gabrielle was about to continue
on that subject, Regina put up a halting hand.
"Please, no more on the subject. I'm trying my
best to forget the cad."

Gabrielle muttered something like, "How's that
working for you?" But then she surrendered and
said, "I need to drive over to Tante Lulu's place
to get some okra. Dagmar is making a gumbo for
dinner tonight."

The two sisters, Dagmar and Inga, had turned
out to be quite the cooks, even in the rustic make-
shift kitchen in the burned-out shell of the old
plantation house. The kitchen had been in a sepa-

rate building and was made of brick. There was no way they could share a kitchen at the castle in Transylvania. Besides, Lizzie had Andrea's help.

"There's someone out on Bayou Black that I think you'd like to meet. Come with me."

"What? Zeb isn't here, is he?"

"Of course not. You know that Vikar considers him a prisoner of war, or some such thing."

Regina didn't want to see the louse in person, but still she felt oddly deflated that it wasn't Zeb that Gabrielle referred to. "Who, then? Oh, no! You're not becoming a matchmaker?"

Gabrielle laughed. "No. Just come. You'll be pleasantly surprised."

So it was that a short time later, Regina was at the small bayou cottage of the most eccentric old lady she'd ever met. And Regina had met some weird witchy crones in her time.

No, Louise Rivard, better known as Tante Lulu, was no witch, but she was a traiteur, or folk healer. Cajun to the bone, and she was a bony little five-foot-zero thing, with tight purple curls, a pink tank top covering nonexistent breasts proclaiming in gold sparkles, "I GOT MY CAJUN ON!," lavender running shorts, orange ruffled anklet socks, and white orthopedic shoes. She had on enough makeup to plaster the Sistine Chapel. In other words, she was rather adorable.

"Welcome, welcome," the old lady said, reaching up to kiss Gabrielle on both cheeks, then surprising Regina by doing the same to her. Gabrielle introduced Regina, and Tante Lulu said, "I been 'spectin' you fer days."

Huh?

"Girl, me and St. Jude been pals fer decades now." She pointed to a life-size statue of the saint who held a birdbath in his hands in the middle of the yard. "Me and Jude heard yer thunderbolt of love all the way down here in the bayou."

Huh?

"Tante Lulu has a theory about the thunderbolt of love hitting people who are destined to fall in love," Gabrielle explained. "Once it hits you, you're a goner."

"It sure happened to you 'n that rascal Ivak, guar-an-teed!"

Gabrielle just smiled.

Regina wasn't buying this crap. "Hmpfh! I haven't felt any bolts lately." Just a stab through the heart.

"Sometimes ya jist gotta be open ta love," Tante Lulu said, patting her on the arm. "Why doan ya sit down there on that bench next ta St. Jude and have a little chat? I'm gonna take Gabrielle over ta mah little garden patch ta pick us some okra."

"Where's your visitor?" Gabrielle asked Tante Lulu.

"He'll be here by and by," Tante Lulu replied.

Regina glared at the two of them as they walked down the yard to Tante Lulu's garden, which was really a rather large garden, or at least a compact one jam-packed with lots of different vegetables. Soon the basket Gabrielle had brought with her was filled not just with okra but tomatoes, string beans, beets, squash, various lettuces, cabbage, radishes, carrots, and whatnot.

Sitting down, Regina glanced around the peaceful setting. It was a cute cottage with a wide back porch, its several rockers facing the bayou stream. Steam heat rose off the water, and it was not yet noon. Normal humid temperatures for this subtropical region. Regina realized in that moment that she could be happy with a simple place like this. She could see herself gardening, which she'd always enjoyed, even when it was only to grow witchy herbs and minimal subsistence vegetables in the cold Norselands. The peacefulness of the setting could fill some empty gap in her lost soul. Maybe.

She glanced up at the statue, which seemed to be staring down at her, with pity, or was it compassion? Same thing!

"So, St. Jude, what's up? I hear you're the patron saint of hopeless cases. I pretty much fit into that category. Any idea what I should do about it?"

Nothing. No magical words from above, or from the statue's frozen lips.

"I've forgotten how to pray. I know, I know. Vangels should have praying down pat, but I've been too busy being snarky and bitter and . . ." She shrugged. She really did feel hopeless.

"I'm tired of being so bitter and unhappy," she confided. "In truth, I don't really want Zeb to be hurt in any way. He's a good man. You should be helping him. Not me." She felt better having said that, as if a weight had been lifted from her shoulders. Oh, she was still deeply hurt, but hatred had been eating away at her for days. And she didn't hate Zeb anyway. Not really. If anything, she hated herself.

"Like I said, hopeless, that's me," she said to the statue. "I'm looking for a sign here, Jude. How about a little cooperation? Something to show you're listening." She laughed out loud at her silliness.

But then, she heard a roar and almost jumped off her seat. A huge alligator had come up behind her, and just as she was about to run for her life, Tante Lulu yelled out. "Useless, behave yerself." The old lady reached into a lidded milk can beside the bench and tossed some orange pellets at the gator, who caught them midair. Over and over, Tante Lulu tossed the treats until the gator was apparently full, and turned away to amble back to the stream. "Thass Useless. Mah pet gator. Holy crawfish, but he does love his Cheez Doodles."

Regina's jaw dropped.

But then, her jaw dropped even more as another car pulled into the driveway, and Tante Lulu's "visitor" arrived. It was Beauregard Doucet, the former Lucipire.

His brown hair was pulled off his handsome face and clubbed at the neck into a small ponytail knot. He wore a white T-shirt tucked into blue jeans, and flip-flops were on his bare feet.

"*Chère*, Ah'm so happy ta see you again!" He reached out and pulled Regina into a warm embrace. "When Tante Lulu tol' me you were here in Loo-zee-anna, Ah jist had ta come over."

Regina glanced at the old lady, who was beaming with pleasure at reuniting what she must have considered old friends.

While Gabrielle and Tante Lulu went into the house to get some spices, Regina sat down beside Beau to catch up.

"They're all gone, you know. All the Lucipires," she told him.

"All of them? Even Jasper?"

She nodded.

"How about Patience and Grimelda?"

"Gone. To Hell, I presume, with all the other Lucies."

Beau made the sign of the cross and looked up at the statue before them. "Ah been prayin' fer jist such a miracle."

"And what about you? I thought you were going to Alabama, or somewhere far away from your temptress."

"Ah decided ta stay here and face mah demons." He laughed at his own joke. "Actually, Ah took St. Michael up on his suggestion that I make contact with Tante Lulu here on the bayou. And that has made all the difference. Honestly, she could turn the worst sinner inta a saint. She's a notorious busybody, but she's got a heart of gold. Everyone says so. And, of course, she's got you-know-who on her side." He tilted his head in the statue's direction.

"But what are you doing? I mean, do you have a job?"

"Well, not a job exactly. Ah'm goin' back ta school. Actually, the seminary." Beau blushed, then told her. "Ah'm gonna become a priest."

"No way! A witch priest?"

"Yep. Ah got a calling. And Ah'm not a witch anymore."

"And the voodoo priestess you wanted revenge on?"

He shrugged. "Ah forgave her. Turns out she wasn't worth all the hatred."

There was a message in there for Regina, but she decided not to heed it. For now.

"And what about the vangels?" Beau wanted to know. "If there are no more Lucipires, what's the point of vangels?"

"I don't know," she answered honestly. "There's lots of speculation, but the decision is in Mike's hands now."

After a long conversation with Beau, and then with Tante Lulu over pitchers of sweet tea and slices of her famous Peachy Praline Cobbler Cake, they all promised to keep in touch.

"Remember," Tante Lulu said, giving Regina a last hug before they left, "the thunderbolt doan lie."

Regina was quiet and Gabrielle seemed to respect her need for silence as they drove back to the plantation. Finally, Regina said, "I need to go back to Transylvania."

She could swear she heard a voice in her head say, *"Hallelujah!"*

Was it St. Jude, or St. Michael, or her own bloody conscience? It was all the same, she decided.

He wants her, he wants her
not, he wants her, he ...

Zeb's confinement in the tower room was about to be over. In two more days, Michael would arrive for the Final Reckoning. One way or another, his fate would be decided.

He hadn't minded his so-called imprisonment that much. It was actually a pleasant room, with windows on three sides and a view for many miles around. The wacky town of Transylvania with its cornball vampire-related shops and restaurants, and then on the other sides, the trim Amish farms and countryside.

Besides, he deserved imprisonment, in his opinion. Jasper's message to him about Sarah's last words, blaming him for abandoning his family, were imprinted on his soul, forever. He had sinned gravely, and for his sins, he'd suffered as a Lucipire and now would suffer through eternity with self-recrimination.

His only regret was that he hadn't been able to talk to Regina, to explain himself. He did care for her. Who was he kidding? He loved her. Not that he could offer her any kind of future together. He had nothing to offer her in that regard. Even if he did, he didn't deserve a happily ever after.

But what about her? Shouldn't she be given a choice?

But there were no choices.

Were there?

At the very least, he owed her an explanation.

Needless to say, he was confused.

At least, the world was rid of Lucipires, and he'd escaped just in time. That was no small thing.

And while the world was no longer rid of evil, terrorism seemed to have settled down a bit. Zeb had a television in his room, and he watched the news practically all the time. There was nothing else to do. And no one was permitted to talk to him, not even those who delivered his meals to him. If the network anchors were to be believed, terrorism was on the decline. At least the madness of the past week was gone . . . the extreme examples of depravity. Those that—he knew, though they did not—had been caused by the Lucipire influence.

Now, if only he could settle things with Regina. Make her understand why he'd acted the way he had. Not that he'd had a good excuse, but that there was an explanation other than complete disregard for her feelings.

All his good intentions were for naught when he got a huge whiff of cinnamon and in stormed Regina. With her red hair wild about her head, wearing the black turtleneck and tight black jeans he'd come to favor, and sparks practically flying from her blue eyes, she was a sight to behold.

Thor, who'd become attached to Zeb like a barnacle on a ship, screeched at the sight of his former mistress and darted under the bed. Regina's upper lip curled with distaste at the traitorous feline. She must think Thor was just like him. Not to be trusted.

"Regina!" he said, and without any forethought, he yanked her into a tight embrace, then fell back on the bed with her atop him.

"Oomph!" was all she managed to get out. He'd apparently knocked the wind right out of her.

No matter! He was kissing her face and neck and hair. She kept swatting him away, but he was not to be deterred. "This will be the first time I've seen you in the daylight. Naked, I mean." He shoved her shirt up to expose her black lace bra. He loved black lace bras. He loved no bras better.

"You're not going to be looking at me in daylight. Yikes! Stop it! That's not why I came here."

He'd managed to undo the center clasp on her bra and separate the fabric, letting her breasts spill out. And spill they did. He smiled, which only enraged her more. He couldn't help but be pleased, though. Staring back at him were large, round, firm breasts with rose-colored nipples. "Oh, Regina! How you look!"

"Don't look. I told you, don't look."

Was she crazy? He was looking, all right. And thank heavens for female hormones because Regina might be fighting his advances, but at least one part of her body was happy to see him. Her nipples were already distended, and he hadn't even touched them yet.

Remembering how sensitive her breasts were, he put his lips to her breast and drew the whole areola and nipple into his mouth. He alternately sucked and licked. She tasted like cinnamon and sugar and heaven.

Regina let out one long moan. "I don't want you," she said. At the same time, she put her arms around his shoulders and caressed his back, then began to tug his shirt up and over his head.

"I wanted to talk to you. I intended to talk to you. I should explain to you first," he tried to say, but his hands had other ideas. They were busy doing the same to her, taking off her shirt, admiring the skin exposed. She was soon bare to the waist, just as he was.

"I don't want any of your explanations. Lie down. On your belly," she ordered.

"What? But I want to—"

"Do it."

He complied. Gladly. And shrugged out of his jeans and shoes in the process. It was amazing how flexible and quick a guy could be undressing when the occasion called for it. This occasion did.

"Oh, that is unfair," she said.

"What's unfair?" he asked, twisting his head to peer up at her over his shoulder.

She slapped his head back down, face to the pillow. "You have the best, world-class butt in the world, that's what! How's a woman to resist that?"

Don't. That's how. He smiled into the pillow and relaxed. Things were going his way without any effort. Why interfere with nature?

He felt her straddle his butt then, and, holy crap, when had she gotten naked? Her bare knees were folded at his waist and her bare behind sat on his bare behind. He could swear he felt her soft curls, as well.

His erection grew, painfully, under him.

He started to raise his head again. "Regina, I think—"

"Don't you dare think," she said with female illogic. "Thinking is what caused this whole mess."

He wanted to ask what "whole mess" she referred to. Her rescuing him? Their lifemate business? His seeming ill-use of her for his own purposes? His failure to reciprocate her words of love? His lying to her about his plans for the final battle at Horror? But any questions he might have asked melted under her sweet ministrations to his back.

She didn't say anything, but she sighed deeply as she traced the scars that crisscrossed so much of his skin. There were many of them, and they were ugly. He knew because he'd been able to view them in the full-length mirror on the back of the bathroom door. But, by the way she touched the welts, and then kissed a path from his shoulders to the small of his back, over and over, he could tell that she didn't see them as repulsive.

He could have wept for that small favor.

But he needed to take control of this situation or it would be over before he could bring her to any kind of satisfaction. Forget about himself. He was already on a runaway train to paradise.

Rolling over, he managed to get Regina on her back and he was atop her. She was still angry, throwing off sparks, even as she panted heavily with arousal.

"I have missed you so," he said, kneading her breasts and rolling the nipples between his thumbs and forefingers.

"Bullsh—"

He stopped her rude word with a kiss. For a moment he lay on her heavily so she couldn't move and shove him off. And he just kissed and kissed her, slanting his mouth this way and that to get the right fit, then plunging his tongue deeply inside, then out. He couldn't get enough of her sweet mouth.

"Your smell," he murmured, sniffing her hair.

"Your taste," he murmured, kissing her again, and again.

"Your feel," he murmured as his palms swept over her body, her shoulders, her arms, the back of her thighs.

"You look like a goddess," he murmured, staring down at her. "My goddess."

She blinked up at him, her eyes dilated with passion. Her kiss-swollen lips parted with longing. Her nostrils flaring to catch a breath.

"Words," she argued. "Just words."

"More than words," he argued back, but instead showed her. With long, hungry kisses. With fingers that parted her woman folds and delved in the warm honey there. With his engorged penis which sought entry and then filled her.

He was the one who gasped for breath now as her body welcomed him with muscular spasms. He loved her then with strokes deep and then shallow, slow and then fast. The whole time, they were enveloped in a cocoon of cinnamon rain. Sweet and erotic. Spicy and erotic. Fresh and erotic. Erotic, erotic, erotic.

At one point when the mattress was creaking under them, he heard Thor screech out a protest from under the bed, where he was still lodged.

"Shut up, cat," Zeb said.

When he was fast approaching his climax, he looked down at her and said, "You gave me your blood back at the island. You took my blood at the cave. In many ways we share the same blood, blended. We are one."

She was beyond words at that point, but he saw tears well in her eyes. To emphasize his point he sank his fangs into her neck, and she sank hers into his shoulder.

When they reached the peak of impossibly intense pleasure, they shattered together in a climax so powerful it caused them both to shut down for a moment. In deep sleep, in each other's arms.

As the first peaceful sleep he'd had in weeks overcame him, he promised himself that he would make things right with Regina when they awakened. He would make her understand.

Even if he didn't understand himself.

Chapter 20

*Eeenie, meenie, miney, moe ... How
to choose, How to choose? ...*

Regina returned to the castle two days later,
after slipping out of the tower room while Zeb
still slept. She'd been embarrassed beyond belief
that she could behave in such a wanton manner
when she'd come to confront the man about his
deceptions.

No one knew where she was or had been, and
that's the way she wanted it. Depending on how
things went today with Michael, she would be returning to that secret place again.

Making sure she arrived just before the Final
Reckoning was to take place, Regina stepped into
the front parlor where close to fifty other vangels,
including all of the VIK, were already crammed,
spilling out into the hall and entryway, waiting
for Michael. She scanned the crowd and didn't see
Zeb until he stepped up beside her.

"Where have you been hiding, Regina?" he
asked, clearly angry.

"That's none of your business."

"After what happened two days ago?"

She blushed. "That was a mistake."

"We're lifemates, you know. You can't call that a mistake."

"Oh, yes, I can. Stop touching me."

He'd reached for her hand, but she closed both hands into fists.

"You can't escape me. We're going to have this out."

Just then, someone yelled, "Michael's here."

A shiver of anticipation went through Regina. This was the day! All other days . . . the rest of her life . . . would be measured from this day forward.

The buzz of conversation in the room halted and the crowd parted to allow for Michael to enter. He was in full archangel regalia today. White gown, twisted rope belt, crucifix on a gold chain, sandals on his feet. And a halo that surrounded not just his head but his entire body. Big, white wings were tucked in and folded at his back.

Businesslike and unsmiling, he proceeded to the front of the parlor and stood before the fireplace. "Kneel," he told them.

Zeb, of course, insinuated himself right up to her side, so they were hip to hip, shoulder to shoulder.

"Let us pray." Michael raised both hands in the air and said the "Our Father." They prayed along with him. When it ended, Michael told them, "The Lucipires are no more. God is pleased."

A sigh of relief went through the crowd, who continued to kneel.

"The fact that thou hast destroyed the Lucipires is a good and holy thing. It does not mean the end of evil in this world, but your job as vangels is ended. As of now, vangels no longer exist."

And just like that, all of their fangs disappeared and their shoulder bumps went away. "Sorry I am to tell you, Vikar, but your wings were short-lived," Michael joked.

"I didn't like them much anyhow," Vikar joked back.

"Sigurdssons, stand!" Michael ordered, serious once again. When the seven VIK brothers were standing in a half circle before Michael, the arch-angel said, "This is what the Lord has decreed. You, and all the former vangels, will have two choices. Thou may go to Tranquility and wait until the final Judgment Day. Know that thy chances of going to Heaven from there eventually are good, and know also that Tranquility is not a bad place to be. Better than earth, a far cry from heaven."

They all pondered this option, which raised other questions. What about those who'd married and whose wives were destined to "die" when their mates did? And what about the children of those couples, both the natural one, and the ad-opted ones?

As if hearing these questions, Michael contin-ued, "If thou choosest that first option, thy mates will go with you, but thy children will not. Thou wouldst have to make arrangements for their earthly care. Thou canst surely see now why I urged you not to connect with human lifemates. The complications!"

Michael waited to see if there were questions so far. There were not. None voiced, anyhow.

"The second option would be to become human

once again and live out a natural life. There is risk in this option. Earth has temptations. If thou commitest some grievous sin again, thou wilt not have a second chance for Tranquility. Dost understand?"

They did. They could still go to Hell.

"Vikar, thy pride is still great. Could thou control it?"

Vikar cringed at being singled out.

"And Trond, wouldst thou become lazy again? Mayhap the military would be too difficult for thy lazy soul?"

Trond also cringed.

"Harek, Harek, Harek! Still no archangel website?" Michael smiled, knowing he was responsible for the delays. "I guarantee, thou wilt be trading stocks and gambling as soon as I leave today. I know, I know," he said when Harek was about to speak, "the evil is not in thy making money, but how thou usest it."

Harek just smiled.

"Mordr, thy anger is a cancer thou still must fight to control. First time one of thy children is threatened, I fear what thou wilt do."

Mordr appeared angry just at being accused of anger.

"Cnut, surely you will not gorge yourself again? But then again, who knows?"

Cnut mouthed silently, "No way!"

"Sigurd, thou, too, must control thy sinful envy. One island is enough?"

Sigurd blushed at having been caught out.

"Ivak, what can I say about thy lustful nature? Best you castrate thyself if you want to survive."

Ivak really, really cringed.

"In any case, the option of one more human life is open to all vangels, and I will explain the details to each and every one over the next two days. Decisions do not have to be made today, although, if Tranquility is thy choice, that can be accommodated forthwith. I would rather you give it great thought. In fact, I will give you one month to make a final decision. No, I will give you until Christmas, if you need that long."

"If we decide to live out a human life, what will we do?" one vangel asked.

"Whatever you want. I will give each of you a small amount of money to start over, but thou wilt have to work to support thyselves, like any human does."

Regina could see that this prospect troubled some of the vangels. Many of them hadn't been trained for anything but fighting Lucipires. On the other hand, there were many occupational talents represented among them, as evidenced by all the electrical, plumbing, and architectural work that had been done on this castle renovation.

Regina looked at Zeb, and he looked at her, as the same thoughts occurred to them both.

Zeb was apparently not going to be singled out for some particular punishment. Michael surely would have mentioned it now. Well, that was good news. For Zeb, anyhow. For Regina, too, because, really, she didn't want him punished any more than he'd already been under Jasper's rule. Punishment by Michael, that was. Punishment by her would be okay.

The other thought was: Regina and Zeb weren't going to be forced to marry. In fact, they might not even be considered lifemates anymore.

Regina sniffed the air.

No fresh rain scent.

Zeb sniffed, too.

Then frowned. Clearly, there was no cinnamon scent either.

Regina couldn't decide if that was good news or bad news.

Michael dismissed them all then, reminding them that he would return at Christmastime for final decisions. Unless people wanted to go to Tranquility now; those vangels, or former vangels, should let him know by signing a sheet that had been set out on the hall table. Then, Michael hurried them on by asking that the next group of vangels be called forth.

"I have assigned a special team of archangels to help you all during this transition period." Michael's glance swept the room as he prepared a farewell statement. "I cannot say, Vikings, that it has been a pleasure working with you." As always, he said the word "Vikings" as if it was distasteful. "But thou art not as bad as thou once were." That was as close to a compliment as the Northmen would ever get.

Just like that, it was over. They were no longer vangels. *Who will I be now that my self-identity has been taken away?* Regina wondered. Others were apparently just as bewildered.

In the confusion and talking among themselves that ensued, Regina got separated from Zeb. That was just as well. She had much to think about.

Not only had she lost her vangelness in one blow, she'd also lost her fiancé. Should she be glad or sad about that?

Even angels need closure sometimes ...

Zeb forced his way through the crowd until he got close to Michael. When he caught the archangel's eye, he said, "I beg permission to speak."

Michael nodded.

"Are you saying that I am free?"

"As free as any others here."

"But . . . but . . . I was a Lucipire."

"Was," Michael emphasized. "Thou does not need to remind me of that unsavory fact."

"I've been 'imprisoned' here awaiting your decision on my fate."

Michael nodded. "Betimes Vikar oversteps himself." Apparently, Michael had been aware of Zeb's whereabouts. Zeb hadn't needed to remind him of that. "For killing Jasper?"

"Yes."

"What makes you think that Vikar's sin of pride was any less for wanting to be the master executioner?"

Zeb hadn't considered that. He frowned, not fully understanding. "The things Jasper told me at the end . . ."

"Pfff! Now you listen to a demon?"

It sounded ridiculous when Michael said it like that. But what Jasper had said couldn't be discounted so easily. "He said my wife cursed me for abandoning my family."

"Sarah forgave you long ago. Where she is now, there is no place for blame or resentment."

"But . . ." Zeb made a motion with his hand to indicate what had just happened in this room. "I don't deserve forgiveness."

"When will people learn? It is for God to decide whom to forgive and whom not to forgive."

"My guilt is huge."

"Mayhap thou needest what modern folks call closure," Michael advised in a rather tongue-in-cheek manner. But then he wagged his forefinger at Zeb. "Stop flailing thyself. Trust in the Lord."

On those words of advice, Michael turned to speak with the next person waiting for his attention. As he was about to walk away, Zeb could swear he saw Michael wink at him.

In a sort of daze, Zeb made his way through the crowd, both incoming and exiting, many of them bunched up around the hall table signing the register for Tranquility. Zeb should have looked for Regina, but first he had some other things to do. Closure, that's what Michael said he needed. In that instant, Zeb made a decision.

He was going home. For the first time in one thousand, nine hundred, and forty one years, he was going back to Israel.

Letting go . . .

Regina didn't bother to wait for Zeb. She'd seen him go up to Michael, and she'd heard part of the conversation. It was about Zeb's wife. Was Zeb being given a chance to live his human life over with Sarah and his two children?

Michael hadn't quite said that with his announcement today, but he hadn't discounted it either. Surely, that must be what Zeb was asking. When Michael had offered the option of living out a human life, had he meant here or in the past? Either/or?

Well, Regina, for one, had no interest in returning to the old Norselands and her life as a witch. But what *did* she want?

Regina decided that she would be the better person, if she was going to live a rocky human life. Despite the pain in her heart, she could only wish Zeb well. Being given a second chance to change the course of his family's history . . . that was a blessing she couldn't deny him. Sometimes, love really did mean letting go.

She made her way through the corridor and back through the kitchen where Lizzie was doing what she always did. Cooking. Regina gave her a little wave as she passed through, wondering what the old lady would decide in her own case. Would she stay or go?

When she got to the rental car that she'd parked in the back parking lot, she saw that Thor was sitting on the passenger seat, waiting for her.

"So, now you're my best pal again, huh?"

Thor just meowed.

"Let's go then," she said. "I sure hope you like gumbo."

You can't go home again ...

Zeb had only been in Israel for a day when he realized how foolish he'd been. He'd never considered himself naïve, but how could he have thought he'd find answers in a land which in no way resembled the place of his birth?

In fact, his old vineyard was now covered by a shopping mall. A shopping mall! It boggled his mind. All these years, when he'd been forbidden to return to his homeland, he'd been imagining it staying the same, or at least that there would still be a vineyard there in the good earth. The only beverage coming out of that ground now was Coke coming out of the counter dispenser at McDonald's.

Alas! Technology had taken over even that remote region, which of course was not so remote anymore with the advent of cars, planes, and other modes of transportation. Not wanting to make his trip a totally wasted effort, Zeb spent many hours in the museums . . . both regional and big city ones, like Tel Aviv.

At Masada, he found his answers. And his closure.

Masada was located on a plateau high atop a mountain in the Israeli desert, not easily accessed by foot. The first day, he traveled up to the top in a cable car, like all the other tourists. Who wouldn't be touched by this tragic site where 967 zealots, including men, women, and children, held off more than ten thousand Roman soldiers for three years? In the end, they'd supposedly committed mass suicide.

Zeb knew differently, or at least he had viewed, personally, a different side of the final outcome there.

After his initial tour of the fortress, he spent his days in the Masada museum at the base of the mountain. Because he displayed an extraordinary ability to read the old documents in their original language, the historians allowed him access to the private rooms. There, Zeb saw a list of those "zealots" who'd lived under siege there, those that could be identified. When he came to the names Sarah bat Rivkah, Rachel bat Sarah, and Mikah ben Zebulan, he gasped and fought back tears. There was also information on his brother-in-law Benjamin ben David, identified as one of the ringleaders of the "freedom fighters."

Writings on parchment attributed to Benjamin were kept in special glass cases. They were a sort of diary, not day-by-day, but occasional entries up until the end. It was the lines on the last page that struck Zeb. "Sarah weeps for her husband. Even yet, she believes he will come to rescue her."

That didn't sound like Jasper's remark that Sarah had cursed him.

Of course, her lingering belief in him hurt just as much.

"Trust in God," Michael had advised him. So, he spent many hours on his knees in a small chapel after that. Finally, he came to the realization: His life . . . his entire thirty human and one thousand, nine hundred and forty-one Lucipire years . . . had been wasted on regrets. What might have beens, what he should have dones. It was time to put regrets to rest. Time to move forward. This was the first day of the rest of his life.

Closure? he wondered. *Is that what this is?*
Yes!
Now, if it wasn't too late!

Rainy days ahead . . .

A week after the Final Reckoning, Regina was working in the small garden of the cottage she'd rented in southern Louisiana. Tante Lulu had helped her find the property, which wasn't anywhere near as nice as hers, but had promise.

It was one of those houses on stilts that were popular in the swampy regions of the bayou which often flooded. The overgrown garden, which was on a slightly elevated area, had been planted by the owner before going into a nursing home.

Regina had half expected Zeb to follow her to Louisiana, to beg her forgiveness, or something, even though she'd heard his conversation with Michael about his dead wife and family in Israel, but after the days went by, she had to face facts. And then, she'd talked to Ivak, who was over at Heaven's End, undecided about whether to stay and fix up the place again or move somewhere else. Ivak had heard, secondhand, that Zeb had gone to Israel, just as she'd suspected.

So, Regina's assumptions had been true. He was going to live his old life over again, with his family. She couldn't blame him. It hurt like hell, but it was probably the right thing to do. Dammit!

"Are you sure about that?" Ivak had remarked. "I haven't heard about anyone else being offered that opportunity."

"Can you think of anyone else who would have wanted it?" she'd countered. Most vangels wanted to forget about their former sinful lives.

"You have a point there," Ivak had concluded.

On her knees, weeding the garden, Regina uncovered still healthy tomato plants and root vegetables, along with lots of okra, which she hated. Apparently, you couldn't kill off okra with dynamite, let alone a few measly weeds. Thor was having a field day sniffing catnip that the former owner must have planted.

She heard a car drive up and stood, dusting some dirt off her hands and knees. She was wearing farmer-style coveralls with a tank top underneath. Her hair was in pigtails. Walking toward the vehicle, her eyes about bugged out. It was a 1960s-era Chevy Impala convertible in a pale lavender color. A St. Jude bobblehead doll still wobbled on the dashboard, and a bumper sticker said "Not too close, I'm not that kind of girl." Sitting behind the wheel, propped up on pillows, no doubt, was the inimitable Tante Lulu.

"Should a woman your age still be driving an automobile?" Regina asked.

"Huh? I ain't that old. Besides, a gal is only as old as she feels, and I feel 'bout twenty-five."

In your dreams! "I thought you were coming over with someone named Lillian," Regina said, going up to the car.

"This *is* Lillian," the old lady said, patting the steering wheel. "Ah brought ya a present, sweetie. It's in the trunk."

Regina opened the driver's door and helped Tante Lulu step down. Today, she had a blond Farrah Fawcett wig on, with big sunglasses, which she removed and tucked into a pocketbook the size of Vermont. On top, she wore a pink T-shirt with the logo "I Got Game" tucked into white pedal pushers. She didn't have any shoes on.

When Regina looked pointedly at her bare feet, Tante Lulu said, "Mah corns was botherin' me."

Regina took the keys that the old lady handed her and opened the trunk. Inside was a St. Jude statue. Surprise, surprise!

"Jist in case ya were feelin' hopeless," Tante Lulu said.

"Perfect," Regina replied. "Thank you."

"I also brought ya some St. Jude place mats and some St. Jude wind chimes and a St. Jude salt shaker. I even got a St. Jude medal fer Thor's collar."

Whoop-ee! "Thank you," Regina said again.

Tante Lulu, for all her eccentric appearance and intrusive interference in everyone's lives, was an accomplished folk healer, and her knowledge of medicinal herbs was astounding. She knew things that couldn't be found in books. And, graciously, she'd been tutoring Regina the past few days on the possibility that this was an occupation Regina might want to pursue.

Regina wasn't sure about that. First of all, could she make a living from it? Plus, she wondered if she shouldn't go to school to learn, not just a trade, but everyday things. Regina had never been to school. Ever.

Tante Lulu left an hour later after also leaving her a tray of homemade cinnamon buns. Regina had commented, "I thought Cajuns were more into beignets and pralines and sweets like that."

"We are, but I just had a yen fer cinnamon buns t'day. It was almost lak St. Jude was tellin' me ta make 'em."

Uh-huh!

"They give me heartburn."

Me, too.

Just before she left, Tante Lulu looked up at the sky. "I think a storm mus' be comin'. I smell rain."

Yeah, Regina did, too. All the time.

Beau showed up then to help her fix the bed frame in the cottage's single bedroom. While he was inside, and Regina was putting the cinnamon buns into a plastic container, she heard another car approach.

What was it today with all these visitors?

She went out on the porch that faced the bayou and noticed that this time it was a Jeep-type vehicle that had arrived.

And it was Zeb.

Her heart skipped a beat, then went into overdrive.

"Do you have any idea how much trouble I've had finding you?"

Not enough! Oh, Lord, I think I'm going to have a heart attack.

"There are no signs on this frickin' one-lane bayou road."

It's the South, idiot. What did you expect? Be still, heart. Be still.

"And I couldn't ask anyone where you live because you never told me your last name. Do you have a last name?"

I do now. Regina Dorasdottir. Regina HeartRacing-LikeaNASCAR. Regina Ithoughtyouwouldnevercome.

"Some crazy old lady . . . a Cajun yenta . . . in a purple convertible almost ran me off the road."

Good!

"And I'm getting a sunburn."

No more pretty vangel suntans!

"I thought you were back in Israel with your wife and children, running a vineyard."

"Huh? There is no vineyard there anymore." He tilted his head to the side, then seemed to understand. "You thought . . . no, that was never an option. I can explain—"

"Don't bother." *Please do.*

"Hi, Thor! What's up? Met any Cajun kitties yet?"

Go ahead, Thor. Pee on his boot. No, no, I didn't mean lick. Traitor!

"Doucet, what the hell are you doing here?"

Regina turned to see Beau standing in the doorway, grinning like a loon. He gave Zeb a little wave.

Another traitor.

"Ah bin jist fixin' the bed," Beau said.

"Get out!" Zeb yelled.

What? "The rope broke on the bed support. He was just helping me," Regina explained, though why she felt Zeb needed an explanation was beyond her.

"Get out!" he told Beau again.

"Hey, you can't order my visitor around," Regina said.

"I can if I want to. What's he doing sniffing around you?"

Sniffing? Zeb must be going loony tunes if he thought Beau was interested in her that way. But she liked it. "I'll have you know, Beau is going to be a priest."

"I was going to be a priest, too, but it didn't stop me from wanting to screw you upside down and sideways."

"Nice talk!" *Picturing it here. Picturing it.*

Then she noticed that Zeb was pulling his T-shirt over his head and unzipping his jeans. *"What* are you doing?"

"Ah think it's time fer me ta make an exit." Beau chuckled and skipped down the steep steps and around Zeb. He winked at Regina before he got in his car and drove away, tooting his horn.

"What are you doing?" Regina repeated.

At the foot of the steps, he tossed his T-shirt aside and toed off his boots. His open jeans hung on his hips. He wasn't wearing any underwear. His hair had grown out enough that it resembled one of Trond's military haircuts. She also noticed that his beautiful eyelashes were half-mast and sexy as hell as he answered her, "What am I doing? I'm getting ready to do what I should have done long ago. I'm going to lay you down and rock your world. About a dozen times. Then I'm going to let you do the same to me. Then you could maybe show me how you masturbate. I've been fantasizing about how . . . never mind. For now. And I might spank you, *à la* Fifty Shades of Perversion, if you beg me. After that, we'll probably get married."

Oh, boy! "Is that a fact?" She put her hands on her hips, but she was smiling.

"Guar-an-teed!"

"You're learning Cajun real fast."

"Wait till you see what else I've learned."

She was pretty sure it was raining somewhere.

Epilogue

As the vangel world turns ...

Regina and Zeb were married a month later at the castle in Transylvania. It was the first time the remaining one hundred vangels had gotten together since the Final Reckoning.

Those who had not already gone on to Tranquility were biding their time on making a decision. That didn't include Regina and Zeb, though. They'd already decided to stay in the present as humans and take their chances that they could live on the straight and narrow. If not, they had Tante Lulu to help them stay on track. They were going to live in Louisiana as honorary Cajuns ... a designation given them by the bayou dingbat ... uh, senior citizen. For the time being, anyhow.

Regina wore a traditional white gown and veil for her wedding. Vera Wang, no less. Anyone who dared to object to a witch wearing white might very well find themselves cursed, or so she threatened.

Zeb wore a black tuxedo, and his hair was long enough now that he could at least brush it wetly off his face. Which made him even more sexy, Regina said to one and all.

Tante Lulu and her LeDeux family gang came north for the wedding and fit right in with the wacky townsfolk in Transylvania. In fact, they stayed two extra days to take in all the sights. The mayor of Transylvania invited Tante Lulu to come back in October for the Halloween Vampire Parade, but she'd had to decline. Couldn't stay away from the bayou on that holiday! She was planning on dressing as Elvira this year.

Vikar gave Regina away, and was heard to mutter to his wife, "And it's about time we got rid of the witch!"

To which, Alex had replied, "Better be careful, or she'll turn your Seventh Wonder into a pretzel." Seventh Wonder was the name she had given his you-know-what of late. Everyone wanted to know what his six other wonders were, especially his brothers who were always interested in anything to do with sex.

Trond served as Zeb's best man and claimed that he knew all along that the former Lucipire would end up with a witch someday. A fitting conclusion to a demonic life!

Zeb had countered that at least he didn't have a wife who could beat him up. Trond's wife was a female Navy SEAL.

The other five Sigurdsson brothers served as groomsmen, along with Beau Doucet. The matron of honor was Alex Sigurdsson. The bridesmaids were Nicole; Camille; Mordr's wife, Miranda; Sigurd's wife, Marisa; Cnut's wife, Andrea; and Tante Lulu, who was actually stunning in a

Donna Karan fuchsia sheath dress and fuchsia high heels, that went well with her hot pink hair. All the attendants wore Donna Karan in different colors.

Thor was left behind to guard the stilted cottage which Zeb and Regina were going to buy. What they were going to do for work later was yet to be decided. They were taking their time, like all the other former vangels. And, no, Zeb had told Ivak adamantly, he did not want to take over his job as chaplain at Angola Prison. In fact, Zeb was looking into the possibility of starting his own vineyard. The bayou lands with their humid temperatures and frequent flooding might not be the best place for that.

Andrea, a chef, worked with Tante Lulu to create a five-tiered Peachy Praline Cobbler Wedding Cake, but it had cinnamon crumbles along the edges, at the groom's request.

There was a light shower just before the outdoor ceremony, but everyone said it lent a fresh rain scent to the entire event afterward.

The priest from St. Vladimir's Catholic Church was supposed to perform the marriage ceremony, but at the last minute St. Michael showed up to do the job. He explained to the congregation, "God sent me. The Good Lord likes nothing better than a lost sheep come back to the fold."

Many in attendance weren't sure if Michael was referring to Zeb or to them. But there was a lot of surreptitious baa-ing going on. Vikings did like to mock each other.

Michael also agreed to a second ceremony in a modified Jewish fashion, in deference to Zebulan's Hebrew heritage. The ritual was performed under an open-sided canopy called a chuppah and led eventually to the Seven Blessings. At the end, a wineglass was placed on the floor which Zeb crushed with his shoe to symbolize the destruction of the Temple of Jerusalem. But some of the Vikings were said to remark that it was the last time Zeb would be able to put his foot down with his witchy wife.

After the ceremony and the meal, catered by Lizzie Borden, of course, the party became loud and raucous. These were mostly Vikings, after all, and Vikings knew how to have a good time. So did Cajuns. At one point when the band was playing "When the Saints Go Marching In" (though none of them were saints . . . far from it!), someone spoke into the microphone, "Hey, how about the Michael dance?"

Over the years, the Sigurdsson men had watched the movie *Michael* in which a crude, cigarette-smoking version of the archangel Michael, did a really cool, snake-like dance to the song "Chain of Fools." And so the Sigurdsson men showed just what moves a Viking man had. To everyone's surprise, Zeb joined in. After all, he'd been practicing Viking for a long time, or so he told the laughing crowd.

Not to be undone, the LeDeux men did a wild Village People version of "Macho Man" in which they changed the lyrics to "Cajun Man." Those Cajuns could dance!

Zeb and Regina were going on a honeymoon to some secret location, which they wouldn't reveal to anyone (can anyone say Caribbean Island hideaway?), but for that night they were staying in the Dracula suite at the local Blood & Guts Hotel. It promised all the comforts of a queen-size, satin-lined coffin bed with cup holders for Bloody Marys and a built-in sound system that played dirge music. They couldn't wait.

A seed was planted that night in Transylvania which answered that age-old question: Could ex-vampires have children?

They could.

Reader Letter

Dear Readers:

Did you like Zeb's story? I wanted this book to be special, to please so many of you who have grown attached to the "good demon" and wanted him to get his well-deserved redemption. I think Zeb touches us because no one is perfect, and we want to believe that second chances are available, even to the most hardened sinner.

Well, that completes the series . . . for now. All seven Sigurdsson brothers have had their stories, along with Zeb, and Karl Mortenssen in a separate novella, Christmas in Transylvania. *Will there be any more Deadly Angels books? Probably not. But who can say? Never say never, right? At the least, there might be a novella.*

I hope you'll go back and read the entire series, if you haven't already. Kiss of Pride, Kiss of Surrender, Kiss of Temptation, Kiss of Wrath, Kiss of Persuasion, Even Vampires Get the Blues, The Angel Wore Fangs, *and* Good Vampires Go to Heaven.

I took poetic license in two instances in Good Vampires Go to Heaven:

—Contrary to popular opinion, the women killed
during the Salem Witch Trials were hanged, not
burned at the stake. I chose to go with the popular,
yet incorrect, fire deaths.

—There really was a tragic event at Masada, a fortress
located atop an isolated rocky plateau in the southern part of Israel overlooking the Dead Sea. For three
years, just decades after the death of Jesus Christ,
967 Hebrew zealots held out against a Roman legion
of 15,000 soldiers. Unlike my story, however, they
ultimately committed mass suicide rather than surrender to their enemy. There was no fire.

*If my books have helped you develop a taste for
Vikings, you've got to watch the History Channel's Vikings series. Many of the historical characters in that series were already in my Viking
historical romances. In fact, some of them, like
Rollo (aka Rolf the Gangr, first duke of Norse-
mandy), are actual ancestors of mine. Honest!*

So what next?

*First off, some contemporaries. The infamous
Tante Lulu wants to get a few more Cajun stories out there, before she gets too old. Look forward to the LeDeux twins from Alaska: Daniel,
the burned-out pediatric oncologist, and Aaron,
the pilot. There are other contemporaries I have
in mind, as well, all with my trademark humor
and sizzle.*

*I also want to write more Viking historical
romances. Those of you who've read my books
know who I'm talking about. Alrek the Clumsy
Viking. Finn Finehair, the vainest Viking to ride
a longship. Tykir's other sons, Starri, Guthrom,*

and Selik. Jamie the Scots Viking. And so on. You gotta love a Viking!

Of course there are those Viking Navy SEAL time travel books. We can't forget these SEALs: JAM (Jacob Alvarez Mendoza), the former Jesuit priest; K-4, Kevin Fortunato; Geek (Darryl Good), the genius inventor of the penileglove.com with the boyish good looks; FU (Frank Uxley), etc. And, of course, there are all those female SEALs, members of WEALS (Women on Earth, Air, Land, and Sea).

Please write and tell me what you'd like to read next. I love hearing from readers. I can be reached at my website, www.sandrahill.net, where you can sign up for my mailing list, or you can get news on my Facebook page at Sandra Hill Author.

As always, I wish you smiles in your reading,

Sandra Hill

Glossary

al-Qaeda—militant Sunni Islamic organization founded by Osama bin Laden, Abdullah Azzam, and others.

Archipelago—an island group or island chain

Armageddon—the final battle between good and evil foretold in the Bible

A-Viking—a Norse practice of sailing away to other countries for the purpose of looting, settlement, or mere adventure; could be for a period of several months or years at a time

Baldr (alternate spellings Balder, Baldur, etc.)—god of goodness and peace, son of the chief god Odin and his wife, the goddess Frigg

Bane—poison

Bayou—body of slow-moving water typically located in flat, low-lying areas, often swampy surroundings

Beowulf—legendary warrior who was hero of the Old English poem "Beowulf" as well as an opera by Wagner

Boko Haram—a militant Islamic terrorist organization based in northeast Nigeria, responsible for many deaths and kidnappings; its purpose is to institute Sharia, or Islamic law, including the ban on all western education

Braies—slim pants worn by men

Broadsword—heavy sword with a broad blade for cutting rather than thrusting

Cajun—Louisianan descended from French-speaking immigrants from Acadia

Capuchin—a religious order of friars stemming from the original order of St. Francis of Assisi

Catacombs—a subterranean cemetery of galleries with recesses for tombs

Chère—dear in Cajun (female)

Cotters—peasant farmers

Creole—a person descended from early French or Spanish settlers of the U.S. Gulf states with preserved speech and culture

Fake-O—synthetic blood drunk by vangels when other blood not available

Gammelost—stinky cheese, rumored to be so bad that it turned men berserk

Gunna—long-sleeved, ankle-length gown for women, often worn under a tunic or surcoat, or under a long, open-sided apron

Haakai—high-level demon

Hordlings—lower-level demons

Imps—lowest level demons, foot soldiers so to speak

ISIS—Islamic State of Iraq and al-Sham, extreme Muslim group

Jarl—high-ranking Norseman similar to an English earl, or wealthy landowner, could also be a minor king

Kaupang—a Viking-age market town, one of the first towns in Norway

Longships—narrow, open watergoing vessels with oars and square sails, perfected by Viking shipbuilders, noted for their speed and ability to ride in both shallow waters and deep oceans

Lucifer/Satan—the fallen angel Lucifer became known as the demon Satan

Lucipires—demon vampires led by fallen angel Jasper

Mais, oui—But, yes

Mancus—a unit of measurement or coin equal roughly to 4.5 grams of gold or thirty silver pence, also equal to one month's wages for a skilled worker in medieval times

Masada—ancient, tragic fortress in southern district of Israel, located on top of an isolated, rocky plateau

Mead—fermented honey and water

Mikvah—a pool of water used for ritual bathing

Motte—a high flat-topped mound; with a motte and bailey castle it would be a wood or stone keep on a raised earthwork, surrounded by protective ditches and palisades

Mung—type of demon, below the haakai in status, often very large and oozing slime and mung

Muslim—a religion based on the Koran with the belief that the word of God was revealed through the prophet Mohammed

Newt—type of salamander

Norselands—early term referring not just to Norway but all the Scandinavian countries as a whole

Northumbria—one of the Anglo-Saxon kingdoms, bordered by the English kingdoms to the south and in the north and northwest by the Scots, Cumbrians, and Strathclyde Welsh

Odin—king of all the Viking gods

Pheromones—chemicals secreted in sweat or body fluids believed to influence the behavior of the opposite sex

Purgatory—intermediate state after physical death in which those destined for heaven undergo purification

Sabre—a light fencing or dueling sword having an arched guard that covers the back of the hand and a tapering flexible blade with a full cutting edge along one side and a partial cutting edge on the back of the tip

Sac-au-lait—type of fish, also known as crappie

SEAL—Sea, Air, and Land

Sennight—one week

Skald—poet

Stasis—state of inactivity or numbness, condition in which the person cannot move

Tangos—terrorists, bad guys

Teletransport—transfer of matter from one point to another without traversing physical space

Thor—god of war

Tranquility—place where dead vangels go until the Final Judgment Day

Tun—unit of liquid capacity equal to 252 gallons

Tundra—level or undulating treeless plain that is characteristic of arctic and subarctic regions

Vangels—Viking vampire angels

Vieux Carré—French Quarter of New Orleans

VIK—the seven Sigurdsson brothers who head the vangels

WEALS—Women on Earth, Air, Land, and Sea

Don't miss the next book by *New York Times* bestselling author

SANDRA HILL

The Cajun Doctor

Coming soon from Avon Books!

Bewitched, Bothered and Doggone Bewildered...

Samantha approached Rose Alley that afternoon with trepidation. After her embarrassing dream, she didn't want to be within a mile of Doctor Dreamy, but she'd promised Tante Lulu she would come to discuss some ideas for abandoned animals to be relocated here, assuming Daniel and Aaron were on board. Of course, it would be a long time before they would be in a position to offer any services on a large scale; work would be needed on the facilities to meet health code specs and zoning regulations for the kennels. If in fact that would be the ultimate use made of the plantation. So, plenty of time for convincing. On Tante Lulu's part, not hers.

As she drove up, she could see that the old lady had turned this into a party, as usual. The landscaping people were already hard at work, clearing away the jungle, with the help of every LeDeux in the world, it seemed. Dozens of them, of all ages. And was that . . . yes, it was that notorious snake catcher Stinky Hawkins. The *Times-Picayune* ran feature articles on him every other year.

Of course the first person she ran into was Daniel. As she approached, they glared at each other. He didn't like her any more than she liked him. He seemed to think she was a spoiled rich girl who'd never struggled a day in her life. She didn't have much use for doctors per se, especially good-looking ones, after her experience with Nick, but if he was going to have the credentials, she thought it was selfish of him not to use those talents. Egotism, either way.

Then, at the same time, they both started to say, "I had a dream . . ."

She slapped a hand over her mouth with horror at her inadvertent admission.

"Oh, crap!" he said. "We had dreams about each other, didn't we? The same dream."

"I don't know what you're talking about."

He snorted his disbelief.

"Bite me!"

"Seems I already did."

"Did you do something to plant those . . . those perverted ideas in my head?"

"You thought they were perverted? Even the suck and tuck move?"

She ignored his question and continued, "You're supposedly a doctor. Bet you slipped me a pill or something." It's the kind of thing Nick would have done in a heartbeat, if he'd thought of it. But probably not with her. He'd want to play out his fantasies with one of his many mistresses.

"No *supposed* about it. I *am* a doctor, even if I don't practice anymore. What you're suggesting is criminal behavior, which I would never participate in. Nor would I need to." He raised his chin defiantly.

"Oh, jeez. No need to get bent out of shape. I didn't really think you gave me anything."

He visibly tamped down his temper. "Let's return to that 'perversions' discussion—"

"Please don't."

"I've never heard about that new erogenous zone . . . you know, the one you showed me in the dream. They certainly never taught *that* in medical school. I figured it was some *Cosmo* kind of thing."

"I don't read *Cosmo*. It wasn't me who . . . never mind."

He waggled his eyebrows.

Samantha was embarrassed. Every single time she met Daniel their conversations seemed to spiral out of control. They threw sparks off each other, and she was at least partly to blame, she knew that.

Time to change the subject. Samantha inhaled and exhaled. Once again, Daniel had managed to bring out this bitchy side of her personality. Yeah, he was a doctor, but she should be able to judge people on their own merits, not by their professions. It was Nick's fault, she decided. That was her story, and she was sticking to it. For now.

"I brought you a housewarming gift," she said, in a forced tone of politeness.

He grinned, sensing how hard it was for her to be nice to him.

"This is Max. A kitty just for you."

He stopped grinning.

Out shot a golden-haired Maine Coon cat with a lopsided red bow tied around its neck. The cat immediately went over to Daniel and hissed up at him.

"That's not a kitty. It's a pony. How much do you

feed this animal? Do they have Weight Watchers
for cats?"

"Max likes to snack on mice."

"Eeew! I hate cats."

"I think Max likes you." The cat was clawing
at his pant leg with one paw. "Oh, isn't that cute?
Max wants a hug."

Carefully, he lifted the animal as if it might
attack at any minute. Which it might. "I hate cats,"
he repeated.

Max licked his face, and he cringed, then hid
a smile. Samantha could tell that he didn't hate
cats as much as he claimed. Bored with licking,
Max jumped down and rushed over to sniff at the
snake barrel.

"Max could probably catch snakes, too. In addition to mice."

"Oh, that's just wonderful."

Just then, Tante Lulu noticed them from over at
the buffet table set out on the ground-floor veran-
dah. "Yoo hoo! Over here."

She and Daniel glanced at each other, remembered the dream, and stomped toward the old
lady for a confrontation.

"Did you put a spell on us?" Samantha demanded to know.

"Huh?"

"I thought you didn't believe in that voodoo
junk," Daniel added.

"Huh?"

"Don't play the innocent with me, you med-
dling dingbat. I know what you're capable of."
Daniel looked as if he'd like to throttle Tante Lulu.

The old lady narrowed her eyes at him. "I doan

like yer tone, boy. If yer not careful, I'm gonna toss ya in one of Stinky's snake barrels." Then she turned to Samantha with a smile. "Did I tell ya Daniel ain't gay?"

Daniel stiffened.

Samantha had to laugh. The old lady sure knew which buttons to push on Daniel. She was always telling people that he wasn't gay. She wasn't sure if it was because he rarely dated, or because of his appearance, which didn't look gay to her, or something else.

But Daniel was learning not to rise to her jibes every time. He just walked away.

"Looks like they're making a lot of progress outside," Samantha remarked then. The wide area between the alleé, or alley, of live oaks, now the horseshoe-shaped driveway, facing the bayou, had been denuded and new grass sewn. The branches with hanging moss of the two-hundred-year-old trees on either side of the road had grown together into a canopy of sorts. Right now a sprinkler system was in operation to get the lawn going, although it rained so often in this semi-tropical climate that it probably wasn't necessary. Workers were tackling the garden on one side of the house and putting paving stones around the *garconniére* on the other side.

Tante Lulu nodded. "Helps when ya got family ta pitch in."

"And money to pay an army of workers." Samantha had heard the two brothers were fairly well off, but she knew from friends' experiences with old house renovations that money wells could soon become money pits.

"That, too." Tante Lulu was in a gardening outfit today. Straw hat, coveralls, and sneakers. Her hair appeared to be purple, or maybe it was a wig. Little dangly earrings in the shape of shovels and rakes hung from her ears. Gardener chic? "C'mon. I'll show ya 'round, 'specially the area where I think they could house some animals, if we kin convince Aaron and Daniel."

Samantha didn't like the sound of that *we*.

"Show me, too," Daniel said, coming up behind them.

Samantha glanced his way with chagrin.

"What? I'd like to know what the old bird's plans are, too, especially since I own half the place. I still don't understand how we could house a bunch of animals here. Who's gonna take care of them? I mean, there would have to be a manager or vet on hand, wouldn't there?" He noticed Tante Lulu grinning at him. "Oh, no! I'm not qualified—"

"A doctor's a doctor, I allus say."

"Forget about it!"

"Whatever you say," Tante Lulu said with a meekness suspicious to say the least.

"And where do you expect me and Aaron to be when this is going on?"

"It's all in St. Jude's hands, honey."

Samantha could tell he was restraining himself from saying something nasty, even sacrilegious.

"Besides, I have the perfect person in mind fer manager," Tante Lulu added.

"Who?" Daniel demanded to know.

"I'll tell ya when the time is right."

"By the way, Daniel." Samantha had an idea.

"Do you know what you need to keep your lawn nice and tidy?"

"Does Hummer make lawn mowers?"

"Very funny. A goat."

"A what? No, no, no! A monster cat, I can accept"—said cat was lying on the grass, munching on something. He hoped it was catnip—"but no goats. No way! And what the hell are you doing with a goat anyway?"

"Thass a great idea," Tante Lulu said to Samantha. To Daniel, she explained, "Samantha rescues animals in her spare time. Bet she's got a goat or two. Bet she could give ya some dogs, too. Or wouldja prefer pigs and rats."

Daniel turned to stare at Samantha with surprise. "You have pigs and rats?"

"Well, I did have a pig. A pot-bellied pig. Not the kind you raise for meat. But no rats; Tante Lulu was referring to gerbils. And, actually, I got rid of . . . I mean, I found a home for . . . the goat this morning. One goat, not two," she said pointedly, glancing toward Tante Lulu. "A farmer from Alabama, in town for the Holstein convention, heard about my goat. And he also took the pot-bellied pig, the goose, and all the ducks, as well. My neighbors are probably celebrating as we speak. There had been talk about goose liver pâté and Peking duck."

Daniel's jaw dropped with amazement, whether at her array of pets, or her as their caretaker, she wasn't sure. But then, his quick survey of her attire ended with, "Been shopping at Wal-Mart, have you?"

Okay, so he had a point there. Samantha did

like designer clothing, some of which might not be animal-friendly. Today, she wore a Pucci silk, one-shoulder blouse in a shell and seagull motif with artful knots at the shoulder and hemline, over stretch cotton, crop pants, Rebecca Minkoff ankle cuff sandals, a floppy straw sun hat, and Kate Spade retro sunglasses.

His sarcasm deserved no response. She could have countered with an argument that quality merchandise lasted forever and never went out of style. Or she could have countered with a comment about his khakis and loafers as inappropriate for the outdoor work to be done here today. Instead, she continued her earlier conversation about rescue animals. "Not to worry about missing out on the goat, though, Daniel. I have lots of other animals left. Can anyone say monkey? Or cockatoo?" Samantha batted her eyelashes at Daniel, hoping to have a customer. As much as she'd come to care for her rescued pets, it would be nice to have an empty house for a change. Not that she'd ever be totally empty. No way would she give away her German Shepherd, Axel, or Max's feline sister, Maddie.

"I do not want any more animals." He enunciated each word for emphasis. "And don't be giving me those come-hither eyes unless you're ready to hither."

The image of their shared dream shimmered in the air between them.

Samantha could feel herself blush.

Daniel just grinned.

"Jeesh! Doan get yerself in a snit," Tante Lulu said to Daniel. To Samantha, she whispered,

"Mebbe ya should ask Aaron instead. He ain't so persnickety."

"I am not persnickety, whatever the hell that is," Daniel protested. "By the way, old lady, I don't appreciate your setting up a medical practice for me, either."

"Oh, did all them poor sick folks come t'day?" Tante Lulu inquired with the innocence of a cobra.

"Where's Aaron?" Samantha asked, trying to defuse the situation, although she had no idea what they were talking about. Another of Tante Lulu's machinations, she was sure. Although, if it had anything to do with Daniel being a doctor, she could understand. It was selfish of Daniel to waste his medical skills. Selfish, self-centered, arrogant. Just like all the doctors she knew! Or most of them.

"He was here all morning. Not sure where he disappeared to," Daniel said, frowning, as if he'd just realized his brother was missing.

Tante Lulu, who had started to climb the steep steps in front of them, had the answer. "He's over at the Doucet gator farm, tryin' ta sweet-talk Del."

"That's just great," Daniel remarked. "He'll be back soon, or I'll go drag him back. He's not leaving me here alone to handle this mess."

Samantha homed in on only one thing. "Gator farm?"

"Don't ask," Daniel warned.

Off Tante Lulu went then, talking away, regardless of whether anyone was listening.

Turns out, the old lady was an excellent tour guide, Samantha had to give her that, as Tante Lulu interspersed her descriptions of the various rooms with a bit of the history of the house and the property that she knew so well. In fact, old sepia photographs of the house as it had looked in the mid and late 1800s were tacked on the wall of the entry hall.

Still other photos showed the exterior and interior of the house as it had been during more prosperous days. Unfortunately, all the furniture, fine Aubusson and Tabriz carpets, and paintings were gone now, even the lighting fixtures, but the painted-over woodwork, ceiling medallions, and ornate crown molding remained, along with the wide, carved stairway that ran up the center of the main floor's hallway and the sliding pocket doors, a Victorian-era addition, separating the rooms. Although they were scuffed and ingrained with decades of dirt, the random-plank cypress floors would be magnificent when refinished. And the tall, floor-to-ceiling windows remained intact, albeit with wavy glass.

Rooms on each of the three floors were separated by a twelve-foot corridor . . . wasted space in today's house designs. On the main floor, there were two parlors, a dining room, library, and office. Eight bedrooms on the second floor and four on the third floor, along with a nursery or schoolroom and servant quarters. There were a total of three full and four half bathrooms, which had been installed at the turn of the last century . . . as in clawfoot tubs and pedestal sinks and shaving mirrors . . . on these three floors, along with the ground level where the kitchen, pantries, laundry, and other storage rooms were located. Only two of the bathrooms were functioning. There was no basement because of the high water table here in Southern Louisiana.

"Did you know the original owners?" Daniel asked.

"Idjit!" Tante Lulu jabbed him with an elbow. "How old ya think I am?"

"I meant the last owners," Daniel amended.

"Oh, okay, then. Yep, the DuBois fam'ly lived here when I was growin' up. Left suddenly 'bout thirty years ago. Rumor was there was some kinda hanky panky takin' place with Missy DuBois and them dogs."

Samantha wouldn't touch that last observation with a ten-foot barge pole.

Daniel made a sound that was halfway between a snort and a chuckle.

Time for another change of subject. "Forget about the kennels. This would make a wonderful family home," Samantha remarked. "I can see all the possibilities for restoration, but also ways to make it a comfortable living space. Children would flourish in this setting." In fact, it was the type of home she'd always dreamed of. Before she'd become disillusioned by Nick and her failed marriage.

Her Garden District home in New Orleans was more than adequate, but not perfect, for kids who needed, or would appreciate, open spaces to run and play, not to mention the bayou for swimming and fishing. If she'd gotten pregnant with Nick (hopefully, three times . . . two girls and one boy), she would have moved. Maybe that was another reason Nick had been unhappy with her. He was definitely a city person.

She glanced up to see Daniel watching her closely before he asked, "Is this the type of home you grew up in?"

"Hardly. We had nice homes, don't get me wrong." In fact, luxurious. "But my father married six times, and changed houses each time. My mother cavorted around Europe, never spending more than a year in any one place. She practically invented the word 'cougar' for older women, younger men."

"And you?"

"I spent most of my time in boarding schools since I was eight. Same for my younger half-brother, Wallace. Way younger. Plus, we grew up in different homes with different mothers. We were never close." Suddenly, she realized how much she'd revealed and turned away from him.

Luckily, Tante Lulu picked up the conversation. "If yer grandma Sophie hadn't been ill fer so many years before she died, things woulda been different fer you, Samantha. I guarantee it. Yer grandpa Stanley and Sophie were good God-fearin' people, but they let their chillren run wild and neglected the grandchillren whilst Sophie was ailin' and then when Stanley was grievin' after her passin'."

"I hardly remember her," Samantha said. "I was away at boarding school, of course, and when I came home, they didn't allow her many visitors." Her grandfather was a good man, and they'd bonded in the last few years, but he hadn't been there for her when she was young, or even in her Nick/marriage period.

"A cryin' shame, thass what it is," Tante Lulu

said, patting her on the arm. "Family is the most important thing in the world, honey."

Tante Lulu stared at Daniel then, as if with some hidden meaning.

"What? I didn't disagree."

"Then do somethin' about it."

"About what?"

"Makin' a family." On those words she stomped away.

He gasped. "Me? Start a family? Is she crazy?"

Samantha burst out laughing, so comical was the expression of horror on his face.

"Go ahead. Laugh. You do realize that she means that I should start a family with *you*."

It was Samantha's turn to be horrified.

Her and Daniel? A family? No way!

But then a blip of a picture flashed into her mind. Her and Daniel. In bed. Doing what usually led to making a family. "I need to get out of here," she said.

Daniel's laughter followed after her.